Blood Among
the Roses

David Rose-Massom

Copyright © 2023 David Rose-Massom

All rights reserved.

ISBN: 9798870079714
Imprint: Independently published

Dedication

TO LYDIA

My ever-patient partner.

Acknowledgements

And huge thanks go to my supportive friends:

Front Cover Artwork – LYDIA ELIZABETH

Front Cover Design – ROBIN LEVY WEISS

Book Editor: JAN LATHEM

Titles by the same Author

DEATH OF AN UNNAMED GIRL

A DELICIOUS WAY TO DIE

Inna lillahi wa inna ilayha rajl'un
Verily we belong to Allah,

CHAPTER ONE

"Bloody rain!" Sam said to nobody on hearing the drumming of the watery pellets on his window.

Bed was a lonely place for Sam, it had been a long time since he had woken up with anyone alongside him, so it always felt better beginning the day with a grumble. In fact, he had discovered some time ago that he was talking more and more to himself these days, and today was just another Sunday, of another week in a long run of tedious weeks. In his mind it seemed he had lived a lifetime of wasted weekends.

With his bones aching and joints creaking he decided it was time to get his body moving, throwing the quilt to the empty side of the bed Sam shivered with the morning chill before standing and taking a second or two to gain his balance before taking two bold but faltering steps toward the window, 'one small step for man' he muttered before pulling back the limp, discoloured, single, curtain and allowing the weak, grey morning light to spill into the room. This Sunday morning was not the autumn of photographers' dreams, no golds, or bronzes or reds of forests undergoing their seasonal change but more grey or dank and very damp. In Sam's world nature had forgotten to pack her colouring crayons.

Sam blinked at the grim and overcast view outside that consisted of charity shop after charity shop, the modern phenomena that seemed to inhabit the centre of every town, including his part of Chichester's central precinct. It was Sunday so they lay still and temporarily abandoned, windows dark. Rain streaked the bedroom's dusty window and ran down in zigzag rivulets diverted from any direct course by the encrusted dust on the outside of the pane of glass. Absentmindedly Sam scratched his balls through paisley boxers, the once brightly patterned shorts completing his night attire ensemble of socks and an off-white t-shirt that hung off his slender frame, skinny legs poked out and seemed to be mimicking the rivulets of rain for shape and thickness.

It wasn't just this morning that was a problem, the start of every day seemed to get progressively harder for Sam Cobby. Each day from morning until nightfall, he felt as if he were just counting down the hours to a time when he could return once again to his single-life bed and let sleep take him away from his tedious life. Sleep made the days go quicker and while he slept nobody could ridicule him and his ambitions toward better things. Most nights he fell into the dreams of how he would become to be the man he wanted to be but come the waking he always forgot how the plan went. Ambition is a strange bedfellow, full of hope when asleep and yet dashed by morning amnesia on waking.

When between the thin quilt and lumpy mattress Sam was a success, a valued member of the local business community with a seat on the chamber of commerce and an active member of the Freemasons Lodge. Come morning though, as he shook off sleep and returned to the real world where he was the same failure he had always been, feeling as if disappointment was his destiny, a birth right if you like. Sliding his feet into worn down slippers Sam headed down to the dimly lit kitchen. He gripped the stair rail firmly, plodding down one step at a time, left foot first (his left stronger than his right), then right foot alongside left before repeating the process with each stair. The last time he had tried to walk normally downward, as most people do, his right leg had taken exception to the activity and had given out. It was almost two hours of painful waiting before the postman had spotted him lying there and then another 30 minutes before the police broke the door down to give paramedics access to the injured Sam. His shop of object d'art had remained closed for two weeks following the recovery from that fall, he never sold much in his rag-tag store, but at least he would normally sell something to put food on the table. No sales, no food! It had been a tough month or so until he was back on his feet with both finances and health.

Descent carefully managed Sam placed an old, black stained kettle onto the gas hob, its blue flame spitting and coughing before going to work. He waited impatiently for the ear-piercing whistle before pouring water onto the teaspoon's worth of instant coffee that he had put into the cup in readiness the previous evening. Sam sat at the head of a 200-year-old refectory table, its surface pitted and stained with a life of service well-lived, meanwhile his bony arse felt every dent and divot on the seat of a well-worn Windsor chair. Each day began the same for Sam, although strangely, Sunday's felt different, felt lonelier. Maybe it was because on Sundays the town was blanketed by the sound of the Cathedral's bells ringing out its call for parishioners and believers to head for prayer. Sam was not a believer, never had been although he had always lived in the shadow of the spire. Maybe God would have been a little more charitable with his life if he had believed; but he doubted it. His day began with a cup of instant coffee, taken black and bitter and with silent musings of what he had done to piss the world off in such a monumental way. Sundays were no different to other days as each new morning brought back the hand to mouth daily grind. Yet when he slept, he always believed the following morning would be the one that changed his life. Each night when his haggard face rested on its lumpy pillow he just knew, tomorrow would be his lucky day. Would today be that day?

He doubted it.

'Be careful what you wish for', someone had once said to Sam, but he had forgotten who said it to him and he had forgotten to heed the warning for all he had to go on was the wish of a better, brighter tomorrow.

As with every morning today was the same ritual. The pain in his back and down his legs would wake him at around seven in the morning. Pushing down the quilt with his feet he would shuffle his old body into an upright position on the edge of the bed where he would then stretch by trying to touch the ceiling, it was an effort to ease the painful kinks in his spine. Then he would stand and make sure he had his balance before hobbling down the stairs and into the scruffy kitchen where he would pour a glass of tap water to help him swallow the first of the daily double dose of pain killers. Sam had suffered for years with a degenerative spinal condition the doctors never quite explaining why his spine was disintegrating, so they used the broad term of 'degenerative'. Over the last half a dozen years the pains had crept up his spine and in recent months had begun to wander down from the neck as well. His body reflecting his life, basically both were a mess and seemingly on a decline.

Standing by the square, white ceramic, Dublin sink he stretched the night kinks away, gazing out of his kitchen window he watched the rain that, since climbing from his bed, had gone from an easy drizzle to dropping like stair rods, that now pelted at the windows.

Disturbed from his sleep and hungry, Wedgwood the cat had merely opened one eye and glared at his human before almost sighing at the disturbance in the room before disappearing back into his sleep. Sam wondered if cats had dreams of more successful and thoughtful owners who would feed them better. Now, as he sipped at his hot coffee, his whingeing cat had arrived in the kitchen to see what was on his breakfast menu.

In the dully lit kitchen Sam checked his last two slices of bread for mould before popping them into the toaster and as he waited for the toast to pop up the cat flap rattled and he caught sight of Wedgwood's white rear end disappearing, tail up and seemingly giving Sam an insult with a wink from his displayed arse. Sam looked at the ceiling as if he could see through to his bedroom and then back at the swinging plastic flap as he sat at the table and managed to scrape enough marmalade from the sticky jar to give a thin coating on his toast, gazing into the empty jar he let out a long and dejected sigh. He silently scolded himself for not getting a food shop in, he had the money this weekend as he had sold a beautiful Windsor chair the day before, the sister chair to the one he now sat on, the English oak gleaming with natural polish after years of wear, he sold it at a premium as it was a 19th Century version with a steam-curved crinoline stretcher linking the back legs, so designed to make more room for the full ladies' skirts of the time, he had been asking £450 but had happily accepted the offered £350 as the dapper looking gent who bought it was paying cash. In the scheme of things that had made this week a good trading week, but he still felt the depression from which he suffered like a dark cloud. With the cat gone Sam ate his breakfast alone, he could not recall when he last had company for breakfast. What did he have to offer a woman, any woman? He often wondered why even Wedgwood had stayed loyal to him.

He brushed crumbs from his T-shirt and placed his plate in the sink, where the object met with yesterday's plate and mug. With one last glance at the cat flap, he headed back upstairs to dress. The climb hurt, akin to a final ascent of Everest, but the exercise was good.

Dressed and ready to take on whatever crap the gods decreed would be his day Sam made his bed by just shaking out the quilt, his effort-free idea of bed-making. Once again Sam headed downstairs and as soon as his feet hit the worn flagstone floor the flap in the back door rattled out the warning that Wedgwood was back, whereupon the cat proceeded to drop a dead mouse from its jaws and onto the hefty grey slabs of flooring. Sam could not believe that in the time it had taken him to clean his dentures, try for a morning shit and shower Wedgwood had found time to go out, catch his prey and return.

Wedgwood gave Sam that look of haughty disregard that only cats could give. The look informed his owner that the mouse would be breakfast if, as suspected, Sam had forgotten to get cat food the day before. As it transpired mouse was the only thing on the menu, so Sam unscrewed the blue cap on his milk bottle ready to let Wedgwood have the cream, but one sniff of the contents told him the milk was not suitable for consumption by man or beast.

With no sense of urgency as today was Sunday Sam promised Wedgwood that he would pop down the road and get some cat food. He would not be opening his shop of shabby-chic-rubbish today, it was his day of rest which meant the day would drag even more than the other six days of the week. Sam hated Sundays.

Truth be known he hated most days!

His coffee mug held one last sip and now sipped Sam rinsed the cup under a cold tap and placed it lip down on the draining board, there was a moment's thought about washing up the debris in the sink, but then he thought better of it. Turning his back on any semblance of housework Sam donned his ancient wax jacket, adjusted his flat cap before grabbing his walking stick and hobbling out of the back door. The weather that day was a metaphor to Sam, dull and grey. Just like him and his life.

He limped away from his shop and began the short trudge further into Chichester town centre, with each step his body loosened, and the pain drifted away to its normal, just bearable, level. Sam had already forgotten his promise of tinned treats for the cat and wondered if the mouse would still be there on his return home. Before leaving he had attempted to pick it up by the skinny tail and deposit in the bin, but a curling growl from an irate Wedgwood had frightened him off, so he left the mouse right where the cat had dropped it. Sam looked forward to arriving back at home and seeing its small furry corpse waiting for him.

CHAPTER TWO

It had been a little over two years. To be precise it had been two years, four months, and two days, but it was only Kobe Kaan that had been counting and even he could not recall the exact timings of that day. A day that had gone from kissing his family goodbye in the morning to saying final prayers for them in the evening.

That whole day was a blur in his memory, although the remembered images were all too clear. In all that time since that evening, he had failed to find peace of any kind, and knew that any kind of mental comfort would allude him for many years to come. As far as he was concerned, he did not deserve better, or for the aching pain to be diminished. Professionals labelled it PTSD but no matter the name it would be his load to carry for the rest of his life.

If only he had gone straight home at shift's end that day!

Now, five hours drive away from everything that his previous life had held dear for him, he still did not seem far enough away, but any further and he would be out in the Atlantic Ocean. When he had climbed into his Alfa Romeo that day with little more than a holdall of belongings, he had no idea where he was going, he just drove, filled up with petrol and drove some more until he ran out of road. The car stopped in Bude on the North Cornwall coast and so did he. Nobody knew him and he knew nobody, just the way he liked it, he did not want to explain how he had arrived or why he had arrived. That first night he slept uncomfortably in his car, managing to buy a hot chocolate and a tray of six cinnamon ring donuts before the canal-side black shack closed its door for the night. It was all he had eaten that day; the Alpha had been thirstier than him.

On day two, he found a small room to rent that was sparse but comfortable, he didn't want much and nor did he feel he deserved comfortable. Day by day, rain or shine he spent his mornings sitting outside a popular floating restaurant that looked across a vast beach and out into the bay where the tide rolled in and out relentlessly. He had watched both calm seas and wild crashing waves since arriving at the Cornish seaside town with its friendly restaurant The Barge, as it was aptly named. It was a cream, broad in the beam, canal boat with the flag of St Pyran flying proudly above its kitchen end, and it was tied to the wharf wall of the canal that spilled its water via the lock-gates out into the bay, it had become his venue of choice. They brewed locally roasted coffee just as he liked it and were friendly without invading his space or privacy, best of all nobody asked questions. The only downside of his refuge was that all the locals were so friendly, Bude was one of those places where everyone said, '*good morning*' and many even stopped for a chat while their dogs, sensing the pain in Kobe's heart would rub against him and stay there while he absentmindedly fussed them. The dogs were okay, it was the humans that were the problem.

Religion had always been a burden for a man who had been born into a Muslim family in a country where the individual loved the freedom of thought and action. It wasn't that he had been a bad Muslim, though Kobe often thought that his religion could do with a confessional where one was able to just own up to your sins, apologise, act contrite and all would be forgiven. And, he had no desire to meet 72 virgins in the next life anyway. Sometimes being Muslim was difficult to live with, and mixing his beliefs with the day-to-day duty of a Detective Inspector on the Sussex force was almost too much a weight of responsibility to carry sometimes.

The fateful day a little over two years ago was to be one of those days where he would always regret his actions, and although he knew he should treat his God with a bit more respect he could not forgive him, or her, for being so bloody-minded about his sins. Even occasionally thinking that it may have been his love for bacon sandwiches that had been the last straw, and if he had only just forgone that simple pleasure all would be well.

Kobe remembered every minute of that vicious day! In fact, he relived each moment, repeatedly, as if it were a film on a loop, it was just that the scenes would jumble up their timeline each time he relived it.

It was a Sunday that had begun simply enough at his home in the charming and historic waterfront village a short distance from Chichester. Legend had it that this was where King Canute had ordered the tide to turn back and received wet feet for his troubles, across the road from the Kaan household was the churchyard where Canute's daughter was buried. Normally Sundays would be a family day when work shifts allowed, and all had begun well enough in the Kaan household that day, rowdy children, and a wife impatient to be getting into her studio shed at the bottom of the garden to begin another painting. The day before had been spent for family, a rare Saturday from work, and he had revelled in every minute of a lazy day spent walking the winding harbour coastline while watching the children get far too close to the water's edge for comfort. He recalled fondly holding hands with his wife and not letting go throughout the whole five-mile walk. Now he was looking forward to a hectic day of arresting bad guys, as his young son Kobe Junior would put it each time someone was asked what his dad did.

Today's raid had been meticulously planned over the previous week and it was to be the second of such raids in less than a two-week period. This was also to be an attack on a drug house that had been allowed to flourish for far too long. This morning's police invasion was at a well-known drug den running out of a terraced house near the railway station, handy for those in need who lived away from the town centre. Unusually, despite the bite into overtime budgets, the surprise raid was being carried out on a Sunday as it would be a day those involved would least expect the local Serious Crimes Squad to be turning up at their fortified door.

As with most mornings in the Kaan household the day began with the usual random dance moves around his two children who always seemed to distribute more cereal around the kitchen than they consumed and Kobe while enjoying the bedlam had too much on his mind to relax. It was still early and after he left the children would probably go back to bed, but home time was family time, no matter what the time and Kobe would playfully tease the children, getting them wound-up and excited while his wife Rae tried, in vain, to keep the breakfast table in some semblance of order. Over-exciting the children kissing wife and drinking thick, black coffee Kobe appeared to be at ease, but all the while he was mentally working out how the job would go that morning. It was a big deal for his squad and the culmination of many months of intelligence gathering, which meant it was a big day for the city, the local press and all the big brass above him. He hoped it would be a bad day for several undesirables but a good one for his crew.

Sometimes he felt that being a DI was nothing more of a job than that of a logistics manager working out the distribution of limited resources with ever-decreasing budgets.

But, for another 30 minutes his morning was about his family. Without fail his two youngsters would make him smile and forget for a moment the huge responsibility of keeping Chichester a safe place and keeping his squad safe on the raid to come. Wife Rae floated around the kitchen/diner with everything under control and all he could do was feel the warmth from his family while continually checking his watch and drinking coffee that was too thick for most tastes, as well as burning lip and tongue hot. Rae pirouetted around the three of them in a well-rehearsed routine wearing a smile that morning mishaps could never displace. Breakfast trauma over, a sink full of cereal bowls and various drinking vessels and it was time for Kobe to leave.

Little Molly pleaded, her tiny voice breaking Kobe's heart. "Why are you working on the Sunday Daddy?"

Kobe looked to Rae for help, she just shrugged her shoulders and the look on her face informed Kobe that he was on his own with this one.

"Sorry Molly, but the problem is that the bad guys don't take weekends off and so sometimes I have to chase them on Sundays." The pout on Molly's lips told him he was not yet off the hook, so he looked for a compromise. "I tell you what..."

"What?" a voice so sweet it clutched at his heart and yet carried so much of a threat if the 'tell you what' was not up to par.

"How about tomorrow morning I go into work a little later and I take you and Kobe to school first." Kobe senior gave her his best smile and under the table crossed his fingers.

Kobe knew how the school run would go, and Rae offered her little warning of doubt.

"Are you sure, you know what bedlam school runs can be?"

"Honey, I am a respected Detective Inspector and I control a team of testosterone fuelled officers." Kobe began in his often-used defence of his offer. "If I can't oversee two small children and complete a school run, what kind of boss would I be?"

"Just saying, that's all." her look told him he was still on his own with the offer, he had been warned.

Kobe knew from past experiences that no matter how careful the planning or how expertly he carried out the tasks ahead it would be a good school run if everything ran just five minutes late before daughter Molly and Kobe Junior were strapped into Kobe's car ready for the off, and before he kissed his wife Rae goodbye, memories of past school runs made him smile and his wife would always know what he was thinking. He would then hold on to the hug that he never wanted to end, but in the end, and as usual on workdays she would push him away with a laugh.

"Get the children to school, safely, and go to work..." she would order playfully.

"Spoilsport..." Kobe would respond with partially fake sadness. The pout never suited his round face but always made Rae's smile even broader.

Molly, always the bossy one and always the last to get to the car, would call from her booster seat in the back, 'Daddy, hurry we will be late for 'ssembly...' Her arms would be folded with a huff across her chest, just like mummy did when she told either of the Kobe's off, both father and son were used to the little girl's bossy ways '...and put Mummy down.' she would scold.

Kobe the younger's usual response would be "Yuk, stop kissing Mummy, its 's-gusting." And he would be sat in his own booster seat next to Molly's and continue playing on his computer game and ignoring everything else, head down and thumbs working frantically, he would merely sigh and continue killing aliens. Kobe loved the mess that was the school run...

Rae interjected his thoughts of long past school runs. "You do know what you are promising?" she asked, and Molly was quick to butt in.

"But, Mummy, Daddy has already promised. He must take us to school tomorrow now." Bossy Molly was winning the morning as she usually did. She was definitely her mother's daughter, but Kobe knew that as she grew older, she would be Daddy's girl and it filled his heart with joy.

Out of the four jobs he believed shaped his life - father, husband, Muslim, and copper – Kobe loved the family parts the best, those moments are what made his life work, it was blissful, it was an antidote to the pressure of being a modern-day copper. As he continued his thoughts of what would happen on the following morning the distraction carried his mind into family moments, and he pushed to one side the logistics of this morning's pending raid.

With promise made, and re-made, Kobe was finally free to head into work Molly hugged her father tightly around the neck and used the moment to offer dad a plea. One last moment of unbridled joy before engaging his brain with the morning's task.

Before loosening her grip, she whispered into her father's ear, "Be safe today, Daddy, me and Kobe needs you and you now have to take us to school tomorrow."

It always amazed Kobe that his children, at such a young age, already understood the dangers of his job. He found it heart-rending that he was stealing a part of their childhood by pilfering a little of their innocence each day. It was a harsh world, but they didn't need to know that at such a young age.

"I always take care darling girl. And don't worry I will be home to say goodnight before you go to sleep." Although he knew he was in for a long day and a long night, he would probably arrive home just before the anticipated school run.

Fear allayed, Molly released her grip and went in search of her brother.

Farewells and kisses done Kobe aimed his car for the centre of Chichester, although a chill morning he had the top down on his beloved Alfa Romeo, and he was hardly out of the village before his smile was gone and all thoughts returned totally to the job. Little did he realise, as once again his mind centred on the morning's logistics for the planned raid on an infamous drug den, that his life was about to change irreparably. In his mind he again went over the plan step-by-step with no idea that the previous Monday morning's school run which had been so full of sweet memories, was to be his last...

Navigation to Chichester town centre was easy even for the casual visitor, all they need look for on the cityscape was the dominant spire of the cathedral and drive toward it. Just one hour into this Sunday morning and to this moment his own God would be pleased with him. No rules broken so far but the strict pathway of the religious straight-and-narrow would quickly fail, as it did on many a morning, before even reaching police HQ. As was the norm he would be breaking his first religious rule within twenty minutes of kissing Rae goodbye. Those same lips that kissed his lovely wife would now taste the forbidden.

It wasn't that he was a bad Muslim. Kobe Kaan just thought it hard work keeping up with the rules and teachings of his strict faith. He was a believer and his faith had never waned, he just found it hard sticking to the rules. Being a devout Muslim was difficult partner to live with, it took hard work and dedication and many years ago Kobe realised that any religion, were it to be followed faithfully would be hard and required dedication to beliefs that he just did not have. For a start he had no desire to meet 72 virgins in this life or the next, sometimes being both a Muslim and a serving police officer collided and was difficult to live with learning early on his career that being both was sometimes just too great a burden to carry, so it was his job that came first and his religion second.

Unlike his strict father, who he believed adhered to every rule every day, Kobe was never prepared to put in the hours, life had a habit of getting in the way. He found it hard to believe that his father had never tasted the glory that was a bacon sandwich. Kobe Kaan believed that he was basically a good man, despite his shortcomings with the odd bacon sandwich aside, and he was certain that his benevolent God would be far too busy to notice these minor indiscretions.

The everyday life of being a police officer was tough, he had a responsibility to those under his command, a responsibility to those who commanded him and the huge undertaking of being responsible to the diverse population of West Sussex. Being a devoted family man, a Muslim and a Detective Inspector put a great burden on his broad shoulders. More times than not his religion would be given the back seat while he juggled family and job to the best of his ability, then there were the rare occasions the religion and the job would clash head on.

By the end of this Sunday that struggle would change his life forever. Kobe's world would collapse in the discovery that his God, one that he loved so much and who had stood beside him on so many occasions, or so he believed, could be so vengeful. Foul punishments for such small transgressions.

CHAPTER 3

The strict, straight, and narrow pathway of religion that he should have been following failed shortly after leaving home and before he had reached Chichester's red-bricked police headquarters. Kobe always likened his place of work to a genteel old school building rather than the stronghold of the County police force.

Sin number one was about to begin a long list of wrongdoing that Sunday and it began while most people were struggling out of bed, hungover and ready for their first jolt of coffee. Kobe stopped at a small café he liked to frequent, loving the 'greasy spoon' ambience, that backed onto the bus station and looked out toward the railway station, a prime location. It was also close enough to the 'old-schoolhouse' of a police station that take-away coffees were still hot when he reached his desk. His original café of choice had long since closed, becoming a shop for the latest smoking trend of vaping, Kobe could never see the attraction of puffing away on a flavoured steam pipe. The decor in the cafe was nothing fancy with the plain magnolia walls coated with posters that showed boastful photographs of the food just in case customers were unsure of how egg and chips looked. Due to the mugs of thick tea and inch thick sandwiches it was a popular haunt with labourers, students and the unwashed. On Kobe's days off he missed the beverages served there. Such as the 'builder's tea' which was served in a polystyrene take-away cup that was in danger of melting due to the toxicity of the beverage. For Kobe though the important thing was how the establishment kicked up to a five-starred restaurant with the culinary art of the inch-thick doorstep of the bacon sandwich. Thick slices of starchy white bread soaked with melting butter and oozing with the aroma of overcooked, freshly crisped bacon, perfection in a brown paper bag that immediately darkened with the grease. This so secret a menu item it was denied a photograph on the café walls and when the rashers sizzled on the griddle it was a sound to Kobe that was like the finest of symphonies. The young girl behind the counter slathered the thick slices of bread with butter before layering on the slightly crispy bacon, just as Kobe liked it. The girl deftly sliced the sandwich into two equal halves, corner to corner as style dictated and

Kobe enjoyed the crunching sound as the blade passed through the bacon. Bacon sandwiches from here were the full epicurean experience. The young girl had already added the spicy brown sauce that she knew her regular liked and as she pressed down with the knife it oozed from between thick slices of bread. Hidden behind the protective wall of the counter she wrapped the offending sandwiches in a plain paper napkin before sliding the package into the brown paper bag. The skinny girl with a nose ring on one side of her pointed nose and a stud through her thin top lip lisped as she called out the order as if the café had been busy and a queue had been waiting.

"Bacon th'andwich, one large ethpretho and latte to go!" she yelled out of habit already knowing who it was for. The flare of the overhead lights flashed briefly off her tongue stud as she spoke.

She would slip the takeaway drinks into a cardboard cup holder and slide the sandwich silently across the polished chrome surfaced countertop, then she would always look over Kobe's shoulder as if to ensure nobody had seen the hand-off of the illicit transaction. Kobe snatched them up and with head bowed he hustled from the sandwich shop. The deal had been done and at that moment he was glad that Muslims had no confessional.

For a tourist town that at one time was over-endowed with touristy tea rooms and transport cafes its main streets were now filled with faux trendy coffee houses, even his chosen purveyor of the bacon sandwich which was once Judy's Cafe was now renamed The Fat Fig for some obscure reason, it was now one of those compromises between the old-fashioned café and the trendy coffee house. As it turned out the mix was a comfortable one, but the name had been taken literally by many of the customers who were more than mildly obese. It did have a lovely family feel to it however and the dishes on the specials board was another mix of cultures where the likes of burger and chips sat alongside the classic moussaka. It was English café mating with Greek taverna.

Kobe had changed his choice of beverage since its renaming from his once loved builder's tea to a coffee that was strong and bitter at the first taste, but from the second mouthful it was the perfect morning drink to kick-start him on a cold autumnal day.

Now keen to get to the squad room and get plans underway his attitude became all business as he stepped back out into the street. DI

Kobe Kaan had settled for take-away that morning with his bad sandwich hidden from sight and held secretly like a drunk with a quarter bottle of vodka for sipping in shop doorways.

Revelling in his first sin of the day, the teachings of a devout Muslim continued to travel swiftly downhill from there. If his father were alive, he would have looked on with total dismay. As with any police officer signing on for a day's shift, only time would tell if his day as a DI would work out well, or at least better than his religious shortcomings.

First port of call on reaching the station each morning was the front desk, to deliver the latte to the civilian worker who was the first face the public saw inside the station. She was just beginning her morning shift.

"Morning Jemma, good weekend so far?" Kobe asked, even though he knew the answer.

"Morning Mr Kaan, that my coffee?" she replied. "You know me, same old thing Saturday pub lunch with my mum before taking her for a push around Bosham harbour, before dropping her off and heading back here into the jailhouse."

"How is your Mum?" Kobe tried to know all that affected those who worked around him.

"Same as ever, never sure what day it is, and this weekend she even forgot who I was. She kept thinking I was her sister who died years ago." Jemma shook her head. "At least she can't wander off like she used to, not now she is confined to the wheelchair." She lifted the lid of the coffee, releasing the steam and taking a tentative sip. "Thanks for the coffee."

Kobe had worked with Jemma for some years and had seen many changes in the young woman. Her mousy-coloured hair was worn loose these days, the black dye having long since grown out and she now wore it down to hang like curtains hiding the stage that was the drama of her damaged face. Scars were livid on her right cheek and mapped the lines of her lips where they had been repaired after her teeth had been driven through them, her once petite nose had a large bump and a bend in it, a scar curved in a crescent shape around her left eye where the socket had been shattered and broken through the skin. The physical scars were nothing compared to the mental ones, her bright eyes that once shone with an intelligent mischievousness were now dull and closed off to emotion.

A light dimmed to reflect the darkness she felt in the very core of her being.

Once full of life and confident, she now cowered from eyes that only seemed to see her wounds. Jemma liked being in the shade of the dimly lit front desk, it was her barrier to the outside world while she learned to once again be part of that life and it still took every ounce of her willpower to turn up for work each day. Kobe still felt guilt, because he abandoned her to suffer the attack, but he had long admired her bravery; certain a man would carry themselves as well as her after the ordeal she had been put through.

Kobe felt responsibility toward Jemma Costello, once she was a serving officer under his command as a PC, but he had left her in harm's way. Lack of resources had found him under pressure, as it did with many middle management officers. Those above him had no real idea of how to run a squad and how to keep them safe, beneath him rank-and-file officers were short in numbers and, in some cases even short of training. That investigation had been a long and complicated case that had spread his resources thin and forced him to rush from pillar to post, even following clues out of county, something would eventually have to give, and it was his ambitious and popular officer who had suffered. Jemma, once a pretty and confident girl, had been attacked by a psychopathic killer who had escaped scrutiny in what was a thin suspect pool. To all appearances the killer seemed to be more victim than suspect, but Kobe knew that his gut instinct should have told him his thoughts were wrong. A copper with his experience should know these things. It was his job to cover every possibility, he had missed the signals, and it was Jemma who had suffered. For the young but ambitious officer it had been a life-changing miss. Jemma had been sent to watch over the seemingly innocent man in her tough role as a Family Liaison Officer.

Undermanned and overworked Kobe had left her to watch over and liaise with Jacob Tubb in her role as Family Liaison Officer. While protecting Jacob, her colleagues across the south of England searched for his brother Lucas, an escapee from Broadmoor, the hospital for the criminally insane and permanent home to some of the nation's most violent killers. Lucas was believed to be the dangerous one of the two brothers. An insane and vicious killer who had escaped and killed a second time, beating the Nanny who had raised them to a bloody pulp. It was believed the old lady had suffered for some hours before she finally succumbed to her extensive injuries. Jacob's thin, but plausible, alibi had been believed. Kobe being drawn in by a smooth operator who seemed to have a talent for talking his way out of trouble. Nobody on his team had expected the way the story unfolded. Kobe had got it wrong, they had all got it wrong, terribly wrong, and it was Jemma who had paid for his dropping the ball with the investigation. While Kobe raced between counties following leads that would lead to the recapture of Luke, Jemma had suffered the blind fury of a very disturbed man. Brutally raped and beaten by the very person she was there to protect and offer support to. When Kobe found her, Jacob was gone and she was battered, broken, bloody and close to death lying on a cold kitchen floor. Often Jemma had wished he had been later in finding her, that way death would have stolen the painful memories she endured daily.

No longer fit for active service and suffering from an aggressive form of PTSD she took medical retirement and chose to take the offer of working the front desk as a civilian in the hope it would bring back her confidence. She turned to the desk as if dismissing Kobe, she could not take eye-to-eye contact for too long, even the gaze of friends made her feel uncomfortable. She felt a freak on show for all and sundry. Kobe was used to her distractions by now, but still felt responsible for her and along with everything else she had lost a promising career on the force. He shuffled off to his own squad room, guilt ridden and not knowing how to make matters right, he glanced back briefly but she kept her back to him, head down and sipping on her coffee. The DI wished he could do more than bring her a morning latte, he had watched the light go out in her bright green eyes two years ago following the brutal assault and he should have done better to protect her. Jemma Costello was damaged physically and mentally, probably beyond repair, and it was his fault.

CHAPTER FOUR

Although he loved antiques, Sam didn't like antique fairs in village halls that much, apart from the fact he had little money to spend on fresh stock he hated the way the stallholders looked down on him. Feeling that each of them were thinking they knew more about the trade than Sam Cobby did. Sam couldn't help but agree with them sadly, believing that both they and he knew that he was truly crap at his job. If Sam knew anything in his grey life it was the fact that he was indeed crap at what he did.

The streets of the beautiful city were almost empty that morning, tourist season was over, and locals thought better than to go out in the autumnal rains. Clouds were thick, black, and threatening as if some sort of Armageddon was about to visit. It had just been a light shower when Sam first stepped into the near abandoned precinct, and he thought the timing right to get to his local Café Nero without a downpour. A tall wiry man hustled past him going in the opposite direction, head down, face buried in his hoodie and with the massive tome that is the Sunday Times folded under his arm. The rain however had increased in strength and as it bounced from the pavement Sam hurried onward, his flat cap giving scant protection from the deluge. The downpour had driven him away from the city's streets and into the historic Council House and Assembly Room where an Antique and Vintage Fair was being held in the first-floor rooms of the imposing Georgian building. In the ante room to the hall Sam hung his head as he passed under the row of huge and ornately framed portraits of past mayors, he was hoping that he had not shamed the bewigged portrait of one of his ancestors that hung in judgement looking down on all that passed beneath him. John Cobby had been Mayor of the town way back in 1805 and again in 1814, obviously well liked or well connected to serve in the post twice, with a family likeness his ancient ancestor was dressed resplendently in the red robes that suited such a lofty position, a gold chain of office painted cleverly in oils was hanging heavily on his chest as with a fixed expression he gazed down on lesser mortals, Sam by far being the least of them.

A building to house the officers of the city had been on that site since medieval times, but new council office had been built on the same site in 1731 as the city's leaders had needed somewhere more imposing to strut their stuff, the Assembly Room being added some fifty years later. The solid redbrick building had stood firm, the exterior columns wrapping visitors in her stiff arms as they entered the building, gazing down from the parapet high above the street a resting off-white lion sat imperiously. The building originally had stood in solid isolation but was now buried amidst an ever-changing shopping centre. In those early days such was the importance of the building to the walled town that in 1840 the rock-god of the era Franz Liszt played there to an audience of swooning female fans, long before Elvis and the Beetles had performed to a similar effect.

The high-ceilinged Assembly Hall was playing host to a less fervent audience on that rainy Sunday and was lit to pastel brightness, its pale peach walls soaking up the glow from three half-shell lights with their large, inverted domes that reflected their surroundings while flooding the floor beneath them with an even radiance. A bustling and noisy crowd of lookers and buyers had got an early start at the antique and vintage fair and were grazing the stalls and tables like keen-eyed vultures scavenging for scraps. The ever-growing herd eyed the table-top displays with the light of greed shining brightly in hungry eyes. As the human magpies searched for glittering things among the mismatched and detritus, mostly it seemed rescued from car-boot sales. As the early birds looked for quick bargains, stallholders continued to load their displays with shiny bric-a-brac, not quite ready to begin trading but willing to serve as any sale was good even if the moment was inconvenient. Tables strained under the weight of glitter on display.

Impatient for better views the growing herd pushed and shoved one another to reach tables and display cabinets before fierce fellow competitors could gain advantage from haggling for the best price, or in some cases, the 'very' best price before coveted knick-knacks were purchased and hurried away. Sam knew that many of those early purchases would be returned to tables at car-boot sales on another weekend.

Almost hidden amidst this throng of potential customers was the inconspicuous figure of Sam Cobby who had not wanted to pass under the banner which advertised the Antiques and Vintage Fair hung and flapping messily over the front door. The Fair had been the lesser of two evils as outside the heavens had continued its deluge of rain that had dampened Sam and made him shiver. A hole in his shoe had allowed the sock on his right foot to soak up every puddle he walked through. That same sock now squished water with every step he took so he no choice but to enter the well-lit and dry hall. Thin wisps of steam drifted from the many wet coats in the warm room.

On entering the anteroom to the hall Sam removed his tweed Bakers-Boy cap, always worn at a slightly jaunty angle which he felt gave him a jolly air. He banged the water coated cap against his leg, spraying even more water onto the well-polished floor. The serious portrait of his ancestor looked down on him with a face full of disappointment and disapproval. Sam unzipped his battered and well-loved wax jacket and shook rain drops from its surface which was cracked like crazy paving. It was an old and battered jacket that was more friend than waterproof coat, but it wrapped Sam like a comfort blanket. People standing nearest him moved away to avoid showers of second-hand rain as it flicked from the old coat. Despite the cap Sam's hair was wet and slicked down across his head, exposing an ever-growing bald patch. Shivering with cold he tried, like a sodden dog, to shake off the chill wetness from the storm he had encountered on his way to the hall, but the dampness would not be denied its presence and it crept into his bones, every joint ached and stiffened. A typical end to a wet English summer and an even wetter English autumn was forecast!

The ancient hall was often used for events, occasionally playing host to am-dram groups, flea-markets, and the occasional antiques fair, one of which was on that wet Sunday. Sam's decision to enter was not one that had come easily but as with any drug, the hit was inevitable. Plus, Sam did not want to waste the one-pound entry fee that the stern looking lady had taken from him. It annoyed him that she totally ignored the plead of 'trade' from Sam.

The bedraggled Sam was a man who felt old beyond his years, tired of life, weary of the hours spent in his empty store with rarely a customer to chat with, and he had grown very tired of the ridicule from his, so-called, peers. He had spent half a lifetime being the barb of their thoughtless and cruel jibes about his scruffy store and lack of acumen when it came to picking-out the good antiques from the fake and worthless. With that in mind Sam had tried to avoid going into shows with their rows of crammed tables such as this, for several years now he had stayed away, but like a moth to the flame he was drawn. He was having a day off from the store, so he may just as well have a day off from the withering looks and the hidden sniggers, but the rain had different ideas. His fellow traders in the business saw him as nothing but a sad joke, a man having poor stock and even poorer knowledge. In their eyes Sam Cobby was the owner of a shabby junk shop, just as his father had been, and failed to fit in with the elite and snobby traders of the antiques world.

Fate had other ideas about how Sam's day would turn out, the incessant downpour of rain had caught him unawares and caused him to have a change of plan. As he walked the streets of Chichester with only thoughts for a decent cup of coffee in one of the City's many coffee bars, he trudged heavy footed with his head down and his mind lost in lonely thoughts. Only lonely people know what lonely people think of when they shut out the world. Nobody to share thoughts or adventures with, experiences wasted with nobody to tell the stories to. Loneliness was an awkward silence, an empty space with the added fear of never having someone to share a life with. What was an experience or adventure unless the event could be re-told? Sam was cracking on age-wise and now never expected to find a partner, which made the loneliness an even emptier vessel. His life felt painfully hollow.

Outside chilled bullets of pelting rain hit the windows which were suddenly lit with a bold flash of lightening swiftly followed by a loud clap of thunder, noise and light filling the very air that surrounded them and shook the windows of the old building. It was as if destiny had invited him in, rubbing salt into the wound of an already bad day.

He had to dig into the deep pockets of his thin corduroy trousers for the one-pound entry fee and begrudged paying it, what with him being trade and all. In the main hall narrow aisles ran arrow straight between the tables and stalls that covered almost every available foot of flooring, additional traders were tucked away into alcoves and side rooms that sat off the hall. As he shuffled along, life had drained his energy, so it was an effort to lift his feet. The cuffs of his corduroy trouser that were no longer ribbed but worn smooth and shiny left a damp trail along the polished floor. Damp turn-ups hanging down over his scuffed brogue shoes, the idea of taking a cloth and polish to the comfortable favourites gone shortly before his right one sprung a leak, with each step he could feel the sock squeeze out water from the damp wool which made him wonder how much water the bloody sock had absorbed. Aged and scuffed like a battered second skin, his wax jacket was now draped over his arm, at least Sam felt better dressed than he normally would because of a stylish heavy knit jumper with its toggled neckline that he was wearing, it was a new purchase from the sales. He had not treated himself to new clothing for some time, usually checking out the myriad of charity shops for some decent clothing.

He felt clean and proud in it, in return the jumper swamped his small frame as if trying to swallow him. He was clean shaved, an unusual occurrence because nine days out of ten he could just not be bothered, this must have been the tenth day plus it was a Sunday, Sam's face slim with harsh cheek bones, pale skinned and topped with a sweep of salt and pepper grey hair that like his clothes was also wearing thin in parts. He would never cut a dashing figure and he knew it. Despite his shortcomings Sam always tried to exude confidence, a man of knowledge and breeding in the world of antiques. The truth was though that his facts were thin on the ground and sadly he no longer had any belief in his own abilities, his cluttered store a junk shop rather than an emporium for quality merchandise. Both shop and keeper's mind were storerooms filled with clutter and both thoroughly depressing.

The traders that were scattered around the hall were a close-knit community where everyone knew everyone else and had each one had an idea about the other's business. The dealers behind the biggest stalls were the ones who were the micky-takers, the ones Sam spent his life trying to avoid. The inclement weather had obviously bolstered the crowds with window-shoppers who shuffled along grazing among the stalls the genuine bargain hunters and Sam had to battle through the throngs that filled the narrow alleyways and as he wandered the aisles he tried to hide anonymously amid those crowds, but like barbed darts he could feel glaring eyes hooking into him, piercing the skin to wound the weary old man.

Sam wished he had opened the store that morning, at least there he was used to the daily pain of a quiet shop and there was no one to bully him. In recent years the old trader had been buoyed by the fact that it was on-trend for mid-century kitsch to find its way into modern homes which was being led by TV designers, lifestyle magazines and fashion. Sam felt that as usual he was being left behind with trends and fashions, there was a fine line between retro and tat, but it had never occurred to Sam that if he cleared away the tat, his store was still full to the brim with the trendy and desirable. So long had he lived the way he did that he no longer saw the woods for the trees, and he was blithely unaware that he actually did own a vast wealth of knowledge, but due to his lack of confidence Sam was scared to decide which to ditch and which to keep. A clear out and a lick of paint for the store, a few light bulbs in polished angle-poise lamps and Sam could well see a change in his fortunes, and that would change the way people viewed him and his store. They say location is everything, and Sam was in a prime location in a city filled with a well-to-do and fashionable customer base. But Sam was scared to move with the times just in case he got that wrong too. In his locked mind, even if he did all that work, what would draw the public into his shop. It always amazed Sam what people spent their money on, he brushed some imaginary lint from the front of his new piece of clothing and could not believe that he had splashed out forty fucking quid on a jumper, something his gran could have knocked out on her thick knitting needles in less than a day. Grandma's hands, wrinkled and arthritic, moving swiftly, flashing needles clacking together while she sat in front of the warming Aga in the kitchen behind the shop. But he did feel good in it, maybe it was time to splash out on a new pair of trousers as well, or even a pair of denim jeans, something his father frowned upon in the shop. Then as his sock squelched out more water, he thought new shoes should come first.

He shook the thoughts of his grandmother and fashion from his mind and began to be more aware of his surroundings. As he approached each table, some of them now sagging in the middle from the weight of trove upon them, Sam eyed the object-d'art with lascivious eyes. The 'old-school' traders hovered behind each table, some of them tall and bent like vultures waiting for prey to die. Others sat on fold away chairs, already looking bored and tired. One looked at the passing clientele over wire framed rims of spectacles like an exasperated school master, Sam's only good memory of his schooldays was when the bullies had left him alone for a couple of days. He knew there had to be a reason why they picked on him, Sam always believing that he, as the lowest common denominator, was the one at fault. He knew his brain worked differently from theirs, it wasn't as if he was smarter or anything like that, he just saw things differently. Nowadays he knew that he would have been diagnosed with some sort of label like Autism or ADHD, or one of those other conditions that became an acronym, but growing up he was just aware that he always saw things differently, and as a result he was always labelled as thick or stupid.

In a space between two well-built shoppers that barely had enough room to let light through Sam had spotted a small pottery vase, gently pinched at the waist and just six or so inches tall, and to the unenlightened a dull jade colour which was known as Celadon, or simply greenware. It was hidden behind more colourful items, two chipped and cracked Imari vases their bright chinois design leaping out at those walking by. He had a good idea what the inconspicuous vase was, and by whose hands it had been made, but he needed a closer look. The overweight couple, currently being fawned over by the attentive stallholder, stood in his way, and didn't look like moving on anytime soon. Sam saw a foot wide gap between their heaving bodies and went for it bravely reaching between them. As his arm snaked out between the gargantuan couple, he thought he may be putting the limb, if not his whole body, at risk and if they moved together like a pair of leviathan tankers at sea, he would surely be crushed. His movement had startled the couple and thankfully they parted by just a few more inches allowing him to wrap his fingers gently around the ceramic gem and he swiftly plucked it from the blue velvet cloth that covered the table.

Sam hoped the human barrier of blubber would keep him well hidden from the dealer, but his ploy failed.

"You cannot afford that so please put it down!" said the trader cruelly and with a thick, contrived, posh accent. He smiled obsequiously at the couple who had now become an audience to the mini drama that was unfolding.

A pair of jowly faces turned toward Sam in slow motion, one a mirror image of the other, obese bookends.

Sam ignored the trader's slight. "Is this an original or a later copy, maybe by the potter's son?" He asked politely, although in truth he felt like a scolded school child being told 'not to touch'.

"It is in the style of Bernard Leach," the trader said looking at the male half of the couple as if it had been he who had asked the question. "...however, it does come from the same St Ives studio, and it is probably made by one of his sons."

Sam examined the rim for signs of damage, then tipped it forward to check the marks on the base, he spotted something and fought the urge not to smile. The trader could not have seen the mark or was unaware of what it signified. Sam could not believe the man had simply ignored it, either that or he was failing in his knowledge of the well-known 'Father of British studio pottery'. Sam double checked and there punched into the base when the clay was still soft was the legend 'BL' fenced in by the square of the stamp, the signature was that of the great potter who had learned much of his styling in Japan. After studying the craft in Japan, he returned in 1920 to St Ives in Cornwall and opened the studio along with his friend Shoji Hamada. It is still running today and is one of the most respected potteries in the world. Among the details at the studio about his life it is noted that while at school he excelled in drawing, elocution and cricket, the perfect criteria for art school.

Sam knew this small vase was an original and he worked hard to keep his poker face, but in his chest his heart was pounding.

Sam pushed his way between the oversized husband and wife, sometimes he was glad of his bony elbows. As he reached the table, he could feel rather than see the stallholder's look of scorn and disdain. The beer-bellied trader hitched up his trousers which had slipped down beneath his huge gut and attempted to shove his shirt back in beneath the heroic belt.

"What's your best price?" Sam asked, keen on obtaining the small treasure.

"If it was an original Leach, it would be well out of your range." he spat. "Close to a thousand pounds." A smug look of knowledge from the cocksure trader as he nodded a knowledgeable face at the couple who were spectating the interchange between the dealer and the strange little man. The dealer thought he had the edge over Sam believing he was correct about it being a much later piece from the Cornish studio. Sam did not feel the confidence though, and his belief in the fact this may be an original was beginning to wane.

"But you have already said, it's not a Bernard Leach. So, is it, or not?" Sam said still playing the game but was growing impatient with the thrust and riposte of tiresome badinage. He knew he was not in the same league as these weekend dealers but at least he felt they should show him respect as a customer if nothing else.

"Four fifty, and you can't afford it so put it down!" the words were almost spat out at Sam, while conversely his face was still smiling at the overweight couple to whom he now directed his remarks. "Sorry 'bout that, Sir, Madam, now how may I help you?" his voice became high pitched, condescending.

The burly man with his even burlier wife who, luckily for Sam had still not closed the narrow canyon between them, watched the verbal battle with interest but the couple would not allow Sam get any closer to the table as they shuffled back and forth with impatience, it was as if they were keeping the gap narrow to stop Sam purchasing the simple item that was the topic of conversation. Sam feared for his life if he became trapped between the blubber mountains. The large man began to breathe heavily as he sensed the obvious tension between seller and possible buyer feeling a bargain emerging amid the trading of insults. Without warning he took a sideways step nearer to his burly wife, Sam feeling himself in danger took a step backward as they almost crushed the slight man currently holding the celadon vase.

"I will give you no more than two hundred for it." the bulky man bid to the dealer, seeing the chance of a bargain here, and he spoke in a strong American accent. He was already pulling a thick wallet from the back pocket of his ill-fitting khaki cargo shorts. The equally weighty wife nodding her approval which wobbled the jowls of fat around her neck.

"Two twenty-five and you have deal." Ignoring Sam totally the dealer gazed at his customers and without further bartering hands were shaken and the burly man unhinged his fat wallet and slid out the required notes.

"You do take cash I presume?" it was rhetorical.

"Always my trading partner of choice." The grease in his voice matching his countenance.

It was defeat. There was no come-back that Sam could give, the insult had been final. The swordsman had thrust and made the strike and his victim's heart had been run through. The simple but beautiful waisted vase with its elegant shape testament to the potter's skill was still in Sam's hand, even though ownership was about to be transferred and notes counted out. Sam turned away and felt like just tossing the item nonchalantly across the table toward the grasping and clawing stallholder, but he was not a spiteful person by nature and the vase had done nothing to deserve such crass treatment. It was a forlorn lover of the vase that walked away feeling defeated on two fronts, one that he had missed out on a little gem and two that it had been purchased by someone who would never know what he had or appreciate it. In the mind of the purchaser the big man had just got a good deal on an item, something he was obviously used to doing.

"Prick!" spat the dealer at Sam with a vicious whisper. Then with an obsequious look at his customer who although within earshot of the insult chose not to hear it. "Sorry about that sir. Let me protect this in some bubble wrap for you."

The clock had hardly passed ten in the morning and a dealer had made his first sale, it was going to be a happy trading day, the dealer felt it in his experienced bones. Ignoring that fact that Sam had offered him more money the dealer felt as if he had wone something, winning being everything in this cutthroat business.

There was only one thing left to do for the crestfallen Sam and that was just to walk away and try to stand tall and proud, a tricky thing to pull off when only five three in his socks, even when one of them was wet. Before skulking away from the stallholder and back into the already fast-flowing river of a crowd Sam attempted to feel a little better about himself, and he fired one last comment back toward seller and buyer.

"And just so you know. You should learn your craft a little better, that piece is an original Bernard Leach and you have sold it for a quarter of its actual value."

The fat man looked from Sam and then to the dealer, and then back again to Sam. The new grin on his face was huge and his cheeks became bright red.

"Really!" the excited American exclaimed. "How can you tell?"

Sam had to respond as he wanted the dealer to know that he was indeed the 'prick' on this occasion. "On the bottom it has the 'BL' stamp on it and that is not on the modern pieces as that is the original Bernard Leach signature."

It was the dealers turn to blush with colour.

Instead of feeling better, Sam felt even more of a failure, he had lowered his own expectations to below those of the dealer. He should have known better, and his body slumped just like his mind. His father had raised him better than that and taught him politeness above all else, visibly his bony shoulders slumped and the feeling of suffering a crushing defeat flooded through him. He wished he had stayed out in the rain. He knew he should have stood his corner and paid the extra, it would have still been a bargain but now he walked away empty handed and felt cheated.

Once again mid-aisle he went with the flow of foot traffic hoping he was now hidden from view fearful of the eyes that he imagined were burning into him. All the while wishing that the rain had not forced him indoors because of its uncomfortable deluge. He should have stayed wet, and his sock still was. He no longer looked at the stalls or the wares sitting on them but walked with his head down and staring at his scuffed and leaking shoes.

Amidst the noise of a typical Sunday market that echoed around the small hall, and under the unfriendly glares both imagined and real from stallholders a kind hand came to rest on his drooping shoulder, the hand felt heavy, but a few soft words entered his ear and eased the burden.

"Take no notice of them Sam, they have no right to be judgmental about you." The voice was from Nick Flax, the only person that Sam regarded as a friend. "They don't know you like I do."

It may have been a strange friendship that had skipped a generation in their respective ages, but it was one Sam valued highly and he was glad, as always, of his friend's company.

CHAPTER FIVE

He cheered up the moment he realised the hand and voice was that of his friend, Sam smiled at Nick in greeting while suddenly feeling buoyant, and quickly agreed that he should not let the buggers at these Flea Markets get to him. As it always did Nick's smiling face and easy demeanour smoothed away the insults that had troubled the older man and the heavy weight of troubles on his mind lifted like morning mist that had been cleared by a warming sun.

Despite their 20-year age gap they had become friends after Nick, the senior journalist with the local paper The Chichester Observer, had approached the old man for some background on an art theft he had been reporting on. Two people could not be further apart in background, education, or even social standing but they hit it off and been firm friends for some three years now. Sam always enjoying the soft banter from the younger man and the chance for stimulating conversation over a fine tea, something they were both fans of. They were a stack of opposites Nick was tall, straight backed and always clean shaven apart from the long curving sideburns that softened his face and emphasised his strong jawline. A full head of floppy chestnut hair swept down across his brow which Nick was forever flicking away, a constant mannerism that had Sam always wondering, but never asked, why he did not have the fringe trimmed. Nick's overall style was one from another decade and always gave Sam ammunition for fun as the tweed jacket that did seem to match Nick's deep green eyes, with its leather patched elbows and always seemed out of place in today's world, especially when it was worn with a button-down blue Oxford shirt and denim jeans. With a surrender to modern trends the jeans were fashionably ripped at the knees, and the whole ensemble was finished off with a pair of blonde Nu-Buck boots. Sam always imagined the editors in the Observer's newsroom shaking their heads in despair at their reporter's sartorial elegance, or lack of it. Sam's clothes sense stopped at casual, and every day was dress down day in Sam's world.

Nick fell in beside Sam as they navigated the aisles and explored tables, and all the while they walked, they talked a little. With tacit agreement, they wound their way through the hall toward the tearoom at the far end and any words spoken were of trivial things, the weather, the football matches due to be played later that wet Sunday and anything else that popped into their minds. It was never about what was said between the two of them, it was the joy of uncomplicated conversation that both enjoyed.

The day had suddenly perked up for Sam, all his troubles forgotten, and the two men were just enjoying each other's company over a refreshing cup of Rooibos Tea and while they chatted they had no idea that fate was busy tearing up any schedule that the two men had set themselves...

CHAPTER SIX

Chichester like many cities and towns across the country is a place of many colours and faces where normal is the everyday norm. It is a bustling city where all types and classes of folk live and work and both ends of the spectrum had learned to rub shoulders with the tourists and day visitors. Kept snug within the confines of its Roman walls Chichester is filled with history and arts all being watched over by a towering cathedral spire that is home to a family of peregrine falcons. The swift, grey hunter can often be seen on one of the spire's minarets staring down upon the town and a possible pigeon lunch.

It may have been just a short mile or so away from Sam's desolate store but here among the housing estates was a different world where a determined detective inspector and his adrenaline fuelled squad of officers, who were all dressed for trouble, had no knowledge or thoughts of the embittered and down-at-heel trader, why would they? Equally Sam Cobby was too engrossed in his own troubles to even consider worrying about someone else, let alone a police inspector who he had never heard of. Life stories have a strange way of intertwining even when linked by the thinnest of threads and as Kobe Kaan was launching his raid on the drug den Sam sat down, his slight legs under a wobbly table, in a café and sipped his perfumed tea.

Sam Cobby had inherited his ram-shackle store with its odd collection of bits, pieces, and half-dressed mannequins shortly after his father's death. Life was spent in the shop while home was the other side of a velvet curtain and one storey up above the scruffy store. Shop and Sam shared the kitchen. He had always lived and worked in Cobby and Son since before he could reach the ancient, ornate till that still rang up pounds, shillings, and pence. The brass-coloured machine was one of the most valuable items in the store that was filled to overflowing with antiques and bric-a-brac that Sam fondly referred to as 'stock'.

The most damaged and bent item amid the antique stock was the miserable Sam, by his own description a sorry excuse for a man whose shoulders were bent and rounded as if the weight of the world were upon them — which to Sam, they were. A man who had never known the joy of family but who would also suffer a devastating loss in what he considered to be his already miserable and thoroughly depressing existence!

Cobby and Kaan came from different worlds and lived lives at either end of every spectrum of living. They may not have met before; but their routes would begin to intertwine very soon ...

'The best laid plans of mice and men'

It may have been a Sunday morning, but a different type of trader was keenly preparing to open their popular shop on the dot of eleven in readiness for the day's business, which they knew would be brisk. With an exaggerated swagger they hustled from the dark confines of a pristine, black BMW SUV that shone incongruously in the run-down street. Gazing up and down the street to look for threats their furtive eyes flicked back and forth while remaining hidden behind dark sunglasses as if they were the US Secret Service, all that was missing was them talking into the cuff of their jacket sleeves. They were wearing the latest designer clothing of baggy jeans slung low on the hips, designer labels showing on exposed boxer shorts and logo-emblazoned hoodie tops, gold chains hung heavily from necks and wrists, the modern status symbol of success.

A short distance away church bells rang calling worshippers to the Cathedral where they would join in prayer to their God, while in this dingy side street well away from the tourists and the Christians others were worshipping a different kind of deity.

The four new-age preachers swaggered away from the 'pimped' motor with its oversized chromium wheels and toward their own ragged-arsed congregation queueing from the front door that had peeling blue paint and the legend '11B' above a tiny brass knocker, each pastor of the flock looked left, then right, the door opened on cue and in single file they entered the run-down terrace house in readiness of opening that door for business on the hour and on the dot. Their boss insisting on punctuality. Even in illegal trade there had to be standards kept, and customer satisfaction. To passers-by it was like any other indistinct terrace row of houses, but to neighbours and residents, it was the house from hell and despite many anonymous complaints to the authorities nothing had been done, the residents of that house, or so it seemed, were untouchable. The low-income red-brick homes had been built in the austere times following the second world war. Utilitarian but practical in a time when most of the country had to be rebuilt and quickly. To those in the know, behind the peeling paint and the aged exterior of eleven B was one of the fastest growing businesses in the upmarket town that was known for its history from way back to Roman times, and its tourism. Over time Roman invaders and Roundheads and Cavaliers had battled hard for the right to live within the city walls and control its rialtos and wealth.

Now the second tier of management had arrived, it was opening time. Prompt, and the same thing every day, just as with any local convenience store the passé group of men opened regular hours for seven days a week, eleven in the morning until midnight. Strangely for their sort of business only closing on Christmas Day, nobody would work on Christmas day they told disgruntled customers, even they had families to spend the festivities with. The rag-tag and worn-down clientele would be queuing in silence as they always did, heads bowed, staring at their charity store-bought designer trainers, their faces hidden in the dark shadows of a grubby hoody. The trainers the only stylish thing about them and they would have been knock-offs or nicked, the price of real Jordan's or Nike equating to a week of highs, a price none were prepared to pay. Each of the furtive customers trying to avoid the eyes of the other and each one knowing only too well how the system worked, punishment for trying to queue-jump a painful shove to the back of the queue, or worse, which was to be denied access for a day or more.

The regular customer base as always were fully impatient and needy for supplies, their bodies crying out in pain for the next fix, feet dancing on the spot and bodies fidgeting or rocking back and forward with nervous energy. Scratching the sores on dirty faces that were gaunt and with grey flesh seemingly melting and dripping from the bones of their faces. Brows were damp with sweat, and frightened eyes offered fleeting and furtive glances at each other and up and down the street. Long before opening time the queue would be hugging the walls in front of the boarded-up terraced properties that stood on either side of the illicit shop, near neighbours were unwanted and had been scared out of their homes, being sold to one old lady within a few weeks of the store opening. The only few residents remaining in the low rent street kept their curtains drawn and their mouths closed. That one old woman now owned virtually every house in the short street and acted as

Landlady to those still living there, and the four men now inside number 11B were her most trusted generals. It was now three years since the grand opening, so called by the villains who had passed through the doors daily because that is what they had taken on the first day of trading, a grand. Since that day they had never taken less, turnover remained high, the business very profitable.

The trail of bedraggled clients, camouflaged amongst the debris and litter that blighted the poor end of town, waited each morning without conversation or intimacy, and not one of them would show enough bravery to knock on the door a second before the 11 o'clock opening, no matter how desperate the need or strong the craving.

Today the waiting queue were to discover that the start of morning business, and their pathetic, drug-hazed day that would follow was to begin a little differently. There was one downturned face in the ragged line that was not lost in a haze of drugs or carrying the pain of withdrawal symptoms, in the dark shadow of the hoodie one face with bright eyes was watching events carefully, mind on full alert mode, his eyes fully alive to the surroundings.

Around the corner, away from prying eyes was an eager group of men and women that were dressed for action and straining at the collective leash. At the head of them their trusted DI who managed the West Sussex Major Crimes Squad and this was all in a day's work for Kobe and his trusted team, so with his jacket off and replaced by a heavy and cumbersome stab-vest, he stood a pace ahead of the armoured team that were lined up one behind the other and hugging the wall in an alley just a few yards from the 'shop'. Tall black wheelie rubbish bins, standing in line like strange sentinel type figures, had been put in place to partially hide the entrance to the alley and conceal the strike force waiting there. Curtains here and there began to twitch, a flash of face through the window appearing and disappearing quickly, nobody wanted to get involved. At the front of the chain of invaders and in charge of the operation, stood Kobe who could still taste the grease that remained on his lips from his earlier bacon sandwich, he felt the guilt of a good Muslim. Despite his earlier sin he quietly asked his God for forgiveness for the violence that would probably happen in the next few minutes and meant it. His teachings were firmly against any form of violent activity, and it was the one rule he tried to adhere to. Anything different and he would be filled with too much guilt, he was not made to hurt people, no matter how evil they were, he did not have to live by the same ruthless set of rules as the villains.

He could feel the tension in the queue of officers behind him, eight of them, standing firm with jaws clenched and eyes wide open behind the Perspex face masks of their riot gear helmets. Bodies twitched with nervous energy, adrenaline filled and ready for the assault on the drug house. Immediately behind Kobe at the front end of the squad and seemingly very relaxed was one team member who was out of uniform and with his shaven head hidden by a woollen hat under the cowl of a grubby hoodie, his facial features were unshaven and dark but from the shadow of the hood beamed a bright smile filled with even white teeth.

As the DI glanced over his shoulder and up at the huge man he had to smile also, it was infectious. "You wouldn't be looking forward to this would you Tiny?" he muttered.

Despite it being a whisper, the baritone notes of Tiny Smith's reply rasped, and its deep resonance echoed along the alleyway. "You know me Guv, always ready for a bit of action." Despite his bravado when there was a job to do, back at the station he was well known and respected for his gentle and reassuring manner.

Under the ragged raincoat that he wore over the rest of his fancy dress, he flexed his right arm as it was being stretched by the weight of a red painted 'Enforcer', the police force's idea of a front door master key. Behind Tiny the other six officers were dressed head to toe in black riot gear and each wearing regulation stab-vests.

Feeling the tense readiness of his team Kobe took that moment to check his watch and briefly step out onto the pavement and as if on cue the Cathedral bells rang out the hour. What he saw at exactly the appointed hour was four men slink from a black SUV and swagger with cocky bravado toward the target house, they were so wrapped up in looking cool and intimidating that they failed to check the street for unusual activity and that inattention would cost them dearly. The rag-tag line of early customers just seemed to melt further into the red brick wall that was holding them up as the 'trendy' thugs walked past them. They were all similar versions of each other, wearing designer hoodies and jeans, very loose fitting as was the fashion. On their feet trainers that Kobe knew cost more than a copper's weekly wage. The unfairness of which was not lost on the DI, but he also knew they were about to get their comeuppance. He could almost hear the cheap gold chains rattling around necks and wrists.

"Ready?" He looked Tiny in his Irish blue eyes; in response the officer nodded. Then a final pep-talk to those in the alley waiting with pent up energy. His voice soft but carrying to every officer in his charge, "We had a very successful raid two weeks ago, good intelligence, and superb work by you guys and that day we shut down a very busy drug dealership. Same goes for today, we have the intel, we know what we are getting into so everybody take care, do your jobs and we will put another dealership out of business and still be home for tea."

"When you've finished rabbitin' Boss!" Tiny knew he could get away with a little subordination when the tension needed lifting.

"After you then Tiny, my lad." and in response the man hefted the enforcer up into a two-handed grip and stepped around his boss.

He was followed by two more of the team who each stood alongside their DI and held a riot shield in readiness, they would protect Tiny against thrown missiles or dislodge stubborn soldiers of the opposing army with a 'gentle' nudge. The gear they wore made them all feel taller, stronger, and their tactical gear acted like a superhero's cape.

At the given time and through his earpiece, Kobe heard the permission to execute the raid from a senior officer at the Station. The nick was just a mile or so away, but the crew still felt remote from the safety of its walls.

DI Kobe Kaan, feeling the tension rise, slapped Tiny Smith on the shoulder and spoke with rising intensity into his lapel microphone, "This is DI Kaan, Go, GO, **GO**!"

Tiny did not need telling twice.

Enforcer firmly held in readiness the big man's smile seemed to get even broader. Talking to the red tool he muttered, '...let's go Annie'.

Briskly he moved forward and calmly passed along the scruffy queue of addicts, all but a few failed to notice Annie being held at the ready or the two black-clad officers behind him carrying the protective, heavy Perspex shields. All they cared about was that some bastard was queue jumping and that was a definite breach of protocol, the gang on the other side of the door always frowned on such indiscretions and it usually ending in a brief beating for any drug-hungry miscreant who broke the rules.

"Oy!" One brief and brave voice from close to the front of the queue called out, "Fuck off, we were here first." He took a step forward, eyes glazed over and face expressionless, his mental fuzz stopping him from realising what was happening.

That one small step was swiftly halted by a firm hand grabbing his hood and pulling him backwards, and almost pulling him off his feet. The plain clothes officer in the queue was earning his wages for the day. Tiny smiled and winked in appreciation of his colleague's effort, he was having fun and Tiny called back to the halted and half choked junkie,

"D'ya kiss yer mother with that foul mouth ya little prick."

All signs of bravado quickly disappeared from the haggard and drawn face as the boy with spaced-out eyes was pushed back against the wall. He raised a fist in defiance toward what he thought to be a fellow druggie who had pulled him back before realising in his drug addled brain what was happening and that it was police that were pushing in. He was now in the firm grip of a man with clean-shaven face and cropped hair. Clearly visible now that the hoodie had been pulled back was a head topped by a baseball cap emblazoned with the legend, POLICE over the peak. Finally, as defeat was all that was left in the situation, the boy who could not have been more than sixteen but with the creased face of a fifty-year-old, buried his head back into the hood of his sweatshirt and sunk hands into pockets. The plain-clothed officer feeling pity for a disillusioned youth with no ambition other than finding his next hit released him but before he let him go stared eye to blurry eye and whispered...

"Fuck off, quickly." He turned his face and nodded in the direction the boy should indeed fuck off toward.

The youth, despite a waning high, turned tail and walked swiftly toward the end of the street, furtively gazing left and right. As his hunched form neared his escape route of the railway footbridge, he saw more officers emerging from the alley and heading for the door of eleven B. With more important targets in the house, they ignored the fleeing teenager. His departure and rapid movement had sent a mental warning along the cue of prospective customers as one-by-one they also began peeling themselves away from the wall and looking to disappear, faces sweating with the longing for their next fix and eyes flicking everywhere for trouble. Although paranoid about capture they were ignored by the advancing force, the drug dealers' clientele were not the targets today.

Kobe watched as Tiny reached the front door, closely followed by the rest of the team who brushed aside fleeing junkies like waves shoving driftwood aside on a stormy shore. Timing was important.

Tiny thumped on the door with his giant gloved fist just as the 'doorman' on the other side threw the security bolt back in readiness for letting the first customer into the store. Tiny with senses on high alert had heard the click of the deadbolt on the inside of the door, then in one seamless movement Annie was hefted up and Tiny took grip with both hands, he drew her back and planted his feet firmly on the uneven pathway, balanced with muscles tensed, he could feel the power in his upper torso build. The rest of the assault team close behind tensed for action, their muscles taught and ready for a fight, even though they were already mentally wired, this was the moment things could go wrong and the air seemed to crackle with an electric charge of nervousness.

Tiny paused, his body fully coiled and ready to strike as a cobra would. The venomous head of Annie was thrown forward. On the other side of the door, there was just enough time for the doorman to hold onto the latch and bring his eye to the spyhole. That shadow across the spyhole was the signal that Tiny had been waiting for.

Tiny swung back the enforcer in a high arc before driving it forward and rammed it nose first into the wooden and paint-peeling door, hitting it exactly where the bottom hinge held it to the upright of doorframe. Hinges were always a weak part of the door and Tiny felt the wood give and splinter, the door began to twist slightly. The officers behind him impatient and not a little fearful of what was the other side of that door fidgeted with their own adrenaline fuelling their flight or fight reflex, not one of them was thinking of fleeing.

In one smooth movement Tiny pulled Annie back, hefted her higher and hit the second hinge with a mighty thud... the door was gone.

Surrendering to the impacts the wood splintered and gave way. It twisted with a loud crack, the movement inwards pulled bolts and latch free allowing the door to fall inwards and into the hall of the narrow, terraced house. Sound waves boomed deeply along the narrow corridor and up the stairs.

His job done Tiny stepped to one side, slipping the oversized mac from his body to reveal the same black body-armour that the rest of the assault team were in, the stab vest looked ridiculously small on his big frame. Tiny allowed Annie to swing from his meaty right fist, beads of sweat dribbled from his forehead as two officers with Perspex shields filed through the slim opening and trampled over the fallen door. Unfortunately for the doorman he was slow in realising what was happening, he was not employed for his quickness of thought, and the door crashed down onto the dim-witted youth who had been too slow to jump clear. The double thuds of the enforcer and then the door caving in on the skinny foot-soldier had also echoed between the terraced houses that lined the street.

Everyone in that street knew that something was going on at 11b. Safely away from the action and hidden behind pulled curtains, some residents smiled broadly and hoped it was the end of their street being a nest for the vultures of the drug trade.

Even though encouragement were not needed there was a nervous shout of 'GO, GO, GO!' from Kobe, as they all charged into the house. The squad's adrenaline was in full flow and if they were not up for what lay ahead now, they never would be. Three darkly dressed young men at the head of the druggie queue seemed unaware of what was happening around them as they remained leaning against the wall with expectant faces gazing down at soft leathered and shiny boots rather than the grubby and worn trainers of other queuing customers. They acted as if they were unmoved and mentally unaware of all that was happening around them, but at the right moment suddenly burst into action as they brushed back the hoods of their grey and baggy sweatshirts to reveal the soft baseball-style caps, an Americanism but rank and file officers liked them, glad the days of the tall helmet for everyday use were long gone. Planted earlier in the morning to get a good spot in the queue they were back-up officers there in case of resistance from the rag-tag row of customers. By nature, those involved in the drug business, customers, and suppliers alike, paranoia is part of their make-up and once those in the queue realised the street was full of shouting and alive with police officers their legs took over from addled brains and rushed them off toward either ends of the street. The team ignored them, the end users were not the target today, the sellers however were a different matter.

Kobe's triple 'go' cry had not only been for the men around him in the street but also loud enough for a second wave of officers waiting and hiding behind a rickety fence just outside the small rear garden. It was a well-timed assault. At the same time as Kobe's group followed the protective shields into the narrow front hallway of the house the other smaller squad arrived at the kitchen door at the rear of the house after scampering through the broken gate in the fence at the bottom of the garden, the same thing was happening behind the two adjoining houses on either side in case an escape route had been knocked through. None of the back-up teams met with resistance. Some officers are often disappointed at the lack of action, their adrenaline had been building all morning and they had no way to burn off the energy that physical action gave them.

Back in the cul-de-sac of a street two liveried patrol cars, with 'blues-and-twos' blaring to enhance the shock and awe of the assault and to intimidate those doing business that morning, screeched to a halt and blocked the road. Swirling blue lights reflecting off windows and walls, while the sound of the two tones bounced and echoed off the same walls. The illicit businessmen in the house had lost their day's trade as the remnants of the queue and late arrivals made up of the needy and addicted scattered, apart from two bedraggled and confused individuals who were too stoned to realise what was happening, and they continued to wander in circles outside the police cordon in the hope that the intrusion would not hold up business for too long.

Kobe now moved behind the initial onslaught of six officers, it was their task to breech the house and clear every room of any possible danger, it was Kobe's task to follow close behind and ensure everything went as planned and that the initial rush of excitement and energy did not cause officers to go too far in protecting the building and any evidence. Court rules were tough on the police and senior officers had to ensure no rules were broken in the heat of battle. The same rules did not apply to the criminals, they had no rules, free to fight, bite and kick as much as they liked to avoid capture. Looking as if he had emotions under control but feeling anything but calm Kobe stepped over the drawbridge of the door, causing more groaning from the skinny doorman under it, the six-eight of Tiny was stood to one side, leaning on the doorframe, and cradling the bright red 'Annie' in his arms like a new-born baby. He bowed and swept his empty arm toward the door in invitation for his boss to enter the house.

"In you go Boss," his harsh Northern Irish accent, boomed about the house.

"Good job Tiny." The big man's grin grew wider still, he may have been a giant of a man, but he still loved to get praise for a job well done, in that respect he was like a big kid, but nobody would ever be brave enough to say that to his face.

A crocodile queue of black-clad officers followed while Tiny remained at his post just inside the door, he hated missing any action, but his job was done for the moment. The final man to reach the door was DS David Martin, Kobe's second in command, and he slapped Tiny on the shoulder, which he had to reach for and offered a 'well done'. Tiny still with Annie in hand offered a 'go get 'em, Sarge!'.

With controlled energy the men charged through the slim building with yells that echoed through every room, up and down stairs and out into the street.

"POLICE! STAY WHERE YOU ARE!" boomed through the building as the squad, now separated into smaller groups of three, went from room to room.

They barged through doorway after doorway, their APS, the extendable baton, laying on their shoulders and gripped tightly in readiness for action. There were strict rules governing how they used the Armament Systems Procedure, but it did help to boost their courage when totally in the dark about what weapons they could be facing on a raid. At that moment of the supercharged entry the output from their collective adrenaline could have powered a small town.

The broken front door lay at an awkward angle as if something had stopped it hitting the floor. The lanky doorman with his acned face remained stretched out beneath it and was holding it up like a makeshift ramp for kids on speedy skateboards, every time he tried to lift the door that covered him like a stiff wooden blanket, boots and coppers would crush it back down on him. The onslaught of officers in the well-rehearsed raid had trampled over the ramp while beneath it the skinny doorman had the breath knocked from him with every black boot that had hit his wooden cover. Doorman was his normal posting; he was the lesser of all the soldiers, so he got the worse task each day. He was regretting his career choices that morning. His job meant long boring days, ten until midnight every day, but it paid for his own habit gave him a bed, albeit a broken down one with a lumpy mattress, on the top floor. He rarely left the house, he didn't need to, so when the last officer had finished trampling over him, he wriggled about under the weight of the door until just his head poked out. He had regained a little of his breath as he had peered over the door and out into the sunshine, he wasn't sure what was the more fearful action to take next. Stay where he was and be arrested or try to slither out further and walk through the gaping chasm that was the front door and into a world that, quite honestly, terrified him even more than the police. Realising that although his head was clear his bony body was still trapped so he had no choice but to choose the latter option and pulling out a bony arm and laying it across his pale skinned face to ward off the sun like a vampire exposed to the light. He realised that once he was free from his horizontal confinement, he wouldn't be able to put up much of a fight, that had all been knocked out of him when big one they called 'Tiny' had burst the door off its hinges. With one free hand he gingerly touched the surround of his eye, wincing at the sharp pain and guessing it was now blackened, it had been the first point of contact as he had peered through the peephole before being trampled underfoot. He had tried to yell out a warning, one of the few tasks he had as a soldier and his paymasters would be less than pleased at his ineffectual guardianship. Now the police would begin questioning him and he knew he would not be brave enough to hold out for long. In the few minutes since taking up his position his already shitty world had turned to even more shit. His only ever job had just turned to crap, and he could only see redundancy in his future.

To him it appeared as if a squad of hundreds were continuing to pour through the house like a river of black, still yelling and disabling everyone they met, in the hallway and up the stairs, there were young men with wrists and necks dripping with golden bling being fitted with new black plastic bracelets. All a little tight and dull for their liking. Just for effect as Tiny Smith, last in the row entered the house he bellowed the police-do-not-move mantra, it was as if the entire house trembled at his roar.

"POLICE, STOP MOVING!"

The towering officer's smile was even larger than usual, he was having fun. Looking down at the lad with his head poking out from the fallen door, he smiled and said, "You alright down there, lad?" The soft Irish brogue of Tiny seemed to calm the Doorman, but the laddie had no breath to answer with.

The shouting was all part of the shock and awe of a surprise entry, it was just one element of everything that went into a successful raid. It was also important for all in the house to know that police had entered. Rules stated they had to call out as to ensure they were recognised as officers, but it was also giving the bad guys time to flee or surrender, though, unlike in the movies where gunfights and brawls broke out, most of the low-level villains capitulated without a fight. All too slow of thought to do anything but stand there with mouths gaping and hearts sinking.

The front-line officers once over the wood walkway split into their smaller groups in the hallway. Three heading into a front room, what some long-ago granny had grandly referred to as the drawing room while three more headed up the stairs. Climbing the stairs, taking the risers two at a time, the thud of their size 12 boots on the carpet-less steps thudding and echoing throughout the house. Others coming in via the unlocked door at the rear charged their way into the kitchen.

Upstairs in a grubby front bedroom with walls of part plaster and part peeling wallpaper they found three dealers, one standing guard while two more of the drug firm's employees sat at an old kitchen table with a scared yellow Formica top cutting up and weighing blocks of cannabis on an old-fashioned set of brass balance scales. The resin block was such a dark brown it was almost black and on the top a gold seal stamped into the soft product, it was known as Pakistani Gold, the badge a sign of quality. An eight-inch blade of a chef's knife which glittered, despite the dullness of the room, was doing the slicing and the scales weighing off exact ounce lumps. It wouldn't do to be overgenerous with the portions. A bit light and the customer would create havoc, a little over and the boys with the bling would take it out of their 'commission' or their skin and neither was a happy prospect. As for shaving some off for themselves, well, that was a big no-no as closed-circuit cameras watched their every move. Being sat there in just their boxer shorts left them with nowhere to hide any illicit cuts of dope, well there was one hiding place but neither wanted the discomfort of shoving a block of dope up there. Both operatives were quickly pushed from behind their makeshift counter and forced down on their stomachs with hands cuffed behind their backs. That task swiftly carried out two of the three riot-clothed officers leant against the door jamb and waited for the rank and file 'uniforms', 'the plods' as they unkindly called them, to appear up the stairs and take their prisoners down. Both men listened and watched what was happening elsewhere in the house. The third member of their mini team was struggling to control the minder in the room who was making it very awkward to cuff, the two men in the doorway watched on with amusement.

"Thanks for the help you two..." he said breathless.

"No problem," one responded, "...you got this."

With a look of resignation, he finally managed to fit and cinch the cuffs. He sat astride his captive and raised his arms like a rodeo cowboy who had just hogtied a calf.

DS Martin passed the doorway, taking a quick look to ensure his officers were safe and secure, he tutted at the sight of one of his officers sat astride the detained man.

"You are supposed to arrest them, not fuck them, Phillips." said in jest but there was hint enough of his displeasure. "And you two, stop lounging about and get your prisoners downstairs."

The room burst into action once more before the DS, shaking his head, hurried into the next bedroom just along the corridor, followed by two more officers in riot gear. A hefty shoulder from the DS was enough to demolish the weak internal door with one swift charge just above the battered and dented brass handle, the door burst inward crashing against the wall, shaking loose a large wedge of plaster, which fell to the floor in a large puff of plaster-dust. The pair of officers with him paused in the doorway, eyes gazing around the room's interior. As if in disbelief they all looked around the room and then at each other, all carried the expressions of puzzlement. Instead of the violent resistance expected they were surprised to hear the soft waves of music filling the room, DS Martin recognised the sweeping music played by Pink Floyd, Dave Gilmour's smooth guitar playing thoroughly familiar to him. Two huge beanbags that were shoved together were holding a group of what must have been, favoured customers or staff on a break. Each of them seemingly and totally unfazed by the loud intrusion. Their eyes looked numb as the four totally stoned hippy types stared back at the police with no recognition whatsoever, lost souls reflected in dull irises.

"Hey man..." was all one of them could manage to utter in what seemed a friendly manner, the others dreamily waved.

On the floor by the eloquent narrator was the reason for his stupor, laying on a grubby tea tray the tools of his life choices, a used needle, blackened teaspoon, cheap plastic lighter and a lump of burnt tin-foil. The room smelled sweet, like a department store make-up counter and smoke from a skinny joint twisted up toward a nicotine-stained ceiling. If ever there were a child who needed to see an advert against drug taking this room and its occupants would have been the poster-boys.

Further along the corridor two officers peered into the front bedroom, heads craning around the door jamb, there was no door hanging in the entrance. Inside the room it was almost bare, a simple table, two chairs with dealers sitting in them and on one wall a curling and psychedelic poster for an Isle of Wight Music Festival from many years ago, Dylan was the headline act. On the scuffed table top the sniffing stock of white powder was ready for today's customers, little twisted bags of clingfilm. This really was the supermarket of choice for the addled and addicted and in this department two scruffy dealers, each with a protector stood flanking them. The minders looked bored, or stoned, and the service personnel had readied themselves to open shop in the cocaine section, in front of them rows of the ready-weighed tiny plastic baggies of the white powder as well as a selection of drug taking paraphernalia.

This was truly a one-stop shop for all their customer needs.

The two officers, a third standing a foot back from them in support, looked at each other in mild surprise through the visors of their riot helmets and then back into the room, the quartet inside did not seem to realise what was happening, almost as if two helmeted faces peered into the room every morning.

The moment was now, and the pair of officers launched into the room, quickly raising their physical input as they moved at full speed and full volume...

"STAY RIGHT WHERE YOU ARE, POLICE!" they yelled as they drove forward.

The two skinny youths and two burly guards were as rabbits in the headlights, frozen to the spot, eyes wide open but still with no recognition of the events quickly unfolding. It was the minders who were floored and cuffed first, being that they offered the biggest threat, neither put up much of a fight and they were handled one-on-one by the first two officers. They were avoiding getting resisting arrest added to their upcoming charges. The two shopkeepers behind the table offered no resistance either, it is tricky trying to look hard when all you are dressed in is tighty-white pants and striped socks. These were just sales personnel not enforcers. So compliant were they that the third copper into the room stood in front of the table and politely asked...

"On the floor please you two, and hands behind your backs." They complied without argument.

All four were cinched and under control in seconds, the officers now felt a little cheated as they had all that adrenaline running and nobody to fight with. It is a tricky thing to handle somebody with a force enough to subdue them and keep oneself safe, but to also handle them gently enough so as the defence of police brutality would not be an issue. DI Kaan's team were always well rehearsed and well-coached for such situations. Miscreants held firmly by their elbows were all stood up and marched outside to the awaiting vans, cage doors open, ready for prisoner intake.

CHAPTER 7

At the foot of the stairs DI Kaan, was staying central so that he could be on hand for controlling the raid and in a spot where he could get to all parts of the house quickly. He fidgeted and tried to readjust his stab vest; these days he was more used to his loose-fitting suit jacket. He hated the weighty vest but the wearing of it was compulsory, too many officers had been stabbed in recent years, criminals were getting braver, or becoming more stupid. A call, with a questioning tone, from the top of the stairs took his mind away from the irritating vest.

"GUV?"

Kobe immediately leant over the bottom upright of the banister and turned his face upward. He found himself staring up at the spotty face of one of the younger coppers staring down at him, the fresh and youthful look making him feel ancient, the lad on the top step couldn't even grow a beard, so young did he look.

"Five up here to go, Boss..." he yelled down, "...and a big chunk of product to watch over."

Kobe answered in a way that meant there could be no ambiguity in his command.

"Who are you with?" he enquired.

"The Welsh wanker, Evans." Was the response.

Kobe heard a muttered response to the insult from inside the upstairs room, it held a distinct Welsh twang. "That's racist, you Cornish twat!"

Kobe could hear the camaraderie in the voices so forgave the banter as he knew this was part of letting off steam when a raid died down to the clearing up stage.

"No need for the racist Welsh tag Lad, he is just simply a wanker." Kobe chided.

"Sorry Boss."

"Right, you two stay close to the product, remember not to touch anything, and I will send up the forensic guys to bag and tag it. He then turned and spoke to Tiny Smith who was still standing on the door, its crushed soldier still on the floor, but now in custody.

"Tiny, have any more uniforms arrived yet?"

"Yes, Boss and the transport has arrived as well."

"Thanks Tiny, get a few of them in here will you, need some sensible ones to stand watch without touching until its safe for forensics to take over." he ordered gently. "And get that poor sod up off the floor will you."

Tiny stepped off the door and easily lifted it up with his one free hand, propping it against the grubby wall. The lad tried to wriggle his way upright, but a size 13 boot placed firmly on his chest kept him in place while Tiny reached down to flip him over and cuff him, the plastic tie clicking as he cinched it tight before the towering police officer lifted the young lad into a sitting position. Both Kobe and Tiny looked down at the forlorn youth with a face spotted and ravaged by drug abuse. Under the bloodshot eyes were heavy black bags, around his nostrils was scabbed skin and from his nose a mixture of blood and snot dribbled down to his top lip, without thought he licked his lip and tasted the coppery flavour of his own blood. A stiff goatee beard was striped black and white like a skunk's tail. It was a face only a mother could love, and even she would have struggled.

Now sitting up and powered by drugs and adrenaline the guardian of the door was only just getting his breath back and regaining a little of his fighting spirit. He always believed he should fight against the 'Man', and his oppressive boot, even if it was a size 13 and belonging to a giant of a copper.

"You broke my nose you fucker!" he screamed at Tiny Smith, who towered a full head and shoulders over him and was smiling.

"Now, now, is there any need for that kind of language when you have guests? I did knock before I came in, not my fault you were standing behind the door." Tiny looked across at his Boss. "No fucking manners this lot Boss!" Kobe let the inappropriate language slip uncorrected from his officer, Tiny was Tiny, and had been around a lot longer than his DI. Although a rank-and-file officer Kobe, as did others in his crew showed him due deference when it came to years of service and experience.

"I blame the education system and a poor up-bringing Tiny." Kobe responded. "They don't have good role models like you to help them."

With the initial assault over everything began to calm down, the release of light banter helped the officers cope with a stressful situation.

Kobe's DS, David Martin, stepped into the hallway from the street and standing on tiptoe peered over Tiny's shoulder.

"Very eloquent individual you have contained there Tiny," then looking down at the scruffy individual. "I think you should apologise to Tiny; you may have hurt his feelings."

"Fuck you too, he broke my fucking nose." Blood was now staining his already grubby and torn t-shirt.

DS Martin tried to look Tiny in the eye but was almost a foot too short, "Better arrange for the duty surgeon to take a look at him, Smith."

"Will do Mr Martin, just waiting for the transport to sort out their passenger list." Tiny Smith was very old fashioned in how he treated and spoke to his senior officers, he had been around for a long time and respected those in authority who deserved it and had earned his respect. Some of the more senior officers in the county, mostly those who joined from university and had been fast tracked to senior status never quite knew which was genuine respect or sarcasm, the twinkle in Tiny's eyes nor his hard-edged Northern Irish accent did anything to help distinguish between respect or discourtesy. The big man had no time for officers who had not spent time on the streets learning their craft, as far as Tiny was concerned, nothing taught in some college lecture room could replace the school of real life. On this squad however, the DS and DI had his total respect, they had been there and done it and earned their rank, he had no time for graduates who just thought they knew it all. To Tiny these inexperienced jobsworths were dangerous to be around.

Noticing that the 'enforcer' was still dangling from Tiny's hand, Kaan noted. "You do know you are supposed to drop that thing once through the door..." His DI nodded toward the red door-opener.

"What!" Shock took the smile from his face. "...And leave poor Annie here for one of those druggie bastards to run off with her." He hefted the heavy tool with affection.

DS Martin, who had just reappeared on scene, had to ask what many before were too anxious to ask. "Go on then. Why do you call it Annie?"

"Not 'it' Mr Martin, she!" He may have been huge, but his smile was infectious. "And when she knocks, she can open '*Annie*' door!" His Irish accent making the word sound exactly like '*any*'. His raucous laughter echoed through the terraced house, doing nothing to settle the nerves of the drug addicts in the various rooms who were now under arrest, a few of whom looked close to tears.

The DS turned away, shaking his head at the big man's humour, but carrying a wry smile. However, the seriousness of the job at hand took over once again and his demeanour altered as he met one of the team from the initial entry who was now thumping down the bare wood and narrow staircase, his riot helmet dangling from his fist.

With a gentle Irish brogue, that apparently charmed women from the trees with its lyrical tones, Bernie Murphy reported the success of the raid to his DS. Unlike Tiny, Murphy was from the southern side of the boarder, not from the *'Norn-Iron'* side, although they did share a liking of Irish whiskey and Guinness the two Irishmen were as different as chalk and cheese.

"All gathered in and quiet, Sarge." reported the soft-spoken uniformed Irishman who had been first through the door as was always the way. His deep and resonant voice always sounded like poetry to his DS.

"You do know we are of equal rank now, since your promotion Murph?" A line often said by the detective. "You can just call me David."

"Whatever you say Sarge." David had to smile. "A few bodies upstairs to be shipped off and a large lump of some exotic substance to be watched over and bagged up."

In his right hand the riot helmet still dangled. The plain clothed sergeant nodded toward Murph's left hand which was grasping the handles of a canvas shopping bag.

"Whatcha got there Murph?"

"Ah...." he replied with a disappointed tone. "Was hoping you hadn't noticed that."

"Guess it's not your shopping then."

Murph placed his helmet on the floor and pulled open the bag and offered a peek inside to DS Martin.

"Fuck me!" Martin stated as he stared down into a bag full of bank notes. Wads of cash, each two inches thick and held together with elastic bands that were straining to breaking point.

"That's just what I thought, don't suppose I can keep it like." he said while closing the bag up again.

Now the intensity of the morning had relaxed somewhat,

Bernie's body language had softened, and his fluid movements became both feline and feminine, like a dancer he moved softly toward the front door. He would have been in for some serious ribbing if his squad ever discovered that he was at music college learning ballet before an injury changed the course of his career. The team had learned long ago, even before it was fashionable that Murph was gay, but not one of them was brave enough to tease him about it and they treated their knowledge of his proclivities with respect, he was well liked by his colleagues. Woe betides any other copper who talked about their sergeant behind his back.

"Me and my husband could have had a proper honeymoon on this kind of money," he added, "Instead of the crap weekend we had in Brighton." And he took the bag full of creased banknotes out to the forensic team to get it safely booked in.

Everything in the house now became routine, prisoners were guided outside to the waiting vans, forensic team members dressed from head to booted feet in pale-blue evidence onesies walked through the house gathering and logging evidence and tutting at all the uniforms clogging up their crime scene.

As they walked along the corridor toward the back rooms of the house, which was in an extension once built by a long-disappeared and proud house owner.

"Any problems?" asked Kobi of his 2IC.

"These guys were shopkeepers, not fighters," DS Martin responded. "...even their minders knew their job was done. There is one girl, who looked so emaciated that I think she will need to be hospitalised and not jailed, although she will probably end up with both and get lost in the system. They all gave up easily." David stroked his close-trimmed beard, something he always did when contemplating things. "They all knew the game was up and had a fair idea that arrest was always an inevitable action in their chosen careers. Mostly they were working, if you can call it work, for the next hit".

Murphy strolled back into the hallway after depositing the bruised and shaken doorman, with blood caking around his nose, to the waiting van outside.

"You ever thought of forgetting the helmet and just polishing your head Murph?" David Martin asked of Murphy, taking note of his baldness and the fact he was a black Irishman.

"Excuse me while I laugh Mr Martin!" Murph was another of those who always showed respect to others he considered his superior rank, or those he respected for doing the job in a proper and dedicated manner. "You do realise that could be considered racist and I could easily take offense. It would be your fault if I was traumatised by such behaviour and had to go on sick leave and unable to cope with the job. And all because I am a tall, ruggedly handsome, black man."

"Bollocks," replied the DS. "I only take the piss cos you're Irish."

"Oh, in that case you're fine." The Irish brogue sounding even more poetic than usual.

They had reached a back room. "You talking of retiring Murph?" asked Kobe.

"Not me Boss, I am just reporting for sick leave because of the racism toward my proud Irish heritage."

"You wouldn't know what to do with yourself if you weren't in the job."

"Me and my other half would travel Boss, see all the places we have only seen in pictures before."

David Martin was first to respond. "What, on a Copper's pension?"

"Plus, all the compensation I will get for the mental anguish you suit-and-tie marvels have caused. Plus, there is enough product upstairs to open my own shop, if you two would look the other way for five minutes while I loaded up the van."

"Was there a good haul up there, Murphy?" Kobe asked, the smile now gone from his face he returned to the serious business. "It would be good to show the shiny uniforms back at the nick that the raid was worth the Sunday overtime."

The DS cut in, "Not as much as I thought we would find Boss, a good-sized lump of Pakistan's finest and a few powder filled packets, but with the queue that was outside I expected to find more. They would have been out of stock by midday."

"Maybe when we start the interviews we will find out if there is a hidden stash somewhere else in the street." Kobe turned his attention back to Murphy. "If everyone is accounted for and cuffed your team can stand down now Bernie. Then we can get out of the way of the forensic guys."

"Already done Boss and a few are already on their way back to the canteen, just a couple of plods on the front and back doors."

"Nicely done Sergeant Murphy, a well-run raid as always," Kobe offered.

"Always a pleasure Mr Kaan, always a pleasure." He turned to head back down the hallway, but David Martin as always needed the last word. But, spoken quietly so only the three comrades could hear.

"Big, black, gay and Irish, what a bloody mixture."

"Don't forget ruggedly handsome, you English prick."

"Stay safe Murph and see you tonight for a pint."

The pair were not just colleagues but close friends and would always have each other's backs.

CHAPTER EIGHT

DI Kobe Kaan was well pleased that everything had gone to plan. All his men were safe, which was vital to him during planning and execution, and just as important a haul of illegal stuff had been taken off the street. Being well prepared meant clockwork precision, and as usual in his job, when things had appeared to go well there always the danger of there being some kind of sting in the tail. It seemed to be a copper's lot that nothing ever ran smoothly. But 'so far, so good' he muttered under his breath. The thought had arrived right on time as from a room at the back of the house a woman's shout echoed along the hallway. Kobe recognised the voice of one of the newer members of his squad, it was her first big raid.

A dark-haired officer, her hair tied so tightly back in its well strapped bun that the skin on her cheeks appeared to be stretched taught, poked her head into the corridor and said with some force.

"Sarge! Mr Kaan! I think you need to see this!" The cry carried with it some urgency.

DS Martin and DI Kaan exchanged glances; it was only a split-second moment between the two men, but both showed concern. Although a yard ahead of his Boss, David Martin pulled himself tight to the wall to allow Kobe to get past.

They found a small room off the kitchen, and to Kobe it made the layout of the ground floor look odd, sort of out of kilter. PC Stella Gold, stood just inside the entrance, hovering between the freshly revealed opening in the wall and the round dining table which she had discovered in the almost missed room, the set up. With its chintzy wallpaper and white tablecloth, it reminded the two officers of an old English tea room, with its fresh table cloth and fine China. Just eight feet by eight feet it appeared more like a quaint alcove, rather than a room. It was decorated floor to ceiling with garish floral wallpaper, the sort that would have been fashionable in a house back in the 1960s. There was even a portrait of the late queen hanging on one wall. In the centre, complete with its freshly pressed tablecloth, was a round table where an elderly woman took tea from a silver teapot and drank from an eggshell China tea service.

"I leaned against the wall Boss, and it sprung open," Gold explained, pointing toward the secret door, before anyone raised the question of how the room had been missed on the first sweep of the house. "...nobody noticed the crease among the stripes of the wallpaper in the kitchen."

"More to the point," added her DS as he peered over Kobe's shoulder, "How come this was not picked up on our Intel."

Kobe felt this was a question for later, and one he would ask quite sternly, "...and you found her sitting there sipping tea?"

Gold merely nodded, feeling that her boss was just stating the obvious rather than needing an explanation.

Gold had been one of the officers that had come in through the back door and the team had failed to notice the door disguised by the wallcovering on the first search, another question to be thought about when business at the sharp end was done, they should have had intel on the layout, mistakes like that cost lives. At the table was sat a frail looking old lady, pallid complexion, confusion on her lined face with its sharp cheekbones and sad emerald eyes, her hair was silvery white and roped into a tight and heavy plait that hung the length of her spine. The taught skin on her face almost as transparent as the eggshell teacup which she held in her bony fingers. Apart from one raised and arched painted-on eyebrow, the other a straight and fine line, she seemed totally unmoved by the events and mayhem in her house. Every inch the archetypal grandmother she had been discovered on a second sweep of the ground floor as everyone had begun to relax while the adrenaline eased in their veins. The old girl was discovered sitting there in an upright wing armchair, the sort that did not look out of place lined up around the walls of an old-folks home, apparently, she was just sipping tea from the bone china cup. On the table in front was the ornate silver teapot, with matching milk jug and sugar bowl. Gold nodded toward the old lady, her head moving like a sprung loaded dog on the dashboard of a car, the motion shaking free her ponytail which bounced on the nape of her neck as she moved.

Stella was a pretty and slight girl with natural jet-black hair and a small turned up nose, artificially pumped-up lips looked strange against her delicate features. Although the pumped lip look was a modern fashion trend, Kobe did not care for it too much. The riot gear Gold wore seemed to swamp her small body, she tried to stretch to gain some height, but she remained diminutive which is why she worked so hard at her job, to make herself big enough to fill the shoes of the experienced coppers beside her.

"Would you like me to brew a fresh pot, if you are staying?" the old lady enquired as she looked up with a simple smile at the three strangers in her room. "I didn't realise there would be company today or I would have brewed a bigger pot."

She gave a very good impression of someone who had lost a few marbles in her lifetime and was happy to see guests in her home, even if they were unexpected. Neither Kaan nor Martin were taken in by the sweet and harmless looking old girl.

Although the room was small, Kobe took PC Gold's arm and led her to a point away from the table.

"How come this was missed on the first go through the house?" He kept his voice low but there was anger in it none the less.

"Sorry Sir," There was a nervous vibrato to her reply.

"I prefer either Boss or Mr Kaan, Officer Gold."

"Sorry Mr Kaan, totally my fault, it was my responsibility to stay and secure the kitchen area, but I missed the door first time, and it was when I was making sure I had cleared the rear of the house I happened to brush against the door." Gold pushed the door closed and then nudged it a second time so her DI could see it open. The old girl still sipped her tea from its floral cup, Kobe almost expected to see an extended pinkie finger while she held the cup.

Kobe decided to leave any other word on the matter for the debrief, Gold knew she had made a mistake and there was no point in harping on about it. The DI would also take the senior officer on the back-door crew to task as it was his job to ensure the safety of his small team.

"We better get Social Services down here to deal with her. Would you stay with her until they arrive?" It wasn't a question.

He glanced back to the old lady who was still sipping her tea, she absentmindedly brushed a few biscuit crumbs from her lap and onto the floor and smiled at her visitors. Kobe noticed the thick plait of silver-white hair that hung down her back and to her waist, he was certain she was not the batty and sweet old lady she was trying to be.

"Are you sure you don't want a cup?" her voice soft and frail but both Kaan and Martin noted an evil intent in her eyes.

"No thank you Ma'am," said Kobe. "We are police officers, and we are here on official business I am afraid." He gave his best public smile.

"Are you here for my boy, he is always getting himself in trouble the little scamp." The old lady's smile did not falter nor did the relaxed expression on her face. Butter would not melt in her mouth. "He is not a bad boy you understand, he just gets up to mischief like lots of young people these days."

David Martin scratched his head. "Just when you think you have seen it all..."

Kobe noted the puzzled expression that crossed his face and then he realised he was not the only one unconvinced by the scene in front of him.

"Would you like me to top your cup up, until we find someone to take care of you." He reached across the table to the teapot as if to pour but instead wrapped a hand around one side of the pot, it was stone cold. He then took the cup from the old woman's hand and realised the tea in that was stone cold also and smelled of dry ginger. The look of elderly bewilderment disappeared from the woman's face, her cheeks found some colour and Kobe was certain, her eyes had turned black with malevolence.

Kobe turned to Gold, "Slap some restraints on this old witch will you Gold."

"Boss?"

"She's drinking vodka and dry ginger, not tea, do you know any self-respecting woman that would do that."

The old woman showed her true metal. "Fuck you and all your scum copper friends." The genteel old lady spat with shrill tones as she threw the dregs of her drink in Gold's direction.

"Go fuck yourself," the venom was flying easily now, as did the cup's contents. "Don't you lay a hand on me, you dyke bitch." The crone was screaming as Gold moved closer to cuff her, she struggled with all her wiry strength as Gold's training came to the fore and helped her to overcome an unhelpful prisoner. The cuffs were slipped over liver-spotted hands, that had surprisingly long and elegant fingers with beautifully manicured nails. And both hands rested in her lap, it didn't seem right to cuff her hands behind her as deference was given to the woman's age.

David Martin was standing in the doorway, grinning at the drama in the small back room as Gold pulled the ends of the plastic restraints. "Make sure to cinch them cuffs nice and tight, we will have none of that homophobic bullshit today."

"Oh, was that homophobic Sarge, I thought someone had told her about me." David liked the smile that was sent his way and hoped he had not misread it.

"Bitch! That's disgusting." The old lady squirmed and wriggled but with hands cuffed she found movement tricky, and the young officer moved around her chair to hold her down from behind, the woman had nowhere to go with her shoulders being firmly held back into the upright back of the upholstered armchair. With no hope of escape, and the joy of 'fucking' with the police wearing thin she gave up the struggle as Gold held her back with more gentleness than she felt like giving.

The cuffed and parchment hands rested in the old girl's lap, the skin that covered them almost opaque and littered with liver spots, Gold hoped that she would grow old a little more gracefully. It felt like a strange thought but in stressful situations the brain does strange things to cope.

"Keep her separated from the others, will you Gold." her DI instructed in his usual firm but quiet manner. "We have the wrong intel, again. It's not her son, who is as well known for wearing cheap looking bling as he is for his violent nature, he is not the owner of this little shop of horrors so it's not so important that we have missed him. The boss is this little old lady, and it seems we have finally caught her with her hand firmly in the cocaine jar."

Gold was smiling, enjoying her work. "Come along Mum, let's find a van all to yourself." It was said with a hint of sarcasm as she gently lifted the old girl from her chair by one elbow, still giving deference to what was a pensioner after all.

With things settled in what they thought was the last room, Kobe and DS Martin turned and stepped back into the hallway. Kobe spoke to his DS as they walked.

"Thing is David, I don't think that she is even the boss, they have been shifting too much stuff for this to be just a local operation." His DS was thinking the same.

"My thoughts exactly Boss, do you think she will talk once we get back to the interview suite."

"Hope so, because it's the bastard at the top I want..."

Kobe's thoughts were cut short as a high-pitched yelp from behind, it stopped both officers in their tracks.

It was Gold offering a sudden and loud cry that almost squeaked from her mouth, a childlike sound of fear.

"Boss! BOSS?"

"HELP, quickly..." suddenly her voice had taken on new urgency, it was part quizzical and part cry for help.

Two concerned officers turned back into the room and as they entered, they noted Gold was staring down at the old woman, eyes bulging. Leaning over the arm of the chair the young police officer was struggling with the wiry old woman. First into the room was Kobe and he tried to get around the two women, the table and the chair, but the room size was restricting too much movement.

"What is it, Gold?" his tone conveying urgency to match Gold's.

There was no reply apart from a grunt of effort. Gold was using all her strength in struggling to keep the old lady restrained, pulling her into a vice-like body grip with one arm, while her free hand was fighting for a good hold on one of the woman's wrists. The crone's free hand tried to scratch at Golds pretty face, fingernails raked down her cheek leaving red welts. She fought hard but was failing to keep the old woman's gnarled hands down. The old girl squirmed around slightly and finally Kobe could see the reason for the shrieks of panic from his officer.

His young PC, Stella Gold was fighting for her life.

David Martin was next back into the room and all he could see was the three people already in the room in some type of swirling dance movement. The melee toppled the table it teetered for a second then turned over, cloth, crockery and vase of wilted flowers all sliding to the floor and adding more noise to the mayhem. It was then that the DS also saw what had caused the sudden panic.

With a firm grip that belied her age in the old woman's gnarled hand was a gun. It was an automatic. It was black, vicious, hard edged and carried a menace with it that was more than reputation. It was the kind of handgun that would look more at home in an American crime drama rather than in the floral backroom of a small drug house in quiet and pretty Chichester. As if they were watching some kind of TV cop movie, both senior officers noticed that with her free hand Gold was pulling back the old girl's trigger finger, almost breaking it as she struggled to keep the finger out of the trigger guard. The old woman screeched, the sound of a Harpy, the half-bird – half-woman of Greek mythology.

As the two men joined in the fight Gold managed a brief explanation in a hoarse, out of breath, whisper.

"She had it stuffed down the side of the seat cushion, it was already out, and in her hand before I saw it." Gold grunted with the continued effort. Fear stopped her grip from loosening.

Even amidst the scuffle Kobe could see a tear in the young woman's eyes. It showed fear but it also showed human spirit as she bravely hung on to the battling crone in the pretty floral frock. Gold would not be defeated.

As Martin joined in the scuffle, he pushed his arm between Kaan and Gold and more by luck than judgment he was able to grab the barrel of the gun, he wrenched it first one way then the other, trying to disarm the old lady who now seemed to have more strength and purpose than her old body had first revealed. The DS decided to just make sure the pointy end of the gun was not pointing at the trio of police officers and as he pushed the barrel away from its human targets there was suddenly a loud crack. The sound of a backfiring exhaust, it hurt their ear drums and echoed through the house, down the corridors and out into the street. David Martin felt the heat in the barrel as the released round spun its way out of the firearm. The old-girl's bony finger had slipped into the trigger guard and pulled on the lethal lever and the gun had fired as the liver-spotted handheld resolutely onto the patterned grip and struck the edge of the falling table. The three officers momentarily froze, and for a split-second the room was as still as a tableau, a photographic moment that when spoken of by them in the confines of safety later would not sound as anywhere near terrifying as they felt as the shot spat out its crackling cough. A shot that left ringing in all their ears, but no one would recall later hearing a cry of pain as the loose bullet had struck home.

As movement returned to the room so did sound as a cup and saucer smashed on the floor. David Martin had now wrestled the gun from hand and he stepped away from the scuffle holding the firearm at arm's length. One by one all four in the tableau looked up and saw who the gunshot's victim was. The stray bullet had hit a dusky native girl in the head, a clean shot into and through the forehead, a kill shot. The bullet through the framed print of a pretty dark-skinned girl who was very fashionable back in the 1960s, but once again trendy as with all things retro that appeared to be on-trend as per the current fashion for things from a previous generation or two. Despite the wound she retained her enigmatic smile, her almond eyes remained bright and alert, but there was no saving her.

Gold kept the pressure with her grip of the gun hand, with wrested weapon finally free and away she dragged the woman face down onto the faded carpet. Thinking quickly the DI pulled a latex glove from his pocket and using forefinger and thumb as a protected pincer he took the pistol away from his DS and with care and slow movement he carried it down the hallway where other officers had filled the passageway to get to where the gunshot had come from.

"All clear lads, thank you." He appreciated the back up from unarmed officers who stepped up to the plate, despite the danger. "Make way so I can get this to the CSO, and he can make it safe." They all pinned themselves back against the walls of the narrow passageway to allow him to pass. In the quaint terraced, Victorian house with its flowery wallpaper, and cheap dated furnishings it was the last place any of them expected to see a firearm.

One of the uniformed officers was first to ask although they were all thinking the same thing.

"Is everyone alright Boss, do you need the paramedics down there?"

"We are all good, thank you. Williams, is it?"

"Yes Boss." The young lad, who was at the front of the heroic onrush, was proud that the well-known DI had remembered his name.

"Everyone is okay but there is a dusky maiden who won't survive." Williams and those in earshot exchanged puzzled looks.

Fingertip pinch still gripping the pistol Kobe held it between finger and thumb in much the same way someone would carry a used condom. He dropped the firearm into a held out evidence bag by the head of the forensic team, warning him of the twitchy trigger at the same time. On his way back along the hallway Kobe had time to take the measure of Williams, who was towering over those stood around him.

"What the hell did your mother feed you on, son?" Kobe

strained to look up at the lanky youth.

"Lots of Greens Mr Kaan, I always had to eat my greens."

"I did too lad, but I never shot up like you." Kobe took a mental note of the young officer's manner and his willingness to step into possible danger. He decided that he was an officer he would keep an eye on.

With hands now released and re-cuffed behind her Gold began to lead the old woman out of the side room and through the kitchen.

"Just a moment Gold."

"Boss?"

With nothing but a hunch and noting that the old woman had glanced back into the room and down at the floor Kobe was keen to see what had caught her attention. The tea pot remained where it had fallen, its lid at an angle alongside it, bright, polished silver against the heavy pattern of what looked like a Persian rug.

"What is it Boss?" David Martin also asked while trying to see over his DI's shoulder.

"There is no tea spilled, from the pot." Kobe responded.

The blue latex glove that was in his hand he now slipped on, tightly pulled on with a snap of the cuff against his wrist. Latex gloves were impossible to just slip on easily. He reached down and picked up the teapot, with his free hand he pulled a pen from a strap on his stab-vest. Poking the pen into the middle of something he slowly retracted it, and with it came a wad of £50 notes held in a round bundle by a thick, red, rubber band. If the wad had been any thicker it would not have fitted through the hole vacated by the lid.

"Christ in a hand cart!" Martin exclaimed. "There must be a few grand in that bundle. Do you think there is enough there to treat the team to a drink tonight, Boss?"

"And some..." Kobe responded, "we could all have shots."

"Have we not had enough shots already today, Boss?" Gold asked, her sense of humour slowly returning.

"Poor choice of words, Gold."

Turning to his female officer Kobe gave a firm instruction, "Keep her a distance from the rest of that motley crew will you, Gold. Stick her in a squad car on her own and you stay with her."

"Sorry I didn't see the gun down the side of the cushion Boss." Her cheeks flushed red. "I should have spotted it sooner."

"You have nothing to be sorry for Gold, you probably saved lives here this morning."

Her cheeks appeared to redden even more as she tugged on the old lady's arm to draw her out of the eight-by-eight room, which, despite its compact size had held so much drama.

"Ouch, you slag, that fucking hurt." The harsh and violent voice in no way fitted the old and haggard face of the senior citizen.

The muffled voice stopped them all. "Don't you hurt my mum!" So softly spoken, and yet perfectly clear.

The three of them were looking at the back wall of the room, but it was the old lady who spoke first, and it was with resigned anger.

"All you had to do was keep your fuckin' mouth shut, you useless sod!" As she spat out her venom, Gold felt the last of the fight drain from her.

Kobe winked and nodded in recognition and spoke clearly. "I know we have missed her son, but on reflection I think Mother there is the true proprietor of this little pharmacy. We have been trying to catch her with her hand in the cocaine jar for some time."

This time the old lady was pushed toward her journey down the hallway. "Come along mum," Gold said sarcastically. "Let's find you a van all to yourself." And Gold took her out of the room and down the corridor, where Williams was still waiting.

"They may need you in the backroom." she whispered and nodded back in the direction she had just come. Williams moved forward.

"Thing is Boss," said David Martin keeping up the vocal pretence.

"I doubt she will tell us, and some high-priced lawyer is either going to tell her to make a deal or just keep quiet." Kobe responded. Parts of the job of a copper were just to frustrate and when it came to the rules of procedure they always appeared to fall on the side of the criminal.

"Can't see her making a deal by naming the smart bastard who will be her lawyer. Can you?" Neither man needed to answer.

"C'mon David, let's go and see them off to the custody suite and let the forensic guys have the house, there has to be more here than we have found, at least I hope there is or I am going to have to answer questions about all this overtime for just a couple of hundred quid worth of dope and some cash."

"We have taken a gun off the street though." A small crumb of comfort. "That must count for something.

Kobe merely shrugged as he wasn't convinced it would be enough to placate the bean counting superiors.

After the gun incident that caused the hairs on the back of Kobe's neck to rise, Kaan and Martin were on full alert. Williams entered the room, ducking under the door lintel as he did.

"Mr Kaan?" The young man looked down at both of his senior officers and the DS gazed upward, distracted by the height of the handsome young officer.

Kobe placed his index finger across his lips, Martin stood stock still and listened. He heard it as well, a rattle, a metallic sort of sound, coming from the corner of the room. Not a movement as such, more of a sniff, the sound a small child makes when they cannot be bothered to blow their nose. In old houses like this the walls were thin, but the sound was close, unlikely it was coming from the adjoining property. Kobe tiptoed around the table, still where it lay after being toppled, and placed his ear to the wall, more worried about putting his ear against the filthy floral wallpaper than what was behind it. He searched for an opening and found the tiniest of gaps between two strips of wallpaper. He pushed either side of the line, nothing. He slowly brushed his hand further toward the corner of the room, seeking out the next split with his fingertips and upon finding it, pushed to the right of it. Just as the first secret door in the kitchen had a second door popped open and swung outward. Kobe smiled and DS Martin just swore.

"Fuck me!"

Then Kobe spoke, "Jesus Christ!" he uttered. Blasphemy, another sin. He was really building his list of them today.

Behind the new secret door and sitting on a pile of what appeared to be blocks of plastic-coated white powder, cocaine was always the obvious guess, was the son they thought they had missed, gold bracelets rattled and jangled on his wrist as he tried to stretch in the cramped space and pull the door closed again, as if that would keep out the boogiemen. The dealer looked out and the two officers looked in and Williams looked over them and down into the alcove. It was another frozen moment of tableau, all three parties stunned by the discovery and both officers noting a smudge of white powder on the space between nostril and top lip of the 'mob-boss' the sound they had heard was that of the dealer taking a snort of his own product. No wonder the mother had remained in charge of the operation. The boy was ginger, and freckle faced, he wore a red bandana under a reversed baseball cap that had the Nike 'swoosh' on the stiff peak.

Martin ignored the stoned youth and began to count, and he was first to break the silence after working out what the dealer's seat was made out of....

"Ten across, five down and five deep, that is around 250 blocks that bugger is sitting on." The DS had quickly calculated.

"And look on the shelves over his head." Kobe observed. "I can't even begin to figure how many stacks of notes that are up there."

The DI reached in and dragged the youth from the room, there was no fight, and the boy was almost dead-weight.

"Shall I take him Sir?" Williams piped up, Kobe had forgotten he was there and was surprised to hear a voice coming from a high up.

"No thanks Williams, Mr Martin will take him. You can stay here and make sure none of the stock or the bank notes goes missing." Kobe trusted all his squad but with so many people about he was taking no chances.

The tall lad merely nodded and stood at his post.

"Are you busy when you get off this evening?" Kobe inquired.

"No, I don't think so, Mr Kaan."

"Make sure you are in the pub just after six, join the rest of the crew for a drink. I think you have earned being a part of the celebration."

Now it was the young copper's turn to blush, and he just nodded to Kobe, he could not help when it came to hiding his smile, he would be a lousy poker player.

CHAPTER 9

The morning raid on the well-known drug house had worked far better than expected, which was always a good thing. Nobody hurt but thank God that things were not a different outcome with the discovery and discharging of a firearm. Though the knowledge that nobody was hit by the stray bullet was pleasing it was the bean-counters that also had to be appeased and the discovery of the mass storage of illegal drugs had made the overtime more than worthwhile, DI Kaan would not have to explain the raid to the Force's accountant officers. It irked him, and other front-line officers, that the force was now run by the so-called 'bean-counters' and politicians. Instead of being up in front of one of those toothless senior officers receiving congratulations for his team and a job well done, he was now sat behind his desk for the rest of the shift smiling with pleasure at being part of a superb team who had closed for good what was probably one of the county's busiest drug dens. There was a great pleasure in shutting down that business along with its little old lady who had spent her days sipping Earl Grey tea, and gin from her delicate china, in the daintily decorated parlour while mayhem ensued on the other side of the fake door.

Even the tiresome and drawn-out task of all that paperwork that goes along with such an operation could not take the smile from his face, this was why he had become a copper in the first place. Kobe was not a cocky man by nature, but he had really enjoyed watching the cuffs being cinched tight onto the wrists of the foul-mouthed old crone, and her son. He had to admit that the gun had been somewhat of a shock for all involved and then the smile did disappear from his face as thoughts drifted toward what could have been rather than what was. The intel he had received prior to the raid was flawed and could have cost any one of his officers their life.

He shuddered!

He had ordered his team, some of whom he considered friends, into that viper's nest without armed back-up. No matter that the raid had turned out well, the intel was poor and that could have been a fatal flaw in their day's planning. He would do something about that on another day, today was a day to celebrate and once the paperwork was done, he would treat his crew to a well-earned drink.

Plus, today was a Sunday and that was sacrosanct to him, it meant that no matter the workload he would find time to head home for the family roast dinner, it was a rule with Kobe that he would, time and job permitting, spend some time with his beloved little family especially on a Sunday. He looked at the photo of the three of them that sat just to the right of his computer screen, and he felt the familiar tingle down the back of his neck that he got each time he gazed at their perfect faces. The photo had been taken on a recent walk around the tidal inlet that was just a few yards from their home, the harbour in the background the sun throwing sparkling diamonds of light across its calm surface. He counted his blessings every day as he knew that he had a job he loved and a loving family he could head home for, the one side of his life that helped him cope with the balance for the other. No matter the evils he saw and encountered daily on his job he always had his family to remind him of the good and innocent in the world.

Many of his colleagues and officers the length and breadth of the UK had suffered the anguish of severe mental illness, and Kobe was fully aware it was his family that kept his brain level and hopeful for the future. No matter the stresses of the job he always had them to head home to. But that afternoon as he gazed at their faces caught within the ornate silver frame, he held his breath for a few seconds. Something deep inside his core was bugging him, a niggle, just a small beep on his copper's radar.

Kobe felt afraid! As a tingle travelled down his spine. He didn't like the feeling!

He put that moment of fear down to the morning's action, it was always a harrowing experience to be confronted with a firearm, and he begrudgingly dismissed the feeling as something separate from his family. Always the perfectionist Kobe could not help thinking that they had just kicked a hornet's nest, it was obvious that the 'sweet' old lady ran the drug house, but would not be the overall boss, what films liked to call the 'kingpin' or brains of the operation, Kobe knew there was a bigger nut to crack. The old girl's son had been a snarling angry youth, but only in her presence, in reality he had been a snivelling child that had neither the intelligence or courage to be a gang leader. An assumption that was backed by the fact that she had the gun while he was hiding in the secret room. What a way to bring up a child, Kobe made himself a promise that his two children would get an extra big hug from him tonight. Maybe if that youth had been hugged more often, he might not have turned to a life of crime, but Kobe knew it was never that easy. He also knew that the house was just an outlet for an even bigger operation, a satellite dealership, and the higher-up hornets in the drug-chain would be sharpening their stings with revenge in mind. Kobe's team had discovered way too much contraband and money for small drug den in the peaceful city they called home. Something was not adding up.

Kobe was married to a strong woman; it was one of the things that made him fall for her. Strength and wisdom were mixed with a brave heart, a woman who would stand in the way of a speeding train for her children. He was boss here in his squad room but at home a different story. Kobe had always had a liking for strong women, but he had no liking or respect for the old lady. Despite the bluster and best efforts from the crone, he knew the old lady was only a small cog in the city's drug trade. There was too much physical frailty in the old lady and not enough muscle around her for her to be the chairman of the board. As pleasing as today's result had been, Kobe knew there was another layer of management, a silent partner was still out there backing the business that went on behind the solid door of number 11B in that disparate row of terraced houses. No matter the intel that his squad uncovered or received they still had no idea who that might be, and that irked the DI.

The afternoon dragged as he coped with the paperwork connected with such a big operation, the file would end up more than a foot thick, except now in this modern day and age of on-line storage rather than manila folders it would be on the County force's hard drive. There would be even more paperwork and red tape to follow as his two sergeants conducted the interviews, they had his total confidence when it came to that part of the job. 'i's and 't's had to be dotted and crossed, for this lot there had to be no escape on a technicality. The raid had been by-the-book, and so it would have to be for everything that followed.

While one part of his squad worked away behind the walls of the red-bricked station the forensic team were back at the terraced houses working on evidence gathering. Kobe's work phone beeped for an incoming message, it was brief, to the point and yet full of information that made the DI smile.

Dogs reacting to fireplace. Bricks slid apart and revealed another mixed buffet of product and a stack of cash bundles...

It was from the head of the scientific team, and he imagined them in their pale blue onesies, plastic over-boots and hair and face coverings all intent on finding the evidence. His reply was even briefer.

Good job. Thank you. Give the sniffer dogs another biscuit treat from me.

He knew from experience that the team would log every find, every print, and every piece of evidence. He had full faith in them. With that small message he had shaken off and forgotten about that weird feeling a few moments before his phone pinged. It was a good time to interrupt his squad. He stood, stretched the tenseness out of his body, tucked his shirt in and stepped out of his office with its ever-open door and spoke to the crew who were busy writing up their own notes contemporaneously.

"Right, you lot, get finished up with what you are doing, keep doing it right though as we don't want any of this going wrong, as we will be off to the pub in an hour. SOCO have found another substantial load of product and some more cash. We have them all clean and clear so far, so no fuck-ups..." Kobe did not often swear but it always seemed to emphasis his instructions at moments like this. He wasn't sure if another sin had been broken, he would have to check with the Imam later. "...we have them all, even that old witch with her teapot and gun, and there will be a long break in their dealing."

A huge cheer and applause went around the squad room, more

for the offer of beer than the fact they had dealt a small blow to the drug trade.

He went back to his desk and checked his watch as he did, hoping that it was almost quitting time, he longed for the loving arms of his family and a fulfilling roast dinner.

Kobe knew very well from experience that someone would have already started filling the gap in supplies for the city's drug addled inhabitants. Supply and demand a constant threat to the area's youth.

He adjusted the keyboard on the desk, as if it had been moved while he had been away for a few seconds and he noticed his hands were still shaking slightly with un-burnt energy. During the raid the adrenaline had been running like a fast stream, now the task had widened like a river and the deluge had slowed to a trickle but was still there. He knew that some on the team, himself included, had hoped for a little more action and were disappointed when most of the drug-house staff had given up without a fight. Even the son, discovered in the secret room, with his low-carat golden bling dangling from neck and wrists and an ugly scorpion tattoo on his cheek offered nothing but verbal bravery. When confronted he had not put up a struggle or resisted arrest. In fact, he gave up rather meekly considering they had found him as he was snorting some of his own stock, tell-tell white powder remained on his upper lip, where a moustache was trying to cultivate itself but failed miserably leaving the top lip capped with a slight fuzz of hair. With the brush of danger denied them, the thrill of the chase was still high among the squad. Kobe knew the evening's drinks would be a raucous affair, front-line officers had a choice, let off steam and get the bad stuff out of their system or stack it all up deep inside and suffer the mental anguishes such as depression or the bad bear residing in the forest of mental anguish, PTSD. Kobe had a moment's thought for the guy who ran their local pub, and it was lucky the landlord knew them all well, being an ex-copper himself.

Their feelings were a bit like a boxer's who had thrown the knockout punch just a minute into a fight, there is a feeling of being cheated, shortchanged after all the preparation and training for exchanging a few rounds of painful blows but was denied that outlet with the throwing of one good punch landing square on the opponent's chin. Kobe's team had landed a terrific punch and even though the fight was over quickly he was still mightily proud of his fighters.

An hour or two of celebrating their rare win would burn off any excess energy. Kobe would only stay for one drink so that his team could then let their hair down without a senior officer on site.

Kobe made a note on a small yellow post-it as a reminder to check with the police surgeon, he would need to make a report on the injuries to the acne-faced youth who had been the 'gatekeeper' and had been trampled over as the door fell on him. The lad was only a lowly foot soldier who had had his arm broken in the raid and transferred from the crime scene in an ambulance and with his one good arm handcuffed to a uniformed officer. He probably had a couple of broken ribs as well but despite being involved with a drug gang Kobe would have a mass of paperwork for that one arrestee on his own even though the youth with sores around his nose from sniffing to much of the wrong stuff was to blame for standing behind the door, the uniforms upstairs, who had never been anywhere near a raid themselves or on the shop-floor so to speak, would be wanting pages of statements explaining how the injuries occurred to the poor lad. Once in court he knew his squad would be seen as the bad guys in the exchange, such was the modern copper's lot.

His attention drifted for a moment and through the glass wall of his office he noticed along the corridor his female team member, Gold, standing alone and sipping from a vending machine coffee cup. Of course, Kobe knew that each of his officers had their own mugs, so he assumed that Gold had needed some space and so opted for the poor excuse for coffee that the machine dispensed. Kaan made his way from his office to the machine, he would suffer the bad taste for the sake of checking on Gold.

"Don't select coffee, Guv. It's rank." Gold warned.

"Good advice, hot chocolate it is then." He knew it was the lesser of two evils.

Hot drink up to his lips, he blew across the surface of his beverage creating ripples of chocolate scum. Kobe leaned back against the same wall and tried to hold a casual air as if he was also taking a break. Without forcing face to face contact with his junior officer he spoke softly so as not to bring attention to Gold from anyone walking the dim corridor.

"You did very well today, Gold, under extreme circumstances."

He sipped the insipid brew and pulled the required face. "No wonder morale is low on the force, when we are forced to drink this swill!"

"It is pretty gross isn't it, Sir."

Kobe thought of correcting her over the 'Sir' tag but then thought it petty to point it out this time. He really did hate the strict formality of the force sometimes.

"Are you okay Gold?" The question asked softly and without drama. Just one colleague looking out for another. He kept his gaze straight ahead with unfixed eyes on the outside world, sunlight was pouring through the south facing window, he purposely kept his eyes from her just in case there were tears. He recalled vividly his first time of coming face to face with a gun and remembered vividly that had almost pissed himself with fear, and when alone in his flat that evening he had cried. Sobbing with a mixture of relief and the fear of what could have been!

"I have never seen a gun before, Boss..." her voice with a slight tremble. "Well, apart from training of course. But this was the real thing, actual life and death moment, and it looked so bloody huge in her tiny hands. I let it throw me off course for a moment." She said, before quickly adding. "It won't happen again Boss."

"We all get that feeling of 'what-if'," he softly explained. "Even those of us that have been doing this for a few years. Even Murphy," he nodded back toward the office as if to cement the identification of Murphy. "...and he is a mad bugger. But even he will have a moment of doubt, that twinge of fear. Nothing much scares him, but firearms are a different thing. And you did well, you kept professional and safe. Can't ask more than that."

"Would firearms training help in future?"

"I don't know, everybody is different. I did my firearms for exactly that reason but in the end, it just made me realise what damage a bloody gun can do, not like in the movies where it gets treated like a bee-sting and they count to ten and get up again. Stay fresh and innocent for a little longer Gold, at least the fear serves to keep you safe, as long as you keep a clear head and remember your training." Usually it would have been deemed 'inappropriate behaviour' to put a hand on a female officer, but Kobe placed a hand on her elbow and chose that moment to go with eye-to-eye contact.

"You did well Gold, you should feel proud of yourself."

Kobe took a closer look at the four streaks of red that ran down Gold's left cheek, where the crone had scratched her. They were not deep wounds and no blood had seeped.

"How is the face feeling," he asked.

"Not sore anymore Boss, Ta." Then she added, "Checked myself in the mirror and put some antiseptic on. I don't think it will show in a day or two."

"That's good, but make sure you fill out an Injury-On-Duty form, as well as on the Electronic Accident Reporting System, or if you want, I can report it as an Assault in Execution of Duty and charge the hag with something else."

"Will do Boss, but I doubt you want the hassle of an extra charge for such a piffling injury," she replied, and Kobe sighed as he knew he would not have to start the paperwork trail again with another charge.

"Now think on what I said and stop feeling sorry for yourself and go and join your fellow officers. Wrap up your shift, go to the pub and celebrate a job well done with the others."

"I might head home for a lovely soak in the bath, Boss."

Kobe returned to being her DI, and not her friend. "That was not a suggestion Gold." Voice still quiet, but now it carried a firmness that could not be argued with. "You will join the squad for a drink, and you will enjoy the celebration, both of a job well done and a life still being lived."

"Will do, Sir, sorry, Boss." She stood away from the wall and straightened her body.

Kobe's voice turned once again to friendly tones. "And stop acting like a girl, or they will treat you like a girl."

"Sometimes I hate being a fucking girl!" A hint of anger now in her voice, although now there was smile on her face. This was more like the Gold that Kobe knew and why he had included her in his squad. He knew she would become a good asset to the team.

"Save the fears and tears for when you get home tonight and give whoever is waiting for a you a big hug." Kobe realised he knew little about his officer outside of work, something he would rectify as he liked to know all about his officers.

"No one to hug Boss, soon as I mention to dates that I am in the job they seem to disappear. Just me and a scruffy rescue dog called

Bear." At the thought of her furry flatmate a glint of happiness returned to her eyes.

"Well go home and hug Bear then, and as for prospective partners in the future show them your handcuffs and they will be eating out of your hand."

Finally, Gold's disarming smile returned, brightening her whole face.

"Ready Gold?" Kobe enquired, indicating if she was ready to go back into the squad room.

A firm nod was her reply, and she turned toward the door.

They walked back to the squad room side by side, no longer boss and subordinate but fellow combatants in the ongoing war against drugs. Just before they passed through the doorway Kobe added, "Believe it or not, everyone in that room is feeling the same, it matters not whether you are male or female, senior officer or rookie on this job. At one time of another they have walked away from their fellow coppers to hide their feelings, me included." He offered with such confidence that there was no room for doubt in her mind.

"Even Murphy?"

"Especially Murphy, you know he is a big softy really, the tough guy is all an act. They all know from experience there could be weapons when we take on a raid, sometimes it's like the bloody wild-west out there. And if you take the pre-raid intel as gospel then you are asking for trouble. We all know that if we fuck up then any one of us could get hurt. But today has been a job well done." And, as they stood in the doorway between corridor and squad room, he stopped, turning to face her. "You spotted the gun and assessed the situation, no matter that it scared the crap out of you. You were professional and did your job well." Now he smiled. "So, go be with your team, finish your paperwork and when they leave shift to go to the pub make sure you are among them. You have earned their respect today, they won't let on of course, but they are proud of the way you helped divert what could have been disaster this morning."

CHAPTER 10

At the antique fair, the shared joy of drinking a classic tea together was relaxing the two strange bedfellows, their choice of the afternoon Earl Grey. Journalist Nick Flax was the first to talk once the choice of tea had been decided from the disappointing range that the tearoom offered.

"You really shouldn't let them get to you Sam." He placed a friendly hand on Sam's shoulder. "They are the ignorant ones, just small people with small lives."

"I know, I know." Repetition of words because he was embarrassing himself by feeling the way he did. After so many years of being bullied the weak responses become almost automatic. "They pick on me, I bite, which makes them bully even more. I am my own worst enemy. I am bloody useless at my job, I was useless at school, useless with the girls and it all makes great ammunition for the buggers. Don't forget the biggest bully of the lot was my old man, even though I love and miss him, he would barely let a let a day go by without letting me know what a disappointment I was."

"If you are looking for sympathy you know you are looking in the wrong place, don't you?" Nick smiled as he interrupted the grumbling Sam.

"I know, just pissed off with it all." he shrugged.

"When your father died, he was close to closing the shop. He didn't have a penny to his name and debtors beating down the door. But you kept the shop going, paid off all his debts and it may be a meagre one, but you make a living. Not a lot of people could have done that."

Sam knew Nick was right, they had had this discussion many times before and the older man wondered once again why his young friend found the company so fascinating. He didn't question their friendship often; he would hate to break it by examining it too closely. Sam was just glad Nick was around.

A noisy fussing around by the tearoom doorway cut his reverie short and he took the delicate cup from his lips, no sane person would serve Earl Grey in a mug. Nick was the first to look up, his journalistic hackles aroused at the disruption. The tranquillity of the entire room was disturbed which was what the instigator of the upheaval had meant to do, he always meant to make an entrance no matter the size or location of the room. At over six feet tall and with shoulders as broad as the doorway the smartly dressed man was busy grabbing and shaking hands with everyone within his reach. Such was his force of presence that even the folk who didn't like him, or had no idea of who he was, were drawn into his electioneering entrance and walk. Expertly weaving through the tables, as a skier on slalom course, he touched shoulders, grabbed hands with an enthusiastic shake while his voice shook the ornaments on the walls as if an earthquake was passing through. The ebullient man reached Sam and Nick's table.

"Nick Flax, as I live and breathe," His voice no quieter even though he was stood next to the target of his query. "What's our local rag's Chief Reporter doing slumming it here at the flea market?" It was a rhetorical question, and the insult was compounded by the lack of his meaty fist being offered for Nick to shake. Instead, the man stood there towering over the table and looking down on the two men whom he looked upon with a distasteful gaze. The voice was as booming and brash as the man, he had intended for the whole tearoom to hear the slight.

Conversation had ceased on every table. Pregnant pauses were rife across the room and Nick merely looked up and said,

"Councillor." Then continued to sip at his tea, his eyes never looking up at the brash man in the loud suit with a shock of salt and pepper hair which was swept back by gel that held the controlled waves.

The lack of response was not missed by Councillor Kenneth Jackman and only those that looked closely would have noticed the slight narrowing of eyes, the stiffening of sinews in his neck and the clenching of teeth, the muscles in his jaw working overtime and visible to anyone who looked closely enough. The grey beginnings of a handlebar moustache were twitching slightly. One of his more attractive, female constituents had told him that it made him look dashing, in a rustic French sort of look, so he was busy cultivating the style. It did cause him great pain and a feeling of bereavement a few months ago when he had ditched a ponytail when it became seemed to become passé. He still missed it; vanity told him it was a good look.

Sam looked up at the Councillor, across to Nick, and then back again. He was giving a slight point lead to Nick on the confrontation when Jackman gave up the battle and turned toward the tea counter and going straight back to his glad-handing with the fake smile back in place beneath the ridiculous looking growth on his top lip.

"I don't know who he is Nick, but I guess you and he don't see eye to eye on much." Sam now went back to sipping his tea, slurping a little too loudly.

"That man is as obnoxious as he looks and sounds, and somehow, he has managed to get himself elected to the City Council." The words leaving a bad taste to the tea in his mouth. "The man is also a crook, which we keep hinting at in the paper, but we cannot get any proof on him."

Nick emptied his cup and caused it to clatter against the saucer as he replaced it on the table. Sam could see the nervous energy caused by Nick's dislike of the Counsellor but chose to say nothing. Nick for his part brought the afternoon tea break to an end.

"I have to go Sam; City team are playing at home this afternoon, so I have to be there to report on it."

"In this weather?"

"It would have to be refereed by Noah before they called the match off!"

"You back in time for Roadshow?" Sam asked referring to their Sunday evening must not miss Antiques Roadshow where over another good pot of tea they would try and outscore each other with valuations.

"Wouldn't miss it..."

With total confidence Nick leaned in for an uneasy man-hug, he was a man totally at ease with affection for his friend, Sam unused to close human contact found it uncomfortable at first but now enjoyed the sign of friendship. A real conundrum for a man who grew up with very little in the way of physical signs of affection.

Then Nick was gone, as the councillor loudly ordered tea and a slice of Battenberg, his encore for the day's meet and greet. Performance over conversations resumed around the cafe.

Sam's whole life seemed to be made up of confusions, he hated his life and yet enjoyed it when people entered his store to get pleasure with the things he held there. For Sam's part there was no finer feeling than when he garnered joy just from the smiles and positive comments.

It was almost as joyful as when he sold something, and yet he hated saying goodbye to the objects he loved. For Sam, there was always discomfort when in large groups of people, and yet he enjoyed the hubbub and conversations surrounding him on that Sunday. To put it simply, Sam thought he was weird, shy and an outsider, yet yearned for the company of a good woman. There had been 'girlfriends', but only a few, in the past, but that was a long time ago and they never stuck around for long.

Now it was time to head back to the misery that he called home and a cat that just used him for food and the odd bit of affection.

CHAPTER 11

Sam sidled through the meandering and narrow gap between the tables and headed out of the tearoom, stopping a moment to work out the route from there to the exit, which would avoid going past the bully of the ceramics dealer, he had suffered enough indignity for one day. So, it was head down and head back through the throng, the room was packed now as buyers mixed with those just coming in from the rain that persisted outside. The hall was steamy and sweaty, condensation covering the tall windows and rain-wet clothes drying in the warm atmosphere.

Doorway reached he looked out at the incessant drizzle that left reflective pools of amber light on the grey pavement and thoughts immediately went to his semi-dried out sock, knowing it was about to get saturated again.

"Fucking weather!" He muttered the words under his breath but obviously not quietly enough.

Looking over his shoulder he noted the prim looking lady swamped by the hand knitted coat of many colours that hung from her scrawny shoulders, under which was a T-shirt carrying the legend 'Lesbians Love...', Sam would have loved to know what it was that lesbians loved so much they would put it on a T-shirt but the rest of the statement was hidden under the folds of her rainbow jacket. The whole of the colourful ensemble was topped off by her severe face and a wild and windswept display of purple streaked hair, she was giving him her sternest glare while still sitting behind the table, guarding the petty cash tin that held the entrance money in front of her. Late arrivals were charged the same as the early birds and a young couple dripping rainwater onto the foyer floor passed Sam and headed into the hall, before being halted and having the 50p per person demanded of them. A key around prim-lady's neck was pulled forward, the lid of the petty cash tin unlocked, coins deposited and locked again. Unless the tin was bolted to the table it seemed like a redundant ritual. His language from a few seconds before had not been forgotten by the colourful gatekeeper.

"Is there any need for that kind of language, it shows a real lack of education." The voice was pinched and squeaky, like her face. "There are families here with children you know."

Sam thought she may have been a primary school teacher in a previous life, and he felt he would like to tell her to fuck off, but that would only add weight to her already low opinion of him.

The rain outside continued to fall and a soggy sock seemed to be the lesser of two evils so without further comment he stepped outside zipping up his wax jacket as he went. Happily leaving behind the fat couple with their new and overpriced purchase, the rude stall holder with his sanctimonious looks, and the loud councillor. As for the gatekeeper, he felt there had been a moment between them, a sexual charge, an instant attraction, and Sam hoped the legend on her T-shirt had ended with *'poverty stricken old junk shop owners',* but he doubted it.

He tugged his flat cap from the coat's pocket and slid it onto his head, at the same time his right foot, the one with a hole in its shoe stepped straight into a puddle, the sock was back at its sodden state. The painful pellets of rain from earlier had eased but the miserable drizzle continued, even the bloody rain could not work up a proper downpour for Sam.

Sam was miserable, the weather was miserable and at this moment in time, his whole life was bloody miserable. Even his cat treated him with disdain, and Sam would never know if he and the multi-coloured lesbian could have had a life together or not!

He plodded away from the hall with a heart so heavy it was dragging him down, further down than the wet sock on his foot. With hands sunk deep in his pockets Sam took a moment to look up and offer a prayer for a slightly better life. He didn't want much, just better. As he had never believed in any sort of God-like deity though he knew any prayer would fall on deaf ears. All he profited from with his glance to the heavens, and he guessed whatever gods where up there were laughing in his face, was rain spattered spectacles that gave him a speckled view of a thunderous black sky finally parting to offer better times with soft flashes of blue sky. The pathway back to his shabby shop remained as grey and uninteresting as Sam.

For most people arriving home, especially on a stormy day, there would be a comfortable moment of warmth, hot food and feeling of welcome from the cosy indoors. But as Sam neared his shop with its scruffy exterior and dingy displays behind grimy windows his heart remained down in his damp boots, it was the worst looking shop on the street, and that included the impoverished charity shops. On summer days with the windows cleaned and a decent display in the window it didn't look too bad but today the shop front looked like an embarrassed old beggar with an empty cap at his feet. As he reached his door Sam struggled to see the keyhole in the late in the day gloom and like a drunk arriving back at home in the early hours, he stabbed the door with the point of the key several times before finally inserting tool into receptacle. The sun had begun to set and say goodbye to another winter's day as more time had flown by than Sam had realised with the clock now drifting from late afternoon and into early evening. Streetlights had come on and as Sam opened the door to the shop, he glimpsed the glow of reflected lights in the puddles that nestled among the uneven paving slabs. He gazed around, aware that someone was watching him and out of the gloom he saw a face across the narrow precinct walkway, it was rounded and grubby, rheumy eyes leering out of the dark doorway of a kitchen shop. Sam thought it a cruel irony that a homeless woman should be sheltering in a place surrounded with the latest in kitchen gadgets and crockery. Realising the watcher was also watching him he had tried to get through his door quickly, but Sam took one more look in the temporary shelter across the way and at the homeless woman who sat bundled up in a shiny sleeping bag, her few possessions surrounding her as if she needed to keep everything within easy reach.

"What the fuck you looking at!" croaked the old girl as unfocused eyes held a mixture shame and anger, the voice drawled with the effect of cheap alcohol. A brown, plastic cider bottle lay beside her drained of its cheap thrills. Her grey hair was matted and a shade lighter than the drooping blackish bags under her eyes and on her forehead the crusty spotted scabs of drying, picked wounds.

Sam turned his face away, guilty of the fact he found the state of the woman fascinating, just as passers-by ogle the victims of a traffic accident and treat it as entertainment. Turning away he shut his shop door quickly and at the same time tried to shut out the guilty thought of shame after spending the day moaning about his lot and the dump of his home and business, but at least he had those things. One more look, this time through the door window and the last remnants of the shop name which once upon a time had been read bold and in gold leaf, *'Cobby and Son, Antique Dealers',* his father had ideas above his station back in the day. He thought for a moment about taking the hag a hot drink and the half packet of ginger biscuits that was in the cupboard waiting to be eaten, but as she once again spotted him watching with two grubby fingers raised sharply, she gave him an angry V sign and mouthed 'fuck you', that took any charitable thought out of his head and he turned away into the gloomy interior of his Sunday afternoon shop. Focussed on the window he thought maybe it was time to change the name of his establishment, maybe Sam's Junk and Rubbish would be more apt, especially as he had no son to hand it on to. Even if he had been lucky enough to find someone and have a family, he doubted any boy would want this legacy. He never had...

He imagined, 'One day son, all this will be yours', the response would be, 'no thanks Dad, keep it!' But as Sam had never found a woman ready and willing to put up with his squalor it was a moot point. He tried to recall when last he had a relationship with that rare breed, a good woman, but apart from one brief affair with the woman who ran the charity shop next door he could not recall anyone special. It was that long ago he could not even recall her name, although he did recall that one lunchtime, she had put up the ' *losed for Lunch'* sign, the 'C' having been rubbed away after years of handling, and they had unsatisfactory sex on the bundles of clothing that had been donated to the store. Sam Cobby was not a good lover and nor was he a good bet for any long-term relationship, that ship had sailed many years ago and he had long ago come to terms with having to live the rest of his life alone.

None of this was cheering Sam up.

Through the shop he took the meandering alleyway between the clutter, broken dreams and junk that was laughingly known as stock, toward the accommodation that lay hidden behind the deep green velvet curtain hanging over the doorway. The walk was like some strange maze, formed by new stock just being dumped into spaces amid the old. A dark oak Welsh dresser with drooping shelves laden with mismatched chinaware, stood sentinel like against one wall. Its drooping facade made it look unhappy with its lot, where once it would have stood with wood gleaming in a warm country kitchen. The depressed dresser was surrounded by scratched tables of both dining and coffee variety, mistreated chairs many of whom wobbled with loose legs and arms. A brocaded chaise-lounge should have added a little class to the furniture section, but it's one padded arm hung down like an injured limb. Threadbare and in need of massive renovation it sat forlorn and jammed into one corner, most of its seat being covered by piles of music sheets that mostly dated from Vaudeville days. Next to it a matching armchair, both in style and condition, had its seat covered in cat fur as it was the chosen place for Wedgwood to get away from Sam. He was a Devon Rex, his coat was a kind of blue grey, hence the name, and it appeared that the chair had more of her fur than Wedgwood himself had. He had chosen the chair as his day bed when just a kitten, using a long ago sold footstall as his ladder to the comfy seat. Wedgwood was now nine, and still his daybed remained in the same spot. Keeping up with a high turnover of stock was not a problem for the cat, or Sam.

On the walls around the shop were inauspicious paintings and prints displaying various levels of competence from the artists, the best of which was a gold-framed print of the Monarch of the Glen, a Royal stag with 12 points on its antlers the original was world famous, worth a fortune if it ever came up for auction and by Landseer. Even with that print the dust had dulled the wonderful view of the Scottish Highlands with its magnificent antlered red deer. It hung at a slightly wonky angle and the tilt had annoyed Sam for years, but to level it up would have meant moving a mass of stock to reach it and he had not the slightest inclination to climb the barricade of furniture between him and the highlands.

As Livingstone did in darkest Africa, Sam forged his way through his own almost impenetrable jungle to reach long-lost treasures. At times it seemed to him as if it were a living, moving mass with very little that remained in the same place and each trek from front door to accommodation was fraught with danger. His store carried with it, especially on dull evenings, a risk of attack and injury, sharp edges and pointed items lay in wait at every narrow crossroads. A moment before Sam pulled back the heavy drape where he would sign with relief after having traversed the shop without injury, the edge of a newly donated coffee table took him by surprise, his shin ambushed a few steps short of safety. The heavy item had stepped out from the crowd and kicked him mid-shin, the thinning material of his corduroy trousers doing nothing to protect his leg part from the sharp-edged assault. A vase that sat on the table, an innocent bystander in the conflict, wobbled on its base at the collision before succumbing to gravity and toppling over and rolling from the table's edge before hitting the floor. The vase's ordeal was not yet over as it landed on one of the few spots on the floor that was not covered by some thin rug or other. The fall ended its century or so long life in a dozen colourful and pointed shards.

"Shit, shit, and double shit!" Sam bent to rub his damaged shin, the forming bruise making him wince, but much like the vase there was no saving his broken and battered ego. The offending and aggressive table remained solidly where it was, immovable and undamaged. Hearing the fuss and noise Wedgwood prowled out from beneath the velvet curtain and chose this moment to greet his servant, who had promised to buy some cat food while out. In a figure of eight movement, he rubbed against the damp legs of his benefactor. Affectionate purring from the cat signalled that it was okay to fuss her and stroke the soft fur. Which Sam did both out of affection and out of guilt as he had forgotten the food. Through to the kitchen and Sam opened the food cupboard, he had to appease Wedgwood somehow. There was a tin of pilchards in tomato sauce, a favourite for Sam on a Sunday evening when heated to put on toast. Tonight though, he lifted the cat's bowl and forked the contents into the dish, placing it on the floor the cat dived in, eating, and purring in equal measure. Sam did not begrudge the cat having his supper, he was good company and Sam had forgotten to go to the shop because of feeling so miserable at the afternoon's events. While Wedgwood ate Sam shook out her blanket that lay alongside the always warm Aga, fluffing it up and making sure the cat had a warm and comfy bed for a post-dinner nap. Sam could have done with one of those himself, apart from the fact he had no dinner, but at least he had a half pack of ginger biscuits for when Nick came round a little later.

Food done with and an empty bowl Wedgwood strolled across to his blanket, stepped on board and circled a few times to tread down his bedding. Collapsing as if his legs had just given out the blue-grey cat was immediately into his sleeping position and Sam lent down to stroke his housemate but being in sleep mode already the cat hissed and flicked his tail with annoyance, cats let owners know when the time is right for fussing.

It used to be that Sam would talk to Wedgwood, after all its why he adopted a pet, it was for the company and as a kitten the cat would pay rapt attention to his master. It wasn't too long before Sam was ignored, the cat showing nothing but disdain by either sleeping or washing though Sam's attempt at conversation. It wasn't too much longer before Sam realised, he was just talking to himself, the cat no longer caring about Sam's boring days. Without noticing Sam had become one of those strange old people who purchased a pet to replace the children, or companion, they never had.

Very much like his father before him Sam never had much to do with the slightly Bohemian people that lived, worked, and produced art to varying degrees at his end of town. Everybody seemed to keep a safe distance from his father believing he was always grumpy, although Sam knew a different man who was always enthused when talking about antiques and their history and lives. It was different for Sam, he chose to stay clear of his neighbours, not that he disliked them, more the fact that he didn't like talking to strangers very much and nor was he very apt in making friends of strangers. His friendship with Nick was a happy accident and although at least a generation apart they seemed to just suit each other.

Flicking the wall switch downward, Sam turned on the overhead light in a vain effort to dispel the gloom, but not by much. Daylight was a distant friend in this part of the house. From another rustic and somewhat warped dresser, each shelf covered in shiny Formica, standing between the curtained shop access and the stairs which at that time of day merely climbed into more darkness, Sam picked a selection of mismatching cups and side plates. As far as Sunday afternoon tea was concerned only the best china would do. He placed an ancient kettle onto the naked burner of his stove, hefting it first to ensure there was enough water to fill the teapot before running that under the tap which now issued hot water and Sam rinsed and warmed the delicate china pot in readiness for the tea infuser ball, now laden with the leaves of tea that were dark and full of flavour. There was a fine art to making a good cup of tea and Sam took pride in his chai making. All was ready on the fine, dark, wood, dresser, the surface of its base pitted and scarred with the cuts and stains of a life well lived. Sam, as he did with all the furniture he collected, wondered about the history of the dresser and with a fingertip he traced the circle of a teacup that had been too hot when placed there by some long-ago owner, or maybe even a servant in some wealthy household. It was a solid piece of furniture with slightly drooping shelves and attractive lines that had cost Sam just £20 during a house-clearance from an old Manse just outside of the town centre, the expired owner having Sam's respect for purchasing such a beautiful kitchen piece.

Sam checked his watch as the kettle sung its one note, steam produced song and he knew it was time to pour water over the silver ball of peppermint flavoured tea. He poured slowly, with almost surgical precision, full of reverence for the humble tealeaf before carrying the loaded tray, complete with a plate full of ginger biscuits, to the hardy refectory table that had sat solidly on the flagstone floor since his childhood. He had eaten dinners, breakfasts and lunches from its worn surface, a surface which had only been polished by the hands that crossed it over the decades. It carried the signature of his family, his mother with small hands and elegant fingers always seemingly preparing food, both sweet and savoury on the surface; his father with brawny hands that became so delicate when it came to renovating small pieces he had purchased, unlike Sam his father was a craftsman. Both parents told stories of their life around this table, so much so it was as if this table were his family tree. Bathed in the warmth from the ever-heated Aga this was where he had sat writing his homework notes each night. When his grandfather had died, so his father had told him, the plain pine coffin that carried his body had spent a night resting on the same solid table.

For now, though it held a teapot with steam drifting from the curved spout, two delicate china mugs, specialist teas being far too elegant for builder's tea style mugs. He felt a pang of guilt when he plucked a biscuit from the plate of gingernuts. Sam easily gave into the temptation to eat one but was careful and wary not to get the sweet taste or the plate would be empty long before Nick was due to arrive. Sam often joked that he never had a half-empty packet of biscuits in his cupboards, they were too nice to hide away.

The old carver chair was as well-worn as the table, its seat polished by years of arses rubbing it to a shine, and Sam sat and poured his tea. The peppermint aroma invaded the nostrils as soon as the first drop found the bottom of the cup and Sam's mouth watered slightly. Gently held between forefinger and middle finger the cup was lifted and the contents sipped, his miserable day perked up with immediate effect. There may have been doubt with Sam's ability to spot a real antique or a good bargain, but he never doubted his taste buds, especially when it came to his teas.

Under the dull glow of the overhead light Sam's face remained grim, at times he felt well used, broken, and scratched beyond repair. Much like the bric-a-brac he tried to sell. Forty-nine years of age but he felt ten years older and when he saw his face each morning in his bathroom mirror, with the silver backing blistering in places and ragged at the edges as was everything else in his life. To Sam he now appeared as a reflection of his father's haggard face shortly before he died.

Sam's life and the shop, along with most of the dusty stock had been inherited from his father just four years earlier, he could not help but miss his father as memories of him were in every corner of the store, and every object carried the story of how his father had come by it and when. Growing up it had been Sam's playground, hiding between turned legs and under heavy drapes, each day a new adventure to imagine. The downside to this wonderful emporium of hiding places was that he seldom went out and played with others of his age. Now it was just a place of heartbreak and broken dreams with Sam only selling the occasional piece and barely making a living. He may have been useless with the business, but he knew nothing else, the thought of a getting proper job, or change of career at his age filled him with dread.

In his Father's Day, it was quite a busy road where the shop was situated, but many years ago the street had been pedestrianised like the rest of Chichester, and the business dried up almost instantly. The whole city had moved on, the entire shopping area now paved, was filled with coffee houses and charity shops, even Woolworths, with their amazing sweet counters, had gone when at one time every town and city centre had had one. Now it was a pick-and-mix sweet shop, a Poundland and the remnants of old trading companies such as Cobby and Son, Antiques Dealer.

Incongruous amidst the clutter and ancient, hanging on the kitchen wall was the one piece of modernity in the building, that was a flat-screen TV with its 40" HD picture which looked more real life than real life itself according to the Japanese maker. Remote control aimed like a silent gun Sam flicked the 'Stand-by' button that brought the electronic anomaly to life in readiness for the regular Sunday evening treat of Antiques Roadshow. As a trailer for some strange thriller about a private investigator with a wooden leg that would air later that evening ran on-screen, Sam thought maybe he should get himself something to eat, but recalling the meagre delights that were on offer in his fridge he opted for another of the ginger biscuits, then a third followed. The sip of peppermint tea now tasting somewhat strange when mixed with ginger. The announcer, with his BBC accent, announced where the show was coming from but Sam missed it as he crunched on his third biscuit, then the instantly recognisable theme tune ran over the titles of a programme that was first aired in 1977, over the years it had never waned in its popularity. The current presenter was also a well-loved newsreader and she had seemed to boost the viewing figures even higher. Knowledgeable experts told tales of old when presented with works of art, vintage toys, classic furniture, and even clothing and autograph books – Sam recalled that nearly all kids from his youth had an autograph book somewhere in their lives. The 'big deal' of every show though were the valuations when disappointed faces were hidden or offered feigned surprise with higher valued pieces. Each five-minute star of TV hoped that their trinket would be the surprise of the show, a piece designed by Faberge or painted by Tubbs or Turner. A long-lost gem or a worthless trinket, they all appeared carefully displayed on camera.

"Has it started yet?" Nick pushed the kitchen door open and hustled in. Wedgwood lifted his head, briefly, before stretching and going back to sleep, the cat was an expert at that.

"Good timing Nick," Sam greeted his friend. "Tea is brewed, and Miss Bruce is well into her stride."

"Have I missed anything juicy?"

It was a well-practiced routine between the two men with Sam repeating the preamble to the show of information about the venue. His version was however, abridged slightly.

"Apparently it's some castle or other in the West Country."

"You are a veritable mine of information, Sam." Nick shook his head, but smiled. "If the antique trade doesn't work out for you, maybe you should take up journalism."

"It hasn't and I thought about doing just that, if you can do it, it can't be that hard."

Before Sam could freshen the peppermint tea Nick asked for a fruit tea. "Have you got something like a blackberry tea, I need to get the cold out of my bones."

Sam tutted. He did not like to hear that one of those new-fangled fruit infusions as being referred to as tea. Without comment though he moved the kettle across on the hob of the Aga to generate a bit more steam for the whistle while he grabbed the fruity teabag from the cupboard.

"What cake did you bring?" It was a tease as Nick had entered empty handed.

"Sorry Sam, the match ran over, and I rushed straight here."

"Fruit teas and no cake, you are a bloody heathen, Nick Flax!"

Nick stepped back outside the kitchen door before returning with a box of Dunkin' Donuts, that contained four brightly coloured and covered ring variety of the doughy treat.

"They didn't have any proper English cakes in the store, so you will have to struggle with American donuts."

Sam was not appeased. "Bloody yanks can't even spell doughnuts, so what makes them think they can bake them!" But he still reached into the box and took out a pink icing topped donut complete with hundreds-of-thousands decorating the surface. One of the things Nick loved about the time the two of them spent together was the freedom of the open verbal warfare.

Sam, taking a bite from the soft ring, nodded at the screen. The game was on.

"Victorian if I am not mistaken, and around one hundred and fifty quid..." Sam's guess was at a small but attractive brooch that was being critiqued and valued on the screen. He stopped speaking to swallow the lump of doughnut.

The on-screen expert asked of the brooch's history, had it been an heirloom, or something recently purchased? She then brushed a wayward lock of ash-coloured hair from her forehead. The camera meanwhile shot the piece from every angle, a wide shot between presenter and owner, a panning close-up of the stones showing their sizes and the glitter before speaking of the three 'Cs', clarity, cut and colour. It was a camera light rather than the sun's paintbrush that lit the jewel.

"I reckon nearer a thousand," said Nick watching Sam for his reaction. The confident way he had spoken of his guess had Sam second guessing his own ideas of value. So, Sam with uncertain upped his own bid by a few hundred.

This was a game played every Sunday by the two men.

"You really should stick with your first guess and gut-instinct Sam." Nick responded with a smile.

Their attention turned back, in silence to the wide screen, where the brooch was now held delicately in the expert's well-manicured hand, her black loupe held up to her eye. "You will be pleased to know..." she said, in her public-school and slightly nasally voice.

The owner's face began to shine with the anticipation of untold wealth but somehow no smile crossed her lips. A stray lank of hair she quickly tucked behind her left ear, the anticipation was murder.

"...it is in wonderful condition, definitely Victorian and at a specialist auction could well fetch between," a pause for effect. "Say, between one-thousand and twelve hundred pounds."

The gasp from the small audience surrounding the camera was barely audible, in days when lotteries make multi-million-pound pay-outs, and footballers earn ten-times that much in a day any four-figure sum was a measly prize. The human list of expressions has real trouble when showing two at once. The woman looked at her brooch with renewed eyes, the smile on her lips said sheer joy at getting that valuation, but the eyes are not so good at lying and they showed utter disappointment as her mental greed took over. As for the small crowd in the background they would have headed home that evening full of stories about their new-found stardom. Fifteen seconds in full view of the camera and their own cameo would surprise friends and family as the recording would be replayed time and time again, with the 15-second TV-star saying coyly... *'They obviously liked the look of me, one of their researchers sought me out and asked me to stand front and centre so the camera got a full frontal of me. I wonder if I could start getting jobs as one of those film extras thingies. Watch carefully now, it's coming up any second, the camera was looking straight at me, any second now...'* Then the embarrassed silence as the outstanding 15seconds of Oscar winning performance was cut to just 5 seconds in the editing suite, or even worse cut altogether. Fame was a fickle mistress, no matter how short.

Back on screen the owner's husband who had been standing

silently alongside her up until that point gallantly explained... "Why thank you, I didn't think it was worth anything and we won't be selling it of course, it was my wife's grandmother's." He of course had not expected to even get on the TV with the brooch, he looked like an out-of-work builders' labourer, his grubby t-shirt stretched over a bulging beer gut. The look on his face was one of how quickly he could get the money and what to spend it on. Sam bet it would go on beer and go quickly.

Both men in the kitchen simultaneously called *'liar'* at the screen. And so, the Sunday ritual continued with first one then the other calling out the values and by the time the programme neared its end they were six all in the count, and in the hour since his arrival Sam had made one cup of tea, while Nick had made two. Sam had moved onto Darjeeling while Nick had stuck with his autumn berry flavoured. It was Sam's turn to make the final cup of tea, while both silently wished there had been a few more ginger biscuits, but something had gotten Sam's attention. The kettle hung uselessly in his hand while the tap ran freely. So, he could hear the TV better, Sam turned the tap off and put the empty kettle on the draining board. Nick was a good journalist and knew when to keep quiet and let a story unfold. He had seen the instant change in the expression on Sam's face.

As always, the show's director had saved the best for last and the final four minutes of the televised show, before the outro by Fiona Bruce, were given over to a small but powerful bronze statuette. In the background the skies were a majestic summer blue, a large crowd surrounded the expert's table, all aware that something special was about to happen. Nick began to make his bid, if Sam was distracted enough victory could be this week, but a raised hand from his friend and Nick did nothing, nor spoke, except to turn to watch the screen that had so captured his friend's attention.

Sam seemed to be holding his breath while on the television and turning under the scrutiny of the camera was a bronze statuette standing just over a foot tall with a sword carried threateningly overhead. In the scheme of things, it did not look that much, the sort of small bronze that could be seen in any dealers' window display. Even Sam would likely have something similar buried at the back of his shop. But there was something about this one object that had grabbed Sam's rapt attention.

The audience gasped then applauded as the suited valuer gave his thoughts on what could be the history of the piece and what it could be worth. It was a huge sum. But then the crowd suddenly went silent as the expert offered a rider to his valuation...

Back in the kitchen Sam said, "He is not even close with that figure."

Nick was dying to ask, but as a skilled journalist he knew when to pick his moments to question, he waited for the programme to finish.

"I say that it may well be worth somewhere in the tens of thousands, but if it is what I think it is, and I will have to check with some of my colleagues, this could be one of the most valuable finds we have ever had in the 55 years of Roadshow surprises."

Sam turned and glanced at Nick as Fiona Bruce wound down the programme by asking viewers to watch this space to find out about the bronze in future programmes.

"He got it wrong!"

"Who did, the valuer?" Nick asked.

Sam looked stunned, "That one is a fake, not worth a bloody thing. It's a fake!"

CHAPTER 12

Kobe eyed up his preferred pint of Guinness and across the half-inch or so of foam he spotted the young probationer Gold, chatting and laughing amid the throng of off-duty officers she had worked so well with. She lifted her gaze for a second and mouthed a 'thank-you' in his direction. Kobe raised his glass and nodded in response, certain that the young and still impressionable dark-haired officer who had handled herself well that morning had a good future ahead of her. Being happily married, a rarity or so it seemed among serving officers because of the pressures of the job, Kobe did not watch the young officer for long, there was something else in the bar that was dark and attractive, and equally as seductive – his pint of Guinness. More Muslim brownie points lost, but he sipped at the heavy tasting drink with great relish. Its body as deep and black as the darkest night, the perfect percentage of soft, white, foam topping the darkness, a snow drift on a dark landscape. The glass was slippery with condensation and felt cold in his hand as he turned and saluted his squad, the glass held high in acknowledgement as to a job well done. Kobe Kaan was a man of few words, and his team never expected a speech, and they wouldn't get one this evening.

"Good job team, enjoy your evening," his eyes travelled to every member. "...you deserve to let your hair down." Every one of them raised their glass back toward him, every member of his crew recognising that their leader had done them proud as well as kept them safe.

No matter how successful their work they all knew that in the back of their minds was the thought that, although they had shut down a major drug player that day, there would be another opening shop tomorrow. It was a never-ending battle but that did not mean they should not try to put an end to the insidious trade. These thoughts of a pointless career because they would take the criminals off the streets and the courts would free them again, it was why morale was so low in the modern police force, and why the mental wellbeing of the rank and file was a growing problem. But, for now it was time to celebrate the win.

After that first illicit sip of the dark beer, the rest slid easily down his throat. As the beer was downed the team were getting increasingly rowdy and their noisy enthusiasm began to make Kobe feel old and out of place. It was time for him to head home to his family, his place was with them and not the youthful crew who would be drinking freely tonight, the last thing they needed this evening was a senior officer keeping their boisterous spirits in check. Kobe drained the last of his pint and placed the glass on the bar, the last remnants of foam drifting down the inside of the glass, he wiped excess foam from his top lip with the back of his hand. Illicit bacon, violence and alcohol, all things in a copper's day, but not good if you were a Muslim, Kobe was glad they did not have a confessional, because he alone would take up the Imam's time. One last job before he left, he passed £50 to the landlord of the pub a man well used to the police using his bar.

"Make sure they stay well-watered, Tony." The rotund man with his trouser belt well hidden by the overhanging belly, replied he would.

Kobe had already texted Rae before taking the walk from his office to the canal-side pub, telling her he would not be home late and that he would be home in time to eat with his family, Sunday dinner with them a perfect end to the week. Rae had not replied, and Kobe assumed that she would have been busy getting the children bathed and ready for bed before he reached home, he loved the smell of freshly bathed children.

Kobe had enjoyed his one pint, but he enjoyed watching his group of officers letting off some steam even more. Well before the chubby landlord called time, they would all be well watered and, hopefully, ready for their walks or taxis home. When they had first arrived the tension amongst them was palpable, they had worked well today but it was sheer luck that no one was shot, intel had been poor and therefore there was no armed response team in place. They would party a little harder that evening, while all knowing how easy it was for the game to go wrong. Only his DS, David Martin saw him leave, the others busy taking part in a particularly noisy drinking game. His DS waved Kobe goodbye and watched as his boss walked out into the fresh evening air. For his part Kobe felt heavy and bloated, not used to drinking, his pint weighed heavy on him, and he was glad of the fresh air as he walked back to the nick to collect his car.

Although it was still late summer a chill breeze ran off the canal and up the street and Kobe thought about leaving the lid up, on his beloved Alfa Romeo Spider. Turning with his back to the still waters of the canal he took a moment to breath in the air, there was a smell of algae coming off the water and it felt almost like a signature of the city, and Kobe liked that smell. To many visitors it would smell slightly off but to Kobe it was the Chichester's signature perfume. Reaching his car, the cherry red of the bodywork gleaming under a mixture of the evening sun and the security lights in the station's car park. It would only take ten minutes to take the hood down and he loved to feel the air racing across his dome of a head as he sped along the lanes back to his village.

Sinking low into the sport's cars bucket seat he flicked the engine into life, he never revved it hard to begin with, preferring to hear the engine burble away on idle. He had purchased the car, mostly to impress the girls, when he was a young copper on the beat with no thought of promotion or of settling down. Then he met Rae, and to date she was still the only woman who had been in the passenger seat. Alphas were well known for being unreliable, and it was totally unsuitable as a family car but he cared nothing for sensible when it came to his bright red toy. It was a 1982 Alpha Romeo Spider, a bright cherry red and its iconic badge atop its ugly and downward facing grill. On either wing its headlights sat up like frog eyes. There was nothing overly fussy about the car, which was part of its charm, but it was an Italian classic. Inside the gear stick stuck out at a peculiar angle from the centre consul, which had taken some getting used to. The Spider was an out and out boy-racer style of car, the interior was a collection of switches and dials, the sound system a simple cassette/radio and it was mainly used to play soul music from the likes of Sam and Dave, Otis Reading and Aretha Franklin, classic music for a classic car. Right hand on the polished wooden steering wheel he slipped her into reverse and pulled out of the marked bay, then with a satisfying purr he pointed the sloping red nose toward home. Looking back down the road and seeing it was all clear, he feathered the throttle and the body of the car flicked to one side, thrown there with the torque of the engine, the purr swiftly rose to a growl that echoed from the walls of the station. He knew it would annoy the station Skipper which made him smiled, then Kobe let the clutch drop and the rear wheels screamed in agony spinning and leaving rubber on the tarmac before finally biting and rocketing away from the station, leaving work and reports behind him, his only thought now was to get home to Rae and the children.

Once in her stride the car was like a symphony and he was the maestro, the conductor, the car's music was an orchestra playing the same erotic tune. It was a well-rehearsed routine, off the throttle, a dip of the clutch, lever down and into the next gear, clutch released, and throttle floored. The Alpha responded to each loving touch, a concerto between man and machine. Rae had often said that he loved his car more than he did her, but it was usually when she had seen a new pair of shoes she needed. She was wrong though, he loved them equally!

He eased off the power as he entered the outskirts of the small village that was perched on the inner reaches of Chichester harbour. Bosham had an ancient history, it was said that King Canute had sat on a wooden throne there and ordered the tide to retreat, way back in 965. Of course, he ended up with wet feet, but it showed his courtiers that he was not a god but a mere man. By all accounts he was not a bad king, his daughter was buried in the local churchyard.

Driving through the small village with narrow roads and the waterfront just yards away, the burbling engine drifted into his ears and echoed off the rows of houses, all with solid walls surrounding small gardens and gates with slots for tidal boards to be slipped into on flood tides. More than a millennium on from Canute, and still no way of stopping the tide when it decided to flood.

Kobe had enjoyed the ride, but his smile broadened wider than ever as he parked the car on the square of gravel at the back of the house. The breeze that chilled the centre of town was gone and here on the waterfront, it was a warm evening, the sun beginning to dip over the harbour. He had brought Rae here one evening shortly after they had met, he had prepared a picnic and he laid out the blanket on the grassy area at the edge of the village. He opened the wicker hamper, and they dined on chicken drumsticks, salad and homemade coleslaw while accompanying it with a crisp white wine. He couldn't remember which wine it was, but he recalled that the picnic combined with a magical sunset where the whole sky burned with shades of red as it said goodbye to the day, it was a painter's sky that was composed of seductive colours. His planned romantic sunset picnic had worked a treat, and she was smitten with him. After three or four more such picnics they both realised that Bosham was an idyllic place to live, the children were safe here and they all enjoyed sailing dinghies when weekends off could be managed. The downside was the expense of living in such an idyllic place, even on an Inspector's wage he would not have been able to get a mortgage for a house anywhere near the village centre and it had only been affordable because of a legacy left Rae by her late stockbroker father. It gave them the freedom to live here and to enjoy a comfortable life with no worries, it even enabled Rae to work on her art full time which she did in a small studio at the end of the garden.

Switching off the engine the orchestral burble of the exhaust was silenced, the engine spluttering slightly as it died, an asthmatic trying to catch breath. At the same moment the masters of soul music, Sam and Dave, that had been playing from the tinny speakers, were also interrupted mid song and Soul Man was silenced.

The sudden silence was disconcerting.

There should have been noise coming from the house, there was always noise coming from the house. He eased his way out of the low-slung sports car and groaned slightly at the ache that made him wonder how many more years he had squeezing in and out of the cockpit. God, he hated getting old! He re-secured the hood back in place and as he clamped the device on the passenger side, he looked down the garden path and noticed the back door was slightly ajar. More to the point why were two very excited children not rushing through it to smother their father with hugs and cries of joy.

The sun had begun its decent into the harbour waters the autumnal colours of the sky almost gone there should have been light from the kitchen window sneaking out into the garden, but the windows were dark and blind. The only warmth coming from the house was a slim sliver of yellow light coming from the back-door's narrow opening and it illuminated the edge of the path. There was something not right and the joy of the drive home and his successful day slid away far too easily, leaving him with a dread feeling. It was his copper's instinct, a feeling he trusted without fail. It had kept him safe on many a day in his job of unknowns.

Something was wrong! His mind thought it and his heart felt it!

Checking his pocket he felt for his mobile phone, paranoia had now set in, and he felt comforted by the fact his phone was there should it be needed. He had had seen many bad things in his job, things he would never un-see and those visions remained with him to this day, like a stain that could not be washed out.

Pushing open the back gate the hinges squealed out a warning, it put Kobe even more on edge, if that were possible. Where were the overtired but lively children who should be running through the door and down the path to meet him? Where was the shadow of Rae that should be stood in that doorway ready to give out the welcome-home hug that she offered every day since they had moved in together? Where was the smell of dinner which would have been laid out just in time for his arrival. And, more importantly, why had Rae not replied to his text saying he was on his way home.

Something was very wrong!

CHAPTER 13

"I didn't know you smoked!"

The voice was soft, almost whispered, but it still startled him. David Martin had been lost in thought as he enjoyed the view down the canal where a pair of swans still looked pristine in their white plumage despite the setting sun darkening the water's surface, David noted they were still young swans as the dropping sun transformed their tan, downy feathers on the neck into a golden fleece. With someone at his shoulder David looked around from his view of the canal to see Gold standing beside him. Her features were partially in shade and David thought it made her look mysterious, her face ethereal, plus it meant there was no awkward eye-to-eye contact, he had always thought her pretty.

He took the unlit cigarette from his mouth and looked at it shamefaced. "I used to smoke a lot when I was younger, thought it looked cool." he responded. "Gave it up a long time ago but some years back when I first worked with the boss, he and I had worked on a tough case. One that got to both of us. An elderly lady who lived alone in her country house had been beaten to death with a hammer and it was two days before her cleaner had found her. It had been a long, hot summer and by the time we were called the result was not good."

"I always wonder how I would deal with such a thing when it comes around." She shivered and David discovered he wanted to hug her. It was the first time he ever realised that he even fancied her. He told himself, that as her sergeant, it was not a good idea.

"Anyway, Kobe always had his growing family to head home to and it seemed to protect him from the horror part of the job. Me, I just started smoking again and turned to the bottle. A pack of king-size and a bottle of Famous Grouse seemed to do the trick until the boss pointed out I was smelling bad, and the scent was a cross between a distillery and an ashtray. So, I joined AA and quit booze, been dry for two years now, and began to just not light the fags. Saved money as well, I have had this packet of Benson and Hedges for nigh on as long as I have been dry."

"Thought you drank Guinness like the Boss..." She could not

keep the surprise out of her voice. "A copper who doesn't drink, what's the world coming to." she added.

"Coke and blackcurrant."

"Sorry?"

"Coke and Blackcurrant, it's what I drink if I have to go to a pub these days. The landlord here knows what I have so he just serves it without being asked. Stops people I don't know well from asking why I am not drinking with them," David expanded.

"I didn't mean to pry, sorry." Gold hoped she had not offended her sergeant.

"Not a problem, most of the squad already know I am tea-total anyway." A sudden thought hit him, and he pulled his ancient packet of cigarettes out. "Sorry would you like one?" he asked as he drew the battered flip-top from his inside jacket pocket.

Gold raised her hand and shook her head as a negative response, then asked. "Can I?" It confused David until he realised, she was nodding at a spot next to him on the canal-side bench.

"Please do." David Martin realised he was smiling, he liked her being out there with him.

Taking a seat at the other end of the bench and she offered a large smile to David, he noticed it and hoped he wasn't reading too much into her friendly manner, but he did like her beautiful face, her thought her smile intoxicating. As the evening light caught her face, he noticed the red welts running in parallel lines down her cheek.

"How is the face feeling, doesn't look as if it will scar?"

He thought he saw her blush and hoped he had not overstepped any mark.

"It's fine," she responded, running her fingers over the wound. "...her nails did not break the skin."

"Are you okay? You know, inside." He pointed to his temple in a clumsy way of checking if she was mentally okay. "That was one hairy experience." It was an honestly asked query. "You don't seem the sort to leave a party early."

"To be honest, I am not that much of a party-girl. Early nights reading a good book with a glass of wine at home are more my scene." Seeing that the DS seemed distracted, she now asked if he was doing okay.

"It's not anything, I was just..." he seemed reluctant to finish the sentence.

"Or did you just need some fresh air because you are a lightweight since joining AA?" She discovered that she enjoyed teasing him even though he was her boss as well. The cider she had been drinking, along with a couple of shots she had been bought, were emboldening her.

"That will be the day, I can keep up with anyone, when it comes down to Coke and Blackcurrant. Mind you, if I was still drinking, I would find it hard to keep up with you youngsters anymore." He was enjoying her company. Out of habit he sucked on his unlit cigarette and blew out imaginary smoke which theatrically drifted away on the easy breeze that was coming off the canal. The charade gave him a pang of foolishness.

"You can put the cigarette away now; you have me to distract you." Gold slid a few inches closer but stopped short of touching. Softer now she asked, "So, why did you come out here, something must be on your mind."

"Not sure what it is, but just had a bad feeling, you know that twist in the gut that tells you something is wrong."

"Coppers' radar for trouble you mean?" She turned her head and glanced at him and saw his head nod in the narrow cone of light projecting down from the streetlamp behind the bench.

The lamps that lined the canal were erupting into life one after the other travelling down the canal, well more of a drift than an eruption as modern bulbs take a while to warm up before throwing down cones of light onto the pathway. With darkness growing the scene offered romantic reflections on the still waters.

"Did you feel it too then?" David now turned to face her, and it was her turn to nod. "Thought it was just me."

"You thinking something is wrong with the raid or interviews this morning." Officer Gold carried a puzzled look as she tried to figure out why this instinct was a troubling one, she had never felt like this before. It was like the first time she felt love, such a strong feeling and yet bewilderment as to what was happening.

"No, I don't think it is anything to do with this morning either." They both held a look of puzzlement, not a good look on a police officer.

In modern policing there was jargon for everything and every action, at police training they would call it something fancy such as

'Professional Judgement'. It was that immeasurable thing that either came naturally or arrived with experience and time on the job.

"I thought it was the onset of evening chill, causing goosebumps on my skin." Gold tried to explain what she felt. "But then gut ache joined in. I did maybe think it was something to do with the gunfight at the OK Corral this morning, that poor native girl, shot through the head and only in her prime." Joking was the obvious release for troubling events.

"I felt that bit myself, it was a something's up feeling or I had drunk too much of the squad room coffee."

"If it isn't today's job what..." Gold didn't finish.

The phone in David's pocket burred with vibration and he slipped it from his jacket pocket, and he lifted it straight to his face which now showed an even stronger look of concern.

"DS Martin..." he stared into Gold's eyes as he listened in silence to the information he was receiving. She in turn knew what he was hearing was nothing good.

"Sarge?" Gold enquired but her colleague was still listening intently, he held up one finger to quell her enthusiasm. She lightly gripped his elbow, almost as if she could glean information via some sort of osmosis.

David wound up the call, "Thanks Skipper. I owe you one and no one will know the call came from you."

"Sarge, David...?" Asking again Gold now realised that both their antenna had been working well, she stayed holding his elbow, not sure if it was helping her or him as she waited for the punchline. She did know that the contact with David felt natural and good, she was not embarrassed by leaving her hand there, she softened her panicked grip.

With his professional face on he told her what he could. "Something has happened at the boss's house. Something to do with his family but all the station skipper could tell me was that it was bad. Really bad to quote him."

"Are we heading over there? I will tell the guys..." She prepared to stand up head back into the pub, where raucous laughter floated out from the bar. David stopped her, it was his turn to grip her arm now.

"No..." it was a sharp reply. "You need to stay here and say nothing." His voice urgent but controlled. "When I know something, I will call you and the rest of the team, but for now..." he left the rest unsaid.

She anticipated the rest of the sentence. "...go back inside, keep this call to myself and tell them you went home early because you drink like a girl." Stella felt a sort of anger rising in her, she had proven herself today and she was not going to back down now. "Is your car at the nick?"

The question stopped him in his tracks. "No, damn it!"

"Well, mine is, but I have had too much to drink, I will be over the limit, so are you good to drive us to the Boss' place."

"I knew there was a good reason for me giving up the demon drink. And you were going to call me a lightweight." Then he said what she wanted to hear. "Come on then Gold, I'm driving."

"Oh great, now they will be thinking you and I have disappeared together, probably to some seedy hotel for the night." It was a nervous chuckle that followed her words.

"You should be so lucky." They would have both laughed if the situation had not been so serious.

No more was said as they sprinted back to the car park, Gold had already drawn her keys from her coat pocket, her thumb already paused over the unlock button on the fob. Their copper's instinct, that unfathomable feeling that they get, the nose for trouble, the Professional Judgement. All their senses were on high alert now, their skin tingling with the adrenaline surge.

CHAPTER 14

There was an eerie silence that seemed to wrap itself around the entire harbour-side village that made Kobe shiver despite it being a warm evening, it felt like one of those eerie horror movies where something bad is hiding in the swamp. He could smell the mud, it was low tide, the normally noisy gulls were silent, and it seemed only quiet locals were drinking and dining at the Blue Anchor pub that evening. All of Kobe's senses were on high alert. The tourism season was all but over and there were no dog walkers on the shore path. It was as if the whole of Bosham had realised something was wrong and were holding their breath waiting for news.

Kobe stood holding the open gate and looked down the path, Kobe junior's bike lay across the crazy paving, abandoned for the night. He assessed his next steps. There was a need to move forward, but he was fearful of what he might find. His feet finally moved, once in motion he walked speedily toward the back door, caution now out of the window. He didn't know why but he knew his family needed him, something was wrong in their pretty cottage. It felt as if his heart had ceased beating, causing a pain in his chest. Legs were leaden and each step hard.

At the doorway he paused, pushed it fully open using his elbow, one foot on the threshold. The same threshold over which he had carried a pregnant Rae just seven years before. Somehow knowing there would be no reply, he still called out for his wife. As expected, there was no reply, the cottage had lost its warmth, now it was cold, threatening.

A different tack, he called for his children. "Kobe..." a pause, then "Molly..." again. "Kobe lad." They could just be playing hide-and-seek with him, and as a comedown from this morning's raid he was seeing and feeling things that were not there.

But surely Kobe Junior would not be able to stifle his giggles for this long.

Again, he called out. This time for Rae. "Rae, Rae honey, answer me. This isn't funny!" His voice now sobbing with fear as he walked along the narrow hall. He had been a police officer for too long, his senses were telling him all was not as it should be.

Passing the kitchen door, he gazed in, the refectory table was laid up for dinner, a dish of cold roast potatoes already out and in the middle of the table and Kobe could smell burning pork. This was not the time to turn the oven off, the pork could bloody well burn. Deeper into the house he stepped, still silence came back at him, an evil deathly silence and he berated himself for thinking like that and still expected Molly to burst out of the under-stair's cupboard, her favourite hiding place. She would come barrelling down the hallway, as she always did, and leap up into his arms, laughing all the while for making daddy so scared.

Police training told him to take care when entering the house, be aware that intruders may still be in there and for him not to taint any evidence, should evidence be needed. Why would evidence be needed, this was only a game of hide-and-seek.

Reaching the bottom of the staircase he turned the corner, using the rounded wooden filial on the bottom of the banister for leverage and he took the stairs two at a time, his footfalls echoing back downstairs as each booted footstep hit the bare wooden treads. With each step he called their names, enough steps and time to call each of them three times.

"Rae, Kobe, Molly." Each call catching in his throat, a sobbing cry left his lips and was filled with agony. This was not a game of hide-and-seek. "Rae, Kobe, Molly." Silence was all that came back. On the landing now he called one last time, only now it had become a whisper. A whisper filled with anguish. *"Rae, Kobe lad, Molly."* He knew now for certain that there would never be a response. Holding on to the banister his fist, gripping so hard, his knuckles had turned a ghostly white.

Instincts built with over 20 years on the force never failed him and he wished just once, just this one time... that his instincts could be wrong.

But he wasn't wrong, a coppery smell entered his head. In his career he had registered that smell too many times.

The first stripped pine door, in the centre of one of the four panels a postcard picture of Elsa, her favourite Frozen character. Using his elbow again he pushed it open, so slowly, he did not want to see what was inside. But beyond the door a neat, tidy bedroom. Molly was a proper little girl, and she kept her room pristine. A place for everything and everything in its place and his spirit lifted slightly because all he saw was normality.

Next door along the hallway, the smallest bedroom and Kobe knew he would find Armageddon. A bedroom, just like his as a child, a mess, nothing in its place and no sight of the carpet they had fitted only last year. Kobe junior's door squeaked as it slowly opened heavy on its hinges, normality again and he noted to oil the hinges. He saw what he expected to see, bedlam in his boy's bedroom.

He tried to calm himself, all was as expected so far. Kobe questioned his concerns but could not get fear to stand down.

Two more paces, that was all that was left to his and Rae's bedroom. It was a room at the front of the house with a sash window that had a magnificent view down the harbour, some mornings they would sit up in bed and watch the early sailors navigating down toward the main harbour. He hesitated two short steps from the closed, stripped pine door, they were the biggest steps he would ever take, but his body refused to move. If he took those two steps there was no going back.

The coppery smell was stronger here.

Shuffling his feet, he moved forward and with his left foot he pushed the last pine door wide open, arms hanging leadingly by his side. This was his and Rae's sanctuary, their bolt hole away from kids and his job. Walls were decorated with bold roses on a white background, Rae's choice of wallpaper, not his. She was an artist for goodness's sake she had better taste than that, but as with every other choice, Rae had the last word. Full blooms of red roses, far too 'girlie' for his taste but Rae had loved the swirling patterns of scarlet petals.

He forced himself to investigate the room, not even feeling his feet shuffling over the bare wooden planks of the landing and caught sight of the full-length mirror on the wardrobe. He stared at the reflection...

There was something wrong with the roses!

He could see his family and they looked peaceful on the bed. Rae's back was facing the mirror, and he could see what looked like her arm over the children. They were just having an afternoon nap and hadn't heard him calling.

Palm flat on the warm wood of the bedroom door to keep it

from swinging closed again, his skin was clammy and sweating and yet felt chilled, as if the blood flowing through his very veins had dropped in temperature. Like a parachute jumper taking his first leap from an airplane Kobe hesitated in the doorway fearful of taking that one big step into the void beyond. There was no going back once that step was taken, he caught sight of his watch, the silver strap shining against his olive skin, on the face it read ten to seven, the children would be cranky in the morning being kept up so late when they had school the next day. With all the willpower he could muster he pushed the door open fully and took one step into the bedroom, but stopped short of approaching the bed itself or the three people laying there. The three of them looked peaceful on the bed, a blanket covering the lower halves of their bodies. Everything was fine and he breathed a sigh of relief and mentally kicked himself for getting so worked up over nothing. He looked around the room, just to double check everything really was okay.

But everything was not okay, there was something wrong with the roses...

CHAPTER 15

A few miles away, back in the tranquil city centre two men sat with legs tucked under a rustic table sipping tea and arguing about the value of antiques that were appearing in high definition, saturated colours and in a wide screen format on the broad black television that looked incongruous in the dim kitchen filled with antiques of its own. Sam glanced over at the Welsh dresser where an art-deco pewter, Tudric clock that rather than standing proudly on its own was surrounded by a pile of invoices that needed his attention but would be left for another day. The elegant blue enamel face sat above a dull grey embossed tree-of-life and read ten past nine on its Roman numerals, Sam had turned the TV onto its on-line content where for the second time that evening it was almost time for the final and most expensive reveal of the antiques show, the one item they always saved until last.

Once again, the camera centred in on a table with a smallish but imposing bronze on its green baize surface, expert Eric Knowles stood one side of the statuette and an overweight man with a horrid, greasy comb-over stood on the other. The latter tried to hide a nervous smile while he avoided eye contact with the camera, just like the young lady from behind the scenes had told him not to. It was a beautiful day for the Roadshow and sunlight glinted from the bronze despite the patina that attempted to dull its surface.

Sam was still sitting bolt upright, elbows off the table, the cup of tea in his right hand being ignored. Wide mouthed and slack jawed it felt like the eyes were popping out of his head. He made a sudden motion, startling Nick and causing the table to jerk on its four legs as they scuffed noisily across the flagstone floor. The sudden squeaking of wood on stone disturbed Wedgwood and he looked up from his blanket by the Aga, seeing it was nothing to concern him he stretched, yawned and went back to sleep. Nick was also aware at the change of atmosphere and with a silent gaze he flicked between screen and Sam.

With expert analysis the presenter chatted on...

'If this had been what I first thought when I saw it earlier today, then we would all be in for a day of lovely surprises.' He had one of those smiles that experts use when they know something that they are

sure no one else does. *'I have to admit I had to share this with a couple of my colleagues and let them examine it as well, and to be honest none of us are exactly sure what we have got.'*

Point by point he went over the statuette of a Roman centurion, which was in perfect condition. The bronze arm holding a short and stout roman sword, or *gladius,* in his hand that pointed skyward above his head, as if being held aloft in victory. On his head a *galeae,* the Roman Helmet its crest, normally horsehair but now bronze and perfectly groomed forever and sweeping back over the crown. Bit by bit the bronze was examined and detailed thoughts broadcast, but Sam was no longer listening...

"What can you tell me about this beautiful bronze?" The expert involving the owner with the quest for information.

"Not a lot really, I saw it in a charity shop window and liked it, so I bought it." The man who had queued under a blazing sun for more than two hours, his forehead now red with sunburn, was milking his part and tried to offer a coy smile, but it did not work on a man in his early fifties with wobbling cheeks, the sunlight caught beads of sweat on his forehead.

Nick responded before the expert could speak again. "Well, that would have been a safe bet, it was either going to be a charity shop or a bloody car boot sale." Nick had failed to notice that Sam had gone quiet.

The owner overplayed his part and could not help but glance into the camera, a big no-no. "I only paid, eight pounds I think." he said adding a puzzled expression for effect. "It's very heavy..." he finished up as if the weight would add value.

Eric Knowles went into full expert mode. *"I am loving the patina on this dramatic statuette of a Roman soldier, a Centurion from the look of his uniform and with that full plume on his helmet. Far too elaborate for a lowly legionnaire."* Even the second time round that evening expert Knowles was having fun with this valuation.

Back in the kitchen Nick could not help himself, he had to put his repeat bid in. They were at six-all with guesses in their weekly challenge. "It's the last item on the show so I reckon, ten to twelve grand." He seemed confident. "Could be more I suppose, but that's my guess. Still not a bad return for £8."

Sam did not respond, he heard the 'bid' from Nick somewhere in the background, but he looked so rapt at what he was watching it seemed as if not to sink in. Neither time had Sam offered a counterbid. Nick was, however, now watching closely and even he looked stunned at the valuation.

"I have looked closely but cannot find a signature." The smooth voiced expert was winding up his piece to camera. *"I suppose you want a value,"* It was a statement not a question. *"I do recognise the statuette, but I have only seen drawings of it until now."* Time was running out on the programme. *"If it is what I think it is then this is a significant find, probably one of the most significant we have ever had on the Roadshow, certainly in my 12 years on the show. That said, I do believe this to be a copy. If this is genuine, and a lot more research will have to be done then the value will be what anybody is willing to pay for such a rare item, a one off. That said I am sure it is a copy but in saying that it is an excellent piece made by a very skilled hand, but still, as I say, a copy."*

The owner now began to sweat beneath his comb-over, the thin hair looking damp and shiny, and he absentmindedly pushed his hair back to reveal his shining dome of a head. He was trying hard not to smile too much, but he also didn't want to appear to be disappointed with the value.

Sam held his breath, Nick held his and the audience on TV that surrounded the viewing table all held theirs.

"If it were real, and I must reiterate, if it were real, which I and others on the Roadshow have no doubt it is not, then we would be talking millions not thousands." A collective intake of breath could be heard through the TV speakers and the small kitchen. *"In simple terms it would be what anybody would be willing to pay to own it. Copy or not it is exquisite, and I would love to own it myself."*

The camera cut back to Fiona Bruce with whichever castle they were at this weekend in the background. Eric Knowles joined her for the outro, now the crowds had gone.

"Eric, can we go back to that bronze of a Roman soldier, you said it could be a significant find, how significant?"

"Several of us have pondered over this for most of the day. None of us have seen the actual original, long lost before any of us were born." He smiled at his small attempt at glib humour. *"As I said, I have only seen drawings, sketches for a work to be produced, in old books. It is either a piece by Bayer, who was one of Rodin's teachers and*

mentors."

"He of The Thinker fame..." Interjected Fiona Bruce.

"Exactly, or it could have been a maquette for a much larger piece done by the great man himself." He was ending. *"It will take much research to discover the truth but just seeing it has made my day."*

The presenter's attractive smile filled the screen, and the expert was cut from the shot. *"It very much looks as if this story has not yet reached a conclusion."* A teaser for the audience at home.

But, neither man in that Chichester kitchen listened to what she had said in summing up as it was Sam who had the last word as he spoke over her...

"It's a fake!" he exclaimed, "I know it for certain."

CHAPTER 16

The roses were still bleeding...

Swirls of crimson that made up the vibrant flower heads were somehow darker now, and spreading, roses almost melting down the walls, as if more blood-red blooms had been painted onto the paper landscape.

In place of the peaceful English garden scene Kobe so disliked when first picked by Rae, there was now something evil in those repeated printed blooms. Summer splashes of delicate flower heads were now dribbling down the bedroom walls, the roses were running red down green stems on the walls of a room that should have been a place of safety, a restful haven for his family. Obscene blooms that were past their best and with no gardener to deadhead them. Blood petals were dragging down the walls, the roses with their thorny stems, cut and bleeding.

Kobe then noticed the snow-white quilt that normally covered the bed with pristine waves like a rumpled snowdrift. Something dark, the source of the coppery aroma, had now turned the wintery landscape into a rough tundra of blood red carnage. Beneath the blood-soaked snow his beautiful and irreplaceable family.

The three of them, Rae spooned into the back of Kobe Junior, his beautiful boy, and he in turn spooned into the back of Molly, his inquisitive and bossy daughter, where each time she smiled up at him his heart would break and shatter with joy. Rae's blonde hair draped across her beautiful face with its delicate features. All just lying there in violent sleep, at rest in their own secretions. The harsh smell of violent death pervaded every corner of the room, the coppery aroma of drying blood and the stench of bodily fluids that had been released at the very moment of death. Smells so acrid and horrific Kobe could taste them on his tongue.

Rae was never one for wearing perfume and the memory of the smell of her hair as they cuddled each night made him shiver, that sweet smell always made him feel giddy but at that moment another smell had captured his senses, and it was one he would never forget. He could never recall the brand of shampoo she used, to him it was just part of her natural beauty, but with a slight hint of coconut.

Like a vicious imprint the image of evil that defiled their 12x12 bedroom would lay burned into his memory for the rest of his life. That and the strange silence that filled the house, a home that normally would carry the sound of music or the rowdy symphony of children playing, laughing and even when their cheers turned to tears, he would still love the bedlam of a family home. The entire house seemed to have died along with his family, the only sound he could hear was the faint whistle of the tinnitus that he had always suffered with but rarely noticed these days.

Like the sounds, his visions would now betray him, because he would no longer recall the sight of his children gazing up at him, their faces filled with nothing but love and trust, that would make his heart burst with joy. Trust... They trusted him, the matriarch, the policeman, their protector. He had broken that trust, where was he when they needed him, drinking beer, and breaking the teachings of his faith. His wife, Rae, his stunning and beautiful wife, no longer to be wrapped in his arms at day's end, the softness of her lips brushing his mouth, the softness of her skin against his hard body.

The visions of three beautiful people had been snuffed out the moment he pushed that door open. Another cruelty of violent deaths would be the memory of violence and not of the beauty of things that had been before. Even the roses would now be for ever bleeding.

He stood there on the threshold of the bedroom, the man, the father, and the husband all wanting to rush into the room and check for pulses, for any sign of life. Instead, the policeman stood there full in the knowledge that none of them could have survived the blood loss, beneath the hair and the blood he could see the broad macabre smiles of the slashes on each of their throats. Red streaks against pale skin just visible. The investigator in him knew that if he entered the room and disturbed the scene then the chances of finding clues as to who had done this would lessen, he had already contaminated too much of the crime scene. It caused another stroke of pain realising that his house, their home was now just a crime scene... The man in him just wanted to hold them and comfort them and take them away from this house for ever.

There was another sound in the room, and it took Kobe a

moment to realise it was a deep moan that was resonating from his own body. His energy gone, he slumped in the doorway, with his back on the door upright he just slid down into a heap on the floor, one leg bent and trapped under the weight of his body, he had no energy to move it.

He was eye-level with the surface of the bed now and he could just make out their beautiful faces, in a row of three across the pillows, but he could no longer bear the grief of looking at his children with their contorted smiles, so he zoomed in on Rae's perfect features. She looked at peace from this angle, but he knew that view to be misguided.

He struggled to get his phone from the pocket of his jacket and while staring into that face he recalled one of their first dates.

As a much younger man, and one who had only just made into the CID which had been a life-long dream, Rae took him on an adventure weekend. All through that wonderful escapade she would have a wicked grin on her face and would mercilessly chide him for his discomfort that lasted most of the day.

They, along with a group of friends, had spent an hour walking around a Welsh mountainside while enjoying the stunning landscapes that surround Abergavenny in mid-Wales. That had been the fun part! Before leaving the cars, they had donned grubby boiler suits and somebody had loaned Kobe an orange safety helmet, complete with chin strap, that had a torch on the peak. He was intrigued but all he got from Rae in answer to his questions was that smile. Now a good mile away from the car he noted a flock of sheep were watching them with inquisitive faces...

"Emergency services, which service please?" The speaker on his mobile phone asked, he hadn't even realised he had pressed the three nines. The voice amidst the silence of the cottage boomed out of the phone's speaker.

It took a moment to form the words in his mouth, but the operator remained calm and professional. "Hello, sir, which service can I help you with?"

Despite the view in front of him he went into professional mode. "This is Detective Inspector Kobe Kaan, put me through to police control please."

Kobe heard the operator put him through and telling control who was on the line.

"Hello Mr Kaan sir, how can I help" Another female voice, and knowing she was dealing with a senior officer the civilian operator sounded a little hesitant.

"I am at my home in Bosham, just arrived after my shift ended and I have just found my family killed, they are all gone..."

He broke down and cried. His mind however, in a vain attempt to protect him, returned to better memories...

The rag-tag group of explorers reached a cave entrance, not much bigger than a cat-flap, or so Kobe thought, in the side of the mountain. It was a weird thing to see halfway up a mountain with nothing man-made in sight, a locked, metal, and hinged doorway. The sheep seemed to lose interest as one by one the six knelt and shuffled in through the door, the guide locking it behind him. They all then, strangely, signed a visitors' book, lit only by the torches on their helmets. For Kobe's benefit, as he was the only novice, the guide explained that should anything go wrong then rescuers would know who and how many were lost. 'LOST?' thought Kobe, nobody mentioned lost or rescuers.

The guide saw the concern on Kobe's face, "It is just a small thing in case we get lost inside the mountain."

Kobe's face made the point, 'what do you mean lost in a mountain?' Rae saw his discomfort and tried to reassure him, but she was having too much fun at the heroic copper's expense.

"It only happens very rarely." She said with a wicked grin.

"Don't worry Kobe. Is it? I have been through these mountains dozens of times, it's perfectly safe."

Kobe decided to just shrug it off, for now, but made a mental note to push them both off the mountain when and if they emerged through the rusted door again. He then looked around trying to see where next, all that was facing him were blank cave walls on three sides and the rusty entrance on the fourth wall. Rae saw his discomfort; in fact, she would watch every uncomfortable moment with great glee.

"We go through that tunnel down there." She said pointing down to the bottom of one wall. Kobe's headlight had been at eye level, and he now looked down into the gloom and saw a black hole, round and with only about a three-foot diameter, and it looked like water lay on the floor all the way through the tunnel.

Not much scared Kobe Kaan, always seeing himself as adventurous. For goodness' sake he had even leapt from a perfectly good aircraft along with the Red Devils, the British Army Parachute Regiment Freefall Team. Not once, but twice and he smiled through every minute of the experience, from taking off the hefty landing even enjoying the thrill of the 'ground-rush' as they reached treetop height. Now he was scared by a small hole in a big mountain. This was far out of his comfort zone, way outside.

Everyone who knew and had worked with Kobe Kaan, knew of his quiet and calm demeanour when under pressure. Always one to just get on with the job and in quiet tones he would control his troops on the ground, he was always controlled and confident, but in this mountain, he was anything but.

His query of how to get through, what was, a 30ft tunnel with a foot of water on the floor, received the response of *'quickly'*. Following the techniques of those who disappeared into the dark hole first he lay belly down in the water and using his elbows for propulsion he squeezed and shimmied his way through. Fearing swallowing the brackish water he was crawling through he kept quiet, but for the following three hours through diminishing holes and crevices into the mountain and another 3 hours back out again he chattered away. Rae had never heard him talk so much, before, or since. If she were able, she would be proud of his stoic silence now.

On that adventure into the mountain, he had never been so scared, and nothing had come close since and it was not fear he felt now, it was abject desolation. When they had reached the centre of that cave network, they had turned off their lamps and sat in perfect darkness, the world around them totally black, no light could creep this far in. He could hear no sound, when they all sat still all that could be heard was their own breathing and the smells of the cave were dank and deep. Kobe felt all those things now while sitting in the doorway to his and Rae's bedroom.

When they finally emerged from the mountain and his panic had calmed Rae just slipped her hand into his, without comment. She had seen him show fear and had not thought less of him, and for his part Kobe knew from that moment she was the girl he wanted to spend the rest of his life with. How he wished right now that she would slip her tiny artist's hand into his clumsy mitts and ease his dread, but he knew that would never happen again.

CHAPTER 17

"How do you know Sam, you sounded so certain?" It was the journalist in him, he had to ask questions. "How can you tell from here when the experts on the ground there couldn't tell for certain?"

Sam stood and refilled the kettle but then plonked it down on the draining board, he needed something stronger. Without yet answering Nick, he then strolled over to the Welsh dresser and pulled down two glass tumblers as well as grabbing a bottle of Talisker Single Malt off the shelf. Sam so rarely drank these days that the bottle had a layer of dust on it, he didn't drink often because it would be too easy to turn his depression and his dismal life into alcoholism. Without asking he poured a small shot for both him and Nick, placing one glass in front of his friend who chose to ignore it while patiently awaiting an answer.

Sam returned to his carver chair at the end of the table once again, its feet scraping on the flagstones, he just sipped on the whisky. The image on the TV was of the Centurion on pause, his sword arm held high in defiance. As smooth a whisky as it was Sam pulled a face as the first shot burned his throat, making his eyes water. He quickly took a second sip to settle his taste buds and calm his nerves. Steeling himself, he pondered for just a few more seconds before responding to Nick's query. His head snapped one way and then the other, as if he were searching frantically for something in the room, but it was eluding him.

"Sorry Nick, right, how do I know?" He was speaking on autopilot as his memory searched back in time before his father had died, long before. "Because, I have seen the original, that's why. The real centurion was here, in this very room. I saw it every day when I was a boy."

"And you can recall it from way back then. Can you?" It was not said in disbelief but in a search for reality, it was part of Nick's job, knowing how to draw out truths.

"You cannot forget something that beautiful." Sam continued, a warmth in his face as if recalling an early lover. "Now that fake version has reminded me, I remember it well. The quality, the weight of the bronze, the coldness of touch, the patina. The skill in sculpting the muscular body, a six pack I could only dream of having, the sharp detail of the Roman's face. Everything about it shouted quality and my father was so proud of that one piece that at the time I could never imagine him selling it, even though he was in the antique business. He was a smart man, smarter than me..."

"Stop putting yourself down Sam, you are a very smart man." Nick would try and boost his friend's confidence whenever he could. Sam as usual was dismissive of his friend's vocal gesture and brush it away with a wave of his hand.

"My dad in his younger days worked for a lovely old removals and house clearance man, George Cooper." Sam continued the tale with no further interruption from Nick, he had his friend's full attention. "According to dad, old man Cooper was a lovely man, a gentleman in every way, his business was built on the fact he was trusted. Always willing to treat his porters with respect and teaching them everything he knew if they were so inclined to learn. Any question dad had for any piece, be it painting, pottery or junk, he would answer fully."

Nick absentmindedly took a sip of his whisky, and the sharp tang made his eyes water a little and supplied a cough to clear his throat.

"The other reason his Porters liked him was his generosity, along with his mild manners, he got a lots of clearance jobs because of that trust and Cooper always gave fair prices, not a common practice among house clearance businesses in those days." Sam explained to Nick.

"Old man Cooper, as my dad always referred to him, was as sharp as a blade and he knew all too well that people were just people and many of them would have no hesitation in stealing from him, despite the fact he paid wages that were over the odds for the day and no matter how much he was liked. Instead of getting angry though he would just put it down to flawed human nature and just end the thief's employment. He thought that a simple act of generosity would stop the pilfering. He came up with a scheme for all his porters, whom all looked professional in their brown overalls, that the first item they picked up on the clearance was theirs, if they didn't take the piss and pick something that was obviously valuable. The rest had to be left alone as they were his. According to dad this worked quite well. There were those who always took liberties though, but they never lasted long with Mr Cooper. Cooper, which was a good thing, wanted his porters to start their own collections and eventually their own businesses.

"The cost of pieces lost on each clearance was a cheap way of keeping the pilfering in check. Why steal when you could obtain honestly. Anyway, dad had never picked anything of too much value, just pieces he genuinely liked, sometimes taking nothing at all. One day they were down Lewes way, in East Sussex, they were clearing this big old house, and it was packed with nick-knacks of all sorts, the man that had left it all behind was a well-travelled bloke and collected just about anything from wherever he had been in the world and it was a huge clearance job, apparently. Mr Cooper had paid a good price for its contents. It was in the very first room dad saw this bronze statue on the mantle over a big open fireplace, according to Dad it looked nothing much as it was coated with black smoke stains, it must have not been cleaned for years. He didn't know it of course but that smoke discoloured piece was the real deal. Not a dud like that one on Antiques Roadshow. Dad claimed it as his Porters-Piece, as they called it."

With the TV off and Sam in full flow every time he took a breath the old kitchen fell into silence, all that could be heard was the snoring purr of Wedgwood. Nick was as caught up in the hearing of the story as Sam was in the telling of it.

"Dad could hardly afford it from his wages, but he offered to pay Old Man Cooper two quid a week toward the cost of it. Mr Cooper though would always stand by his credo, he was a church man and honest through and through, a man of his word. He told Dad that there was enough in the clearance for everyone to be happy and if it is what he wanted then he could have it. In the truck back from the clearance that evening dad kept the Roman on his lap as if protecting it. Before they arrived back at Cooper's warehouse the old man asked my dad if he knew what he had in his hands. Dad had no idea and said as much to his boss, he just said 'I like the look of it, the weight of it'. Then Mr Cooper said something which my dad thought of at the time as very strange. He said, 'you have something very special there in your hands...' and dad offered to give it back if it was too much. 'No, you have it, it's yours and you have earned it with your hard work and honesty. But one day when the time is right you will use it to set up your own business, or make sure your family are well looked after. So, take care of it.' ...and dad did. I had forgotten it until this evening."

Nick interrupted, "Your dad bought you up with those same principles Sam, its why people always take the piss with you, because you are far too nice." Sam blushed. "Those people, like that dealer at the market today have no manners and no time for honest folk, because they are crooks at heart, and because they are, they think everyone else is."

"So, what happened to the statue, did your dad sell it to get this shop." Nick was into the story now, not for his paper, he was not made that way, but because he was genuinely interested.

"Dad kept it for years," Sam's mind was deep in recollections, "...up on the mantelshelf it was. I never thought of it much, it was just always there, shining brightly once dad had gently cleaned it, and every now and again he would take it down and gently buff it up with a clean, soft cloth, nothing abrasive, it was kept over the open fire in the lounge and dad never wanted it to get blackened by smoke again. I think it was still there, and gently polished, when he died." He paused trying to recall what had happened to it. "No, it couldn't have been, or I would remember moving it."

"How long ago did he die Sam?" Nick's voice was soft for the fear of upsetting his friend.

"Must have been 20 odd years ago when his heart finally gave out, I had just turned 30, but his ticker was weak for a long time before that. He stopped coming with me on house clearances at least five years before that, and that was when he started clearing a lot of the stock out, trading on to other dealers and the like, he must have moved it then, but I never recall him selling it."

Nick was deeply engrossed with the tale of the statuette, as a journalist he always had an enquiring mind even if there was no story for him at the end of it. "So, where is it now, just tucked away somewhere?"

"I have no idea, Nick. Dad always referred to it as his collateral and it would always be there if he needed it." Another thoughtful pause. "Dad said that as long as the Roman was on the mantle, the business was doing okay."

It was the question Sam did not want to hear.

"Don't keep me guessing Sam, for god's sake!" he had to ask, it wasn't in his nature to ignore a question when it needed to be said. "So, where is it now?"

"Gone!"

"Gone?"

"Yes, fucking gone." A raised eyebrow from Nick, and Sam knew he had to tell it all. "I think I sold the bloody thing."

It was hard but Nick remained silent. Sometimes as a journalist it was the best thing to do, just keep quiet and your subject will always keep talking because they were nervous to have gaps in the conversation. True to form, Sam kept talking...

"I'm sure that I sold it Nick, I didn't mean to, it was just in a job lot of bric-a-brac that I sold on. Dad was right about one thing; the business was okay while the Roman was on the mantle. This was a time when he wasn't up to working much more, due to his bad health, and things were not going too well. So, I had a clear out and sold boxes of junk that on their own were not worth much but if I sold enough, at car-boot sales and the like, I would make enough money to keep the lights on in this place and feed myself. I didn't mean to sell it, Nick. I think it may have just become caught up in the clear out."

Nick reached across the table and just put a warm hand of friendship on his friend's arm, and still he said nothing.

"You know this place well enough Nick, it's like an impenetrable forest at times, and you really cannot see the wood for the trees. Walk through the shop on any day and it's like a winding footpath through dense undergrowth, every now and again you come across a sunlit glade where you get to see flowers of growth and you believe things will be different, but the clouds soon loom and before you know it someone has picked the best flowers."

"You do always try and look on the bright side of life Sam, but other times you really are a miserable bugger, aren't you?"

"It's part of why I am so popular." Sam said with sarcasm on his tongue.

"It still does not answer the question though, how did you know that the one on The Roadshow was fake and not the one your dad picked up as his Porters-Piece."

Again, Sam chose his words carefully, "There was something about our piece. Gravitas I suppose you would call it, it had a weight to it, and I don't mean the weight of the bronze." Nick nodded to note that he was aware of what Sam meant. "I know that I am not very good at this game, crap if the truth be told and I have never felt I was any good.

I know dad loved me, but he always seemed disappointed at my valuations and stuff. That said though I do seem to have muddled through over the years without trying too much. I suppose you end up with a knack, or a good eye for the good stuff."

"You put yourself down way too much Sam, you are far better at this game than what you think. You just let the other dealers do you down." Nick always tried to bolster his friend's feeling of self-worth. He had always believed in Sam, its why he enjoyed his company so much despite the near 15-year gap in their ages.

"There is something intangible when you have been in this game for a while. Could be the wrong brush stroke in a painting, or the sheen or shape of a piece of pottery, or with the likes of the statuette there is that certain something indescribable, unaccountable. In the end it is down to gut-instinct, a feeling that something is just 'off'. And there was something 'off' with that statue tonight," he said pointing at the frozen screen. "It wasn't right."

Sam felt tired and Nick thought he looked it. The old man looked defeated, so Nick took pity on him and stopped with the questions. A short silence fell at the table and all that could be heard was Wedgwood's continued purring as he slept by the Aga. Sam had certainly had enough of being bad at his job for one day and thought of a remark he had often made down the past two decades, and that was he wished his dad had left him a fish and chip shop. He liked fish and chips and had come to hate antiques and the world around them. He relied more on the staple of English cuisine for his life than he did in making money with all the old crap he carried in this shop.

"Do you want another cup of tea before you head off Nick?"

Nick stood to go and slipped his jacket back on as he spoke, "Not tonight, Sam, thanks, I had better get home to Suzi, she said there was something we had to talk about tonight and I will get it in the neck if I am much later."

"Anyone would think she's the boss in your house."

"The problem is *she* thinks she's the boss, and, apparently, I have no say on that subject."

The two friends said their goodbyes with a friendly man-hug. Sam used to feel uncomfortable hugging another man, especially as Nick always kissed Sam on the cheek, but it was just the way that Nick was, and Sam would now miss those intimate moments with his friend if, God forbid, he was not around. Nick's parents had worked in theatres all their lives and so were well used to all the 'lovies' with their hugs and kisses. To Nick it was the ultimate sign of affection and belonging. And, to Sam affection between men was something alien, even with his father, the father/son relationship was a marvellous and loving one but did not involve physical contact. Now Sam looked forward to Nick's kind of friendship and was totally at ease with the affection which was always offered so freely and without inhibition. The hugs were now returned with the equal love of brotherhood. Sam said goodbye to his friend, and both looked forward to the next Sunday's instalment of their antique quiz, courtesy of the BBC. Sam picked up the remote and flicked the television to off, seeing the Roman soldier so large was getting tiresome.

"Give Suzi a hug from me Nick." Sam said with a hint of wickedness, knowing full well that his friend's pregnant girlfriend did not understand the bond between the two men, given their generation gap.

She had never been rude to Sam, nor though did she offer anything nice to say. She merely accepted the weird friendship although she often questioned it with Nick because of its weird mix of generation and type. To Suzi it was as if Nick had a lover in the background.

"I'll try Sam, but as I am running later than usual, I may give it a miss and just blame you for my tardiness."

And the door closed and as it was for most of the week, it was just Sam and Wedgwood left in the kitchen. It was a moment that Sam never liked each week as for the next hour or so the place would feel even colder and emptier without the warmth and companionship of Nick.

Nick made the drive home swiftly, but safely, a smile on his face but all the while hoping Sam still had his Roman Centurion hidden amongst the rest of the debris that was his shop. For now, though, all he wanted was to get home to a pregnant Suzi.

CHAPTER 18

As he climbed into bed Nick lifted the quilt gently not wanting to disturb his partner. Suzi headed early to bed these days as her growing bump seemed to tire her quickly. Suzi lay centre of the bed, arms and legs spread like a starfish, sprawled across the bed it was almost as if she were setting a trap, he would not be able to climb in under the quilt without waking her. She released gentle grunts with each slow breath, and Nick gazed at the round bump that held their unborn child, gender not yet determined – they wanted to wait, and he was in awe of this beautiful woman who picked him and then decided to have a child with him. It took a strong woman to put up with him, and now she had volunteered to go all in and share a family life with him. He watched in awe as she slept.

He whispered, "I love you Suzi, and I love you little lady...." He was cut short from telling a possible boy that he loved him too.

"Told you it's not a girl, it's a boy." Suzi surprised him by being awake, normally she would sleep through a storm.

He kissed her belly anyway, "Whatever you are I love you anyway." he softly said to the bump.

Nick Flax knew he had a blessed life, a job he loved doing, and that he was good at. A wonderful woman to love, and more importantly who loved him, and a new human to dote on and marvel on as they grew. Until 'it' too was an adult and put him in an old folk's home. It was almost too much to take in, a little over a year ago he had been a single man, who lived for work. Now he lived for Suzi with a little work on the side. She pulled the quilt back over her swollen midriff and told him to get into bed. He gazed in awe at her flawless face, lit only by the streetlight outside the window, even in the low light and with shadows she was stunning with her blonde pixie cut hair and cute nose, and her mouth, soft and thin lipped, a mouth he always wanted to kiss. Nick never was one to take a liking toward the modern trend of pumped-up lips, Suzi was perfect in every way as far as Nick was concerned.

It read a little after ten on the bedside digital clock as he climbed into bed and as he moved Suzi watched what she referred to as his *'Little Johnson'*, bounce up and down, barely touching his thigh as it did. It always embarrassed him, and she had mentioned it more since becoming pregnant, he put it down to hormones.

"It's lucky you are a grower and not a shower, Nick Flax, or you would never have had the chance to make this baby." She rubbed her stomach affectionately.

"Thought you were tired and wanted to sleep, and stop being rude about the Mighty Cock."

Suzi giggled.

"You better have cleaned your teeth; I am not kissing you while you taste of one of those kinky teas that Sam likes so much." She wriggled closer to him, a move she instantly regretted. "Christ, your feet are bloody freezing." But she hugged him anyway.

"I have cleaned my teeth, and how do you know I have been with Sam?" Nick asked as a tease because she knew only too well where he had been.

"It just seems an odd friendship is all." It was an often-repeated refrain. "I wouldn't mind if you were out with some bleached, blonde tramp or came home pissed like normal blokes, but you haven't. Yet you still come sneaking back home like a wayward husband with a guilty secret, and instead of the second-hand smell of scent or lipstick on your shirt you come home with kisses tasting like perfume from your boyfriend's stash of teas." She moved her leg away from Nick's foot as it wasn't getting any warmer.

"I don't sneak anywhere." Nick tried not to make his voice confrontational. "Anyway, you cannot tell me off, as you still haven't agreed to marry me, thereby leaving me free and single to do what I want."

"Nor am I likely to say yes, at this rate." Suzi grunted as she rolled to one side and hefted the weight of their child slightly to ease the pressure of the little fidget that she would soon be pushing out into the world. She looked forward to meeting their child but was not looking forward to the pain of childbirth. And once her angelic little boy was born, she would not let Nick anywhere near her again.

"Sorry Suz..." He knew she hated her name being shortened and he only did it to tease. "It won't happen again." Nick slid down into the bed and placed his hand on her stomach, imagining he had his hand on his daughter's head.

"You will be back there next Sunday with you two playing

Bargain Hunt." Her voice softened as he kissed her forehead, most women would hate his constant attention, but she loved the fact he was always in contact with her, holding her hand, kissing her and stroking their child. "It would serve you right if I decided to bring Junior into the world during Antiques Roadshow."

"And, as soon as the programme finished, I would be here like a shot to take you to hospital." Nick fired back quickly. "Just think yourself lucky my girl that I don't run off with another, less grouchy woman."

"The only thing you are likely to pull at your age is a hamstring!" Suzi tried to look cross, but it wasn't working. "...and you wouldn't dare come home if you ever went with another woman." She chided. "You are mine and don't you forget it."

Nick rolled over to face her, careful not to put any weight on her swollen belly, but he revelled in the warmth and smoothness of her skin. He had gone to sleep with his hand on her stomach every night since Suzi had announced she was pregnant.

Before Suzi his one true love was his work, he loved being a reporter, spending his time between the office, his one-bedroom flat and those Sunday evenings with Sam. The man was simple company and Nick could forget any hard news he had covered that week and just enjoy his time drinking tea and chatting.

Suzi was ten years younger than Nick, and she wondered now and again why their own friendship worked, and it surprised her when the friends turned into lovers. She loved him with all her heart, he had come along when life was at its lowest and had kept her head above water as mentally, she felt she was drowning after her parents were tragically killed. To begin with the age difference bothered Nick but Suzi was such easy company he just went with the flow. He had just turned 35, and she was just 25, and just recently had lost both her parents which is how they met.

Father English and Mother Chinese, she had a little of both their looks. Her skin a soft yellow, almost jaundiced, Nick thought her complexion to be a soft shade of golden, huge almond eyes that when she wanted to Suzi could use to her advantage, big time. Every time he looked into those beautiful eyes, he felt like the luckiest man alive. Nick had only ever seen her parents in photographs, he would have loved to have met them as they sounded a lovely, intelligent couple. Suzi spoke of them often, and always with pleasant memories, they had been a close family and with Nick letting her speak often about them it had helped her come to terms with the unending grief that she felt at their loss.

They had been killed a little over four years ago, Suzi was just 21 and had been in the back seat of the family car when it was involved in a tragic accident on the main trunk road that by-passed Chichester. He and the Chronicle's photographer had been called out a little before midnight on Christmas eve to a fog-bound multi-vehicle pile-up. The A27, although a straight dual carriageway, was always a road of confusion and accidents. Drivers felt they were safe on or over the 70mph limit with it being a straight road, but as the road passed close to the city there were several roundabouts linking either to the city centre or the nearby coastal resorts. Those roundabouts caught inattentive drivers unawares on bright summers' days, but that night it had been a thick peasouper that had drifted in from the coast and it only took one thoughtless driver driving way too fast for the conditions to ruin several lives that night. Suzi was one of those who had lost everything that night and she still carried bad dreams about the crash. Meanwhile the careless driver, as often happens, had walked away unhurt, and then walked free from prison after just four months in jail for causing death by dangerous driving. There is no price for stealing away loved ones but surely, they were worth more than just a few weeks of lost freedom.

They estimated the car's speed to be more than 85mph, when he lost control and hit the metal stanchion of a footbridge, that crossed the dual carriageway, before spinning across both lanes and hitting the central reservation crash barrier. On the way he caused a truck to swerve, hitting two other cars and blocking the whole road. The driver of one car was killed, and the front two seats in Suzi's family Peugeot were obliterated killing both her parents, they were both so damaged they were left unrecognisable. Suzi, by a sheer twist of fate was thrown clear and left with just bruises.

Nick found her shivering sitting on the central reservation with her back to the damaged crash barrier, a small trickle of blood ran down unnoticed on her forehead. No ambulance crew had treated her yet, after checking with one of the on-scene coppers, who he knew well from his police contacts said he could sit her in his car if she was okay to walk and he would come and talk to her soon. It was never any fun reporting on serious road incidents especially when it left three dead and one young lady traumatised for life and leaving her parentless.

Nick took his jacket off and draped it around the young girl's shoulders, pointed to his car which was visible on a side road leading from the accident, and walked her there. He took her hand to help her up and she didn't let go again until they were in the car.

With the single ambulance crew available busy, Nick drove Suzi to the hospital, and still stunned from the accident she refused to let go of his hand even when she was checked over by the A&E team. She did not want to go home and was panicked by the thought of going back to her house, she had never lived away from her parents, being entirely happy living at home. Now, though she could not stand the thought of going there and being left alone. There was a tacit trust between them both and Nick took her back to his small apartment, made a bed up on the couch which Suzi insisted she sleep on. She had been prescribed pain killers for her bruises and small head wound and Diazepam to calm her nerves and hopefully make her drowsy. Whether it was the trauma, or the medication Suzi did fall asleep that night, while holding Nick's hand as he sat on an armchair next to her.

Four years later and they were still holding hands, and now Suzi was about to start a family of her own.

"Actually, it's nice to have you home, I wasn't really expecting you until morning, or even later." Her voice, as it did that first night three years ago, was slipping into sleepiness.

"Not home until morning?" Nick lifted his head from the pillow. "Why would I be out all night?"

"Mainly because I thought the office would have contacted you, they tried you here when you didn't answer your phone." She was now suddenly a little more alert herself, "I was expecting you to come home telling me the gory details of the murders you had been called out on."

Nick sat bolt upright in the bed and said, "Alexa, turn the lamps on," and both bedside lamps slowly lit the room. He looked around for his phone which he had put on silent while watching TV, "What murders Suzi?"

She struggled to sit up, wobbling from side to side like a drunk trying to sit up straight, she was suddenly wide awake now. "You know that nice detective we have met at a couple of functions?"

"David Martin?"

"No, his boss, Kobe, Kobe Kaan, is it?"

CHAPTER 19

At that moment in his life when he needed Rae the most, she could not be there to help him. The last time he had needed her this much and to whisper softly to him that everything would be okay, he was still an hour or two before he and the rest of the caving group would be out of the dark and dank cave with its rock walls caving in around him. It would be alright; Rae was beside him!

Everything would always be alright if Rae was beside him.

Now at the time he needed her the most she was marooned with their children in a billowing sea of white foam stained with red. It was now a room he dared not enter, could not enter, would not enter. The analytical mind of the copper told him that nobody would blame him for entering the room and taking his family up in his arms, he was only human after all. 'Checking for signs of life', he would tell the investigation team, and he would know the team by name, having worked with them all before. But they would not show him any favouritism which was only right. As soon as he reported the killings, the word had raised quickly into the ears and across the desks of his superiors, they would be sending for officers from another station within the county force to investigate. He wouldn't know them personally; they would only know him by name or reputation. The practical side of his professional mind told him that the less he disturbed the crime scene, he almost broke then, his home, his family were a crime scene. Incomprehensible! But he knew deep inside that the more he disturbed things the slower the investigation would go as they would have to rule him out first and foremost before ever looking for someone else.

Kobe calculated all of this from where he was rooted in the doorway to the bedroom. All the time knowing that his family were dead.

So much blood among the roses, experience told him, gut instinct told him, nobody could have survived.

Since that weekend away in those dark caves and narrow rocky tunnels the thought had never crossed his mind that one day he would be without Rae. A scenario where she was not in his life was unimaginable. And since the children had come along, beautiful, and chatty Molly and her big protective brother Kobe Junior, the quiet thinker, meant the thought that one day he would be without them went into the realms of sheer fantasy.

Sat propped up in that doorway into the bedroom of carnage Kobe's heart pounded. He could feel it in his chest, hear it thumping in his head. He could feel dribbles of cold sweat on his neck and running down his spine. Everything else was numbness and fear.

He could not stop looking at them, it was like a horror movie where one could not tear eyes away from the scenes unfolding on the screen, no matter how terrifying.

Sweet little Molly her nightie covered in rainbows and unicorns was coated in her own drying blood, the beautiful, printed colours almost hidden now. Arms stretched out in front of her, as if reaching for her father, were laid across the only part of the quilt still white. She was reaching out for him; but he was busy drinking with colleagues. For the first time he noticed laying on the floor just two feet from him was her favourite teddy bear, that had most of his stuffing hugged out of him. Kobe reached out and took it, making a mental note of where it had fallen so he could tell investigators later. He hated thinking so clearly about some things and being so confused about others. He held the limp bear to his chest; it held but a crumb of comfort.

Kobe, the smaller version of his father, serious and protective of his sister was curled into his sister's back his left arm draped over her body. He was like his father and only wore boxer shorts to bed, they looked baggy on his slender frame. Growing up he had always seen his father strolling around the house, first thing in the morning sipping from his first cup of coffee dressed in nothing but boxers and slippers. Before putting on his school uniform his boy would strut about the cottage emulating Kobe senior. Tired of trying to get either of her macho men into dressing gowns Rae would just shake her head in amusement.

Behind his precious children lay his once beautiful wife, his still beautiful wife, Rae. The angle of her head, her hair matted and twisted with blood had turned her English rose beauty, with her almond eyes staring to the ceiling, into a bloody mess. Her throat wide open, a gaping wound distracting eyes from her strangely serene face. Would he ever again remember a face that he so adored, without seeing the blood and carnage.

He wondered if she had been made to watch her children die first, or, and even more horrifying, had the children been forced to watch their mother suffer.

It appeared from his limited view from the doorway that Rae's brown and fluffy dressing gown had been pulled down over her shoulders to trap her arms by her side, but it seemed that in her moment of dying she had managed to free one arm and throw it across both of her children. Her action had left her left breast naked, pale white, small, and pointed, the flesh coated with splashes of dried blood and again he wished that he dared to enter the room so that he could cover his wife and give at least a modicum of dignity in her death.

What sort of God would meet out such horrific punishment. What sort of God would allow children to suffer so, and Kobe hoped that whoever did this, did not let the children see their mother being slaughtered?

His beautiful family transformed into the grotesque, but he still loved them, still adored them, still wanted them.

Unable to look any more he threw one arm across his knees to cover his eyes in the crook of his elbow. Eyes were squeezed tightly shut but the vision, although now hidden, was burned into his brain. It would be unforgettable. He knew there would be no answer but still he called out to their tortured, quiet bodies, this time his voice a barely audible harsh whisper.

"Rae, Kobe, little Molly." He was right, there was still no answer.

He wanted numbness in his head, he didn't want to think anymore. Still, he considered going into the bedroom but who would he go to and hold first, who would he touch first. Would he be caring parent or loving husband. Finally, he was glad he could not go into the room. He would not have to choose between son, daughter, or wife.

In a guttural voice that came from deep inside him and was filled with anguish, Kobe looked for his own God, and began to chant...

"Inna Lillahi wa inna ilayha raji'un." Quoting the prayer automatically. At first a whisper. Then over and over he chanted it with a stronger voice that to his ears sounded as if said by a stranger, not recognising where the sound of the prayer was coming from.

Despite his name Kobe Kaan and the fact that he was born in England, Kobe considered himself as English as it was possible to be and was probably one of the reasons why he had never followed being Muslim with any sort of commitment. Although his parents were strictly religious his home life had been Westernised in all other ways even before his birth. While at Oxford University earning his degree in Criminology and Psychology in Criminal Behaviour, he had loved the freedom of being a student and letting his hair down, so it was easy to let the teachings of his religion slip while he studied the next-morning effects of alcohol and sleeping around. He was a lapsed Muslim but now it offered a small amount of comfort amidst the unrelenting agony.

"Inna lillahi wa inna ilayha raji'un." He chanted over and over, 'Verily we belong to Allah and truly to him we will return'. When death was around it was not the time to abandon or denounce Allah, and even though Rae had been raised Catholic Kobe knew he had to prepare her for her onward journey the only way he knew how, the Muslim way. The same went for his children for whom the choice of which religion to follow had not yet become an issue. So it was that he continued to offer the prayer over the bodies of his family.

With the prayer chant taking on a rhythm and cadence of its own Kobe began to rock his head back and forth from his crouched spot in the doorway. His family's end may have been brutal, but their crossing should be peaceful and blessed.

As a man and a Muslim what should happen next was dictated by his long-buried beliefs, firstly he must close their eyes and jaws, but his core belief in the law of the land and its process of gathering evidence and forensics overruled his religion and meant his must leave the bodies untouched, for now.

For the first time in his life Kobe Kaan felt totally useless and did not know what to do with this alien feeling, apart from wearing it like a heavy cloak, or more in keeping with death, a shroud weighed down by misery.

CHAPTER 20

His upper torso continued to rock back and forth, his bent legs, arms wrapped around them, were cramping up, but he felt nothing to do with the physical. The mental pains were driving nails into his temples. Cold tears stuck to his cheeks and the weeping made his eyes sore, his chest was tight, and he found it hard to breathe. It took a monumental effort but finally a small part of the level-headed Kobe, the man, and the copper, who could deal with any problem returned and he managed to draw his mobile phone from the sheath that was his inside jacket pocket. Looking at the phone he hardly recognised what it was in his hand, finally with the tip of his thumb he hit the nine three times, at least it felt like three, it could have been more, but the other end began to ring anyway.

"Emergency Services, which service would you like please?" asked a well-spoken voice on the other end without any sense of urgency. Her voice calming, assuring.

Finding his own voice was a little harder for Kobe, at first, he thought he was unable to speak at all and when words did form in his own mind they were without coherence, he was babbling. Hardly able to form a sentence the girl on the other end knew just what was needed.

"Take a breath, and your time sir," The call centre operator knew when a caller was panicking. "You are through to Emergency Services sir. I am here to help you." The faceless voice held a modicum of concern, it would only be human, but she was also well trained and would be professional no matter what. "Can you tell me what you need help with Sir?"

Despite knowing what he wanted to say, deep in his brain somewhere a voice was telling him not to ask for help, or he would lose any control that he had over the operation.

His mouth uttered the words without any help from his brain. "Police please..."

All the operators could hear was the rasping breaths in her earpiece. She remained silent for a few moments, experience telling her not to rush the distraught caller, it gave Kobi time to level his breathing and compose himself. Although he never thought it at the time, but later he would commend her level-headed actions.

Kaan repeated himself, but clearer this time. "This is DI Kobe Kaan, police control please." Keeping his voice calm was hard but panic now would not help his family. He almost laughed at the thought that nothing now could help his family, but it was a laugh out of grief, not humour.

The woman's experienced voice continued to be calming, "Putting you through to the police control room Sir, so please stay on the line."

He thanked her. Then heard her announce who he was to the police control and the number he was calling from. Somehow in those few brief moments he was able to control himself a little more, and yet he felt guilty for being calm at such a catastrophic time.

"You are through to police control; can you please repeat your name sir and where you are calling from?" The voice cold, the operator well trained and used to disaster daily, he sounded almost bored.

Kobe had been listening to the phone on speaker, it lay in his lap cradled in the palm of one limp hand, but now he brought it up to his ear and took a deep breath. Now the professional part of his brain clicked in, as a senior officer with the lives of his team on the line every day, he had to have a natural ability to remain calm, or at least pull calmness up from his boots or else the rank-and-file officers would be in danger.

He no longer wanted to stare into the room at his destroyed family, but from his seated position in the doorway it was hard not to. His eyes were unable to close or turn away, he simply continued to gaze at the devastation before him.

"*Inna lillahi wa inna ilayha raji'un.*" he prayed over them one more time, his voice softer.

"Sorry sir, I did not catch that, this is police control." More insistent this time.

"This is DI Kobe Kaan, of West Sussex Serious Crimes squad, out of Chichester." The operator remained quiet, waiting for the DI to give him more info.

"I have just arrived home to find my family dead." Saying the words out loud made him choke, phlegm in his throat, hard to swallow.

"You say you found them dead Mr Kaan, are we talking an accident here?" The boredom in his voice was now gone. He was having to coax whatever information he could.

"No!" A huge intake of breath to steel himself. "No, they have been murdered, my wife and both my children."

"Are you sure sir?"

It was as if someone had turned a knife in his own gut.

"Am I fucking sure?" Kobe broke. "They are lying here with their throats cut and blood all up the fucking walls... Yes, I am fucking sure."

The operator kept his voice level, this was no time to show emotion. "I know that was hard sir, but I had to ask."

Kobe had no room to argue or time to apologise.

"I will need your address, Mr Kaan. Then I can get someone out to you." his voice gentle, coaxing the information from Kobe, who told him what he wanted to know. "There are cars on the way to you already Mr Kaan, they will be with you soon." A second or two of silence as if the operator were doing the correct actions at his end of the phone. "My supervisor is here with me now and he is already contacting your Chief Constable, and an ambulance is also on its way, Mr Kaan."

Kobe thanked him, he was not angry at the operator, the man was just being efficient. Now with almost excited tones the operator came back on the line.

"It will take the nearest car about 15 minutes or so to reach you Mr Kaan. Bosham is a bit off the beaten path as you know sir." Kobe felt the voice begin to have a calming influence. "I will stay on the line with you until the first officers arrive, so talk or don't talk, it's all up to you Mr Kaan. Can the officers obtain entry easily Sir or do you have to let them in?"

"I think I left the back door open; my family and I are up in the bedroom."

Despite all his hopes that this was all a bad dream, and he would wake at any moment, the call to Emergency Services put the stamp of reality on the evening's events. Maybe, he thought to himself he had accidently sniffed some cocaine from the morning's raid, and he was now hallucinating. But the harsh reality was that he really was on the phone to police control and his family were indeed just six feet or so from him and yet so far out of reach. The harsh reality was that after saying the words, 'my family are dead', he knew they had been massacred and lay on an altar of white bedding and surrounded by bloody roses.

There was no way back from here.

Kobe felt useless and helpless. Selfishly he considered himself as a lesser man for not being able to protect his own family. It was his main job in life, and he had failed them, self-pity was not Kobe Kaan's style.

"Mr Kaan, Sir..." Kobe had forgotten the phone was in his lap and live, he responded with a softly spoken 'yes'. "You should be hearing a car arrive at any moment, the first officer is in your village now. Is there anything else I can do for you before I ring off?" There was nothing much the civilian could do but he was keeping his caller on the line a little longer. "I am sorry for your loss Sir!" Although a civilian, they were all on the same team. Normally with such calls an operator would not comment, but this time he felt it was the right thing to do.

It made Kobe jump, but there was a shout from downstairs. The operator heard it. "I can hear help has arrived Mr Kaan, I will hang up now. I wish you well Sir." And the phone went quiet.

From downstairs, a shout. "Hello, this is the police." It echoed in a house that sounded empty and hollow. "This is the police, and I am coming up the stairs." It was a voice that sounded confident, at first and then a little hesitant. "I am coming up Sir, are you armed?"

Kobe thought he had said 'harmed'. "No, I am fine, I am not hurt its my family."

Big boots climbed the stairs thumping heavily on each step, strangely Kobe hoped he had wiped his feet or there would be hell to pay from Rae, she hated muddy boot marks through the house.

The phone now silent in his lap all he could hear was heavy breathing from the young officer who was climbing his stairs. Soon any responsibility for his family would be taken from his hands, and he hated the thought.

The constable's head poked around the corner of the stairs and looked straight at the distraught fellow officer. "Mr Kaan?" It was a question, but it did not warrant a reply.

Kobe mentally found himself breaking away from his family, now he had to let go while others did their jobs and there was nothing for him to cling onto. Cracks appeared in this thoughts, lucid thoughts came crashing down.

Kobe Kaan's mind began to unravel.

CHAPTER 21

Long after Nick had headed home to be with Suzi, Sam had just remained sitting at the table. A cold cup of tea in front of him, untouched and forgotten. The television was off, Fiona Bruce and the Roadshow crew long gone. Sam had just been sitting there, all-in-all it had been a thoroughly depressing day. Oblivious to her owner's depression, Wedgwood slept on. The overhead light with its weak bulb dropped nothing but a dull yellow light down onto the table and it seemed to sum up Sam's life, dull and uninteresting. Sunday nights with Nick were all he had to look forward to, and they were over far too quickly, it was surely the dullest life that had ever been.

Finally, Sam got up, scraping the chair's four feet across the flagstone floor as he did, the screech made Wedgwood look up, his furry face full of disdain. Sam took the cups to the sink and rinsed them under the cold tap, leaving them to drain on the side. With his back aching, damp weather always made his body play up, Sam decided on an early night and Wedgwood followed him upstairs and within seconds he was curled up on the frayed quilt long before Sam got into bed. He was tired but it would prove to be a restless night as he drifted in and out of sleep. Although physically weary, his brain was on full power and would not shut down. Through his thoughts on waking, and his dreams in brief moments of sleep, he could see only one thing, the image of a small bronze Centurion.

The Roman soldier's body was toned and muscular, the brass six-pack rippled with fine-tuned muscle, the short, glittering sword held aloft in his right hand, the pose was that of a soldier readying for attack or brandished in victory. The helmet carried a thick bronze brush from front to back, in his dream Sam saw the crest as bright red, as it had been in the history books at school, and the bronzed body that of a swarthy Italian with tanned leathery skin caused by days of serving in the sun. The soldier's whole demeanour was that of someone ready to fight, it was the aggressive stance of a gladiator offering strength and power. It could only have been portrayed and accomplished by a skilled artist who had carefully moulded the bare muscular torso. He was a study in the warriors of his day and in his dream, it was Sam who was being attacked.

After a lot of tossing and turning, Sam finally awoke, covered in sweat and still feeling tired as if he hadn't slept at all. It was still sometime before sunrise, but he swung his legs out of bed to sit on the edge of, what was, a lumpy mattress. Sam winced as he stretched his body, he was never sure if the pains in his body were because of his spinal condition or was it just because he was getting old. He just knew his body hurt. Wedgwood raised his head, opened one blue eye, but realising there was still no food on offer he closed the eye again and ignored Sam.

If he had paid attention to his minion, Wedgwood would have noticed something strange this morning, something he had never seen before. Sam was smiling!

The broad grin on his face, which was hurting long unused muscles and causing his face to ache, Sam must have dreamt something good amidst the normal horrors his dreams brought about, because this morning he felt so good, it felt strange but somehow, to Sam, it seemed to suit him. Sam threw an old, moth-eaten jumper over his upper body, it may have been tatty, but it was warm and comfortable. He rammed his feet into threadbare slippers and almost took two stairs at a time heading down to the kitchen. There he topped up the kettle and put it on the hob, making sure the spout had its whistle fitted, he didn't want it boiling dry if he got stuck into clearing the cellar. He took a mug from the draining board and readied it by emptying a cappuccino sachet into it. He took care when making his beloved tea infusions, but for coffee it was boil the kettle and pour over the powder. Sam thought it must be something like seven in the morning and was puzzled by the fact that the sun had not yet begun to rise. It was early for him but felt there was no point going back to bed now, he was far to hyper.

Full of optimism he opened the door to the cellar, which complained with screeches as hinges, unworked and unopened for at least two, or could it be three years, gave way to a rejuvenated adventurer. He made a mental note to squirt WD40 over them, it was a good panacea for all things squeaky. He pulled the chord that hung down just inside the door and so dim was the ceiling light that Sam thought it was drawing light from the room rather than brightening it. He had a decent torch in the shop and so he fetched it, not believing that it was so early, and the shop was in darkness he was surprised by a tall-case clock in the far corner of the store as it clanged out four times enforcing what he thought was a very early start. Inherently lazy, Sam rarely saw or heard a clock much before nine in the morning. When he returned to the kitchen the kettle whistled loudly to say job done. All Sam did was turn off the gas ring, he was too hyped up already to add caffeine to the mix.

He was ready to dive down into the murky cellar, when he recalled what he dreamt about, the story that had eventually woken him.

He was back at the car boot sale two summers ago, he hated them as an event, as it was a day lost working in the shop while hanging around in a field haggling over prices of 50p for this or a pound for that. So much effort for so little return, but he needed to eat and buy some home essentials and he felt this was a form of begging, but it had to be done. He thought to the old wooden crate, the one that carried wine in a previous incarnation, and that day small pieces of virtually worthless scrap held within its rough wooden walls. As soon as the car boot lid was lifted, it was like the pulling up of the drawbridge to an invading hoard of warriors as grabby stall holders descended upon him and his stock.

Before he could drive them all off and leave something for the paying public one trader, with hair slicked back and shiny with some sort of hair gel, had grabbed the old wine box that held the ephemera of items. The dealer obviously had seen something worth his trouble as he asked Sam with urgency and no politeness, 'how much?', he had to get back to his own stall and there was no time for niceties.

"Twenty-five," said Sam.

"Twenty!" replied the dealer.

"Done!" said Sam, pleased that he had at least covered his petrol costs and the fiver it cost him for his compact 3mtr x 3mtr sales pitch.

To be truthful Sam was quite happy with the deal, he had folding money in his wallet which had been starved of notes for a couple of weeks at that time, it was a hard diet. He had not diddled the dealer either, he would at least double his money on the trade, but Sam still thought it poor return for a day's work.

There was nobody to witness it, but Sam felt embarrassed walking into the lounge, not a room he used often, especially in winter when this was the coldest room in the house. Why sit there when the

Aga was keeping the kitchen so warm and toasty. He opened the door and swung the torch beam the length of the mantelpiece, just to check that it was not still there. It wasn't but at least he had checked.

Taking the steps down carefully to the basement, Sam thought back to the box and remembered some of the tat that was in there. A small but charming ginger jar, not a chip on it but with no lid, and the blue willow pattern that was on it shining as brightly as the day it had emerged from the kiln. Which could have been in the last decade or the last Century, Sam had not worked out how to read the Chinese stamp on the bottom of the piece. For all he knew it could have said Tesco on the bottom in Chinese characters. A pair of porcelain figures depicting Bo Peep and some unnamed shepherd boy, gaudy and twee but some folks liked them, she was perfect, but he was missing his shepherd's crook – and the hand that had held it. There was a complex Meerschaum pipe, very ornate, and alongside it costume jewellery and cameo brooches. All perfect fodder for a car boot sale.

What Sam could not recall from that box of ephemera was the figurine of a Roman Soldier cast in bronze, the very one that had been seen on TV the previous evening. Maybe for once his luck had changed and he did still indeed own the original. He would tear the large basement apart until he found it. With the hairs standing on the back of his neck he began to rummage, moving stuff from one corner and back again. His father had often told him that his fortune could be found in the shop, but Sam had always believed that to be a generality and not a specific. Since waking this morning, he believed dad's words did indeed mean his porter's-piece. He never could figure out why it had not remained on the mantle shelf.

Wedgwood, who had returned to the soft cushion of the quilt was disturbed by the noise emanating from the room two storeys below. Crates were being moved, the odd piece of crockery being smashed, each time something broke Sam cursed loudly. It was too much for the cat and she slunk downstairs, looked mournfully at her empty food dish and then clattered her way through the cat flap. He blinked at the low sunlight and slunk off along the weed-riddled path.

"One day, Sam, you will find your way in this life, maybe even find your fortune. That one, beautiful piece that will change your life." Sam recalled this oft held one sided conversation with his father, but always thinking it was his way of making sure Sam kept the shop. "You may think this is all junk and that your old man does not have the keen eye needed for this business, but I have not done too badly. There has always been a roof over our heads and food on the table and trust me son your treasure is buried away in here for a time when you will need to find it."

Sam always felt the chats were apocryphal and meant to be taken with a pinch of salt. His father would always smile after his little speech and tousle his son's hair and Sam took that to mean it was a light-hearted tease and not to be taken too seriously. Now though he suddenly believed that the time was right in his life to find that one special item, the life-changer. Every wheeler dealer, cheat and true trader believed that one day something would turn up and their ship would indeed be coming in. Sam was beginning to think this was his day, so vivid were the images from his dream.

Two hours later and still nothing but an increasingly despondent Sam kept digging, moving, and shifting. He even found an old Welsh dresser, in fine condition but brown furniture did not sell well. Alongside that a beautiful three-seater settee, Sam didn't think of their value but wondered more how the hell his father had got them down into the cellar. It was as if he were digging one hole and then another but storing the soil from that one in the last hole. He did have the slim hope that he would tidy up down there and create a stock list of what would sell. But, like most of Sam's plans nothing would come of his ambition, he was just moving shit from one place to another. The dust in the enclosed cellar was choking him and causing him to cough but he didn't want to stop, but maybe a short break as hard work was not one of his good characteristics. Back up to the kitchen and he looked at the kettle that he had abandoned long before the sun came up. In fact, he was surprised to see that the sun had indeed arisen. Opening the till in shop, and it always opened with such a pleasing clatter, he checked for some cash and there was a ten-pound note and change, so he grabbed the note and went two doors down to get a proper coffee from one of those well-known chains of coffee houses. The friendly girl behind the counter with bobbed black hair and a pretty turned-up nose, asked him if he had been in an accident, a strange question he thought, before he looked down and saw that his clothes were covered in grey dust.

"Oh, all this no, just moving some stock around in the basement." He smiled back, surprised that he still felt positive and happy despite the worthless search so far.

The girl with a tattooed wrist and hand pointed at his face. "And, you have cut yourself."

He touched his forehead where she was pointing and there was indeed a trickle of blood being stopped by the thick dust.

"Do you have plasters?" she asked with a concern in her voice that said so much more. Basically, she was saying without saying a word, 'you are man, living alone and of course you haven't'.

He shook his head, if he did have a first aid box, he had not come across it in the search so far.

The young Barista had finished concocting his cappuccino, the steam noisily hissing from its nozzle to get the drink to just the right temperature and the right amount of capping froth and handed it across the counter in the takeaway cup. Take a seat and I will clean you up the girl had said and was gone from behind the counter before he could argue. Sam took a seat in the window and sipped at his coffee through the lid, it burnt his lip slightly, but it was a pleasant feeling and the coffee tasted strong and without bitterness, he preferred a smoother coffee. Swiftly the girl was back, and Sam noted the brief flash of reflected light from the ring that was piercing one side of her nose. Like a battlefield medic she had returned with cotton wool and a cleaning solution which stung when applied to the cut on his forehead. With a sharp intake of breath he winced, Sam tried to be brave and not flinch, but he couldn't help himself.

"Don't be a baby." She said after hearing the gasp of breath from her patient.

Sam liked her smile, not in a creepy, fancy you style but as a father would enjoy a child's smile. Her face exuded warmth and friendship and it made the older man feel comfortable being in such proximity, it was so easy today for people to get the wrong idea. Some people just gave out a friendly vibe, as did this girl. Finally, she patched up his wounded head with a square Band-Aid. He was good to go, and he stood examining the handiwork in the large mirror that was fixed to the wall behind him. The badge on her work shirt carried the legend of 'Annie', and he thanked her very kindly and told her to keep the change from his tenner, he couldn't really afford to be that generous, but it seemed cheap to do anything else, especially as he was digging for a massive pot of gold. Although she argued he insisted, saying that if she didn't want it then to put it into one of the charity pots on the counter. And Sam headed back to work and telling himself that he was a wastrel, giving away £10 for a cup of coffee. Okay, she had stopped him bleeding to death or worse, getting the wound infected, but that change would have been a week's food for Wedgwood.

Back to his shop he went, sipping the hot coffee as he walked. Back in the cellar he began burrowing and working again and it was a good two hours later before he stopped again. He was weary and getting hungry for lunch, but he was on a mission now, plus his only money, apart from odd change in his pocket, had gone to Annie for her kindness. So much effort had gone into the search that Sam had broken out into a sweat, something he never did, it felt strange and rewarding at the same time. Any effort spent would be well worth it if the statue were there. Wedgwood would never be hungry again, nor would he if the truth be known. He was about to plonk himself down in an old armchair that he had recently uncovered under a pile of very dusty sheets and a stack of, now crispy with age, broadsheet Daily Telegraphs with the top one showing an illegible date sometime in 1974 and bearing the headline 'SLIM MAJORITY IN WILSON'S GRASP'. Sam assumed it referred to the long-ago Prime Minister Harold Wilson. Dust and newspaper scraps flew into the air when they he disturbed the long-ago heap and when that dust finally settled a battered old chair emerged from the debris. Sam could not even recall it amongst his stock. He was just beginning to recognise it from a long-ago memory when he heard the front door rattle causing the bell above it to jangle out a warning. Sam wanted to continue diving amongst the junk, but thinking he had locked the front door, so he went to investigate. Unusual that he should attract a customer on a Monday morning, so with reluctance he trudged up the stairs once again, his back was feeling the activity of the morning and his legs were feeling weak as he trudged up the staircase, he would pay for all this activity over the next few days. His body was already complaining about the effort.

Pulling the heavy drape back to gain access to the shop he was surprised to see it was the young barista from just along the precinct standing there.

"You've stopped bleeding…" she said. Sam could never recall having her confidence when he was young, Christ, he did not have that kind of confidence, even now.

Sam merely touched the strip of plaster above his eye and thanked her again. She could see puzzlement on his face as to why she was there.

"I just finished my shift and as it's a quarter past lunchtime, I thought you might be hungry, so I have bought you a tuna-melt sandwich." She held out the triangular packet, and with a little hesitation he took it, and he must have looked concerned because she added with a cheeky smile and a tilt of her head, "Don't worry I didn't steal it. I bought it with your change and still put a few coins into the charity pot. I hope that was okay?"

"What a lovely thought," he said while offering a smile through the dust on his face. "Too many people take advantage these days, so it is nice to meet someone caring, who is not out to make a quick buck." He looked at the floor as he spoke as he was unused to speaking to people outside of a business environment, or outside of his age-range.

Before he could even think of anything else to say she just said 'bye, offered him a dazzling smile, spun on her heels and she was gone, leaving the bell over the door jangling in her wake. Today was turning out to be a good day for the old antique dealer.

Sam sat on the top stair leading down to the cellar and was glad the dust had settled as it was irritating his throat. He ate his sandwich, a little nervously at first as he had never had a tuna-melt before. It was delicious and filled the void that he had in his stomach. Weary from working so hard and now sated after his lunch it felt good, his mind was also in a good place, something that never happened much in Sam's depressing life. Just maybe, things were turning up trumps for Sam Cobby, at long last.

CHAPTER 22

Sam startled himself awake with a loud snorted intake of breath, the pig-like oink echoing down into the cellar. His body ached and his neck was stiff, then Sam realised he was still seated on the top stair that led down to the cellar, an empty sandwich pack in his lap. He thought of, Annie, the pretty barista who had brought him the sandwich and again appreciated that not all people were only out for themselves.

The backroom and cellar had never been an organised storage space, more a dumping ground for excess stock as well as for every useless nick-knack, cracked pot and broken chair back that was not fit for display in the shop. It was a thin line between hoarder and collector and Sam had passed that benchmark many years ago. It had to be said in his defence that his father was no better, *'don't throw anything away, you never know when you might need it, or if someone may want to buy it.'* It was a mantra, of which his father had many. For years, the discarded, worthless, and unsellable were piled upon the forgotten jumble of stock that was the lot of being an antique dealer. All through that morning and, it seemed for much of the afternoon, Sam had worked through seams of debris, cushions, and terrible works of art. From the top stair where he now sat, Sam looked over his shoulder and into the shop and realised he had been down there longer than he thought as the sun had now begun to drop behind the charity shop and barber's opposite, the alley outside bathed in growing shadows. He had been at it, apart from sleeping a chunk of the afternoon away, since before daybreak. No wonder he felt stiff and knackered. He would have trouble sleeping tonight as he knew his body would complain at the physical effort.

Before shutting the cellar door for the night, he went back down once more to remind himself of how far he had reached into the detritus in search of the Centurion. Boxes had been torn open, or just tipped up, to reveal their contents and a whole tea service lay shattered on the concrete floor. Sam felt guilty about that, he may have been searching for the proverbial Ark of the Covenant, but that was no reason to smash things that had once graced somebody's home and only been bought out for special occasions. He picked up a handle-less cup and examined the pattern, it was awful and unbelievable that a skilled potter somewhere had thought this to be avant-garde and beautiful enough for someone's Sunday best.

Sam had not worked up such a sweat, or felt his body ache this much, since the last time he shared his bed with a woman, and like so much of the stock in his shop, that she too was overpriced and not worth the expenditure. Lesson learned he had not bought another like it and had showered more times in the following 24 hours than he had in the entire year before the on-call escort's visit. Despite her being attractive, in a cheap-trampy sort of way, he still felt unclean and queasy at the thought of ever doing that again. But loneliness was a burrowing worm that ate away at your self-esteem and confidence.

Sam had locked the door behind the barista so, when a rattle from upstairs echoed down into the basement it could have only been Wedgwood clattering through the cat-flap. On his way to his blanket next to the Aga, the cat had looked down into the basement with the sort of haughty look that only cats can give. Sam tried to trot upstairs, firstly two at a time before he tripped on the first riser and cracked his shin, then one at a time, before in the end he just stepped up at a speed his body could keep up with.

While popping to the coffee house Sam had remembered to go into the newsagent next door and get a couple of packets of food as well as cat biscuits. Wedgwood meowed loudly as Sam approached her blanket, cats could be very forgiving of their owners, especially if they had food. Sam knelt and tickled his cat behind her ears, and she quickly broke into a loud purring sound that resonated through her whole body. Her slave then ripped the top of the sachet of food and emptied it into a bowl, squeezing every morsel out of the sachet. Immediately Wedgwood was up from her blanket and lapping up the meat and gravy. Sam filled her water bowl as well as putting down biscuits. Wedgwood was a very contented cat.

Feeding the cat, it made Sam consider feeding himself, but being a man of small appetites, he found that the sandwich had been enough for him. Plus, the fact was he was far too tired to eat. Despite his powernap on the stairs, he was exhausted both from lack of sleep and the hours of rummaging, searching, and throwing stock from one corner to the next and in some cases, back again. Sam was not a man used to physical endeavours and so far, those efforts had failed to uncover the valuable artefact he was hoping would still be down there. Pleasingly he had uncovered a threadbare and slightly battered armchair that had been hidden by the linen sheet, several rolled-up rugs and a neatly folded pile of newspapers. Sam could recall that it was once his father's favourite chair but could not remember when it had been interred in the cellar. Before it was just him and his dad, his mother would shout at Sam, and tell him to get out of his father's chair before he arrived home and caught him in it. He could never make up his mind whether his mother was just joking with him, or if his father would have been annoyed. Sam never stayed in the chair long enough to find out.

Sam felt guilty when he failed to recall what year it was his father had actually died, he was lousy with dates, but he did remember his father sitting in the chair, with the curtain between shop and home drawn back so he could keep an eye on the shop, sometimes snoozing while waiting for the door chimes to ring out the fact a potential customer had entered. His father never failed to respond to the jangling bell, even if he was asleep in the big comfortable chair. Years later it was the first sign of illness when every now and again, his father began to miss the bell ringing, looking confused at the strange sound that echoed through the shop. For as long as he could remember it had just been Sam and his dad. When Sam left senior school, with five GCEs, including one for 'woodwork' it was the most education anyone in the family had achieved, he was planning to go to college to study furniture making, he was quite good with his hands and making things with wood. But his father was lonely and began to suffer with depression, an ailment that nobody understood back in those days, and the doctor would just tell the old man to buck up and get on with life. So, Sam was needed increasingly to cover the old man's shortcomings. Those shortcomings in later years turned to Alzheimer's, which was not something that appeared on the news, back then nor was it talked about in any positive way. Back then it was just someone old gradually losing their marbles. As the years passed by Sam also began to feel lonely; his mother having died when he was just a small kid, and now it seemed as if his dad was dying, but doing it bit by bit instead of just keeling over with the effort of living. It was a customer who had found his father slumped dead in his favourite chair, but by then his father had no idea who Sam was or what they were doing in a room full of old stuff. Sam missed him but thought it a blessing he was now gone, although even thinking that gave Sam a mass of guilt but he did think it fitting that he had died in his favourite, tatty armchair. His guilt was doubled by the fact that at the moment he left him unattended was when his father died, on a quiet February day in the shop he decided to pop out and get some essentials from the local Sainsburys. He could have not been gone more than 30 minutes, but he had not been there for his father's passing. He could not even get that right. The potential customer who had found him would never return and was annoyed that he even had to stay to make a statement to the police who he called when not knowing what one did when finding an unexpected body.

That was then and this was now, and Sam was knackered by the hours of rummaging, searching, and throwing stock around the room, the effort was exhausting. Not a man used to physical labours his back ached and his legs were wobbly, but he was determined to find his legacy. And then sell it! All he could think of was that if this piece were there, and it was what he thought it was, and he could find a buyer, and he would show them all not to take the piss out of him. He would be the smug bastard for once!

After taking over the family business, Sam, attempted to upgrade things and become more professional. For his whole life he had watched as his father struggled every day to make ends meet for himself and his son. Before old-age and his mind began its vacation from reality his dad had kept the books, with everything smartly written into the sales ledger, there was no fancy computer programme to do the adding up and keep a check on stock costs and levels. It was just the way it was, and Sam often thought it was much easier and more efficient than on-line accountancy and on-line tax returns, and the rows of ledgers, their spines spotted with mould, were still on a shelf down there in the musty cellar. During his search he had also discovered a shoe box, it felt weighty but that was because it was filled to the lid with invoices, there must have been four- or five-years' worth of them. Sam was little better at keeping trace of receipts and invoices, he kept his in A4 envelopes, but at least each year's receipts were individually 'stored' in the clearly labelled manila envelopes.

One of the first things Sam did on inheriting the shop was to buy an inexpensive laptop computer, for keeping track of his sales and purchases, along with its neat profit and loss column. He soon stopped that last column, it was far too depressing and each March he would struggle to make sense of the data, but at least the taxman seemed happy with his on-line delivered returns. He marvelled at the technology available and often pondered over the magic of modern wizardry, promising himself that one day he would do an evening course at the local college for basic computer skills. But the thought of doing such a complex thing scared him off, so he continued to just muddle along with the mysterious thing sitting on his desk. To Sam computing was some kind of hocus-pocus and was to be avoided at all costs.

Then he found Facebook and social media, and suddenly the world shrank in size as he gathered a world full of friends and contacts who he never got to know personally or meet face-to-face. He kept the laptop, along with stacked in-and-out trays, on a classic, leather-top pedestal-desk to impress customers with his prowess and acceptance of the modern day, but still with an eye for the old. The bright red gizmo looked odd sitting in the middle of a sea of embossed, green leather. He kept the desktop and mahogany pedestals well-polished and buffed to a shine and it all looked so professional with his mahogany Victorian Captain's chair, if he had to sit in a shop full of crap he would do so with a certain amount of style. Since setting up his internet voice he had sold several pieces online, one piece was even sent to the USA, where it had arrived broken, and he had to pay a full refund. He became so enamoured with himself in the elegant chair behind the fine desk, that on quiet days (and there were too many any of them) he began to author a novel. He had always enjoyed writing at school, although he was always getting into trouble for writing, and thinking, too much, they would ask for a 500-word essay for his homework and the following week on the due day he would give them 5,000 words. The text just seemed flow from him but instead of encouragement to write he would be punished and would then have to explain to his parents the C- he would get on his report card. He put it down to his teachers being too lazy to read his pieces properly. If he could write five thousand words by hand in a notebook, writing 50,000 words on the laptop would be a doddle. Before writing the first word of his epic saga he wondered the number of words went into a novel, and began to panic, not knowing if he even knew that many different words.

They say write what you know about, and so he began to write about his father's interesting life as an antique dealer. A dreary Monday morning had settled greyly outside of the shop and apart for a few hairy individuals arriving at the barbers opposite, he saw nobody else through his window that day. It was the perfect morning to begin and so he lifted the lid and fired up the old laptop. For an hour or two the screen in front of him remained blank, so he went onto the media websites to see what was happening around the world and before he knew it, he had prevaricated right up to lunchtime, and then stalled some more until it was time for the mid-afternoon tea break. Words refused to flow.

Finally, just before four in the afternoon the title came to him, 'My Father's Life with Mr Cooper', it was hardly the snappy beginning he had hoped for. Day two of the literary masterpiece came and went, he did have an excuse for that day as a customer did come into the shop and strolled around the maze of junk. After producing that magical title, the days turned into weeks and the weeks into months and before the year's end, he had forgotten all about being a writer. His professional life had already been chosen and foisted upon him without any form of consultation.

He realised as he shifted more boxes of his house-clearance ephemera, that a couple of years ago he had sold the smart, green leather, topped desk for just a small profit, and the laptop with its novel title written, had not been opened since. Maybe it was time he should have another look at his book. They, whoever '*they'_*were, had said that a novel could take up to two years to complete from opening scenes to its dénouement, (whatever that was?) and even longer to find a publisher. He had more chance of selling a valuable item from his shop, but neither enterprise looked like succeeding.

If he did find the laptop, maybe Nick would teach him the enigma that were spreadsheets, but all that thinking was mentally tiring Sam out, so once again he got stuck into the search for the Centurion and as he moved around, dust motes filled the air and shafts of light streamed down in the cellar, like crepuscular rays on a cloudy day, through the one narrow window to the outside world. The dust motes when lit by the rays looked like fireflies dancing on evening air.

All around the expanse of the basement he saw more damaged goods than a tornado would leave behind. Over the coming weeks he would have to fill his 1984 classic Range Rover with debris and take it to the tip. The thought crossed his mind not to walk too far from his mustard-coloured monster or else someone might chuck that into the metal skip. It was like him, old, dented and wheezed a great deal when pushed – but still loveable.

Wiping tears of sweat from his forehead with the sleeve of his jumper, Sam was beginning to think he had got it wrong and that the bronze had indeed been in that job lot at the car-boot sale. From the foot of the stairs, he looked around, and the mass before him only offered Sam a feeling of loss. There was nothing left to move, nothing else to lift or look under. He had selected items that would refresh stock upstairs, but more would enhance a good rubbish tip. Sadly, there was still no sign of that Roman soldier. Just maybe it was a dream after all, a bit like buying a lottery ticket, a couple of days of dreaming of what could be, only for hopes to be dashed when checking the ticket numbers against the draw. Abject poverty had become his housemate, and it was not about to be evicted any time soon.

Last time he had sat in his father's chair he had lowered himself gently down on the edge of the seat not knowing how strong the chair was after all this time, as well as not wanting to disturb cushions full of dust. But now he was exhausted, and with the ache in his back nearing a seven-out-of-ten pain level, he limped to the chair on his very weary legs before taking a deep breath to avoid dust inhalation, and just dropping into the deep and once-plush cushions of his dad's armchair.

Suddenly the pain in his back shot up to the top of the scale and forced a grunt from deep inside of Sam. He slid, rather than leapt, from the chair, and ended up kneeling by it as if in a sign of homage. Sam had a high pain threshold but this pain in his spine was something new. It was sharp, penetrating, deep within the bones! For a moment he panicked, worried something else had given out in his crumbling spine.

Sam was like most people with lifelong afflictions, in that they choose to ignore what the body tells them, and just getting on with life. There was always someone worse off, so what did Sam have to complain about, it was his load to carry and no amount of moaning and complaining would change anything, so he just learned to live with it. Leaping up so quickly gave Sam another sharp pain as he managed to crack his head on the one low beam which stretched the length of the cellar. Being a short-arse, he was not used to banging his head on low things, unlike six-four Nick who hit his head on about everything.

So, with his left hand rubbing his lower back and his right

rubbing the tender top of his head, at least it did not seem to be bleeding this time, which was good, especially as the girl from the coffee house had finished work some time ago. Still rubbing the invaded parts of his body, he stopped rubbing his head long enough to remove the bottom cushion from the chair and fluff it up to see if it made it anymore comfortable.

If Sam had been from a previous generation who used such words, he may well have cried out 'Eureka' for midway between the padded arms of the recliner and previously hidden by the cushion, was the Roman Centurion.

Lying flat on his bronzed back and looking up from the shadowy bronze hollows that were his eyes, the statue was mesmerising. Sam stopped rubbing everything that hurt and just stared down into the chair, the bronze was trapped between the hessian on the bottom of the chair and the webbing just under where the cushion was, it had been well hidden which was why he had not felt it when he first sat down. He thanked a God he did not believe in for keeping the bronze safe for all these years. Another time and Sam could well have taken the chair to the dump, but his father must have known that Sam would not get rid of his favourite chair.

Sam also took a moment to thank any deity that was listening for not allowing him to land on the bronze sword which would have impaled his buttock as he dropped onto the antique. Try explaining that one to the junior doctor on the casualty ward.

Sam rushed upstairs to find a sharp knife with which to slice through the webbing and free the bronze warrior who had remained in hiding for more than 20 years.

Even though he had just sat upon the bronze statuette, a move that would have damaged lesser mortals, Sam held a smile of triumph as if he were the fighter in the gladiatorial ring, he lifted his vanquished foe with care and reverence. As gently as a first-time father would hold his new-born and with delicate fingers and an open palm he brushed and puffed away the first layers of dust before holding the brave soldier up to the limited light sneaking into basement via that one narrow window. It shone, glittering in the dusty rays and Sam imagined he saw the Centurion blink at the stranger that was sunlight. It could not have been held and handled with any more lightness if it had been composed of eggshell China rather than rugged bronze. Dust clung to parts of the muscular torso where the patina was the dull green of moss, so Sam grabbed the first piece of cloth within reach, a red scarf emblazoned with the badge and name of a football team that played 250 miles away. He used it to rub away years of Verdigris in the folds and loin cloth of the centuries old soldier. Finally, without damaging any of the natural ageing he revealed every contour of the warrior's face.

Sam was lost in the sheer magnitude of what he was caressing, and he looked around the cellar to see if anyone was watching this moment of love and affection. Holding his warrior in one hand he lifted the large cushion and replaced it in the chair before plonking himself down in its folds. More dust was propelled upward and Sam's backside downward as the cushion sank where the webbing had been cut allowing the Roman's escape.

As Sam gazed into that weather beaten face, with its hollow eyes and its striking Roman nose, he knew that his life would never be the same again. He also realised he had remained in the basement of his shop because he knew that once he, and his soldier, rose above ground level things would change in an instant. The tickle in his throat from breathing in the floating dust made him cough, breaking the myriad of thoughts and imaginations that were cascading through his head and made him notice that his cheeks were damp with tears. Sam Cobby was crying. He did not know if they were tears of joy, sadness, or fear. The fact that he was still in the basement answered his own question, it was fear. The stairs back up to ground level would be the longest and hardest climb of his life as everything about his life would change the moment he emerged with that small bronze figure, a Roman soldier with a bold expression and his sword triumphantly held aloft.

CHAPTER 23

Kobe was knackered! His body ached in the way a hungry man craves food and yet with no appetite to eat. His thoughts were a scrambled mess and travelling far too fast to make any sense. It was as if he were a computer asked to conduct too many instructions at the same time by an impatient operator, his curser was frozen on the screen, the background wallpaper a picture of carnage within a blood-stained rose garden. Every time he slid his mental curser toward an image of himself walking together with his wife around the gently lapping waters of Chichester Harbour, it disappeared only to be replaced by the horror that were the images in his mind. Thoughts of watching his children run in and out of the shallow waters at the edge of the gently lapping harbour tides, their wellingtons being of little use as water splashed up their legs and into the boots, everyone laughing all the while as their socks soaked up the cold seawater. He now only saw their bloodstained faces. The harbour was a wonderful place to inspire the artist in Rae and to bring up Molly and Kobe Junior, beautiful, fun, and safe. It was why they bought their beautiful waterside cottage; it was safe, colourful, and away from his job.

Now it was a desolate wasteland that encircled him.

The mental tableau of that lost paradise immediately transferred to one of a living hell. Instead of children blissfully playing in the waters close to their home they were laying in the arms of their bloodstained mother, never to run into the sea again. The blood soaked bedroomed continued to burn and carve its way into his every thought and no sooner than he tried to relive one of the gorgeous moments of their life together, then the never-ending loop of destruction would take over again.

As a DI he was used to logistically separating events, whittling down every minor detail and producing an answer for every eventuality, it's why his team followed him without questioning his authority. They were safe in his hands as he thought of everything before stepping toward confrontation and danger. In his hands they were protected despite the perils of being a modern-day copper, but no longer. Kobe's normal working process of separating fact and diversion was broken, he could not protect his own wife, his own children, how could he now say to his team they were safe in his charge. Everything he had trained for no longer counted for anything.

For now, he was lost blindly in the short prayer that he continued to chant, his voice deep, cracking with dryness...

"Inna lillahi wa inna ilayha raji'un" repeatedly... *"Inna lillahi wa inna ilayha raji'un..."* Verily we belong to Allah...

It bought him slim comfort.

Kobe and Rae had a shared love of theatre, the dramatic, the musical, dance and even opera, which Kobe up until he had met Rae thought he would hate. She turned him onto opera, he introduced her to Jazz, even though he thought she said she liked it just to please him. In brief moments of blessed relief, he began to see the scene before him as if it were a scene in a blood-thirsty play. Shakespeare at his tragic best, each player playing a part with a stunned audience watching on from the auditorium and revelling in the Bard's bloodlust.

Only there was no one sitting next to him in middle of 'Row F' or 'Row G,' their preferred seats at Chichester's famous theatre. His beautiful Rae, no longer there to prepare him for a discussion about the good and bad bits of that night's performance, there would be no after theatre debate which normally continued long into the night over hot chocolate and crackers. The players were all in place but there would be no encore tonight, instead they held centre stage until the backstage crew moved them into the wings and out of the spotlights. And this drama was nowhere near its final act. That had not yet been written and in Kobe's mind, there was no visible end to the story.

A voice from the foot of the stairs finally broke the tension and asked. "Mr Kaan?"

It was one of those questions that would never need an answer, not really. But Kobe croaked in reply, "Yes."

Heavy-footed, a lanky uniformed officer climbed the stairs, trying but failing to make as little sound as possible with each step. Warren Finch, known as 'Bluetits' to colleagues on his shift did not want to fuck up on his first solo shout. It had been less than a year since he had come out of Probation and this was his first major crime scene, let alone multiple killings. PC Finch was aware that when he reached the top, he would be officially on his first murder. It was the not knowing of what lay ahead that scared him, he had seen dead bodies before, admittedly only a few, but he had seen them. Without realising it he slowed down as he neared the landing of the small cottage, he liked the look of the place and strangely thought he would like to live in a cottage like this, and for a moment he envied the DI until he recalled why he was there. He could hear somebody muttering words in a language he did not understand, thought it sounded like an Arab, or even a Pakistani. Would he be called racist for thinking things like that, and if so, should he put it in his report. He settled on saying he did not understand what the detective was saying, which coincidently was the truth, but during training nobody had mentioned anything about recording the truth, it was whatever fitted the scene.

Suddenly from where Kobe sat hunched in the doorway, he saw the constable's head pop up over the landing floor. The young copper's eyes were out on stalks, like the preverbal animal in headlights, the fear of what he would find on his first murder shout had drained the colour from his face giving him a near, clown-like appearance. Despite the horror of it all he reminded Kobe of a Jack-in-the-Box he had as a child, he would wind the handle like crazy and the jangling music would prepare him for what came next. He knew that the clown inside the tin box would leap up at any moment, but no matter how often he reloaded the clown before making him leap out again, its sudden reappearance would scare him every time and startled he would leap up with heart pounding, and a giggle in his throat. It was always a comical moment for the young Kobe, but he was not laughing now. The young man's shoulders were curved trying to disguise his true height, in the dim hallway he appeared like a human caricature of Punch, the seaside puppet, husband, and wife beater.

Bluetits left the stairwell and stood next to the doorway, towering over Kobe who was still slumped where he had fallen and still reciting the prayer to Allah. It was then that the acrid smell hit the young officer in both nostrils before he saw, what would-be officially described as, the crime scene.

"What the fuck..." He could not help himself; he had never been to a murder scene before, let alone one this bad, thankfully for him the DI on the floor did not react and the young officer hoped he hadn't heard it.

Finch could not control his emotions or his physical being and he gagged again as more bile crept into his mouth and the taste was vile, but he knew he didn't dare actually throw up because not only would he contaminate the crime scene, but he would also be the subject of much mirth and mickey-taking. But that smell, it was overpowering, he could taste it. And, he had never seen such an horrific sight. He joined the force to help people not be subjected to such a scene that was before him now and he stood rooted to the spot, hardly able to breathe, unable to avert his gaze.

"Mr Kaan, Sir..." he could not finish the sentence, his throat coated with the taste and smell of the room, his eyes switching between the blood-soaked roses on the walls, and the bloody, mutilated, corpses laid together on the bed. "Are they your children? Are you sure they are..." Again, he could not spell out what he felt he needed to say.

Even in the dense fog that filled Kobe's mind, he was still first and foremost a police officer, and he heard the young officer wretch and looked up to see his body tighten up trying to hold the nausea in.

"If you are going to throw up lad, take it outside and well away from the scene." There was no kindness in Kobe's voice, just cold professionalism.

The sound of the voice in the doorway shook Bluetits from his stupor, but before turning to leave, even though he wanted to get outside, where he would throw up the coppery taste of blood that seemed to leech onto his tongue, he bent to touch Kobe on the shoulder, maybe help him up and out of the building.

Kobe's voice was harsher this time, impatient. "Don't touch me you idiot!" Not the DI's best moment but why would it be. "I am part of the scene now. I need to be processed the same as everything else. At least try and act like a professional."

The inexperienced officer began to stutter an apology, but he needed to keep on track, and strangely taking control of the scene seemed to bring Kobe back from some sort of cliff-edge of total despair.

"You need to get outside lad," His tone had softened as his own training kicked into automatic mode. "Secure the house and the scene, try not to touch anything on the way out as every step you take contaminates the scene and I don't want you fucking up any future prosecution on a technicality."

A little professionalism came back to the youngster. "Sorry Mr Kaan, will do Sir."

Despite his heart still breaking with every second Kobe was

stuck where he sat crunched up in the doorway; he softened his approach with the boy. Christ, they were getting younger every day.

"Good lad, I know you are first on the scene, but I have no doubt your sergeant or maybe even someone higher, will be close behind you." Kobe was now in 'job' mode. "It may even be someone higher up the chain so get your game face on and at least look like you know what you are doing."

The lad had to listen carefully as Kobe was now staring at the floor, finally able to get his eyes away from his family and he gave the officer, still standing over him, a silent thank you for being a diversion. And Warren backed away from the bedroom and the distraught father/husband.

"Sorry Sir, of course Sir." It was like an over subservient waiter were backing away from the table after taking the meal order. Kobe wanted to verbally tear him apart, but just did not have the energy.

As for the young PC, his first death-call would linger long in his memory and the rancid smell and taste may never leave him, he gagged again so turned and literally hurtled down the stairs and out into what was a swiftly darkening evening, Hopefully, in the dim light nobody would see him throw up. As he placed a hand on the tail end of Kobe's beloved Alpha Romeo, the metal feeling cold on his sweating palm, he finally let go of his stomach contents. Unfortunately for him just as he lurched forward and vomited, he was picked out in full technicolour by the headlights of an approaching patrol car carrying his sergeant. It was not the young copper's finest moment and not what he imagined, he realised at that moment that a policeman's lot did not come as advertised.

CHAPTER 24

Sam Cobby was now a rich man, not in monetary terms, nowhere near that just yet, but certainly in kudos and assets, he felt rich, and that was something he had never felt before. No longer would he be seen as a failure, in an industry that had shaped his life both good and bad up until now. They would not laugh at him anymore, better still they would envy him as the dealer who had made the find of the Century. Hitting him like an electric shock he knew that the dealer who had belittled him just yesterday would now want to be a reluctant friend. The mind plays strange tricks when the romance of life has a turn of fortunes. Sam could imagine the local TV station interviewing that obnoxious dealer, his sanctimonious smile large on the screen as he told them of his friendship with Sam and that only the day before his find that they had been in friendly negotiations over a pair of china figures that Sam had coveted. The thought gave Sam another reason to smile as those that had belittled him would now claim to be confidents and friends.

He needed to call Nick, tell him of his great find. It would be good for Nick's career as well to break the story; it would even hit the Nationals if it was a slow news day. It would be a fine repayment for the years of true friendship that the reporter had given him. And he wanted Nick to tell everyone. Sam wanted the world to know, he wanted those detracting and insulting bastards that he did have what it took to be a great dealer, he wanted the bullies to choke on their smug attitudes.

That one item, that lonesome and forgotten Roman was his own Holy Grail, the one single item that everyone would covet, they would covet Sam's success. He was enjoying every single moment despite the fact it was only he that knew of his find, for now. There would be no more Sunday village antique fairs, no more clammy over-crowded town halls with their gloating part-time dealers. No more would Sam have to utter those words, 'Is that your very best price?' as he hunted down a bargain.

Sam had found his new future, and the grass did indeed look greener on the other side, and he was going to revel and enjoy the rich grazing that came with success. Every week Sam would dream of what he would do if he ever won the Lottery, this week he had not even been able to afford the small cost of one ticket for the Saturday night draw.

Telling the world would have to wait though as an exhausted Sam, still sitting in his father's battered recliner and hugging the Roman as a child would hug a cuddly bear, had nodded off. It transpired that it was demanding work being this successful and more tiring than Sam would have thought. He dreamed of better things, of having a swish new gallery where he would have clientele, not customers. They would have to make an appointment to enter his glittering showroom where ornate frames would hang from the walls, keeping sumptuous oil paintings wrapped in their ormolu arms. Polished mahogany and teak furniture would stand on rich Persian rugs that would spread across the floor, and in the window, displayed behind bulletproof glass would be that regal Roman with his sword held high.

It was the best dream that Sam had ever dreamt.

CHAPTER 25

Through the thin net curtains, he could see the gathered audience of nosey neighbours and intrigued passers-by gathering on the kerbside, tickets should be going on sale soon now that the teasing trailer of gossip had tempted them out of their homes. Both Kobe and Rae hated net curtains, seeing them as something their parents would hang, but being in such a beautiful place to live they had to endure the stares of over-zealous tourists who thought everything was fair game for their visual entertainment. It was lucky that Kobe could not see that around the next corner, in the village's carpark, handily placed next to the red-bricked block building that was the public toilets, a burger and an ice cream van had set up to feed the hoards attracted to the gore-fest. As soon as they had lifted the flap and slid back the windows, they were serving coffees and ninety-nines, even the police were thoughtlessly taking advantage of the catering services. The crowd were baying for blood and did not want to miss a moment. The feeling among some of the spectating crowd was that if they could have been forewarned, fairground rides and bouncy castle would have set up and making the scene a Mardi-Gras. As with hangings and public executions of the Middle Ages, murder had become entertainment. Death a thrill ride all on its own. When it came to having fun there was little better than watching someone else suffer.

In the modern technological world, shrunken to the size of the screen on a mobile phone, the entire planet was now being streamed the events from that small harbourside village. Within moments of reflecting windows being filled with the reflections of blue swirling lights, and the streets echoing with the sound of sirens video recordings were being beamed around the world and the ghouls were watching avidly.

Word on the street and the internet was that there had been a triple murder, a woman who was a 'well-known' artist and her two beautiful children, who had died in her arms, and the fact they had been butchered by her blood splattered husband. To make it worse, so the word travelling among the crowd by locals who wanted their 15 seconds of fame, he was a high-ranking and serving police officer.

Butchered his family they said, dismembered one neighbour had said wanting his story to be better than others in the village, walls dripping with blood they said. All were guessing and spreading growing rumours, and it was their idea of fun and they were proud of their part in the tragedy. While chatter spread all around, eyes would not leave the house, they all wanted a glimpse of the blood-spattered walls, sight of the accused being dragged, handcuffed and under a blanket, from the house to the waiting police van with its strong mesh cage inside. 'He was an animal; he should be caged' they opined.

The sad thing was that even the neighbours who knew the family and chatted with them, as people do, living in small villages, would be complicit in spreading rumour, rather than fact. Those that kept quiet and refrained from rumour helped spread them, doing nothing to stop them. Nobody would come to Kobe's defence.

Peering over the low brick wall they craned their necks seeking that perfect view, hopefully a glimpse of the murderer of which two neighbours were agreeing that there was always something shifty in the way he looked, even though he were a police officer, there was something not right about him. The young copper who had been first on the scene now stood guard over the roadside gate and he could clearly hear the tittle-tattle being said about one of the force's most respected officers, and with each erroneous statement holding his tongue was getting harder. He also figured out that in among the swelling crowd were journalists looking for tomorrow's headline.

One pinch-faced woman puckered her lips, took a deep breath and dived straight into the deep end of the chatter as she told her overweight and three times divorced friend...

"I don't know why they employ foreigners and refugees in our police force, all I can say is that they must know that no good will come of it." She said it loud enough so all could hear her opinion.

Her friend responded in a slightly softer but still able to be heard by those close by, one of whom was busy taking notes in his reporter's notebook. "I heard he is one of them Muslims, I wouldn't mind betting that this is some sort of terrorist attack."

He knew it could cost him his job, but he could no longer keep quiet as the officer who he had admired was unable to defend himself, he would jump to his defence. "How can you talk like that about your neighbour?" he asked in a voice just as loud as pinch-face. "He is one of our finest officers and he has just lost his family for Christ's sake. Have a bit more respect."

He knew he should not have spoken; officers are told never to lose control and not to speak out, especially as he was now watching the journalist who was busy writing his comments down in shorthand.

The crowd were not satisfied though as they turned into a baying mob calling for swift justice against the Muslim terrorist who had slaughtered a beautiful English family. The murderous crime of the Century had visited their quiet waterfront hamlet, if violence could visit them, it could visit anywhere. Nothing was out of bounds now as reporters drifted through the crowd thrusting microphones in people's faces, the cameras picking out candidates for soundbites. A police officer, one of those Muslims, had murdered his family in some sort of ritual and eaten his own children's hearts. Plain murder was no longer enough to feed the voracious appetite of the spectator, simple facts no longer able to hold their attention for more than a moment. The crowd shuffled and fidgeted sharing their time between watching the house and watching to see if they were in line of the camera, some even swept hair back in subconscious grooming.

When, from inside the house, someone had pulled the curtains blocking out the exterior view all that remained for the spectators was to exchange gory details and make up scenarios that buffed up their own self-importance. Nothing ever happened in Bosham, well not since King Canute went for his ill-conceived paddle, and the village folk were going to make the most of the excitement.

Except at low tide there was only one road into and out of the village and now that was clogged by TV trucks and more onlookers who arrived in a ragtag convoy. Trucks complete with satellite dishes so the news from this sleepy part of West Sussex could be beamed instantly around the world. With current technology, the 'news' came long before the facts. Modern news gathering and broadcasting was a fast-moving beast that often ran out of control. The thrust of the reportage, until some more juicy facts were known, was about the quiet Muslim who had lived in the village for several years undetected, even by his own force.

This was going to be a good news day for the press as they were getting the stock story of the police officer and his murdered family. One neighbour wondered how the TV trucks could send images and reports around the world, when he could not even get a fucking signal on his mobile phone!

'No, they did not know him well...' and 'he always kept himself to himself...' and of course, 'no fault of the children or their poor mother...' and 'things like this just did not happen in little villages like ours, but that's how terrorists fly under the radar, isn't it...'.

The mob are always good at getting at the flesh around a story, and now *Pinchface* was being interviewed...

"Don't look at the camera love, just look at me as I ask what you know about the family and what has happened here this evening." It was not just the neighbour who knew them so well getting the chance of stardom, this could lead to bigger TV jobs for an ambitious local presenter.

"Oh, his surname was Kahn, or something like that, a foreign name you know." Despite her instructions, Pinchface was looking straight down the lens, she wasn't going to let a chance like this go begging. "He is one of those Muslims, so no wonder this has happened. Those Muslims are different, aren't they? They see things different to us." The interview had turned into her soapbox of fear and outrage. "What I want to know is how they get to be in our police force, how can we feel safe on the streets when they allow terrorists to be running our police. We shouldn't be employing them; we should be sending them back where they belong and live by their own funny laws. What his poor wife must have been going through, and she a good Christian girl by all accounts..."

But nobody was listening any longer, even the journalist had lost interest because this bigoted woman was not going to help his career travel in an upward trajectory. He moved away from her while she was still in mid-rant, then before moving on to his next victim he took a moment to preen. A youthful and handsome face but his hair, wavy and carefully cut showed grey streaks at the temple. He searched the crowds for someone with darker skin to get their opinion, but Kobe was the only dark-skinned resident in the village.

"They are all white and middle aged." Said the one reporter to his camera operator. "How am I supposed to get a balanced report with this lot." Now preened and peeved, he moved on to his next victim, while hoping his last interview would end up on the technical cutting floor.

Thankfully in any crowd there is always someone with an opinion and few are unbiased, most very judgemental. And, as usual there were plenty to choose from, many of whom were standing under the odd streetlight so as to be noticed. The public demanded their moment on camera, and they were duly obliged, it was not every day that murder visited the streets of quiet, rural villages such as Bosham, and the witnesses who had seen nothing and only heard gossip were determined to make the most of their chance in the spotlight.

The curtains were pulled closed in the cottage and the crowd's disappointment was palpable. At least when they could see the theatre of shadows moving behind the nets there was a chance to make up their versions of the facts. But now the curtains were closed, and the stage laid bare, the theatre inside the house that was act-one of the murderous play was done. All that remained was the action backstage, which even the most avid audience member could see was just not so enjoyable. A few even drifted away for home and a late-night cocoa, tragedy had become boring.

A new rumour began to circulate, and the buzz quickly spread. Someone in the crowd realised that the photographers, reporters and cameramen would pay good money for videos and images of the street scene prior to the curtains being drawn. They may not have their moment in front of the camera, and a few were genuinely camera-shy, but there was a fame of sorts to have their names linked to the images. A kind of street market opened as press agency guys, and TV folk bartered and offered best prices for what had been recorded on mobile phones. Instant media! At every event that offered entertainment or scandal there would be people holding their phones up above their heads while recording every dull moment of every dull event. There were no eyewitnesses anymore, only mobile phone witnesses. People would rather watch it later than view it in real life, only to rush home and watch the video before watching other's attempts and then comparing footage. They would boast to friends about how their footage accompanied the lead story and was, they hoped, introduced by somebody like that nice Fiona Bruce, with her soft and proper English accent. Murder once again was good business.

"Oh, I knew the family very well," Said another 'near' neighbour, who had never met the Kaans, she was from the other side of the village. With a serious look on her face and dressed in baggy, tie-dye clothing, her feet strapped into paint spattered sandals; the hippy artist was taking her turn to answer the handsome reporter's questions in her quest for moments of fame. "...they were a quiet family, the children always polite and well behaved." She flicked her heavy dreadlocks back over her shoulder and would not speak ill of the dead, "And she was a wonderful artist, a little naive with her work, but coming on nicely. She always exhibited at the village open-studio event, although she never sold much of her work." A self-centred grin was on her face as she had sold her own credentials as an artist very well, no harm in a little self-promotion, she thought.

"Well, no! I did not know he was a police officer. They let Muslims into the police force, do they?" Another said, voicing her opinion, "Are they not vetted before being accepted? So how did he get to be an Inspector or whatever he was. No wonder we can never spot a terrorist before they go on their rampages..." The camera had already gone dark long before she began her misguided vitriol, the journalist already turning away looking for his next victim.

Each interviewee would have their own biased opinions on what is good or bad, their ideas on race and religion biased from too much media fearmongering, which drove anger and dissent into ordinary people. For too long people, especially in small semi-remote villages like theirs, were told that different was dangerous and to have someone dark-skinned like him in the village, well it was only a matter of time before something bad happened.

Kobe had been arrested, charged, and found guilty of his family's murders long before bedside lamps were turned off that night. The ones among the onlookers who had no opinion and were there just to gawk and had nothing to say, and had no opinion either way, for them that Sunday evening was simply good entertainment and great dinner-party gossip.

More police vehicles arrived at the back of the house with both uniformed and plain clothes arriving, no other vehicles were getting near as the main road in and out had been policed for the last hour. As for the only other road access, well that was impassable due to a high tide. Back along the road, beyond the outlying post office and stores cars were being turned around or abandoned on the lane-side as the drivers and passengers walked to the village, in his report later the officer on the blockade would state that he was surprised at how many people lived in such a small village.

Among those turned around were DS David Martin and PC Stella Gold, even their Warrant Cards failed to get them into the village, the officer on duty at the makeshift barricade of six red and white cones had obviously been ordered not to let anybody through from Kobe's squad. David had filled Stella in on his phone call from the Station Skipper during the swift and short drive from the city centre to the normally peaceful village but, all he knew for certain was that Kobe's family had been killed, and that he was still on scene.

"How do we get in then?" Gold asked as David wound up his window and prepared to turn his car around in the narrow lane. "I am assuming we're not taking Plod's word for things are we." Stella had a good poker-face he thought and made a mental note never to play cards with her.

"Plod?" he queried. "You know he is the same rank as you Stella, right?"

"I know, but he is still a plod, and will be until he retires or finds a better job. That is why he is on the gate and not in the village in the thick of things."

"You are wise beyond your years PC Gold."

"So where are we going now?" Like a dog with a particularly juicy bone, she would not be letting go anytime soon.

"Are you assuming that I am going to break the chain of command to enable us to get into the village and see the DI?" Even though they both realised it was just banter between them, Kaan's squad were nothing if not loyal to the man and his rank. Nothing could break the concern for their Boss and friend, and no 'Plod' would keep them from getting to him.

"No, what do you take me for? I like my job too much to suggest such a thing." She sounded hurt by his remark but had a ready response. "I did assume however that you would know of a footpath where we can slog on foot into the village. I hear tell it is a wonderful view of Chichester Harbour from down there."

"I certainly do, and the scenery is magnificent." The thrill of the chase got their adrenaline pumping, each felt their own hearts racing. "Now swing this heap of rust around and turn right at the end of the road."

"This heap of rust got you here, didn't it?" Then she conducted a tight and efficient three-point-turn, before racing to the end of the road.

The officer on the barricade was left with nothing except the smell of burning rubber and he had a fairly good idea that the next time he would seem them it would be across the other side of his barrier as they were escorted away from the crime scene.

Back outside of the besieged cottage the crowd were now held back at a respectful distance to allow the forensic folk to get their valuable work done. They remained with craned necks and stood on tiptoes to get a better view. The craft centre, which also functioned as a cafe in the summer season, had even opened its doors, but at least they were giving the police officers on the ground free coffees and teas. Like spectators at a bullfight, the crowd were baying for blood and waiting in anticipation for the matador to be gored by the bull, or at least the blooded copper to be walked in full view of the audience, and when the moment arrived - they would yell '*Ole!*' or something similar. At the very least they would be baying for the blood of the Matador in this scene.

Residents of the small community, as well as disaster-tourists who had beaten the blockade, stood gawping. Rumour and Chinese Whisper were still flooding the crowd with exaggeration, part-truths, and downright fantasy, and they were revelling in every moment. In future years they would tell anyone who was interested enough to listen about the day they witnessed a gruesome murder, and how the blood-soaked culprit was a serving police officer – one they had known personally. All were waiting for the moment they would truly become part of the story as newspaper hacks, TV presenters and radio newshounds picked them out of the crowd for their comments and take on the events as they unfolded. It seemed the press never tired of asking the same questions, to get the same answers.

Out on the A27, the broad main road that swept traffic past Bosham, and far enough away from the narrow lane that gave access to the village, Stella Gold parked her trusty VW Golf half on a grass verge and half in the road, she pulled the passenger's sun visor down so that the sign attached to it could be easily read. 'Police Officer on Duty'. It looked official but would never carry weight if she got a ticket, she relied on the fact that no officer would give her a ticket, just in case. David just gave a half smile in recognition of the subversion... He kept his in the glove box of his own car.

They found the footpath a few yards further down, it appeared from the bushes at the end of an attractive inlet, the tide was out a little way, and on the shore, the snowy-white plumage of little egrets showed up as the end of evening bled into nighttime. Swans drifted lazily on the ebbing tide and at any other time both of them would have enjoyed the hues of sun kissed reds and golden light that reflected from the harbour waters, it truly was an idyllic sight, and yet such was the state of their mission, neither noticed nature's glory in all her splendour.

The trek was over well-trodden ground but still deserved a careful consideration for each step, risking a soaking they rushed on close to where the calm waters gently lapped against shingle. Most days tides would flood the path before the ebb when once again it revealed its worn trackway. Shoes were getting muddied, trouser cuffs getting wet, but nothing would stop them in their quest. The Boss would do it, and more, for them. Neither spoke as they trudged on for close to a mile around the water's edge, the sunset continued to burn amazing colours but David, who was leading the way, disinterested in the view, he was too busy watching each footfall while trying not to stumble. Close behind Gold watched his colleague's feet trying to follow them step-for-step.

Finally, they were at the outskirts of the village were the rustic footpath turned to potholed tarmac which circumnavigated a blunt finger of the harbour. Down the centre of the road was a line of seaweed, indicating the height of the previous tide. Steps on the other side led up to houses where the gardens ended with low brick walls and gates that had slots for flood defence boards to be slotted in readiness of spring tides, it was the cost for living in a street with such exquisite views. Lights had gone on in a few of the houses, other windows remained in a blind darkness, both officers felt that many remained that way as the tenants were off enjoying the show in a village where little happened apart from the occasional flood. This weekend there was murder and the circus that followed such events on their very doorstep, too good an entertainment package to miss.

Having been at the Kaan household many times before David Martin still led as they neared the main village road, which travelled up from the water's edge and past a delightful tearoom. As he turned the corner David saw parked, below the high-water line where in summer the ice cream van would be trading until the incoming tide sent it packing, four squad cars as well as two silver saloon cars that could only have been CID transport. The bean counters several years ago decided that silver cars were more value when it came to resale, what they had not figured on was that the sudden glut of silver cars on the market all at the same time would make the original thought totally redundant. Without thought, David grabbed Stella's hand and pulled her around the end of the wall which was in the shadows but led up to the Kaan household where out the front the clamour for positions was still unveiling itself as people jostled for a better view, where journalists looked for their next quote for tomorrow's papers, and photographers stood ready-eyed for that front-page pic. Just two uniforms had been allocated the job to keep them all at bay, well their constant gaze and yards and yards of yellow tape with the legend **'Police Do Not Cross'** writ boldly ad-infinitum along its length.

David realised he was still holding Stella's hand and dropped it as if from an electric shock, in return her face looked as she had received the same shock. Martin thought a DS should not be holding a PC's hand, even if she was an attractive girl, then realised he had never thought of her in that way before. Time to say something to avoid showing the blush that he felt had just appeared on his cheeks.

"Front or back?" David Martin looked at Stella for her input, making her feel a sense of belonging in a tight team for the second time that day. She also thought she had seen something else in his look.

She considered the options for a moment. "Well frontal assault means we will have to navigate that lot," she pointed to the ever-moving throng as if it were a single living entity. "Is there a back entrance?"

"There is."

"Well, what are we waiting for?" And this time she took his hand, it felt natural, and it puzzled her as she had never thought of him that way before.

They ducked around the throng, keeping eyes and heads down after David had said to keep low in case an eagle-eyed local reporter spotted them. This was not the time to be collared for comments. As they traversed the end house, they both spotted Kobe's beloved Alpha with its sleek lines still shining in what remaining light there was. A uniform was propping her backside up on the curving bonnet, it did not look very professional, in fact it looked sloppy. Both of Kobe's team looked at each other and knew it was their moment, so they walked up to her and David threw his sergeant's stripes at her.

"Is that any way to be seen while on duty at a murder scene officer...?" he waited for an answer, Gold stood slightly in the shadows, hoping her stance showed gravitas.

"Sorry, Sir!" she was in black combat trousers and a black stab vest, the only light caught the pale skin on her face, "Sorry Sarge, Cummins. It is Cummins..." she stammered and then realising her mistake she finally stood up straight.

"This is a murder scene, and the home of a fellow officer." Although an experienced officer Cummins looked embarrassed at her moment of misjudgement. "What if the press had caught you leaning on DI Kaan's car, it would have made a fine front page shot on the morning papers wouldn't it? Right alongside the headline of 'Senior police officer's Family in a Bloodbath."

"I really am sorry Sarge. I know it's no excuse, but I have stood here for a good couple of hours now and have no idea what is going on."

Her sergeant finally took pity, he did not want to alienate her, especially as she would be in serious trouble once it had been discovered she was the one who let them walk into a crime scene. "Just behave with a little more professionalism Cummins." His voice softer now. "Plus, I assume the forensic boffins have not worked over the car yet..."

"Um, no, I don't think so."

"Well, it's part of the crime scene and its going to show your finger and arse prints now."

The conversation was over, the officer feeling suitably crucified. Martin and Gold had opened their route into being with their boss. They both knew that they would be in trouble for entering a crime scene, Martin especially realised it could cost him career-wise, but to them to be with their DI was all that mattered.

Cummins turned her back to the house and stood in an at-ease position, back straight, feet apart and hands clasped behind her back. If anyone had looked closely, despite the autumnal evening chill, they would have spotted a bead or two of sweat sat on her forehead.

The back gate was open and Gold, led by Martin, passed

through the final barrier. They could see through the back window that forensic team members dressed in pale blue paper onesies, were busy in the kitchen bagging up things while others dusted door handles and door jambs.

"Well, we made it, Gold."

"We did that Sarge, good going."

And they slowly walked down the path, not really knowing how to things would work out once through the back door. A forensic kit bag sat beside the doorstep and DS Martin took out a pair of plastic blue over shoes, handing a pair to Gold when, over her shoulder, he spotted two men approaching Cummins, they did not look like press corps. Before David could decide what to do next, any further movement was swiftly nipped in the bud.

"And where the fuck are you two going?" The voice was loud, deep, and harsh. It stopped the two on the garden path in their stride, Gold balanced, and hopping on one leg trying to get the plastic bootie over her chunky Doc Martins. "If you think you are going inside to fuck up my crime scene then fucking think again."

David Martin recognised both the man and his voice. It was well known he could not finish a sentence without swearing, however, put him in front of a busy court or a higher-ranking officer and butter would not melt in his well-spoken mouth.

"I think I asked you a question, DS Martin?"

Suddenly the brusque man brushed past Gold as if she were not there and was right in the sergeant's face. She was between the officer who reminded her of a Sgt Major, and the inconsequential DC that accompanied him. She would not be bowed by him, despite his smug grin which was boosting his self-importance.

"What the fuck are you staring at junior?" She said with an authority that she did not feel, her face like thunder, dark and menacing – Gold played the part well, he did not answer but instead blushed vividly, his face lit by the light pouring out from the house, forensic lamps boosting the cottage's moody lighting.

His smile disappeared and Gold strained to hear the whispered conversation going on between the two Alpha-males in the quartet. Her concentration in trying to make sense of what was being said was broken when Martin gently touched her elbow and steered her back down the footpath that they had worked so hard to traverse, he said nothing, and she decided not to ask the obvious question.

Out through the gate once again, and well beyond Cummins hearing and steely pissed-off gaze. Martin lifted one foot to remove the bootie and then the other, he tucked them into his jacket pocket rather than litter a crime scene. Gold took his lead and took the one she had fitted off as well.

David brought her up to speed, "He quietly reminded me that if I took one step further not only would we be arrested but it would probably cost us both our jobs as well."

"Were those his exact words?"

"Not really..." A small smile came to his face, and it felt alien given the circumstances. "He said, 'get the fuck off of my crime scene and get fucking well away before I place you both under a-fucking-rest and get you both fucking fired."

"Eloquent fucker isn't he." Gold offered. It was not the right time to laugh, but they had to, and it released a little of the tension they were feeling.

"But he also said he would tell the Boss that we tried." Martin shrugged and offered... "Cup of hot chocolate Gold?"

"It's Stella when off-duty David, and after all the handholding that's been going on this evening, I think we should be on first-name terms away from work."

"That's Mr Martin to you Gold." His voice stern and Stella was unsure what to do or say next. She tried humour.

"Does that mean the offer of a hot chocolate is off the table then?"

Nothing more was said, and they both walked toward the impromptu catering van with its bright lights and chalked menu board. Their shoulder's rubbing as they walked closely together. Once they had their warming drinks, they would stand across from the Kaan's back gate and watch as their boss was marched out to a waiting car. They wanted him to see that despite his loss, he was not alone.

CHAPTER 26

Martin and Gold leant back against a fence where they had an unobstructed view of The Kaan's back door, they watched as suitably booted and onesie wearing officers and forensics marched in and out of the once charming cottage. In the night light they appeared like spectres drifting in and out of the back door.

Gold glanced at her DS, and he knew what the question was and answered before it was asked. "The foul-mouthed one is a Detective Chief Inspector, goes by the nickname of 'Ghost' but don't ever let him hear you say it."

"I take it that is not a compliment."

"Far from it." and David explained. "He thinks it is because his first name is Casper..."

"You're joking, who would christen their boy Casper?"

"No idea, his parents had one strange sense of humour but that's his name, but we mainly call him Ghost because whenever there was the boring work to be done, like paperwork or babysitting a prisoner, he would go missing and become invisible." He told her.

Casper Jones was a short stocky man, with a shaven head and a blonde moustache which covered a weak top lip, ice-blue eyes sparkled with meanness. Despite his lack of height, he still managed to offer being an imposing figure, always dressed in sharp suits which were dark and matched with a white button-down shirt with no tie, unless for court appearances and then they were always plain and dark to match his suits. This Sunday evening the suit was dark blue and double breasted, the shirt open at the neck was crisp and clean, on his feet a pair of brogues, brown and well-polished even though they showed plenty of wear, if DCI Casper was going to be called out on a Sunday evening his feet were going to be comfortable.

With blue booties covering the shiny brogues he had entered the house, the young DC, who David did not know following close on his heels, and even from across the road they could see the youngster was in awe of his DCI.

"In there, Guv." Inside the house a forensic suited officer pointed to the lounge where Kobe was now being detained. Without a word of thanks Casper entered the lounge with the DC close on his heels. As well as Kobe in the lounge there was a uniformed constable keeping an eye on him. When Casper had told him to 'fuck off', he was relieved and happy to leave the room.

"My name is DCI Casper Jones, and I am to be the Senior Investigating Officer." He glanced over his shoulder at the young DC. "This is Detective Michael Cross, and he will be my note-taker this evening." Cross flustered and fumbled as he tried to get his notebook and pen from the inside pocket of an oversized blazer.

Kobe did not acknowledge either man, they hardly registered in his tangled mind. He vaguely had a recollection of meeting DCI Jones previously but at that moment he did not care from where or when.

Casper was a stickler for rules and procedure, so his first job was condolences for Kobe's loss. It sounded insincere, which it was. As far as Casper was concerned, he was looking at the guilty party, there was no need look elsewhere. Jones' lazy mind was already made up. Experience told him there was rarely any need to look outside the home with a family murder. He made no attempt to shake Kobe's hand or sit opposite him to level the playing field, sitting down would have wrinkled the sharp lines of his suit. Behind him Cross looked around for somewhere to sit but on realising his DCI would remain standing, changed his mind, and just remained where he was with pen poised over a blank page in his notebook. At five-six Casper preferred to stand when in this kind of situation as it made him feel superior, behind the pulled curtains of the lounge he stood over Kaan who had not even looked up. His lack of eye-to-eye contact partly from disdain and partly to hide away the pain. From his temporary lofty position looking down it would normally give the interviewer the advantage over his subject, except Kobe had used this strategy many times and he could not be intimidated, his greatest fear had materialised in the violent loss of his family and there was nothing that would scare or intimidate him anymore, not in his frame of mind.

Outside the closed curtains on-screen reporters, stood neatly preened, ready for any breaking snippet and despite their thirst for a good story were unaware of what was unfolding inside the cottage. They all waited for the two main events, the bodies being taken out of the cottage and placed into a plain undertaker's ambulance, and then the husband/father/accused/officer being led out cuffed and looking sheepish, but at the moment the journalists were frustrated, cold and hungry, but dare not go to the burger van for fear of missing any kind of movement. They all knew it would be their jobs if any of them missed anything.

Back inside the front room lit only by a dim overhead light, the energy saving bulb surrounded by a paper Chinese lantern, the kind that first gained popularity way back in the sixties and seventies. This meeting gave Kobe his first glance of the officer who would be his nemesis for the next, however long it took. He did not recognise the smartly dressed DCI by name or sight but knew him by reputation and it always concerned him when police officers in civvies looked too smart and trendy, it usually meant they were all substance and no experience. Even with everything he was suffering this tragic evening, Kobe's brain still worked on the external things and took him beyond his thoughts of loss and horror, and he judged this Casper Jones to be a ladder-climber and not a true copper who got to where he was with grit and determination. Kobe did not like him from the moment he entered the room. Kaan's fears were brought to life when Jones notified him of his rights, the moment he entered the room, and he was formally arrested for the murders of his family. No open mind there then, nor any slack for a fellow police officer, not that he ever expected to be awarded any slack, no matter what the accusation.

A forensics team member, masked, gloved and booted for action entered the lounge with large plastic bags which held a dull grey track suit and Kobe was asked politely if he would be kind enough to get out of his street clothes and into the fresh tracksuit. At least one investigating team member offered him due respect.

"I would like a Federation Rep here please before I say or do anything." Kobe was trying to fight his corner except his voice was weak and lacked conviction. He was beyond caring about what happened to himself. The only thing he needed was to take care of his family's needs, both as a man, and as his religion dictated, but he knew he would not be allowed anywhere near their blood-drained and still bodies. Indignity was added to the list of the evening's proceedings as he was forced to strip in front of the forensic officer, the young and inexperienced DC and DCI Jones who from the look on his face had already judged and convicted Kaan. To be honest, Kobe was beyond personal feelings and rather than being pissed off about his treatment he felt extraordinarily little, he blessed the numbness he felt. He just wished he were upstairs lying beside his family, spooned behind Rae, his long arms draped over the three of them and his own life's blood draining from opened veins, it is where he should have been. Although not a vengeful man, Kobe felt the need to stay alive long enough to discover who had done this to his perfect life. Who had so brutally killed his beautiful family, cutting all their ambitions and dreams short. What sort of animal had done this? The questions were racing around his thoughts and mixing with his sorrow, who had he so mistreated that they felt this was the answer to their own problems. He wished his mind could sit still for just a few minutes.

Thoughts were interrupted when a pair of old trainers that were kept in the rear utility room were just deposited at his feet. One piece by one piece he removed his clothing, most of them bloodstained from when he had dropped to the floor. Kobe stuffed them into individual plastic evidence bags which were being held out by the forensic guy. He was down to boxers, and stopped, plain white as Rae liked the look of white boxer shorts next to his olive-coloured skin.

"Sorry Sir, those too," forensic guy ordered, but in an apologetic way as he continued to show respect for an officer who he knew and liked.

Kobe slipped them down and off, dropping them into the final bag. He felt no embarrassment at being naked in front of the trio of officers and slid slowly into the oversized tracksuit that had been handed to him, before slipping his sockless feet into the loose fitting and grubby gardening trainers.

With the dark corner that was his detective brain, his thoughts conjured up a scenario, he was not out to get just one person. No this was the work of at least two. Number one was the killer, a psychopath, someone who enjoyed their work no matter how horrendous. It takes a special kind of killer to murder children, especially in this harsh and blind-to-pain manner. Worse than him... 'or could it be a female killer, despite the vicious nature of the killings'... was the person who ordered these killings and why did he hate Kobe so much. What had he done to so anger someone?

"I asked you a question DI Kaan!" The DCI was short to reach temper level, as well as short in stature. He needed something to replace his physical inches, and over the years he had learned that being a bully was the way to go.

Kobe had not heard the question, nor did he want to hear it repeated. Instead, his thoughts continued a wild and uncontrolled journey. One moment it was full of the evening's images and the next it was revenge, then he wondered what sort of mind he had that despite all that was going on he still had his copper's brain that was currently trying to work through the mental files that were his list of possible suspects. Whoever they were, they would pay when he had that one figured out.

"It will do no good to keep ignoring me, it only makes you look guilty." Jones was like an alligator with his jaws firmly clenched and his teeth deep into his victim, he was just waiting to drag him to the bottom of the criminal swamp where he could complete the death-roll and tear the flesh from him to reach the truth, well, his truth anyway. And his truth was the only one that mattered.

Kobe responded this time, and with strength, although he could smell the tears that were rolling down his cheeks. "I told you once Sir, I will say nothing until I have a Fed Rep with me, as well as my solicitor."

Jones smiled, a shallow and mean smile, he had his man. "That just makes you look like the guilty bastard you are, and I am going to have you." He leaned into Kobe's face, noses just half a dozen inches apart. "You are going to pay for what you did today."

Kobe wanted to react and tell the smug bastard that he was already paying but he held his own council.

The forensic officer who was still writing on the evidence bag labels did not like to see or hear such disrespect, not just for a serving officer, for anyone, and he had to say something.

"I don't think you are being very respectful Detective Chief Inspector." He said fearlessly, despite the fact he was talking to a superior. "I heard Mr Kaan ask for his Fed Reb and legal representation, and you should abide by those wishes."

"Nobody asked you to butt in, just go and do your own job and leave me to what I know and what I can and cannot do." Jones pointed the way out of the room as if he were dealing with a recalcitrant school child.

Before he left the room, he looked Kobe in the eye. "Sorry about him Mr Kaan, and sorry for your loss Sir." He held the glance for a moment longer, before finally turning and leaving the room.

Kobe did not recognise the eyes, which were the only part of the scientific officer showing, but he was thankful for the kind words amidst such anger.

Up until now, events for Kobe had been drawn out as if in a slow dream. Suddenly, now he was out of his bloody clothes, life became a whirl of activity that felt to Kobe as if it were a film where time lapsed into a series of sudden happenings. He knew it was time to be taken from his home and his heart strings plucked even harder at wanting to remain here with his family. He knew now as he was cuffed by the young DC who still had spots on his childlike face that he would never again be in this place, his home. The home where he and his amazing wife with her huge almond eyes had raised two beautiful and intelligent children, the home where Rae had produced such stunning works of art, the home where usually Sundays (was it still Sunday?) were taken up with morning papers, afternoon family walks and evening dinners, before stories were read at bedtime. That bliss had become long lost dreams in one evening of madness.

Lost in his random thoughts he vaguely recalled the cuffs going on, the metal cold against his wrists, the pinch of skin as they tightened. The only missing feeling was shame, he had nothing to be ashamed of as he had nothing to feel guilty about, no guilt equalled no shame. Filling his vision was the fresh-faced DC who could not look him in the eye while putting the cuffs on, an officer should never feel intimidated by his prisoner as right should be on your side, this officer was ashamed of his actions and showed it.

From around the back of the house, where Gold and Martin were still waiting to show support for their friend and Boss, gossip quickly spread among the few photographers and reporters who were stood there patiently waiting for some sort of event to unfold and without warning they suddenly sprung from their starting blocks and raced around to the front.

"The Ghost is fucking taking him out the front..." Martin exclaimed, the anger in voice obvious.

"Surely not." Gold responded, but both followed the fleet footed press.

Sure enough, there out front with the caged van were two waiting escort vehicles. From the Kaan's front gate, across the public footpath and to the van with open back doors four uniforms stood, two either side, with arms spread to hold back the press and onlookers. Kobe was walked down the path, he tried to hold his head high, but it was not easy, his wrists clearly cuffed in front of him, he was being paraded for all to see. There was a brief media frenzy, and tomorrow's papers would all show a decorated police office being arrested and shamed for the cold-blooded murder of his family, still-cameras were held high to catch the action and flash guns sparked light like strobes into the night sky while TV cameraman further lit the surreal scene and filmed every inch of the walk from the front door, for the half a dozen paces down the garden path and across the path and into the waiting van. For the voracious public with their appetite for scandal and news, this was food to their hunger and drink to their thirst for someone to blame. The police officer had done it, he had murdered his family, those poor innocent children put to death by their Muslim fanatic of a father. Why would they have paraded the prisoner in such a way if there was any sign of innocence?

Casper Jones, in his new store-bought double-breasted suit, followed one pace behind at the tail of the short procession, a stern but smug expression on his jowly face, and from the moment the entourage stepped out into the real world his five-foot-six was now stretching to six-foot-five. For today, he was the big man, and once his prisoner was in the van, he would make a short statement to the waiting press. He would also ensure his voice was loud enough for the crowd to hear his every word.

Kobe stepped up into the van and once he was above head height, he could hear the baying of the crowd that had gathered, hear the shouted questions the press wanted answered, hear the accusations that the world would now hold. He was now a murderer and a cold hearted one at that. His position as a police officer was loudly being questioned and his Muslim faith was being denigrated by frenzied lips and overactive minds.

Suddenly with the slamming of the back doors his world descended into silence, he could still lip-read those with opinions at the front of the crowd through the darkly tinted windows, he was pushed into his seat and a safety belt clicked into place. The young DC continued to closely watch his charge. Kobe had forgotten his name already.

Outside the back doors DCI Jones took a moment to look at his reflection in the same blacked-out windows, with a show of vanity he checked to see if his clothes were straight, shirt collars down inside of jacket, jacket buttoned. He decided he was in fine fettle to face the cameras and he mentally prepared his short statement. He thumped the tinny back door to inform the driver he was to go. The white van reflected the flashes of a dozen cameras as it pulled away down the narrow street, and on past the arts and craft centre, one of the patrol cars whipped out in front while the second tagged on at the rear, for Jones this was a magical sight, the stuff of movies and of police heroes being made.

Kobe looked straight ahead, still able to see through the smoked glass and at the rear of the crowd he saw his friend and sergeant, David Martin standing alongside Stella Gold, the young PC who had handled herself so well back at the start of this strange day. He knew they were not part of the crowd, but there to support him. He thought that knowing his sergeant as he did, he would have bet money on the fact that David would have tried to get into the house, he was that sort of friend and that sort of colleague, and no doubt Gold was made of similar stuff. Even in his time of loss he thought that they might actually make a cute couple, and he noted they were stood with shoulders and arms touching, he would have been happy for them if he had any idea what happiness was any more.

Kobe dropped his eyes to his feet and took in the fact he was wearing his paint spattered trainers, they were a visual distraction as he did not want anything to do with the outside world anymore, he neither wanted to look at it or live in it.

Kobe Kaan was done!

CHAPTER 27

Sam, following a fitful sleep, finally awoke fully. He recalled nodding off in the comfortable chair last night while still hugging his Centurion, being a success was more tiring than he would have thought.

Thinking back on the restless night Sam had small fragments of dreams that ran like movie trailers through his mind's eye. Instead of the junk shop that was waiting for him upstairs, the same messy emporium that waited there for him every day, there was a stylish antique studio filled with classic paintings that hung in ornate frames, polished furniture that smelled of beeswax, broad chairs and chaise lounges that were wrapped in rich tapestry covers, all sitting on priceless Persian and Moroccan rugs, and centre stage standing on a marble plinth some four foot high and weighing an absolute ton was the Centurion, his sword still held triumphantly above his head and his bronze torso still catching the light from the carefully placed overhead spots. A heroic figure with a well-designed six-pack and a pert but muscular arse, not the original of course but a well-made reproduction, the making of his fortune would have been sold at the first opportunity.

It was the best dream Sam had ever had, and that including the teenage one that he had about his biology teacher, Miss Moffatt, and for all the good it did him he even joined her ballroom classes which were twice a week after school and that never cured the fact he had two left feet, or his teenage fantasies about the delicious Miss Moffatt.

Being rested, Sam did not need to look at the clock, the sun was up outside, and his good night of delicious dreams had come to a conclusion. Ahead lying in wait, what for him, would be a genuinely exciting day. He took his mobile phone from the stretched pocket of his patchy woollen cardigan and hit the quick-dial number '1' button, such was his social circle it was the only number he had on speed dial. At the other end Nick's phone buzzed and vibrated on the top of a bedside table putting a stop to the lovemaking he had just persuaded Suzi to join in with, since getting pregnant she did not seem that interested in sex, although Nick had heard things much to the contrary about pregnant women in general.

Sheepishly he plucked his phone up from the bed side table,

and saw it was Sam calling. Suzi saw the guilty look that had crossed Nick's face and merely tutted.

Beyond the 'tut' she added, "Why does he always call at such odd times, he is a nuisance, and I will never understand how you two became friends?" Suzi swung her feet out of bed, her bump was growing and she looked over it saw with dismay her swollen ankles and part flounced and part waddled out of the bedroom, she was always good at flouncing here and there, even more so, since she had become pregnant.

Nick pressed the answer button on the phone's screen but before he or Sam could speak, Suzi poked her head back around the door, her beautifully rounded stomach appearing a second before her face. Nick smiled and once again wondered if he would make a good father, he had no hesitation of thought about whether Suzi would be a good mother, she would be a great mother.

"After I have peed for England, would you like a cup of tea?" She forced a smile, she never stayed cross with her partner for long. "You really are ruggedly handsome, you know." She added with a flirty smile.

Nick blushed. "Yes, please Suzi," and then he turned his attention to Sam. "Have you any idea of the time Sam?"

"About nine-ish, or so..." The fact that the question had even been asked put Sam on the back foot and looking around at the few clocks in the basement he noted they read everything from midnight to midday. "Sorry Nick, I just woke and thought it was later." Glancing finally at his watch he was disgusted to learn it had only just passed 5.30 a good four hours earlier than he had thought.

"Are you OK Sam, its far earlier than you would normally be awake, you are always a late riser like me."

There had been enough idle chatter, Sam needed to get to the point.

"Nick, I found it!" It was Sam's eureka moment.

"What, the statue?"

"No, the pound coin I lost behind the sofa cushions!" Sarcasm was a Sam speciality. "The Roman, I found him. Or should I say he found me with the tip of his bloody sword!"

"Sam, this could be life changing or break your heart," Nick always saw both sides of any story. Down the phone's earpiece Sam heard the toilet flush and wished he had made tea first his throat parched, his mouth gummed up.

Licking his lips to get some saliva on them Sam continued. "It's the real deal Nick. I have the original, and it is sitting here in my lap." Now he was saying the words, it begun to feel unreal and not reality as he expected. Sam put it down to fear of failing again. "It was in the cellar all along, my father had hidden it in the stuffing of his old chair, and I think he may have done that so as to give me something for later in life, a sort of nest egg."

"Sam that is awesome..."

He heard Suzi in the background. "Nick, tell Suzi I am sorry I woke you both, I didn't think to check the time I was so excited."

"Suzi says Hi back..."

"No, she didn't Nick," Sam said without rancour, he knew she did not think much of their friendship.

"Morning Sam." She said loudly so he could hear down the phone, then to Nick. "I am going to sit in my chair downstairs, join me you when you have done." Suzi leant down with an arm around her stomach as if protecting the bump, and kissed Nick gently on the forehead.

He looked into her beautiful, narrow, oval eyes, sculpted like that because of her mother's Chinese heritage, her dark hair was cut short and dyed blonde which Nick thought brought out her Asian skin tones. Her eyebrows remained dark and thick, contrasting with her hair. She was so beautiful, even with her bed hair sticking up all over the place. Nick had lost his heart from the first moment he saw her.

"I am back, Sam."

"I was about to say that things are going to be different in my life now, Nick. They will not be able to take the piss anymore, I will be ahead of the game for once and they will have to respect me now." Sam could not hide his excitement, even if he had wanted to.

Nick was more of a realist. "Don't get yourself excited just in case there is a fall ahead. Remember what the rapper Eminem sang, *'The truth is you don't know what is going to happen tomorrow. Life is a crazy ride, and nothing is guaranteed.'* And I don't want you to find out that your statue is fake as well, Sam."

Sam had no idea who Eminem was, or why he would be singing such lines.

"You can be such a killjoy Nick." Sam was excited and steaming ahead with no thought of the consequences, somebody said a long time ago, beware that for which you wish. "I want you to write the story Nick, you can have the exclusive story."

"You are getting ahead of yourself Sam, and I would be reluctant to let the world know about it if I were you. Sometimes a story is not in the public interest and can have severe consequences once it is out there."

Later that morning and back in Sam's kitchen at the well-worn table Sam and Nick stared at the Centurion who stood like the proud warrior that he was in the centre of the worn wooden surface. Until his friend had arrived Sam had continued to sweep small patches of dust from the soldier's cracks and crevices with a soft-headed toothbrush. Every now and again he would reach forward and stroke the bronze surface in much the same way as lovers might caress each other.

Nick, now watching his love-struck friend asked again. "You are sure that one is the real deal?"

"I am and it is. For certain."

The reporter had never seen his friend so blissfully happy, and he felt good for him, but still something about the whole event felt to Nick as if it would all unravel somehow. He was not normally a pessimist, but his journalistic hackles were up.

"And you want me to print the story." he said with concern in his voice.

Sam just nodded.

"If you are sure I would love to write the story, but you do realise that because that fake was on the Roadshow the story will probably go national, maybe even international." Nick, if he was being honest with himself, was champing at the bit to start writing the story. "And, you know that it will keep running long after you have sold it at auction because of its life-changing value."

"I know all that Nick." For a moment, the joy left Sam's face. "I have been the butt of people's strange ideas about what is humorous for most of my life, and I am aware that I have not been particularly good at what I do, but I get by, which is more than some. I was bullied at school because I didn't have a mum, and because my dad was a junk-shop owner. Well, I am tired of just getting by and being bloody well insulted every time I go to an antique fair or auction, I am fed up with my money not being good enough for them. That prat yesterday on his stall, he sold that porcelain for less than I was willing to pay because he just wanted to make a point. Now I want them to know that I am not a waste of space and that now I have hit the big time."

"You do know it won't change much, don't you!" Nick tried to explain, but he knew that Sam was beyond listening. "The people that have a go at you are not intelligent enough to realise that they are the losers Sam. They will still find ways to get under your skin."

Sam pleaded once more, without realising he had already worn his friend down. "Please tell my story Nick, I would never trust anyone else to write it. I just want to be seen in a good light for once, a little fight back against the bullies."

Sam looked away from the Roman soldier with his sword held high and gazed at Nick with puppy-dog eyes. Nick the journalist and not the friend gave in to the entreaty and against his better judgement surrendered to the look, took his reporters' notebook from the leather satchel that Suzi had bought him the previous Christmas and opened it on a clean page. Nick was old fashioned and preferred shorthand to recording on a device, and so the story began that would change lives. Nick began writing in shorthand on his pad and began to tell the story about his friend Sam Cobby and the tale of his long-lost Roman Centurion.

CHAPTER 28

Arriving at the newly built custody suite of Chichester police station was another strange sensation for Kobe. The square block of a building constructed of blue tinted glass stood out like a sore thumb against the red brick of the main station and looked more like an architect's idea of a theatre frontage than a place where the villainous were charged, printed, and posed for mug shots. Kobe handcuffed and uncomfortable in the back of a police van arrived without really noticing where he was, but the fact he was the wrong side of the divide that night did not go amiss. Normally he would arrive for work and stroll through the front door stopping to chat with Jemma Costello and hand over her latte coffee. He had not asked, but he assumed, that they would not be stopping for coffees and bacon sandwiches that night. He hadn't seen her, or anyone else outside the station for that matter, but standing and waiting even this late into the night Jemma was outside the main entrance to the nick and watched him arrive. She hoped he would see her friendly face and take a crumb of comfort from her being there.

The three-car convoy bounced across the shallow ramp of the kerb and kept a little of the speed up as they entered the car park, either side of the gate were a dozen or more press photographers, a couple of TV cameramen and a crowd of baying spectators none of whom had ever seen a murderer, let alone one that was so well known in the area. As they shot through the gauntlet of press, camera flashes bounced around and lit the whole street. It was a surreal experience for the copper turned prisoner.

Kobe jumped in his seat, startled. He had been looking down at the floor when a loud thump on the window had echoed through the car. One of the spectators had broken through the press cordon and attacked the rear window, while yelling at the guilty man in the car. Kobe only just made out his racist ranting.

"I hope they hang you, you fucking terrorist, murderer, fucking Muslim." The rant was only a few seconds long but long enough for photographers to capture the scene and one of the TV cameramen to record every syllable, in high-definition colour and sound. The middle-aged protester was about to get his 30 seconds of fame as a popular television reporter swiftly grabbed him and pulled him to one side. It was not what most people viewed as an anarchist attacking a police car, the man was dressed in a knitted tank-top that looked as if it was either knitted by his mother or was a charity shop reject, the rest of his ensemble was baggy brown corduroy trousers and brown sandals. Protester, camera operator and pretty TV journalist moved away from the throng to the front of the custody suite, she did not want the other journalists to overhear the interview and get free copy.

Inside and at the custody sergeant's desk there was a welcoming party of suits and uniforms. Some to gawk at the fallen DI and a few to offer support. In truth though few of them would continue supporting the once popular officer for fear of damaging their own careers by being linked to a possible murder suspect. Guilt or innocence had no place there in the custody suite, it was all about perception. A hand was thrust forward for Kobe to shake, he ignored it, or more likely never even registered it was there. The voices wanting his attention were a cacophony of sounds, nothing melodic, just voices talking over voices, no single voice could be distinguished. Out of the small crowd stepped a man with a rumpled suit, a striped shirt, and a paisley tie, this was not a trendy look. But he had a friendly face and a quiet manner.

Placing a hand, gently, on Kobe's shoulder the scruffy man introduced himself as one, Peter Jordan-Reeves, but Kobe forgot the name in less time than it took to say it. The one thing he did say that made Kobe take note was the fact he was the Police Federation Rep, and he would be alongside the DI throughout the interview procedure.

It took only a look from the Sergeant on the booking desk, and the small gathering of the curious disbanded, disappearing through doors and along corridors, nobody thought to offer condolences or even offer help. From the most popular officer at the station, Kobe Kaan had become toxic.

Now alone in the Custody Suite, apart from the Federation Rep with the forgotten name, DCI Jones and his weasel looking assistant, while the other side of the booking desk was the Custody Sergeant Chris Carne, who was thin on top and bearded, and he was not enjoying the evening's events. Sgt Carne was an old friend of Kobe's and now he had to do the worst job of his 22-year career, it was his duty to repeat the Caution again and he looked totally embarrassed at doing so to a fellow officer and colleague. He had booked serving officers before, of course, but he knew this to be a waste of time. Kobe and he had worked together many times, and he knew how much he loved his family, he would never harm them. With the booking process completed Jordan-Reeves in his role as Fed-Rep repeated his earlier words to Kobe, asking if there was anything he needed or wanted.

With all that was going on around him, Kobe's mind was in utter turmoil, the only thing he wanted or needed was to be with his family and to grieve as a father, a husband and as a Muslim. He wanted to beg them, plead with them, to let him deal with his family. There were rituals to conduct, duties needed to be done and only he could do them.

"I need to see my family. There are things I need to do for them." His voice was soft, so soft the detectives who remained at his shoulders hardly heard the words.

They did not understand the strength of his pleadings, nor know anything about his religious teachings. If the truth be known, neither of them particularly cared. They just assumed he wanted to somehow tamper with the evidence the three bodies would offer up. That was not going to happen on Casper Jones' watch, and as far as he was concerned it was another hint of the guilt of Kobe Kaan.

Every now and again a uniform, a CID officer and even a cleaner or two had wondered through the custody suite to get a look at the evening's superstar arrest. When another small crowd had gathered, they should have staggered their timings, but all wanted to get a good look so later they could say they were there. If guilty they would say they knew all along and if exonerated, they would say they had been there to support him. Only those not on duty or who had decided to stay away from the custody suite would have nothing to say on the matter, they were not there, and they saw nothing – but that never did stop anyone gossiping before.

Carne's patience had run out with those cluttering up his suite, "Give a fellow officer some room and some respect for fuck's sake!" he barked and the loud bollocking did the trick, and everyone apart from those who had to be there dispersed once again. Then the Custody Sergeant leaned across to Kobe. "Sorry 'bout this Mr Kaan, we both know it's the rules." he said looking straight into Kobe's tired eyes. "And sorry for your loss, Boss, they were a beautiful family."

Kaan may have been brought in as the prime suspect in the

murder of his family, but he was still due the respect that a Commended police officer deserved, and Carne was an old school skipper and as much of a fixture as any of the cells or furniture. He held Kobe's gaze a few seconds longer and the damaged man appreciated the words and the gesture. The sergeant slowly moved his glare to the pair of detectives who had destroyed Kobe's career, guilty or innocent, mud like this stuck to a man. The older detective was a poorly liked career man and was used to disrespect from other officers, but the youthful Michael Cross shrivelled under Chris Carne's malevolent stare.

"All booked in now, Jones..." If words had carried venom Casper Jones would have been writhing in agony on the ground by now.

"That's Mr Jones to you Sergeant."

Carne did not correct himself; he had been around too long to be intimidated by a senior officer who only got to where he was because he had a university degree and friends in higher places.

"I think you can remove the cuffs now." It was not a request from Carne, and few people were brave enough to disregard him in, what effectively, was his custody suite, his domain.

The two suits looked at each other, the older one shrugged and nodded to the youth. Kobe lifted his hands without invitation and Cross removed the cuffs, the bracelets had left a red welt on each wrist.

"Again, sorry for your loss Mr Kaan." The Station Skipper, spoke with a clear and intentional voice.

Jones did not miss the use of a respectful title.

CHAPTER 29

Things were moving swiftly, Sam's head was spinning, and it was only day one of, what he now perceived as, his new life. He was back on the first floor of the old town hall and standing under Mayor Cobby's 17th Century portrait looking up at him and feeling as if he had at last honoured the family name. The photographer from the local rag felt it made the perfect backdrop, far better than the scruffy old store out in the precinct. He may have only been a regional photographer, but he did have standards, even if they were only modest ones.

Sam stood proudly in front of his illustrious ancestor, finally proud of his family name and his own achievements, he no longer felt as if he belonged in the shadows as he posed for the images that would be in The Chichester Post, maybe even front-page news, unless someone started a war or robbed a bank in the quiet city. The old dealer was knackered, who knew it was this tough being in the public eye, the real celebs who he saw in the tabloids everyday must have great stamina for all this PR work. Nick had arrived at Sam's kitchen at half five in the morning and apart from a powernap in the old armchair, he had been hunting in the cellar for hours before discovering the Roman. Over copious cups of tea Nick had asked questions, changed quotes, advised on good answers, and moulded Sam's words into interesting and intelligent copy. The experienced reporter had also managed to leave out the words, 'I found it Nick, I finally bloody found it!' which Sam had spent most of the morning repeating, still partially in denial of his good fortune.

Nick had called the photographer, the unfortunately named David Bailey, before he had even left for the paper's office, if truth be known it was even before he had slipped from his dressing gown and poured his first coffee. Bailey, as he was referred to at the office, in the paper and on their web pages, was not known for being an early riser never reaching the office before ten in the morning, and here he was out on assignment already and it was only just gone nine. He could slip away earlier this afternoon; he thought while posing Sam for yet another arty-farty shot.

The early start was doing nothing to his mood, he was grumpy when he arrived and was getting more annoyed by the second. His subject, not the most photogenic person he had worked with, kept closing his eyes in anticipation of the artistically bounced flash. Bailey would have preferred an artier style of shot in natural light, but he knew the picture editor just wanted, what was known as, 'dead-people-standing', the most economical way of getting more faces on the pages. More faces meant more sales, as copies would be bought for friends and relatives, a half-lit, moody style of shot was not the way to go. Pity, because the early morning sunshine had pushed beams of glorious light through the windows and into the vast room, the other, real, David Bailey would not have put up with this shit.

"Sam..." Make friends with your model, so first name terms. "You keep screwing up your eyes."

"I am sorry, I find the flash a distraction." He said in his defence.

"That's okay let's try something a little different. I want you to close your eyes..." Bailey spoke slowly as if he were talking to a school child, but Sam had not noticed, or was beyond caring. "Hold the statue just a little higher, now close your eyes gently, do not screw your face up. Take easy breaths and I will count to three, and on three, open your eyes."

Sam did as asked, and the photographer seemed pleased, or at least he was no longer talking to him as if he were a troublesome ten-year-old.

"And again. One, two, three..." A few more clicks and flashes. "Once more. One, two, three. Got it!" He thanked Sam for his patience, but then followed up with just a few more, these shot with natural light which was beaming through the large window. He wanted some arty shots in the camera just in case the story went national.

Nick could not help but smile as he watched the youthful photographer, who nobody considered to be in the same realm as his namesake, drop to one knee and shoot upwards while once again doing the countdown for Sam's benefit. It was a far more dynamic angle, and the snapper knew that the better shots could well make the Nationals after his paper put the words and pictures out through a news agency. It irked to know that it would be the company that would take the fees from the Nationals but at least he would get the recognition with by-lines. Worth its weight in gold when it came to moving up in the photojournalistic world.

Nick was now sitting on the side lines, his story about his friend and his historic find having been written and submitted to the sub-editors, but he felt it only right to keep an eye on his friend so that he wasn't exploited. Nick had argued long and hard with Sam about doing this, although his journalist's hackles were well up at the thought of an exclusive story that would go nationwide, if not even further. The problem was always the same though, as soon as anyone found an iota of fame or did something good there would be those wanting to ride the coattails to claim their small part of the glory, or to bring the culprit back down to earth. Nick was only to aware that once sent out into the limelight there was no way back and the 15 minutes of fame did not always work out well for the recipient. Call it reporters' intuition but Nick had a gut feeling that the near future for Sam would not all be good news. As he watched the photographer shoot Sam and his Roman statue, he did so with trepidation. Nick Flax feared for his friend and his well-being. Sam was no worldly-wise man.

Trepidation alone would have been a bad enough feeling, but as Nick quietly sat by watching he felt an involuntary shiver, a bystander watching a collision unfold and not being able to do a thing about it. A chill travelled up his spine, making the hairs on the back of his neck stand on end. He felt it was a definite portent of things to come, when all he should have been feeling was a shared joy and elation with his friend. Put it down to the human response of fight or flight, or years of journalistic experience, but something was not right here. Nick was suddenly aware that Sam was looking at him and he was also wearing a look of fear, but he smiled at his friend realising that he must have been showing on his own face, what it was he was feeling.

Just as he relaxed his expression, and his mood, the warnings that he was triggering took on something more palpable as somebody with the bluster and force of a tornado burst into the room and insinuated himself in the middle of proceedings. He obviously saw some advantage to being invited up onto Sam's bandwagon. It was the Councillor that Sam had met at the antique fair just yesterday afternoon, Kenneth Jackman, and he wanted his slice of this publicity pie.

The slick and smiling interloper revealed himself with the loudness of his gruff voice long before Nick saw him charge into view. The Councillor looked every part the slick politician with his greying hair carefully combed back, small curls of almost white strands flicked out around his ears. He wore a deep blue suit with a red satin lining, sharp and distinguished, worn with a pink shirt the button-down collar open at the neck. Although in his mid-fifties, which he would deny vigorously, he still had the face and a complexion of a man 20 years younger, so he was still a young looking man except the open-neck shirt showed off a wonderful reason to wear a tie, for the skin 'V' at his neck was showing off liver-spots and creases of skin.

Without invitation he inserted himself into the photoshoot, never one to miss an opportunity he had heard about the press call for Sam, but needed reminding who indeed, Sam was. This was a news opportunity to ride on the tails of and which may help his plans for Mayordom.

"Morning Councillor." Nick was quick to place himself between the sharp politician and his naive friend.

A small breath of air dared to blow free a carefully combed wave of grey hair and leave it drooped across Jackman's brow, it was swiftly, and deftly brushed back into immaculate place with the fingers of one hand, the move hardly noticed. Jackman was a man who thought appearance was everything, well, that and his natural charm.

"Good morning, Mr Flax, lovely day for a photoshoot." The voice thick and gravelly as usual and yet as smooth as honey.

Although Nick stood between Sam and the councillor, Jackman just swerved his way around and was upon Sam in a flash, like a lethal hunter taking down his prey. The councillor with hand extended as he neared his quarry, Sam could do nothing except take the offered hand and shake it. The camera flashed again. The skin felt cold, the grip firm and while being held by the right hand the left snaked up onto Sam's shoulder where it gripped the bony joint firmly but without discomfort. The camera flashed and Sam blinked again. The councillor equipped with an election winning smile which he released into the open at every opportunity. Sam was snared and the camera flashed again.

"Sam, isn't it?" He knew damn well it was but getting conformation meant they were communicating, and Jackman liked that.

"Councillor!" He could not think of a witty response, so it was just the one word he uttered.

"We met just yesterday, Sam, at the antique fair that was here." Jackman's gaze was not centred on Sam's face but secured onto the bronze face of the Centurion which reflected a golden glint of greed in the councillor's hazel eyes.

Not one to leave early when an opportunity raised its head, the photographer continued to fire away as the councillor moved in for the kill, right hand still in the firm grasp of right hand but the left had now snaked around Sam's neck like a boa ready to squeeze the life out of its prey. Sam heard the clicking and blinked at every flash as the young photographer grasped the opportunity to keep snapping, with the technology of the digital age and no film to reload the press photographers' lot was a much easier one. For his part Sam would regret it later but now he was enjoying the attention, it was not everyday an important town councillor took interest in his electorate and here he was treating Sam like his best friend.

Nick could do nothing to stop it and any kind of intervention could well get him banned from council press calls and that would not please his editor. He reluctantly became a bystander in the drama unfolding before him, and it worried him.

As they posed, both smiling broadly for the camera, Sam's now with a fixed grin with teeth naturally aged a slight creamy colour, while Jackman's was a full on, bleached white beam of an opening, every tooth level with its partners on either side, a perfect smile that had cost close to a thousand pounds. Jackman chatted easily about the Roman Centurion that Sam still had in his hand but at some point, the councillor had grabbed one leg and now seemed to be handing it to Sam as Royalty would hand over the FA cup. Sam liked the feeling, never having won a thing in his life.

Between smiles and snaps Kenneth Jackman drew the story of the bronze out of Sam, telling of his regular Sunday evenings with Nick watching Antiques Roadshow and spotting the fake Centurion, as good as it was. But Sam knew he had the real deal somewhere in the basement of his shop.

Sam explained how the search had ended in the early hours of the morning when it was discovered after a four-hour quest, in the base of his father's favourite chair down in the dank basement of his small shop. All the while Nick was carefully recording the 'chat' in shorthand on his pad, writing furiously so as not to miss a single word. If there was any wrongdoing following this, so called, chance meeting then Nick would have a record of what was said.

"I called Nick right away, and he arranged this photo shoot after he had interviewed me." Sam told his new best friend. "He thinks the story might be picked up by the national papers..."

"Does he now? And I think he may be right; it is an unbelievable story of a man who has been brushed aside for so long but now has the attention of the antiques world upon him." Jackman knew Sam would love getting the compliments so was 'bigging' him up further than he had already grown.

Jackman was looking and thinking beyond this moment, he could see way beyond a mere photoshoot while standing under one of the pompous arseholes who had been mayor, totally missing the fact that the 'arsehole' he was under was one of Sam's ancestors. He had not yet figured out how, but he knew there was money to be made here. Also, there was the Kudos that went along with stories such as this, maybe when this gets out, he could be considered as a prospective candidate for MP. That would suit him, being a Member of Parliament and sitting in the Commons. Bugger just aiming for Mayor.

There was an opportunity here to attain greatness. Maybe then his wife would stop nagging him about money. She never understood that you had to spend money to make money. Simple economics!

"You say this bronze figurine could be quite valuable then Sam, if it should come up for auction." Somehow the benign smile of a minute ago had turned to something much more sinister and only Nick noticed it. It was a smile of avarice.

If a light went on overhead as it did in cartoons when somebody had a clever idea, then a giant searchlight had gone on over Jackman's head. It was beaming all the way to a bright future, all he had to figure out was how.

Then it hit him!

"You need to be careful if this does turn out to be valuable Sam." Jackman was thinking on his feet, "Where will you keep it? Until the Auction if you are preparing to sell it, at least."

Sam had not considered this before, there had not been time since its discovery. "Well, probably in the shop, it's been there all these years, and nobody has broken in. Maybe I should put it under the bed." It was a flippant comment and Sam embarrassed himself by saying something so crass.

"Yes, that is as maybe." A plan was formulating. "Before today nobody knew it was there, not even you, but now the world will know. Is your shop that secure?"

Nick knew it was time to interrupt. "What are you getting at Councillor? If you have some sort of scam going on in your mind..."

He did not have time to finish his sentence. "What do you take me for Nick Flax, that's the trouble with you journalists, you always think the worst of people." Jackman had anticipated the interruption and aimed his reply at Sam. "You say this is likely to be highly valuable Sam," First name terms, they were now buddies. "Then why don't you keep it here." A smile of victory now crossed his face.

"Here?"

"Yes, why don't we at the council take care of it for you." Jackman was in his stride now, like a Churchill tank he was now barrelling forward, and nothing would stand in its way. "It is something that your city should take a pride in." Friendship and a promising idea were now becoming a duty and service he could give the city where he grew up, and it was 'we' now and Sam liked the sound of that, it made him feel as if he had finally arrived and belonged. "We will put it on display and guard it at the same time." Jackman was gently nodding his head as he spoke, it was a prejudged movement as he knew that if you nodded at people they too would nod, and you could not nod and say no at the same time.

"Would it be safe?" Sam asked and Jackman knew he had snared his prey.

"Safe as any of the Council artefacts and works of art, look around you Sam, valuable paintings, the chains, and regalia of the mayor, they are all kept here safely. We have spare glass cabinets which are lockable and separately alarmed, as secure as the Tower of London Sam, and when did you ever hear of anybody stealing the Crown Jewels." He hoped he hadn't pushed his point too far. "Plus, your wonderful Centurion, and he is magnificent Sam, should be on display for the whole city to enjoy. At least until you take it to auction." Jackman took a breath before adding. "It is a shame that the city will not be able to buy it so we could keep it here Sam, even though we have this wonderful history going back to Roman times." he added knowing that Sam had been bitten.

A final nail to hammer the idea home. "All free of charge of course Sam, the city would love to do this for you." Added the councillor on seeing the expression on Sam's face change to one of weighting up the costs.

Sometime in the conversation Jackman's voiced had dropped into low and conspiratorial tones and Nick could only glean the odd word from the conversation, and that was worrying him. He pushed his chair back to stand and go and save, or at least support, Sam. He felt movement behind him, and a strong and yet elegant hand planted itself on his shoulder, pushing him down into the seat. Holding him there, Nick was amazed at how easily he could be held still by such bony fingers. He continued to start to rise but the hand hid a strength that its elegance belied.

It was Councillor Jackman's driver Fiona Webb, an enigmatic soul who often switched roles from chauffer to minder and it was the fact that she switched the two things so easily that troubled people who had come face to face with the woman. Being a reporter for all his working life Nick never felt intimidated by anyone, but this woman scared him for a reason. He had often asked the question as to why a mere councillor should have a chauffeur anyway. The answer had always been the same, that Jackman paid her wages, and she was down as one of his employees. As much as the rest of the council disliked the fact, there were no council rules against it.

Nick stayed put at the back of the room, the photographer had packed away his gear and was heading out of the door, he needed to get back to his editing suite on the computer and submit his photos to the editorial team. He gave the reporter a brief wave and he was gone. The gripping hand, with its pointed and painted nails, remained on his shoulder, and for good reason the power of the grip scared him, Nick did not want to remove it. It was a strange feeling of being under control, but he seemed unable to break the imagined firmness of the hold.

Sam, over by the rarely used stage, was being drawn in further to the idea that it would be great for the city if he allowed it to display the Centurion. It would be good for him as well as it would have his name plaque on the glass cabinet. 'Loaned to the City of Chichester by Sam Cobby of Cobby and Sons Antiques'. His dad would be so proud of him. Overnight he had gone from being a ridiculed junk shop owner and a nobody, to finally being a somebody. And he liked it. Nothing and nobody would be able to take this away from him or spoil his moment.

"We could even have another press call Sam," The lid of Jackman's deception was being firmly screwed into place and Sam was in a jam all of the councillor's making. "We can put the Roman on display, it will go nicely with the history of Chichester as we already have the museum with a Roman villa and artefacts displayed in there. Your Gladiator..."

"Centurion!"

"Sorry!" Jackman did not like interruptions when in full flow, but he let it go.

"You said gladiator, but he is a Centurion." Sam was now knowledgeable about such things and did not want to be misquoted and made foolish again.

"Okay, your Centurion," Jackman corrected himself and tried not to show irritation in his voice. "...will bring the history of Chichester full circle."

Nick watched on helpless as a handshake sealed the deal. Then, as suddenly as it had arrived the pressure on his shoulder lifted with the hand releasing its grip. He had also noted that it was a subtle nod from Jackman's head that had caused her to let go. He was surprised at such a fine-tuned bond between a councillor-come-businessman, and his driver. He made a mental note to discover more about Fiona Webb. With the hand holding him in place now gone he headed over to Sam. The Councillor was already heading out of the building, he had work to do and to him that meant his money worries would soon be gone.

Without a word passing between them Sam and Nick headed into the coffee shop, where they had been less than a day before, but so much had changed since then. Old Mayor Cobby in his grey wig watched them go and he was scowling under his mayoral tri-pointed hat with a grand feather in it. As they sat sharing a pot of tea Sam told Nick what Jackman had offered to do, for his part Nick decided that it would be wrong to deflate his friend with nothing but gut-instinct to guide him. So, he smiled and congratulated him, letting Sam revel in his moment of success.

Sam, not normally perceptive, could see trouble in Nick's eyes. "What's up Nick, have I done something wrong. You look a little serious and I thought you would be happy for me."

"I am Sam, I truly am." Lied the troubled journalist. "All those people who over the years have taken the piss out of you and your shop will now have to eat their words, you have finally put the bullies in their place."

They clicked teacups together and over an aromatic Earl Grey they toasted Sam's success.

Once out into the street and well out of the glare of the 18th Century Mayor Cobby, Jackman nodded to Fiona to come closer, sharp heels clicked their way over, the tap-tap-tap echoed under the entrance to the hall. High stilettos were a turn on for Jackman, but he liked weaker women that he could control, not strong women like Webb, or his wife.

"I have a job for you." he whispered, and Fiona knew not to interrupt. "Get up to my office and watch last Sunday's Antique Roadshow will you, you can get it on 'Catch Up' and find out who the bloke with the fake Gladiator..."

"...Didn't he say it was a Centurion, not a gladiator."

Jackman gave her a fierce look with anger in his eyes, but his moods did not bother her, not much did.

"Okay, a fucking Centurion then..." he continued. "We are going to need whatever fake statue he has, if the experts say it is as good as it is supposed to be then we could be in the money."

"Does it bother you how we get it?"

"No, it doesn't, I just want it."

CHAPTER 30

Kobe had been in the grey soulless room for almost two hours now and was strangely, for him, sitting on the side of the table reserved for the lawless and suspected. It was as if he were in an alien landscape seeing the room for the first time from this side. The walls opposite were the same colour, the view side to side the same, and yet somehow, he had had never seen this alien world. As if he had not been through enough already this was throwing him mentally sideways. First and foremost, Kobe was police officer, and one who took great pride in his work and the training of the officers around him, despite all that was happening he made a mental note that if he ever got through this, all his junior officers would at some point spend time this side of the table being questioned, it would give them valuable insights.

He felt ragged, bruised, lost and fearful; all feelings that were not his normal, and it scared him, just as the thought of a life alone scared him. He wanted to fight the feelings, but he had no strength for any more battles that night. He was not afraid of his interrogators or their repetitive questions, he only had truth as his weapons. Plus, he had been in too many interviews, both job and with suspects, to worry about the process, it held no surprises for him and there was nowhere that his questioner could make a sneak attack from.

No, the fear that was gripping him, causing him to sweat, was the fear of memory. The biting fear at revisiting that bedroom, in his statement and in his answers. They would make him tell his story repeatedly, forwards, and backwards, looking for the slightest deviation. In his mind the images were in full colour, high definition, and 3-D, and they continued to play on the widescreen format in his head. It was as if someone were rerunning the same horror film over and over, and now he had to review the film in fine detail, not just once but repeatedly.

He was awaiting a solicitor, well a retired barrister, if the truth be known, but it was someone he had dealt with in the past and trusted. It had been on opposite sides three years ago when he first met Robert Berry QC and it was someone from the legal profession he liked and applauded for the simple and quiet way he dealt with matters. Berry was the Godfather and defender of Lucas Tubb, a psychopathic killer who had been sent to Broadmoor for the murder of a young woman, sadly and despite his tenacity at solving riddles Kobe had never been able to identify those traits within the young man. It was strange case for Kaan, who at the time was a Detective Sergeant and it eventually helped him climb to the rank of DI. Police would not normally be aware of what happened to a body once forensics examinations and the case had been settled but Kobe needed to know what happened to the young lady, he felt that someone should care and at least mourn the girl. There was nobody fitting her description on the Missing Persons Database, nor did anyone claim her, it was a sad end for any life, let alone a young girl. On the order of the coroner, she was placed in a *Paupers' Grave* in the local cemetery with the essential parts of a basic funeral but with no headstone or marker, there was just a record of where she was lain, and a number for a headstone, she could well have been with a couple of other unidentified bodies. Kobe and two other officers who investigated her murder went along to the most basic of ceremonies out of respect, for some poor souls there was no dignity to be had, not even in death.

The case, which had been closed by investigators, later reared its head again when Lucas Tubb escaped from Broadmoor, a rare feat, and he had gone on to prove his innocence as well as have the finger pointed at his half-brother Jacob. The twists kept coming for the investigators and it remained strong in the memories of all those involved. The murder Of the unnamed girl was never fully solved, and her killer was still out there in the world somewhere, but nobody was looking for him. For authorities the case remained closed, there were more recent murders to deal with, but for Kobe the task was left unfinished.

Robert Berry was the Godfather of Lucas and had defended him. The, then DS, Kaan appreciated the way Berry had worked and managed himself. Defence lawyers are not real favourites of the police as they seem hell-bent on finding a way to reveal technicality failings and get cases thrown out of court. But Kobe had respect for the retired QC, both men appreciated the professionalism in the other.

Kobe clearly knew of his own innocence, but he was extremely aware that others would think otherwise. Many would mark him down as a killer simply because of his dark skin, some because of his religion, while others just hated it and were quick to point fingers when police officers were too close to a serious crime. In the media though, it was simply the fact that there would be no smoke without fire. Which is how, Kobe was sure, that the DCI who was waiting to start the interviewing was relishing the fact that he could smell burning somewhere in the middle of this tale.

Kobe's Fed Rep had said he would be happy to contact Robert Berry only to discover the music loving, guitar playing Barrister had been in Weymouth overnight, having played a gig with his blues band The Deadbeats. On contacting him the call had been brief and Berry had immediately left Dorset and was now making an early start on his way back to Sussex as a special favour, he recalled Kobe Kaan with fondness and liked the man and how he did his job. Kobe recalled a quiet man with grey hair, a grey goatee and sallow skin, it was as if he had never seen sunlight, which he hadn't between courts and nightclubs. He was a retired Barrister and now, in his new life, an itinerant blues musician with a gravelly voice and a sweet-sounding old Fender guitar, the only thing that was more battered than the player.

Kobe wished he were here already so that this could be done with, and he could get out into fresh air and away from people. His mind was in obvious turmoil and driving at great speed in any number of directions, on the main road the thoughts that he would never see and hear his family again, something he feared more than anything else. On the side roads of his mind, he was the investigator, the man who for all his career had worked on the enigmas of crime, and he would forever be travelling lanes of thought as to who could have done this. But now he was stuck in the heavy traffic of the legal system, sitting at red lights waiting for a 'go' signal to get the next few hours over and done with. He knew his interview would take up most, if not all, of the day once Berry had arrived. With the same questions asked repeatedly, the investigator believing repetition was a sure way to trip the accused up. Each time questions asked in a different tone, or in a different order to throw him off his stride but all intended to make him slip up, to expose inconsistency in his story. His interviewer did not want his brain to have time to rehearse the answers. Kaan was an experienced DI, although now the suspect, who knew the tricks. He was an expert interrogator. Most crimes that crossed his desk were solved here, in the interview room, and the rooms were grey and bland for good reason, there was nothing there to distract the mind. There was nothing better than getting, by fair means within the law, a confession from someone. Unlike the movies the accused could not be beaten into submission, nor could they be tricked, but with experienced questioning and that meant having what you believed the answers to be already in your head, it was possible to get them to just admit what they had done. Modern day criminals knew how the system worked and to a degree they knew the game was up, prison was just the downside of their business. Kobe had learned long ago, do not ask a question you don't know the answer too, it was too risky to be taken by surprise, and he knew that there would be some tough questioning coming.

He also knew the questioning would be relentless, the cocky DCI Jones was going to make his name today and for the future. A top career move would be on the cards after Kobe Kaan had been brought to justice, and Jones would be relishing the challenge. For coppers like Casper Jones, when it came to their career advancement, the facts meant truly little.

The door swung open, gently though, not with vigour as an interviewer would open it. Kobe did not look up, not at first, as he was bracing himself for what was to come. However, it was not the two suited officers coming through the door with stern looks and reams of evidential paper, it was Jemma Costello standing in the doorway. A sheepish look on her damaged face, she rarely smiled these days because she was aware the tiniest of mouth movement highlighted the scars around it.

She rarely raised her face to look people directly in the eye, far too conscious of her scars, but this morning she stood upright, found a strength she did not know she had anymore and looked straight at Kobe. She never once blamed him for what had happened to her, but Kobe had never stopped feeling the guilt and was sorry for leaving her in the situation where she was open to the threat of being attacked. Out of a sense of duty but also friendship and support for a fellow officer he, and his family, had been beside her throughout her recovery, and helped with both her physical and mental repairs. Some nights when she was too scared to go home to be on her own, she would sleep on the Kaan's couch, and his children were always delighted to see her in the morning. They never noticed her injuries or scars and she loved them for that. Now his family had gone, he realised she would be there for him.

"I thought you might need a coffee, something strong." she said.

It was then he noticed in her hand the cardboard cup with steam rising from its rim, and then he smelled what he assumed was a double espresso.

"Perfect," he said, "I think I will need that." There was no smile accompanying the remark.

Jemma placed the cup on the scarred tabletop and stood back, she wanted to hug her friend and boss but knew cameras would be watching her every action, nobody could blame her for taking him a coffee but any longer in the room and it would cause them both difficulties. So, she backed away to the door and as she slipped through, she said in a loud whisper...

"See you when you get out!" It was a throw-away line with a gentle smile that almost elicited one from Kobe as well.

"You shouldn't have come in Jemma, they could sack you for this." he warned, "But thank you for the coffee."

"Don't worry about me, the bosses still feel guilty about the lack of manpower available when I was..." she still could not say the words, nobody other than the victim will ever know how hard it is to say 'attacked' or 'raped' after the event, it made the victims relive the pain and shame of such an assault, physical wounds could heal easily, the mental ones never left them. "Anyway, they would never sack me, can you imagine the resulting tribunal, I would have a field day."

Despite his position and grief, he could not disguise the chuckle that caught in his throat.

"Thank you. For the coffee and the support." He tried once again and failed a smile.

"Your DS, David, said to tell you that he has everyone out listening for any words on the street about who may be responsible. Chasing up all their informants, or at least they will be when upstairs is not paying too much attention." Jemma explained. "The whole squad are out there asking questions, Boss, but they have all been warned off by the Deputy Chief Constable. Even at this early stage and before they have truly begun an investigation, they are worried about the bad press."

"That is about all the support I expected from upstairs, Jemma."

A noise from outside the interview room made her turn her

head. "Time I was going." And the civilian worker turned and walked out the door, just as the DCI Jones walked in and collided with her.

Jemma just brushed past him as she would a stranger in the street, leaving him muttering and full of bluster in her wake. Jones did not know whether to shout or not, and who would he shout at. Kobe saw that the incident had cost the officer in charge a touch of his cool exterior, but Jemma was right, there was not a lot they could do. Kobe just sat thinking and sipping the hot and strong coffee, it was a bitter taste, but he liked it. It needed to be strong and bitter to get through to his numbed senses.

Kobe had heard all the rumours regarding DCI Jones, his reputation was not a good one. Bad policing was something the rank-and-file copper disliked and distrusted, those working with 'Ghost' made sure that the bad reputation rumours spread quickly. He was one of those officers who was promoted out of jobs, according to HR rules there was no way to sack or demote someone who was merely incompetent, so department heads simply promoted him to his next posting, just to get them out of their own hair. Kobe did not like what he had heard about the man back then and he liked him even less now. To Kobe, at that moment, it did not matter if he was good at his job or not, he was the man keeping him from seeing and dealing with his family as his teachings told him to. Jones was one of those fast-tracked officers who joined the force straight from university, he may have been clever, but he had no street smarts, nor did he ever get much help from the rank and file beneath him, he never knew how to gain respect, he always demanded it. He achieved results with bullying tactics, not from respect from fellow police officers.

For most of the night he had been kicking his heels and sharpening his mental knives so as to carve huge holes in Kobe's story and now he was ready. He took the chair opposite Kobe and crashed a thick folder on the table as a means of intimidation, it did not work. The young Detective Constable, who was always at his hip, seemed reluctant to even enter the room but he eventually did with great hesitation and finally sat down next to his Boss in a very timid manner. While Jones was immaculately turned out in his fancy suit and polished shoes, DC Cross was rumpled in a cheap charcoal grey suit that had shine on the elbows and knees, and under the cold lights in the interview room showed flecks of dandruff on both shoulders. His short hair was greasy and if Kobe had been his normal alert self, he would have noted that the boy would do well to buy himself a nailbrush.

"What was she doing in here?" The assumption was that he meant Jemma Costello, and it was asked with a tone of voice that already carried a poor temperament on it.

DC Cross made his first notes.

"I asked you a question, Kaan..."

The door opened again, and it was the Fed Rep, Jordan-Reeves. "And you were told, DCI Jones, not to begin any questioning of Mr Kaan until I, and his solicitor, were here and had chance to talk to our client."

"We had to come in and begin as he had an unauthorised visitor in here, and..."

Jordan-Reeves interrupted the man. "And he had control over that, how? You should have had an officer on the door to stop any such visitors from just strolling in." He appeared to be enjoying himself a little too much, it was obvious he did not like the DCI either. "We are not off to a good start are we!" he continued. "Now if you wouldn't mind leaving the room while I talk to this Federation member and await his solicitor."

Jones bristled and his face reddened, "You do not come in here and tell me what to do..."

Again, he was interrupted as the door opened again, this was not turning out to be the promotion grabbing morning he thought it would be.

"He may not be able to tell you what you can and cannot do, but I can." It was Robert Berry QC, and he was very used to dealing with those who thought they could treat the rules as if they were something to be ignored when it suited. "Now fuck off will you and take your chum here with you! While I chat with my client." He said it quietly, but it sounded like a barked order and in his Eton-educated voice even the curse words sounded like a reasonable request.

Knowing they were beaten, they left the room, the DCI tried to do it with elegance but failed when he bumped into Cross. Jones slammed the door after he had passed through it, and it shook in its hinges as he was also told to ensure the cameras were off.

Berry sat next to Kaan on his side of the table and the Rep took a spare chair in the corner of the room, he was only there as a witness and support for Kobe Kaan and would take no part in proceedings.

"Good to see you again Mr Kaan, it's been a while." He held out his hand and Kobe shook it without enthusiasm. "May I call you Kobe when it is just us?" Kobe nodded. "And you are?" he turned and asked the quiet man in the corner.

"Sorry, yes, I am DI Kaan's Federation Rep, Peter Jordan-Reeves," He held his hand out but it was ignored, not out of rudeness but because of Berry getting his legal pad and paperwork in place on the old table, which was so old it still carried the scars of stubbed out cigarettes. Jordan-Reeves continued. "...and if its okay with you I would like to stay in the room."

"Pleasure, and I have no objections but please stay quiet, I have a great deal to get through. And client-solicitor privilege works for you as well. Fair?" The rep nodded his assent.

Robert Berry was not your normal Barrister, and he never was even before retirement. He had arrived after a three-hour drive from Weymouth and that followed only two hours sleep following his gig at a seaside pub. He slipped his leather jacket off and just dropped it on the floor behind him, underneath he wore a black shirt with sleeves rolled tightly to just above the elbows, on his right arm a tattoo of the tail of some big cat or other snaked down and around his arm. Beneath the desk he was wearing old jeans and cowboy boots.

Kobe had liked him when they first met, and he liked him now as he waited for his instructions. He did not want to talk at all, let alone reliving the previous twelve or so hours, had it been only last evening he had discovered his family? Time had no motion anymore, there was just a blur, a crippling, heart breaking long misty film filled with images. Being used to holding his emotions in check had helped him, but now he was under someone's care, someone he trusted. It was if at last he could relax and that was the moment his resolve broke, and the tears began to run. Sobs wracked his whole body, convulsions bent his back, pulled at his gut.

Jordan-Reeves stepped around the table, but Robert Berry grabbed his arm and nodded for him to sit down again, when he tried to say something, Berry just shook his head and gave the Rep a hard glare that almost turned him to ice. But he understood what Berry was doing, he was letting Kobe get it out of his system, they would not be able to speak to him while he was like this.

The door swung open again, and it was the two detectives.

"You've had more than enough time to speak with your client, we need to get this conversation underway."

Rob Berry was not impressed. "Firstly, I will let you know when I have had enough time with my client and secondly you can see DI Kaan is in no fit state to be interviewed." Casper Jones was about to interrupt. "And, don't bother interrupting me because I have not yet finished, I need the police medical officer called in as my client has obviously suffered a great trauma with the events of last night and, this is only my opinion of course, but I think questioning him about last night will only cause more damage to a man already made fragile by events. So, I want him examined by a suitable doctor before I allow him to be involved with any questioning."

"You cannot be..."

That was as far as he got with his argument before Jordan-Reeves repeated the statement on behalf of the Federation. It stopped Jones in his tracks, he was not used to being out of control but both men on Kobe's side of the table had vast experience in dealing with jumped up Uni-boys. Both men faced down the DCI and won the staring contest as the flustered detective gathered up his folders and stormed out of the room, once again. Not until the door closed, and the red light went out on the room's video camera did anyone speak.

Kobe had regained just enough composure to speak clearly.

"We are not going to get away with stalling for too much longer and I would like this to be done with and get out of here so I can see my family."

"It's not that straight forward Kobe, I can call you Kobe?" Kobe nodded. "I have spoken to the custody sergeant, who is an old friend of mine, and someone who has respect for one side of this table and not the other, and he tells me that Casper Jones has already decided that you are the guilty party in this. According to him they have forensic evidence to prove you killed your family and then that you tried to tamper with the crime scene before you called in about their deaths."

Kobe had no answer, so he gave none.

"This will be the hard part, Kobe." Robert put a hand on Kaan's forearm, offering a gentle form of solace and friendship and held it there until Kobe took a deep breath and steeled himself for the return journey to hell. "I need you to go through yesterday's activities, all of it..."

"Yesterday?" Kobe asked with a baffled expression.

"It's Monday morning Kobe, you have been here all night. Just take your time and recall to your best ability." A little reassurance was needed. "You have done this a million times before, just not from this side of the table. Just tell me what you think you would like to hear if you were doing the interviewing."

"How far back in the day?" Kobe asked, he was frightened of repeating any part of the day, the first part could break him. Remembering the last family breakfast, the promise of doing the school run tomorrow," He suddenly realised he should have been on the school run at that very moment. He could feel panic rising in his chest when he recalled the final kisses goodbye. The joy he felt with those kisses, and the strain with now knowing there would never be anymore kisses. Kobe and Rae had shared their final kiss at it was so brief and fleeting, in their young lives.

"Right from the start, we need to show your state of mind in the morning and through the day. It may be important." To show he was ready for business, he withdrew from his briefcase a Mont Blank fountain pen, he always loved to feel the glide of a real pen, he didn't own a ballpoint pen, he found them scratchy and lacking any form of style and it was too easy to record nothing but scrawl, with a real nib your writing flowed and therefore would always be legible. As a back-up he also pressed record on his mobile phone.

Kobe took a deep breath, closed his eyes for a second and began to picture himself arriving down in the kitchen from their bedroom, their desecrated haven, he walked around the table and put his arms around Rae... And so, the day's story began, and Kobe related every minute. From those magical kitchen kisses, right up to discovering the blood among the roses.

Never once did Robert Berry interrupt him, he let the story flow, and he speedily and correctly wrote down every word Kobe had uttered, a lifetime of experience taught him to write everything and write it at speed, no shorthand for him, he needed to see the words, all the words, it was his job to miss nothing, and he never did.

The door opened again; it was a busy doorway. Casper Jones, with a very frustrated look on his face demanded that the interview begin. Berry told him directly that he was not done yet. If truth be known he was done, but he wouldn't let the DCI know that he needed to control the interview room. Now red-faced with anger, Jones turned to make his exit, yet again...

"Just one thing, Chief Inspector." Berry stopped him mid-doorway. "My client has been here all night, he needs a coffee and something to eat," Kobe went to butt in, but Rob squeezed his arm again, stopping him. "A bacon sandwich should do fine; I know he likes them."

The Fed Rep, Jordan-Reeves, said he would love a coffee as well and Casper Jones swiftly closed the door behind him so as not to let this farce continue.

"Continue Kobe,"

As if there had not been any break in the narrative Kobe continued, he recalled as much as he could remember of the morning's raid and the only time the QC broke into his story was to go over the gun incident two more times. He thought it a vital part of the story as he realised the other side may make a big deal out of it, it would give them ammunition regarding Kobe's mental health for the rest of that day.

Again, the door swung open, this time with a gentle squeak of the hinges. It was Jemma with a tray of coffees and sandwiches. Robert Berry remembered her well and offered his best smile and despite where they were and what was happening, she smiled back. It was a shy smile because she was well-aware that the scars on her face puckered and lined around her mouth. Kobe looked up, and quietly thanked her. She noted the blank state of his stare, all emotion had gone from his face, which hurt her. She knew he blamed himself for what had happened at the hands of Jacob Tubb, but she never did, she should have been more aware of what was happening in that kitchen, that day, two years ago. Jemma was simply happy that Kobe had stood by her, made her part of his family, and helped her get the civilian job. Jemma Costello would not have survived the attack if it had not been for Kobe and Rae Kaan. She felt herself welling up as she thought of his wife and their children so she left the grey interview room quickly to find somewhere she could let her emotions out in private.

Finally, Robert Berry relented and let them begin the interviews, after a bathroom break of course, where they had cuffed Kobe for the walk of a few yards along the corridor. Although Kobe hated the thought of telling the story again, especially knowing that Casper Jones would be butting in whenever he felt a question would trip Kobe up, or literally allow him to hang himself. Berry would let the story flow again, the sooner the story was told the sooner that Kobe would be released.

And so it was that Kobe Kaan's latest ordeal began and would continue unabated for some three and a half hours with only one more bathroom break to ease the torture. Whenever Kobe struggled with a question or a part of his story, Robert would place a steadying hand on his arm. If there had been any outsiders watching the interview Kobe appeared to be the same tough, but fair, professional that he always seemed to be. But if they could look into his eyes, which normally blazed with passion for life, home, and his job, they would now see the coldness of a man that had lost all control of his senses, his life and his loves. A small part of him was dying with each minute and with every word. Harder than repeating the story though was the fact that he was being denied the opportunity to guide his wife and children through their last moments on this earth, he had a task to fulfil, the last task he would carry out for this family, and he could not do it from this interview room.

The interview continued with a relentless rhythm. Each repetitious question thrown at him with such great force demanded that he change his story. Each time Casper Jones stopped the storytelling to force Kobe off at a tangent, but this was getting harder each time the story was told as after the fourth or fifth time the tale sounded rehearsed. Kobe's heart grew heavier, his body tired, he had not slept since yesterday morning when he woke to head down to breakfast, that last, wonderful, funny, family breakfast.

Hate toward his interrogators was building with each passing moment, even DC Cross was in receipt of Kobe's loathing, and he had not uttered a word all morning, he just sat there on the opposite side of the table taking notes his back curved like a hunchback as he leant over writing. Beside his notepad were four pencils, two of them blunt with their tips now broken.

Jones was picking at every aspect of his and Rae's life, personal moments had to be shared, dissected, moments he should not have to share as they were private to Kobe and his wife. Jones even entered into the world of fantasy when he discovered that Rae Kaan had her own money, that she had been bequeathed a fair amount of money, the house was all paid for and it was in a desirable position and Jones admitted he would not be able to afford it, not even on a DCI's wages. Kaan was in line for a tidy little pay-out if he survived his wife.

At that moment even Berry had had enough, Casper Jones was reaching, stretching things to a new height without any scrap of evidence to take him there. The barrister watched his adversary carefully and he had aged visibly during the morning, his interview technique was poor, his ideas of what was and what wasn't evidence were weak, but every misstep would help his client in the end.

Off to one side of the table sat the Fed Rep, and he too was taking copious notes, jotting down anything that meant his Federation member was being, he wasn't sure of the word to use to describe what he was looking for... Railroaded came to mind and from that moment that's what he was seeking, signs that Kobe was being railroaded. He would not let that happen.

Kobe took a sip of water, it had warmed in the glass, but his mouth was dry, his tongue sticking to his lips. Also, by holding the glass in both hands in front of him formed a barrier between him and his inquisitors. Jones knew that was exactly what his prey was doing and so wanted to take the plastic glass away from him, to give him an edge in this interview. At that moment Jones seemed more dishevelled and tired than Kobe. His facial expression was jaded, a grey white under the interview room lights, his eyes were watery and looking dull, like a fish's eye after spending too much time on the fishmonger's slab. At one point Kobe realised he was looking at a comb-over as the sweat on his head and had caused the hairs to slip apart. Casper Jones was taking on the look of a caricature drawing of himself, while Cross sitting alongside him had even nodded off a couple of times with his head dropping and jerking back up again and each time it did it shook more dandruff onto his jacket shoulders. Kobe would never allow any of his officers to get in such a state during interviews, he would train them to take breaks and stay fresh and alert.

As Midday rang out from the Cathedral tower, everyone in the room was tiring and Kobe felt pangs of hunger as his stomach growled in complaint. But he desired no food, no drink and he thought that if he did take anything other than water he would vomit. Another question fired at him, another answer passed his lips, but now it was all robotic, his actions tired and slow, his words muffled and low.

The only person in the room who remained seemingly unruffled was Robert Berry, who was as fresh as the moment he had walked into the room, which was surprising seeing as he had travelled from his home in Hampshire to Weymouth, played a frantic gig of blues music before driving for around three hours to Chichester after an early morning start so he could protect a client, who had once been his adversary. The barrister had worked long and hard hours throughout his career so as to build up his stamina.

CHAPTER 31

Kenneth Jackman strode in and out of Chichester District Council Offices as if it were his own domain, the king entering his realm; as far as councils and local government go this was a small pond, but Jackman felt like a big fish in it. As with everything in life, for him it was all about things looking good. When Barbara his wife was younger, she was a real trophy wife, rich, elegant, and beautiful, with her on his arm he had arrived, and it made him feel good. Perception was everything with life lived in the public eye. Next year he would be Deputy Mayor, and he hated being on the second rung, but he had already ensured that nobody would vote against him for being Mayor the following year. He had sought out dirt on his fellow councillors so that he could make it to Mayor. With a little digging and a little detective work the current incumbent Deputy Mayor had been caught with his trousers well and truly down. Jackman had shown him photos taken in a Brighton massage parlour where he was being worked on by a pretty girl with big hands. When the culprit had enjoyed the ceremony of mayor-making next April Jackman would modestly accept the offer of being selected as his Deputy. Jackman was an impatient man so it would be frustrating to wait for Mayordom, but from there to County Councillor would be a breeze and on the next step toward a seat in the House of Commons. All he had to do was grease a few more wheels and he would rise from local businessman to national status. He had the money, thanks to his wealthy wife, and a few dodgy business deals. The vote in the chamber today was only about cutting repair funding for street lighting, but he was there to be heard, and people had better listen, or he would have to repay the substantial fee he had charged the county's main lighting contractor.

With his smart suits, his shiny car with its own driver and rugged good looks he gave off a distinguished air, the perfect politician for the modern era where everything was conducted in front of the media, and cameras loved him. He looked good all the way from Council chambers to building sites, which is exactly where he began his working life. He was willing to work his way to the top, but it was far easier to get the boss's daughter to fall in love with him, and it did no discourtesy to his dreams when he discovered that 'Daddy' was also a County Councillor. He quickly discovered he preferred a suit and tie to a trowel and hefty boots with steel toecaps, and it suited him.

His new wife Barbara was heartbroken when her father refused to go to the wedding, he had never approved of his daughter's rough choice of a suitor. Rough diamonds were okay, but not in his house, despite the fact he began as one himself. It was while the newlyweds were on honeymoon on the Italian Lakes that news came through of a building site accident that had killed her father, which she found strange as he never visited the sites anymore, he had people to do that. Barbara was intelligent but not thought to be business minded, and so it was Kenneth Jackman that took over her father's business, but mainly as a figurehead. Frightened of destroying her father's legacy, she did have reservations about her husband's business acumen, but surprising everyone he proved to be a good at the job and quickly took the building firm to bigger and greater things. It had always annoyed Jackman that although it was his hard work, and penchant for making deals through violence and intimidation, which made the company grow, it was still her money. She still sat at the head of the board and held the strings to the business purse. He knew that she knew that he would never walk away from this lifestyle, and she always pulled the strings. It suited her, and the tough building trade, to have a man at the helm, but it was Barbara that ran the ship, she was her father's daughter.

He grew a persona to match his life, dressed sharply, kept his salt and pepper hair to just the right length and waviness and travelled in expensive cars, always driven by his 'assistant'. Barbara never liked his 'assistant', or his fashionably long hair, often asking him to get it cut, but he liked what he called his 'poet's hair' which he thought made him a dashing figure. As for the assistant and driver, well after Barbara had checked her out and discovered she was committed to the lesbian cause she let that matter drop, she would only accept a fight when it was a fight worth winning.

Jackman thought his look was ministerial and that was where his naked ambition would be taking him, then he would divorce his harpy of a wife and find someone suitable for a Member of Parliament. He had always been a dreamer which is why his wife always kept a tight rein on him and her money. Good looks, charm and personality were what would take him to the top, and if that failed, well violence would always move barricades to success. To the outside world he gave the impression of a serious man doing serious business, whether that be for his company or his constituents. Life, however, was a game to him, played by his rules and with roguish charm. Crisp, white shirts showed off his perma-tan, and matched his bleached-teeth smile. In public life he was an honest man, happily married with a strong moral compass, except the needle never stopped spinning. He started life the middle child of a poor family and he quickly became the toughest kid in the playground and as one of his council opponents had said, 'the bastard took no prisoners', he was still the toughest kid in the playground, and proud of it!

Mud had been slung at him in the past, the local paper seemingly made it their life's work to drag him down, but several threatened court battles had always got the paper to back down and retract.

Leaving the council building, after being the cause of an increased budget for lighting repairs, he stood tall and carried a huge smile. It was a small but busy family run electric firm that had always kept the streetlights burning, it was their most profitable contract. With the revised budget it would take them just a year or so to recoup the £50,000 fee paid to Jackman. Strutting from the building with a smug smile on his face he reached another love in his life, his prized Jaguar, and his driver Fiona was stood beside the gleaming bodywork holding the door open for him.

"Where to Councillor?" Her voice soft, the accent a hard East End of London, she made it sound both seductive and threatening at the same time.

"I need some company Fi," he was the only one who ever got away with that, she would always prefer Fiona. But working for the Councillor had its advantages so she put up with it.

She closed his door, which shut with a pleasing and soft whump of a sound. "Not home then I am guessing?" She asked, knowing the answer.

Pulling away from the town centre he knew heads would turn toward the car, people wandering who the chauffeur driven celebrity was, and Jackman looking out through the smoked glass windows at his adoring fans loved the feeling. Fiona Webb strutted around to the driver's door, her long, blonde ponytail flicking from side to side, and she slipped into the driver's seat. She was slender, long legged, and pretty. Striking electric blue eyes made her look stunning but a second glance and admirers would see the two-inch-long scar above her left eyebrow which she carried like a badge of honour, especially as the man who had cut her lost his left eye in retaliation. In work mode she always dressed in sleek black suit, a white linen open-necked shirt underneath and this was set-off at the end of her gazelle type legs with a pair of electric blue Christian Louboutin heels, distinguishable by their famous scarlet red undersides. Apart from the violence she meted out on others, shoes were her greatest joy. The stylish heels made her appear much taller than her five feet eight inches, in those shoes she towered over her boss, it bothered him but not her. She revelled in other's discomfort.

Fiona had been recommended by a friend who was retiring to Spain to hide his considerable criminal assets, Kenneth would miss him and his tales of derring-do against the legal establishment. Jackman looked up to him as a sort of Robin Hood, the benevolent outlaw. In truth he almost made the infamous Krays look like misunderstood nice guys.

Jackman had agreed to meet the girl as from the description he had been given it would be nice to have someone attractive to drive him around, and the fact she was a devout lesbian would mean his wife, Barbara, would have no objections. If he had bothered to ask his wife, he would have discovered she was beyond caring one way or the other. Another part of Fiona's CV had intrigued the Councillor, he had been warned of her penchant for being a fighter, and one who never came off second best. Her physical description went totally against the character flaws. China white, porcelain skin, cheekbones that were sharp, and defined her facial features. On meeting her Jackman almost lost all composure, she was stunning and just what he found attractive with her small, pointed breasts and long slender legs. It took him a while to figure out, but one other thing attracted him to her, he was afraid of her, and not many could cause fear in the Councillor.

She had been the Councillor's driver and minder for two years now and they had a great working relationship. For her driving skills and just being his right-hand person, he paid her well, but each time she went beyond the law for him he purchased her a new pair of shoes, mostly Louboutin but also whichever fashion house launched a new range, the shoes were expensive, but she was worth it and anyway, his accountant had found a way to add them to legitimate expenses.

Most people would underestimate both her power and her talents, they would not do that twice. Despite her exotic Eastern eyes, an English rose in appearance but she carried the pointed barb of a thorn.

Today she was in her favourite 'uniform,' crisp white blouse, open at the neck and showing, if any man had dared glimpse, just a hint of red lacy bra. She looked more sexy office worker than minder. High-waist black trousers were sharp with a crease from beltline to shining, black stilettos, towering heels that appeared sharper than a fencer's epee. When she agreed to work for him Jackman always thought with his charm and rugged good looks, he would be able to cure her and get her to swap sides with her gender preference. Fiona was tougher than him, carried more confidence; Jackman preferred his women a little more subservient, he wanted his women to be obeying in the bedroom and stunning when out. For her part she had become fiercely protective of her boss, he may have been a misogynous pig, but he gave her the opportunity to release her sadistic side and she loved him for that. Her eyes may have sparkled, and she may have the facial features and carriage of a model, but at times those brown, almond shaped eyes held nothing but a cold, malevolent stare. They never went a degree above freezing when she was working.

The car glided silently down the road from the council chambers toward the Cathedral and sitting in the back Jackman, with a puffed-up ego felt an almost childish joy of being driven around by an attractive chauffeur. He checked his fob watch, slipping it from his waistcoat and flipping the gold lid where it revealed the exact time with its elegant and slim hands, it kept perfect time and was still beautiful to look at. The 9-carat gold Waltham Hunter gleamed in his hand and was as perfect as the day it was when first wound into life in 1920. It showed a few minutes before 4pm and he was not due home to his wife for at least another four or five hours, so plenty of time for relaxation.

In the driver's seat Fiona knew where he was heading and hit the speed dial button on the car's phone app, which was linked to her own mobile number, not her boss's. It rang just the once before being picked up as if the girl at the other end was waiting with hand hovering over her mobile.

A soft voice made for seduction answered with a simple, "Hello Fiona."

"We are on our way." And Fiona cut the call, curt and to the point.

The Councillor reclined in the back of the luxury car and let a broad smile crease his face, he was longing to relieve the itch in his groin. As a councillor he had been voted in by the public on an election mantra that had strong moral agenda, and he marvelled at the voter's gullibility.

The car radio was on in the background, Jackman liked keeping up with local news to find causes to fight, poor people to help and soundbites to make for the next bulletin, every little thing he could find to boost his popularity amidst folk who didn't know what a vulture he was picking at the carcass of people's rotten lives. The newsreader chattered on about this story and that and like a speed-reader with text Jackman grazed on snippets especially when it came to the Government cocking up yet another thing, things would be different when he got to parliament. His ears pricked up for the 'and finally' story, a mainstay of regional commercial stations and usually about a local, the newsreader playing the part of a village gossip. A little light news handed out to leave the listeners cheerful and hopeful.

"Finally, a Hampshire man almost won his own lottery this weekend," the voice finally upbeat. "Portsmouth man and retired road sweeper, Jason Benny, appeared on the latest edition of Antiques Roadshow with a beautiful bronze statuette of a Roman soldier. Sadly, for Jason the expert decided it was a copy, a particularly good copy but a copy none the less. Mr Benny was happy when he was told it was still worth between four and five hundred pounds, but had it been authentic it was estimated to be in the millions..."

The 'out' from the smooth-talking reader was ignored by driver and passenger. The Councillor smiling as the story had told of what he already knew, and Fiona his driver was checking the interior mirror as she felt a reaction from behind her.

"Fiona," he asked in a tone like a child asking for an obvious favour of a parent. "I need you to find the address of that unlucky chap in Portsmouth for me, and we need to make an appointment to go visit Mr Benny and his bronze Roman."

Fiona knew when her employer had a money-making scheme in his head, and she smiled as she felt the chance for action coming on and it would be the sort of action that was her idea of fun. Mentally she had already selected her new shoes.

Meanwhile in the back seat, the wily Councillor was thinking long, hard and fast. He had a severe cash flow problem, and he was worried that word may get out and the knowledge become weapons for his enemies, in the past couple of weeks two of his very profitable business ventures had taken a big hit. More worrying about the news of his lack of cash was the people he did business with, and they were not patient men when it came to settling debts. These debts were substantial. Barbara, his wife, had closed her purse a long time ago and she no longer backed his shady deals. On that Monday evening his brain took a more positive route, and he knew that the future looked good, he could rebuild the businesses, pay his debts, and get his reputation back. Maybe even get rid of that tight bitch of a wife and her knotted purse strings.

He thought back to the morning's press call with that funny little junk shop owner and his belief he had the real bronze.

Wealth and his redemption were coming together nicely.

CHAPTER 32

Night slid into day, with no thought for those working and suffering through it all. The morning sun had moved on past the back of the police station and the only external light entering the interview room was dull and shadow free. Kobe Kaan's interview had passed the three-hour mark, although the time in that room had blurred into one set of differently worded questions to the next. The only thing that time meant to Kobe was that all the time he was in here, he was not out there searching for the people responsible for destroying his family.

He had been permitted a brief bathroom break and could do with another, he also wanted a decent cup of coffee, even in his jaded state his taste buds knew the difference between a good coffee and the stale tasting station, bitter brew.

Each time he walked to the toilets he had to pass fellow officers, colleagues he had worked with, commanded, and befriended. Now they all looked to him as if strangers. Looks of concern for their boss and colleague mingled with the fear of, '*had he done it?*' Every experienced officer knew that sometimes, just sometimes, it was the least likely suspect who was the perpetrator. Kobe just hung his head and gazed at the floor, unwilling to see the pity or accusations pointed at him.

To the uninformed viewer Kobe appeared the same tough, unbending professional he had always been. He always thought he had a good understanding of how the families of murder victims felt when informed of their loss, and he was careful when forming his questions to glean the information he needed in his investigation without extending the hurt too much. He knew how far to push to get the truth, but when to hold back from causing more trauma. In that stark interview room, with Casper pushing every button he could find, Kobe realised he absolutely had no idea how they felt, you had to walk hand in hand with grief and loss before coming even close to any sort of understanding.

The DCI that sat the other side of the table had no idea about empathy, it was word not in any of his useless university degrees that got him his job and rapid promotion. He fired questions relentlessly, often forgetting to give Kobe time to answer, he liked the sound of his own voice far too much. A good interviewer knew when to stay silent, giving room for their subject to talk themselves into trouble. Kaan had tried to be helpful during his own endless interview, his brain was filled with all the answers, but he was unable to bring them to the front because of all the noises in his head. Helpful and compliant with the interrogation would be the fastest way out of the grey room and onto the street. He needed to talk to his DS to find out what he knew, he vaguely recalled Stella Gold standing next to David when he was frogmarched out of his house, she could be useful if that was the case. They seemed closer than just colleagues, or it could be he had just imagined it, they were an unlikely couple, but somewhere at the back of his thoughts was that he was pleased for them. More now than ever he believed everyone should have another someone in their lives.

With its relentless rhythm the interview continued. Each repeated question and accusation were thrown at him with varying degrees of verbal force, there was no subtleness in the probing. Casper Jones just fired away, believing his quick-fire style of interview would trip up Kobe Kaan. All he wanted was one slip of the tongue, one contradiction from earlier answers, and he would happily charge Kaan with the multiple killings. It would be onward and upward for Casper Jones, and his belief in his own infallibility would be given a huge boost. Kobe's Fed-Rep and his barrister were also running short of patience and as for the lowly DC taking notes, had no idea what was going on. To him it was like a film plot unravelling on the screen where the storyline had yet to reveal itself.

Jones demanded that Kobe should change his story. He believed his subject was just one step away from revealing himself to be the killer. Jones had him where he wanted him, at the end of the noose, and continued to try and trip him up with his answers. Jones was convinced Kaan's responses were all total fabrication. Casper Jones had his man, and he did not intend to let him get away, there was no need to waste resources on looking for anyone else. There was always a great deal of pressure on the SIOs to get a result, he always liked the sound of that, Senior Investigating Officer, and it was their job to identify the perpetrator as swiftly as possible. Domestic Homicide was a despicable crime, a crime where the trusted spouse was always the guilty one. Jones' bosses would be congratulating him for years to come on his ability to crack crimes swiftly and make the force look good with the press.

Jones had read the book, and he knew that Domestic Confrontation murders accounted for more than half of all homicides and it was typically the current or divorced spouse and almost always the male of the family who was the guilty party, the wife being the victim. Vicious offences such as the one he was investigating now, were usually conducted in the family home and feature a weapon of some kind that could be found in every kitchen drawer.

Kobe Kaan ticked all the relevant boxes for Jones.

Casper Jones knew who his man was, and he was sitting right in front of him.

Each time Kobe spoke of his tragic discovery the evening before, was it only 18 hours ago, so his heart grew heavier, his mood grew blacker, thoughts grew darker. He had lost count of the number of times he had told the story, each time Jones wanting it told from an unfamiliar perspective, and he pushed and harried Kobe. Each time he did then Robert Berry would interrupt and push back at Jones a little, each time he would ask for evidence, or let his client go so he could deal with his family.

Kobe realised that the DCI's plan was to make him angry, make him snap and show his true violent self, but Kobe knew exactly what was happening and he fought to keep emotions in check. It would do him no good to become enraged now, and in this room. He kept his anger bottled-up and directed toward the real killer. Inside he was seething with rage, but to outward appearances he was in his normal and controlled manner. He hated his accusers, they appeared like a comedy duo from a long-ago black and white Hollywood movie, one big and blustering the other small and nervous, he was being interviewed by Laurel and Hardy and these two on the other side of the table seemed to have the same amount of onscreen clumsiness and ineptitude as the old comedy duo.

Kobe knew plenty of good officers and he wished that it should have been one of them interviewing him, and as he had that thought there was a light rapping on the door, and it was pushed ajar. He did not care what the interruption was, it would give him a few minutes respite and a chance to have another chat with his Barrister.

Jones noted the interruption for PACE, checked the time and paused the machine before taking the few steps to the door, he was not amused by the incursion into his interview. He had been following the

'PEACE' way of working an interview, Planning and Preparation, Engage and Explain, Account with clarification and confrontation – Jones thought himself to be brilliant at that part – and finally, Closure – which he would reach soon – and then all that was left to do was Evaluation and his own self-centred memory of events so far was that he had carried out excellent work.

After mutterings beyond the door Jones stepped back in and suggested a short break, nobody objected. Kobe took the time to look his accuser, eye to eye, as he peered around the door, he saw Jones was a man worn down with workload, tired eyes with the dark skin beneath them swollen bags. It looked as if it had been him put through the ringer rather than Kobe. He hoped he looked fresher. He asked for a glass of water, sipped at it, and asked Robert Berry to find out when he could go and see his family. Berry, with a face soft and impassive, told him to be patient a little longer and he would be out of that room. His Fed-Rep, who could take no active part in the proceedings remained sitting, a bored look on his face but he asked if Kobe required any food. He received a simple 'no, thank you.'

When Jones re-entered the room, he saw Kaan slumped in his plastic chair appearing crumpled and beaten, shoulders were round, chin was on his chest and his eyes glazed over. And if Kobe were asked to describe his mood it would have been just that, down, out and beaten. They now saw something different in Jones, despite his tiredness of a few moments before he now seemed as if he were refreshed and brighter, Jones suddenly had a splash of vigour about him, he was like a marathon runner who had broken through the pain barrier. Both men knew that could mean only one thing, Jones had something he felt he could use against Kobe Kaan.

CHAPTER 33

Jason Benny sat in his scruffy front room that smelled of stale cigarette smoke, in the ashtray beside him a skinny plume of smoke rose into the air, twisting upward from a previous roll-up that he had not stubbed out properly, the dog end still with a faint glow of red at its crushed tip. Jason, a lifelong chain-smoker wheezed heavily as he sucked on a new slim ciggie which he was busy lighting. Success on the third inhalation and its smoke joined its compatriot rising to the nicotine-stained brown ceiling. He coughed and a lump of phlegm hacked from his throat, but, disgustingly, he swallowed it back down.

Even though it had just been lit, he attempted to knock ash from the rollup's tip in a nervous, automatic tap with the brown stained tip of his index finger, a small red ember missed the full ashtray and burnt yet another dark hole in the arm of his old and battered armchair. Apart from a couple of rickety dining room chairs it was the only seating in the room, not that he ever had visitors to sit on them, but you never know when somebody might drop by, and it was only polite for them to have somewhere to sit.

On the only table in the room, a black melamine topped coffee table from somewhere back in the seventies, sat his chunk of a TV. It was not modern, but it had a decent enough picture, and if it ever went wrong, it would probably just remain in situ, it was far too heavy for Jason to lift. The video tape he was watching stopped as it came to an end, he simply leaned forward and hit the rewind button to take the taped recording back to start, and he would watch his minute and a half of stardom on that antique show all over again, for the fifth or sixth time that afternoon, there was nothing else to watch because none of his quiz shows were on that afternoon. He wished his old Mum were still here to watch, then she might finally be proud of him. The only time he had been on TV in the past left her ashamed and not proud at all, the news report about him being in court for exposing himself near the school gates was the final straw and she had kicked him out of the house. If she had not died of a heart attack less than a week later, he might still be homeless.

His statuette was a fake and it had cost all the money he had left from his benefits, £8, that he could have spent on more tobacco, but he wanted that statue. It just meant he would have to roll thinner cigarettes for the rest of the week. But that expert had said that it was worth a few thousand even if it were a fake, what he did not say was who would pay him that much for the bloody thing. He could get one of those new thin televisions that he had seen advertised at the supermarket with that sort of money as well as one of those satellite dish things to connect it too. That Eric Knowles, 'Eric no-alls' more like, took away his fortune even before he had got it. He had bought it because he liked it, but the more he watched the Roadshow, the more he hoped it would be valuable and then when he heard the popular TV show was coming to the stately home nearby, well it was too good a chance to miss, and it was fucking heavy so had to be worth something. He had nearly said the 'F' word on screen but stopped himself before it popped out, his mother would not have liked that especially on a Sunday evening.

He gazed across at the Centurion, still holding that sword in the air, and still shining on his bookshelf and wondered where and when he could sell it, the sooner it was sold the sooner he could buy real cigarettes and a new TV. As a final thought before he hit the 'play' button again, he promised himself to go to one of those pub carveries and have himself a Sunday roast, it was years since he had eaten one of those and he did love a Yorkshire pudding.

With the low valuation any recent dreams of moving from this shithole he called home had now been put on permanent hold, it did no good to dwell on such things and he never did. Initially he had been hurt when the truth about the Centurion unfolded during filming, when they kept going off and checking with other experts, he thought he had hit the jackpot, more like a piss pot, when they finally told him. Didn't even warn him, just starting the camera rolling and let the world watch his disappointment. Bastards!

Benny briefly thought of his rent arrears, then rejected them as he had more important things to buy. He had lived in the tiny two-up-two-down for all his life, it was all he knew. Nowadays the small rooms were strangling him, it was claustrophobic living there. If they threw him out for rent arrears, then the council would have to rehouse him, it was the law, and anywhere was better than here. He could start all over again, maybe buy a new chair. Jason had already spent far more than he would get for the bronze, even if he could find out where to sell it. Hopes and dreams, that is what they gave you on television, then just when you started to believe them all those hopes would be dashed. Did these posh twats on television know they were messing with people's lives, just in the name of good ratings.

His hand, without thought, delicately brushed his ever-thinning strands of hair back into line with the rest of his greasy comb over, then he dried his hand by rubbing it down the side of his trouser leg. Only 42, and he was already balding, overweight and with features aging way too fast, apart from the one on the bathroom cabinet he had removed every mirror and reflecting picture frame from his house, what the eyes could not see the mind did not fret over. Out of habit, as his roll-up was so short it began to burn his tobacco-stained fingers, he would stub it out and light the next. The skin of his face was sallow and creased from years of damage from the toxic smoke, he coughed another wheezy, chesty bark. Time for another cigarette, and he had trouble rolling it because of his stubby fingers, it would not roll as tight as he would like but it would still be smokeable. The craving was getting stronger with every second he went without inhaling and he hurriedly flicked the flame onto the lighter and drew breath. Smoke went deep into his lungs as he inhaled strongly and it pulled a cough out of him that ripped at his throat, but he knew a second drag would ease the pressure, and it did.

His doorbell rang! His doorbell never rang. Jason Benny had no friends, no callers, no one came to visit. He had only just had a caller from the council about his rent arrears, so he was not in fear of opening the door for that reason. He took a long puff on his latest cigarette so as to last him until he got back from answering the door and laid the thin stick on the full ashtray and pulled himself up out of the depths of the chair, there was a layer of floating smoke just above his head, hanging there like low cloud. He thought of peering out of the window, but the garden was far too overgrown to see anyone on his front pathway. It would not be thieves, he had nothing to steal, apart from his Centurion and he had no intention of inviting anyone into his lounge to see it shining amidst the dimness. The stranger that was his doorbell rang again, the chime echoing down the narrow hallway. If it were a Jehovah's Witness asking him if he wanted to be saved, he would just tell them to *'fuck off,'* like he always did, that would stop them coming around for a few months.

He hoisted his trousers up over his overhanging gut, and brushed ash from his shirt front. He did not want to let himself down on the looks department, even if he did not know the caller, and he was sure he didn't. The lino floorcovering through his thin socks, a big toe poking through the left one. Whoever was out there he hoped they would not keep him long. He turned the latch and pulled the door open and was surprised to see a very well-dressed man, with an equally smartly turned-out woman behind him, and she looked young and pretty, even if she was foreign looking with her slanty eyes!

"Mr Benny?" The voice was as smooth as the owner. Benny just nodded and wondered what he was selling, whatever it was he couldn't afford it, just yet. "May I call you Jason?" Without invite the man just brushed past him and into the hallway, it was as if he did not want to be seen on the doorstep of the rundown house.

There was no offered handshake from the man, or the girl who followed on his heels. Bloody rude, Jason thought.

"In here, is it?" And the man was through the door and in the lounge, just as on the TV, Jason was about to be given the valuation on the Roadshow all over again, except the well-worn tape juddered and froze just as his face filled the screen.

"Fuck it!" Jason exclaimed, blaming the two interlopers for this latest disaster. He rushed to the machine and hit the 'eject' button, the cassette bounced out and the unravelling tape followed it.

As Jason followed the smart dressed man and his woman into the lounge he turned round and was nearly blinded by the whitest smile he had ever seen, the teeth were bleached a shiny white that did not seem natural. Grey-streaked hair was swept back in flowing locks, whoever this man was he was the exact opposite of Jason who tried not to reply to the smile because what few teeth he did have left were all brown and angled. He had only just opened the door and already there was this smart man with impeccable looks and manners standing in front of the open coal fire which was dwindling in the hearth. His girlfriend, or whatever she was, looked as if she were about to plonk herself down onto one of the dining chairs, but then thought better of it. Jason was disappointed even though she was wearing trousers, he would have liked to watch her as she elegantly crossed her slender legs, even in her crisply creased black trousers he could tell her lower limbs were long and slim. Her blonde ponytail was pulled back tightly and yet the skin on her face was not stretched, her face was flawless, her eyes the brightest things in the room, even brighter than his Centurion. He liked elegant legs and elegant hands, he visited a massage parlour many years ago, when he could afford it, and the massage therapist was tall and sexy in her white coat. Watching her work on him, with the longest fingers he had ever seen, was an image that he had kept in his mind for years, and he watched mesmerised as those long fingers wrapped around his tiny cock and stroked him close to an orgasm, which hurt because he felt so hard. She had then used just the talon-like scarlet, polished, nail tips to drag up the shaft, and he had cum in no time at all. He felt cheated of the forty pounds he paid but these many years on he still fantasised about those long slender fingers with dagger-like tips. With his attention now back in his grubby lounge he was disappointed this time to note that this girl wore gloves, which he found strange as it was such a warm day out.

Jason slumped back into this chair, almost knocking the ashtray from the arm, just catching it before it spilled out the contents. He looked up at the man by the fire, his face impassive, then he looked across into the girl's face and all he could see there was disgust.

Trying to show a little bravado, Jason asked. "What's your name and how can I help you?" A deep breath, which forced out a small cough. "You can't be police because you would have to have a warrant or something and show me your identity card or badge or something."

"How rude of me." Jackman said, "I am Councillor Kenneth Jackman." It was stated with confidence, like it meant something.

Jason Benny knew it, he guessed, they were from the bloody council. "I had a visit from you buggers just a few weeks ago, I said that when my benefits come in, I would catch up with my rent. So, what are you doing here? You should not harass people like this, I got depression you know!"

"Oh, I am not your local Councillor far from it and any rents owing are not from my department."

The suit still had not offered a handshake as a greeting, surely Councillors were supposed to do that sort of thing. "I thought you had to give handshakes and stuff when you introduce yourselves." He tried so sound more miffed than he was, Jason did not want them to think they ruled the roost in his own house.

"Since the Covid thing Mr Benny, we have been advised to keep personal contact to a minimum, just to protect you, you understand."

"In that case shouldn't you both be wearing masks, or something!"

Benny was becoming tiresome, and Jackman had no time for tiresome people, in fact they were a nuisance. It was the downside of being in politics, he thought, having to put up with fucking morons once an MP he at least would be able to keep them on the other side of a table during necessary clinics.

He looked across at Fiona, wanting to move things along but also to get this man onside. "Make us some tea would you Ms Webb, so Jason and I can have a chat."

"You didn't employ me to make tea." She replied in a huff, but Fiona walked out to find the kitchen anyway. It was more of a hovel than even she had imagined, quickly finding the tea bags, and feeling as if she should have worn plastic gloves instead of her fine leather pair, which she also had in brown and red for different outfits. The smell of rotting food that pervaded through the kitchen almost made her gag, but the thought of a new pair of shoes for her collection overcame her nausea.

"What was your name again?" He was being a belligerent bastard and Jackman was starting to lose his cool, he did not suffer fools at all. "Aint, you suppose to give me at least a business card or something or show some ID." Jason pressed.

Jackman bit his tongue, this ordeal would soon be over, and he would leave the greasy little weasel and his dirty little house, Benny looked lost on his little island of a battered armchair that in turn was stranded on a threadbare beach of carpet. He felt small and insignificant even though verbally he thought he stuck up for himself quite well.

"How rude of me." Jackman thought of giving a false name, but then didn't bother, nobody would ever know they had been there despite the 'posh' Jaguar sitting out there on the kerbside in the rundown council estate. The residents would only remember a shiny car, not the registration plate. Like magpies they were, attracted to shiny stuff. "I am Deputy Mayor Kenneth Jackman." His self-imposed promotion should impress the greasy little man.

Business was about to begin, as Fiona walked into the room carrying two mugs of tea, both in chipped mugs with the Arsenal badge on them. For no other reason than to make Jason think they were friends of his Fiona asked,

"An Arsenal fan, are we?" Such was her distaste of talking to such a weasel, that the simple query sounded as if it were barked.

The response was terse and to the point, "Fuck off, don't even like football, they were cheap in the charity shop."

She placed one mug on the ash covered side table next to Benny's chair and the other on a dusty mantle shelf behind Jackman, knowing all too well he would not even touch the mug, in fact Jackman still had not taken his hands out of his pockets, he had no intention of touching anything in the house, not even the delightful Mr Benny.

"As much as I like to chatter, let's get straight down to business shall we Jason."

Jackman wanted to sound benign, but his voice emerged as an order to a recalcitrant dog. "I am very interested in purchasing your bronze Roman..."

"It's a Centurion, and I don't think that even you could afford him, so he is not for sale."

That struck a barb into the Councillor's psyche, if truth be known he could not afford to buy the statuette, he was out of funds for the moment after taking the last £300 from his account at a cashpoint, it left a measly £7.45 in the black. Jackman wondered for one more time why he was bothering with this charade, but it was the easiest option to just purchase the thing and leave as quickly as he had arrived.

In full intimidation mode he moved a step closer to Benny and towered over the seated man, smoke rose from an unextinguished cigarette end and invaded his nostrils, he could not decide which was worse, the body odour of the disgusting man or that of the stale tobacco. Jason took a closer look at the bullying man's clothes, he had never seen such a sharp, crease-free, dark blue suit, the trousers pressed to a knife's edge. Red socks showing between the trouser cuff and the highly polished Oxford brogues. Jackman brushed the back of his hand across the jacket lapel to brush off a flake of ash that had floated onto him.

"Your recent appearance on television fascinated me, you looked very smart on the Roadshow by the way..." he did not wait for a reply to the hard spoken compliment. "I saw the disappointment in your face, we all felt it, even in our own homes." He looked across at Fiona to ensure his statement was being supported, she nodded and agreed with her boss. "So, I would like to ease your disappointment by purchasing your... Centurion. I have £250 in my wallet right now and I can add your bronze to my own little collection. Despite my looks I am not a wealthy man, Fiona and the car are what the council supply me with, and the suit is a ready-to-wear job from Marks and Spencer, up market I know but I do need a smart suit for my work. I think what I am offering is a fair price for, what is after all, a fake statue." He had offered the low bid to leave room for negotiation, but he was not able to go much higher anyway.

"Why would you want to buy it knowing its a fake then?" he had a point, but Jackman had already thought that through.

"I collect small bronze figures, a hobby if you like and like I said, I am not a wealthy man, but I do love statues, especially bronzes."

Emboldened by the admission that the posh bloke was not that rich, Benny blurted out his starting offer. "Three grand and its yours, that bloke on the Roadshow said it was worth a few grand even if it was a fake, it was a good one, he said." The rotund man tried to relax wrapped in his old armchair and confronted by his two aggressive visitors, it felt good bargaining and although he felt he could get more elsewhere, his greedy mind thought three grand in the pocket was three grand he didn't have.

Jackman's patience was gone, just like his money. He knew that there was no point offering the last fifty pounds in his pocket or anywhere else for that matter. He looked around at Fiona and shrugged, the nod was enough for her. She knew the contract on the disgusting man was offered and she gladly accepted with a simple nod, she would soon be going on-line for more shoes. Even more though she was delighted to be closing off the gene pool to this kind of inbred scum.

Jason, believing himself to be in a good bargaining position, readied himself to be the tough negotiator and the Councillor may not be rich but the fancy bugger had more than the measly amount he was offering and the Council didn't just let every tom-dick-and-councillor take the firm's car and driver on a jolly.

He was not expecting the outburst that came next, surely Deputy Mayors were not supposed to speak like that.

"I made you a fair offer, you fat, disgusting, little man! And you throw it in my face." Jackman showed a little more of his true self when he just spat in Jason's face, globules of phlegm dribbled down his forehead and onto his nose. Even Fiona was a little shocked by that unexpected move, she knew her boss was an evil bastard, but not that base and nasty that he outdid her own brand of evil.

The mood in the room had plummeted and it seemed to Benny that the temperature had as well, he felt fear, a bladder loosening fear and clenched to avoid pissing himself. Jackman stood up straight, moved back from the disgusting mess in the chair and reached out snatched the Centurion straight off the shelf. Despite the dullness of the room, light reflected gold off the sword's blade.

"You grubby little fuck of a man, who do you think you are dealing with! I have scraped better things than you off my shoes. Take care of this little shit will you Fiona." Jackman's face was red with rage, Fiona half expected blood vessels to burst, the muscles in his neck were strained.

Benny felt, in the coldness of the room, a warm glow spread across his lap and down his thighs. Despite the smell of piss, the petite and pretty woman was walking toward him as Jackman left the room with his Centurion.

"You can't just take him you thievin' bastard. I will have the police on you, you just wait and see." It was an idle threat, Jason already realising this was not going to end well for him.

Benny tried to rise with a little elegance from the deep chair, but that was not easy to do when you were pissing yourself, he also realised he was now crying. He wanted to beg, but he was not sure what for. What could she do to him?

The pretty woman in the dark clothes and the shiny shoes moved like a dancer, lithesome, or like an elegant and sinewy snake until she stood just two feet away from him and he waited, for what he had no idea, but it scared him. Would it be a fist or a slap from those long and slender gloved hands. He noted the coldness in her dark eyes, he wanted to say he would accept the £250 offered, but he could not get any words out, he could hardly breath he was so scared. He wished he had rolled another cigarette.

In his eyes it was like a Hollywood thriller where the action moved to slow-motion mode. She swivelled slightly on one of those dagger-like shoes, he thought she may be turning to leave just like her boss had just done. Instead, her right leg tucked up against her standing leg, coiled and powerful and Benny saw the pristine red soles, which he strangely thought was a good match with her rich-red lipstick. Her slender body leaned in the opposite direction, the perfect counterweight. Then he noticed the long, pointed heel, its tip pointed toward him like a fencer's sword. It was the last thing he recalled seeing before the right foot shoot forward, a cobra striking. Its target the size of a clenched fist. The strike hit Benny's chest just to the right of his breastbone and entering between the 7th and 8th rib, the aim was unerring, the force unstoppable. The shoe designer to the stars had never forged his shoes to be weapons, except ones of seduction. The long heel of the Louboutin shoe was a perfect dagger and thrust rapidly forward between the two ribs and pierced deep into the fat man's heart. The whiplash like strike caused his heart to stop and so ending the life of Jason Benny. He never felt a thing. Fiona's leg recoiled and she held the pose for a few seconds, in much the same way as a golfer holds the pose at the top of his swing to enjoy that moment of pride after hitting the perfect shot. She smiled at the perfection of her position and the purity of her strike. To her the hit had been a thing of beauty, elegant, powerful and, most of all, deadly! She was having fun wiping out another disgusting man and lent back again, perfectly balanced. Benny was staring, his brain confused and still not catching up about his lack of life, the foot shot forward once more, this time the heel penetrated the left eye and Fiona was certain she heard a squelching sound as she reversed her foot's direction before standing and admiring her work with the two quick thrusts.

Two mugs of tea, now cold, remained where Fiona had put them but there was no forensic evidence with which they could lead back to her or her boss, they were both careful that way. Alongside Benny's mug on the chairside table was a Zippo lighter, and with one last job in mind she picked it up and flicked her thumb over the rough wheel of the lighter, and as it always did with the reliable Zippo, a flame leapt out of the petrol-soaked wick. Holding it for a second or two to the torn fabric of the armchair she watched as the flame did its job, investigators would think that Benny had just nodded off and dropped the lit Zippo, the delay in discovering the true reason for his death would cause problems with any investigation.

Contract fulfilled, she left the room her jacket now unbuttoned with the effort of her strike, the crisp white blouse under it had also separated slightly leaving an arc of white breast showing above the scarlet bra, she did love red, it was so erotic. Benny would have loved the view, pity he was no longer there to see it. Back in the nicotine-stained lounge, Benny quickly bled out, the ash on his shirt front, now red with blood the colour of the Louboutin sole.

Walking out to the car she was smiling at the perfection of her strikes, she would have liked it if he had taken longer to die, she loved to watch the ultimate moments, just as a pyromaniac loves to watch the flames, the fruits of labour. Jackman was waiting at the rear of the car, a black bin bag in his hands. Leaning against the car Fiona first bent one leg, for Jackman to remove the shoe with his latex gloved hand, then repeated with the other leg before dropping shoes and glove into the refuse sack.

"Did you splash any blood on your trousers?" he asked trying not to look but doing so all the same as Fiona leant forward exposing one white, pointed breast. She did not mind; she was used to his leering looks and it pleased her knowing that he knew extremely well he would never get to touch them.

She didn't even bother to look for blood on her trouser cuffs, there was no way she was slipping out of her trousers in front of her boss, plus she loved the Armani suit she was wearing, a good dry cleaner would do the trick. A glance of her breast was one thing, seeing her stood on the roadside in a scarlet thong from Victoria's Secret was something else altogether.

Now in her chosen driving shoe of a black velvet Jimmy Choo Bing Slipper, a reward she had bought herself when last in London with her on-off girlfriend, Fiona headed back along the M27, the south coast motorway. She never exceeded the speed limit; it was not worth the trouble of having a checkable location at a certain time. The Port Solent Marina, with its Mediterranean style houses and moorings, was just off to their right as the first fire engine blasted past them, hurriedly charging in the opposite direction with lights flashing, a minute later a second flew past. Both trucks in 'hurry-up' mode. On arrival they would find a house ablaze, with neighbours standing on the roadside enjoying the spectacle but hoping the fire would not spread to their homes. They wondered if the creepy man who lived in the house was still in there. Evidence of any crime, and Jason Benny, would be burned to a crisp in the heart of the fire, its voracious flames spreading quickly through the piles of hoarded newspapers lining the walls in the hall, adding fuel to the fire.

By the time they would be able to enter the house safely not only would any evidence be gone, so would the culprits. Neighbours would tell the fire crews, and the odd journalist from the local press, that the creepy man with a comb over would have been inside, and that it was highly unlikely any other bodies would be in there as the strange man did not have any friends or family.

Fire crews in breathing apparatus would come across the charred body slumped in an old-fashioned armchair with no fire-retardant to be seen anywhere in its construction. Only on the morgue slab would it be noticed he had a hole in his chest and heart, and he had one eye missing, and the mortician would have no idea what caused the wounds. That was if he noted the wounds among the charred flesh in the first place.

Benny's burnt body had only just been discovered, the fire crew still damping down the glowing embers of the chair stuffing, when Fiona had ordered her new pair of Christian Louboutin heels from an on-line store, free delivery the next day, and from her favoured designer and it would be paid for from the £1,000 bonus she had earned while doing what she considered to be a fun hobby, it infuriated her that Jackman would owe her the money, but he was good for it; he knew only too well what would happen to him if he stiffed her for the money. Back in her waterside apartment she had changed out of her suit and blouse, both bagged ready for the dry cleaners in the morning, showered and slipped into a blue silk kimono. The English rose with pure white porcelain skin was back, wet hair resting on her shoulders, and she was sipping on a delicious and refreshing glass of Pouilly Fuisse from Burgundy. Normally it would be an earthy red after an extra-curricular job, but she fancied something refreshing today, after the heavy smells from that creep's house that left a nasty taste in her mouth, she had earned something light to refresh her tongue. As she sat in her modern and minimalist lounge looking out to the lights of Chichester marina reflecting on the still waters that continually lapped against expensive boat hulls, she thought of the day's work. She did enjoy her extra duties, but realised a long time ago that her boss was not someone to be trusted, there were no worries about the money, he would not dare try and get out of paying her fee, but he was a weasel, and men like that were not known for their bravery or their loyalty. Jackman would throw her under the bus without a second thought, and with that in mind she made a mental note to get on the internet and figure out how to sell her... she juggled words in her head before it came to her, her 'skillset', that was a perfect description, *skillset,* to a wider international market. There must be others who want the services of an attractive female assassin, and she did love to travel.

CHAPTER 34

"Of course, the room was full of my bloody prints you fucking moron, it was my bedroom." Kobe was tired, dog weary and in no fit state to be questioned but he had refused a break, he wanted this finished. Worst of all for the conscientious DI Kobe Kaan, he was embarrassed to belong to the same police force as his interrogator, with his shoddy knowledge of the most basic rules of how a good copper works.

Berry slid a calming hand onto Kobe's forearm, a small movement that had gone almost unnoticed by the others in the room. He leaned across to Kobe and spoke softly in his ear, it was not a whisper, as such, but soft and with clear diction.

"Kobe, I know you are tired and angry, but keep calm and let them pile up the mistakes. We will be out of here soon; you have my word." It had the effect of calming Kobe, and he took a deep breath before steadying his breathing and thinking of Rae and the children, they would not want him to behave like this.

Across the table DCI Casper Jones allowed his stern exterior to give slightly, his body language eased, and he enjoyed a smirk that everyone had seen, he had been baiting his murderous prey and he had seen the anger flare. DCI Kobe Kaan had a temper! While Kobe's eyes were dark and threatening, Jones' eyes now had a bright glint to them, as the outburst and raised voice revealing a loss of control elicited the smile of triumph and the glint of success.

"Is that the temper you lost when you murdered your wife and children?" It was stated in a tone that was almost gloating. "Did she and your children burn your fuse a little too short. I can understand the pressures of mixing your job and family life, it can all get to be just a little too much to bear, we all understand the pressures of this job. Kobe." The hook was in, and he was dragging a thrashing Kobe Kaan to the shore.

Robert Berry was a master of timing and interview techniques, he had been a Barrister for many years and just because he now preferred to picking his guitar strings and dressing like a bluesman, which is what he was these days, but he had not forgotten how to do his job. He thought the time was right to calm proceedings and give Jones notice that he was pulling on a short leash.

"If you want to just bait my client to get a reaction then we are out of here, so far we are here as a courtesy and you have not charged DI Kaan of any wrongdoing, but tread carefully Detective." Berry looked at the DCI fiercely, it unsettled the sweating police officer. "You will always refer to him with respect, he is not Kobe or just Kaan to you. He is a high-ranking police officer, and you will treat him as such."

Eyes downcast it was Kobe's turn to place a hand on the Barrister's arm this time. "Let's just get this over with Robert, sooner I can get out of here, the sooner I can go and see my family and pray with them."

The thought of his family and their frail, almost bloodless, bodies posed on the bed in such an affectionate way, as if the killer were sending some kind of weird message. Kobe's mind was flickering between light and shade, one moment he was lucid and clear, and the next he was off into a land of fantasy where his family were alive, and this was all a horrid dream. At that moment, at least three hours since he had last been outside of the soulless room, he was in lucid mode and felt it was time to push back.

"Okay smartarse..." Kobe began.

"I will ask you to keep a civil tongue in your head and remember that you are talking to a superior officer." The smile had gone again.

"You might be higher in rank, but you will never be superior to me or any one of the officers on my team."

"You don't have a team any more *Mister* Kaan, remember you have been relieved of your duties."

Berry broke up the fencing match, "Do you have any evidence or not Mister Jones." The *Mister* and its sarcastic tone did not go unnoticed, it threw the DCI off his game for a second or two.

Ignoring Berry, Jones went back to his questioning. "As I said we have several sets of 'fresh' fingerprints putting you slap-bang in the middle of the carnage you created. Would you care to explain." Jones really did think he had laid a trap for Kaan.

"So, where are these prints that you are putting so much store in." Kobe asked again.

"I am asking the questions Mister Kaan, not you."

"Where, where did you find the prints? In a house full of my prints."

Robert Berry was getting as annoyed with the questioner as his client. "That is a fair question to ask Detective Inspector Jones. If, as you say, you want to get to the truth of today's events."

Jones glared at the Barrister, he hated having his interviews interrupted, but still aimed his comment at the man whom he thought he had close to a confession. This would be a feather in his cap, his superiors would see a determined officer who could take on any job, a conviction here and he would be able to name his own career path and job future.

"If you must know, in the hallway and the children's bedrooms." Was this the death knell of Kaan's defiance? "And, for good measure we also found plenty of your prints, clear as day in the main bedroom, where you arranged their bodies as part of, what, some kind of macabre ritual."

"I know you didn't find any in the bedroom, on top of the blood, because I didn't go in there." Thinking again of the room, their bedroom where both his children were conceived, and where he and Rae would have their quiet moments, now his only vision was of his family posed on the bed in that bloody tableau. Tears filled his eyes, and he choked back an audible sob but continued to stand up for himself. "If you found any prints in the bedroom, they must have been under the blood. I wanted to go to my family, more than anything I wanted to hold them, love them, clean the blood from their faces; but I have been in this job too long to go and ruin evidence although my whole being was telling me to ignore what my head was telling me, so the doorway is as far as I got. You would not have found any prints on or in the blood."

Jones felt his chance of conviction, and more horrifyingly any chance of his career moving forward, slip just a little. "The prints in the hallway and on the children's bedroom doors were all yours, and they could only have been put there after the blood had been spattered around the upstairs of your house." It had the tone of empty threat.

"You really are a fucking idiot!" This time it was an educated voice that cursed the DCI.

The note taking detective constable, the Federation Rep and even Kobe turned to see who had uttered those words, words that would be forever recorded on the PACE machine.

"I am sorry to be so blunt but really..." Robert Berry sounded pissed off and astonished. "Can you really be that thick and desperate as to hold my client because you found his fingerprints scattered around his own home, the place he has lived for the last ten years or so."

Kobe felt like a hiatus had arrived, Jones had left a gap wide enough for him to squeeze through and get out of the station.

"Can we leave now, please." Kobe ignored the blustering and stuttering DCI, who was trying to impress on everyone that the interview was not yet over.

Berry saw it differently. "This interview is well and truly over. You have held my client here for the whole of last night and for most of today, and all without due cause. Please do not contact him again without going through me first. Plus, and this will come as no surprise to everyone else in this room, I will be reporting this debacle to the Independent Office for Police Conduct, you have done nothing today except bring the force, and my client's reputation into disrepute."

Robert Berry did not suffer fools, and he was not going to suffer this one any longer. Looking down at his client he could see the man was almost drained, the bright overhead light reflected off the drying tears on Kobe's cheeks, the normally vibrant man's eyes looked dead. Dead eyes, looking out to nowhere, what war photographers in the Vietnam conflict had labelled *'the thousand-yard stare'*.

"Let's go Kobe, we are done here." Berry took a brief look at Peter Jordan-Reeves as if looking for any objections, all he gained was a shrug and smile from the Fed-Rep. They did not need his permission but with that nod it was given anyhow. "You are more than welcome to get a magistrate to give you an extension on holding DI Kaan, but I seriously doubt you would get one with your so-called evidence.

Before anyone else could pick up their paperwork, or even stand up, Robert Berry and Kobe Kaan had left the room. The door into the grey space slammed behind them, Jordan Reeves thought he saw dust motes dropping down from the ceiling and floating in the beam of light from the metal grill protecting the overhead lamp. The red light remained lit on the PACE recording device, until it was pointed out to Jones by his junior detective. It was an embarrassed stutter that called an official end to the interview and with a hefty clunk the machine stopped recording and the red light extinguished.

CHAPTER 35

At the end of the corridor Kobe saw David Martin and Stella Gold sitting on the rigid plastic visitor chairs, both in civilian clothes that he was sure they had on the evening before. The evening before; it appeared as a long-lost memory when life was still good, and he had a family and home to go to. If he had been aware of anything other than his great loss, he would have noted that they both had mud spattered legs as well as looking as tired and dishevelled as he felt. They looked at Kobe with rheumy eyes, both also carrying the grey bags of sleep deprivation under them and signs of pity deep within their gaze. They had been nearby all night waiting for him. Together they pushed themselves up from the chairs and headed down the corridor toward him, moving with urgency knowing time was brief.

David met his boss first, "Boss..." Then thought better of the official affectionate terminology. "Kobe, don't go out the front way, the press is ten deep in the carpark, TV cameras, photographers, the lot."

Kobe did not care, he just wanted out of the station, wanted to go home, and see his family. Treat them in the way a good Muslim should, send them fully prepared and ready to put before Allah. Being too confused to make his own decisions though he followed David and Stella. Robert, his Barrister, grabbed David's arm, it was a gentle but firm no-nonsense grip, pausing the onrush out of the station, then said to the pair who were Kobe's colleagues and friends.

"You get Kobe out of the back door; I will head out the front and keep the press occupied for a few minutes." Then to the disappearing threesome, "Always like to give the press a few soundbites, and I have plenty to say at the moment." He smiled as he plotted a legal revenge on the DCI, then he remembered something and called after the fleeing three. "Kobe, rest easy and give me a call in a day or two" Kobe stopped to give his thanks, to a man who last time he had spoken with him had been on the opposite side of the table in the interview room, but Robert saved him the task. "You are more than welcome Kobe, now go take care of your family."

All the time Kobe had been answering the inane questions in

the grey room, his family were at the mortuary being dealt with in the same way all victims of violent deaths were dealt with. Treated with all due respect but not in the Muslim way. One after the other they had been taken from their home and were now all laying on cold metal mortuary tables with just a thin white sheet covering their ravaged bodies and awaiting postmortem examinations.

Traditional Islamic texts forbids the cutting up of bodies as they believe the body continues to feel pain after death. Even so autopsies must be held to serve justice. Even though he was a lapsed Muslim, Kobe felt their pain and agonised over the fact he would not be able to prepare their bodies in the Islamic way. Their beautiful bodies once again had been invaded by a knife's unforgiven edge.

Two innocent young bodies, who had not yet had time to enjoy the fullness of life and all the loves and adventures a normal lifespan has to offer. And his beautiful wife Rae, artistic, delicate and yet a ruler with an iron will inside the home, Kobe knew, that given the chance, she would have fought like a tiger to protect their children. That should have been his job, he agonised, his job to protect all three of them. They were all each other had and he failed them at the most basic level.

Kaan had no idea what was happening at that precise time, but he was a copper who had worked on murders before and knew what indignities the near future held for his family. It only caused him more pain, gut-wrenching, physical pain that tore his heart apart. Even after the vicious death there was no peace or return to dignity as they would be sliced again, organs would be removed, weighed, examined. Their innocence defiled all over again.

Out of the rear door of the station three shadows scampered across a darkened asphalt yard, Chris Carne the station Skipper had turned the exterior lights out so they could avoid any obvious emergence back into the real world. Hopefully away from eyes and lenses of the press that would be everywhere. At that same moment Robert Berry stepped from the station's front doors and engaged the gathered press, he had their undivided attention. Meanwhile in the yard at the back of the station, David bundled Kobe into the back of a marked car and told him to lay low, meanwhile Stella had leapt in the front and started the engine. At the same time as the engine fired up the yard appeared to be hit by lightning, multiple bursts of white light that lifted the evening gloom as several flashes from cameras bounced around the whole yard. But the hidden photographers were too late, they would have nothing on their digital flash cards except two officers heading out of the yard in a patrol car. Stella hit the switches for the blues and twos, hoping the swirling red and blue lights would throw the photographers off their stride. In a frantic hurry she drove from the yard at a pace quick enough to be on an emergency call out. But still controlled and slow enough so as not run over any journalists, that would have been bad press.

Dusk had dropped a grey veil over Chichester and the swirling blue lights lit up buildings, faces, TV cameras, journalists, and the vans with satellite dishes ready to send images around the world. As for the press crews all they had to send to their respective agencies was another patrol car doing what patrol cars did, leave the yard at speed.

A few hundred yards along the familiar road they took a harsh right-hand corner and David looked across where only 24 hours ago he had been with Stella on the wharf side and taking the call from Chris Carne to confirm that the strange gut feeling he had was the real thing. Stella checked mirrors and glanced out the back of the car to make sure they had no followers and seeing that all was clear gave the okay for Kobe to sit up. Stella took one more paranoid look at her surroundings to make sure nobody had figured out the cloak-and-dagger ruse and followed them. Seeing all was clear she switched off the 'blues-and-twos' and dropped the car's speed to that of the speed limit.

As he slid his way up from the rear foot well, Kobe looked all around and was surprised to see it was dark outside, being sure he had seen daylight squeezing through the narrow window in the interview suite. He let out a huge sigh, so big it caused David to turn around again and check he was okay while Stella kept wary eyes on rear-view mirrors. David was the first to speak, he tried to keep it light despite wanting all the facts and happenings, he was a copper and that was just his instinct.

"Hey Boss, how you are doing?" Kobe was slow to answer, needing to reassess what was going on.

"Not good David, not sure what is happening to be honest." In the back of the car Kobe's face looked dark, almost menacing. His olive skin had lost its normal sheen and both head and face showed dark, stubble growth. Stella took one hand off the wheel and handed a water bottle over her shoulder to Kobe, which he drank from, taking the liquid in huge gulps as if it were his first drink in days.

David continued looking at Kobe, it was more like an examination than a caring gaze. He noted that Kobe's eyes appeared black and vicious, the kindness he usually saw and was used to was gone, but that did not surprise him. Kobe looked around outside the windows. He screwed the cap back on but was not even sure his thirst was sated. He was unsure if what he felt was hunger or thirst. He wasn't sure of anything anymore.

The world outside the car seemed like an alien landscape, not sure what he should be seeing, aside all the other emotions that were worming their way through him he now had panic adding to the mix. In his work Kobe knew how to control emotions, put each small detail into individual pockets so they could be sorted one by one, his brain was an efficient office with everything filed in place, today it was as if a tornado had spun and crashed through that mental office. The streets of Chichester that he knew so well, with its surrounding grey walled fortress now seemed strange. The one and a half miles of Roman walls that surrounded the city were as familiar as his own face in the mirror, and yet those meandering brick ramparts were as strangers. It would have looked no more different if they had emerged into the aftermath of a nuclear attack.

"Are we going home?" His voice so soft David and Stella barely heard it, she gazing at the rearview mirror one more time to look at the boss who had treated her so well just the previous day. "Are we going home Stella? I need to go home." David and Stella exchanged a glance, Kobe did not notice. It was Stella who started to answer, but a look from David told her that he would do the talking.

So, Stella concentrated on her driving, and was thankful that she could escape telling Kobe about the last twenty-four, or so, hours. It made her feel cowardly, as if David were protecting her, escaping explanations to the man she now considered as a friend, and she felt sorry for, what was now, her man. Even though he was the experienced officer who had done any number of, what they called 'death-knocks' in his career. One look at the determined look on his face told her Kobe was in safe hands.

"I don't want to drag things up that you would rather not remember Kobe." He spoke softly but as was always best did not pull punches, it was preferable to be straightforward and honest. "Has anything since last night stuck with you, it's been a hellish time for you I know, but if we can help you know we will."

"I know I found my family butchered and covered with blood last night. My entire perfect life cut down, three beautiful people gone and those arseholes back there questioning me instead of running a good investigation." His mood and tone did not fit with his words, they should have been said with any amount of venom, with anger, even with revenge in mind. Instead, he spoke in a monotone voice, devoid of feeling and character.

Kobe then repeated himself, with a further request to take him home. Again, the two in the front of the car exchanged awkward glances.

"We can't take you home Kobe," David continued to leave it upon himself to answer. "It is still an active crime-scene, no can do I am afraid. Stella has a spare room at her place where you can stay, and nobody will find you there. And if the suits need anything else from you, they can reach you through me.

Mention of the word 'suit' and Kobe examined what he was wearing, pulling at a grey sweatshirt which had somehow found its way to him from his office. David explained that he had been allowed to go to Kobe's office, supervised of course, and fetch his sports bag with running gear in it.

"Neither of you should be doing this, especially you Stella, being so new on the Job." Typical of Kobe Kaan, thinking of others over and above his own pain. "Sneaking me out like that could be an offence that will get you sacked." He paused as he realised what car they were in. "Especially as you borrowed a car to do it."

It was Stella who responded first. "Fuck 'em if they can't take a joke!"

Despite the seriousness of the situation David could not help but release a small smile and he exchanged it with one of Gold's own. The more time he spent with Gold, the more he was liking her, not his brightest idea with his being a sergeant and her just out of being a Probationer. She had not moved from his side since they had left the pub on the canal the night before and he admired her strength of purpose and stamina. Plus, she was pretty. Jesus was that all it was, just one day on. It did not seem possible, but then again nothing was seeming possible now. Kobe just sat in the rear of the car and looked out of the window as Chichester rushed by, he still felt imprisoned. The car fell silent, and David tried to recall the last 24 hours, as best he could, he would need to tell Kobe when he was able to take it all in.

It was hard to fathom that it was only yesterday the squad had raided the drug house, and despite a firearm being found, after intelligence had reported, no weapons on site. Despite that glaring error it had been an extraordinarily successful raid. One of the Force's biggest ever. Stella had done well, spotting the firearm, and getting it away from the old crone, who had it tucked down the side of her chair.

What at first had seemed like an average day and a very average raid had turned into a proper fuck-up before becoming one of the biggest drug hauls in Sussex police history and all hidden in a fake room along with the old lady's drug dealing son. There had been enough brick-size packages of cocaine in the wall to make himself a comfortable armchair out of it. At the end of the day, they had gotten a record amount of product off the streets, making for very unhappy dealers and happy senior officers all the way up the chain to the Chief Constable – and as usual with officers on every level trying to take the credit. It was Kobe and his well-trained team that should be the ones taking the plaudits.

End of shift it was off to the pub to celebrate a job well done and it was, as always, a blast to let off steam with colleagues that all liked each other, as well as drink to the successful raid with no casualties on their side. Then while getting a breath of air and drawing on an unlit cigarette, it was hard to give them up straight away after being a confirmed smoker for most of his adult life, he at first felt, rather than saw Gold coming out from the pub. The noise from the bar and the lights spilled out and onto the quayside and he noted her trim figure in silhouette and outlined with a halo of light.

It was then he had seen the Boss drive past in his Alpha Romeo heading toward his home, and for no reason his usually alert copper's gut instinct left him feeling queasy. As he watched the distinctive taillights disappear around the corner he felt real concern, no idea what for but also no idea of how to quell the feeling. It wasn't comfortable and it wasn't nice. It was then he felt somebody watching him and he turned to see Stella standing just behind him on the side of the canal. Apart from that strange gut-warning, he had been enjoying his solitary moment on the small quay, he had a feeling though that he was quite glad it was Gold who had come outside to join him, he felt relaxed in her company.

The feelings of trouble from deep within his core were not long in being quantified. Gold had fetched them both another drink, she a disgusting sounding Coke and blackcurrant and he another lager. He had no idea how long they had been talking on, what was a warm evening on the waterfront, before his phone vibrated in his pocket. On the other end was Sergeant Chris Carne, the station skipper, who alerted him to the fact that something was going on at the Boss's house and it was nothing trivial. He could not say anymore at that moment.

Since then, it had been a night and day of frustration and heartache. Kobe was more than his boss; David also considered him friend and mentor and owed him a great deal in helping his recent climb from the rank-and-file to detective sergeant. The boss had helped and guided him every step of the way. Now it was time to repay the kindness and friendship. He and Gold had traipsed over a muddy footway and shoreline shingle to get to Kobe's house unnoticed and although they never got into the house they were at least nearby. One moment, however, would stick in his mind for the rest of his days, he saw a vision that he never wanted to see as a police officer ever again, but he felt it was his duty.

A plain dark blue van, without logos or signage, drove into the lane that led to the village's car park, it was waved through the taped police lines without question, both he and Gold had seen the van before. It belonged to the on-duty funeral director, and it was their job to collect the dead and ferry them to a mortuary in readiness for their autopsy, tonight they had a job lot, three for the price of one but he did not envy them their task that night.

Across from Kobe's home, Stella took David's arm and moved him to one side from where they were stood in the shadows watching events, it gave them a better view, a view that neither would have wished to watch but they felt they were doing it for the Boss, not for cheap thrills as the crowd outside the front of the house were doing. The first body in a black bag was carried on a gleaming chrome trolley and it emerged from the back door, along the pathway almost tipping as wheels caught on the crazy paving like a wayward supermarket trolley. Undertakers badly guiding the body of Rae to their van paused at the gate, which the young PC Cummins was watching. The inexperienced officer had a look like a startled stoat, rooted to the spot, mouth agape, he had never seen such a thing before. It was not just a body, it was the remains of a well-respected copper's wife that they were wheeling out, and his eyes could not pull themselves away from the scene. That moment of indecision was all that was needed for another group of silent spectators, behind the fence of the next terraced house along, was a small gossip of news people and they appeared out of the darkness to get, what they refer to as 'the-money-shot'. Suddenly the evening at the back of Kobe's house, which until then had only the light of one streetlamp to lift the gloom, burst into a darkness shattering display of light and colour. A video camera operator turned on his powerful lamp that bounced off the gleaming red of Kobe's Alpha as well as lighting half the street, mixed in with that were a whole barrage of flashguns from stills photographers. It was as a silent war zone with explosive flashes going off one after the other.

Rae was not yet in the van and already her dignity was being stripped even further by photojournalists in search of the salacious and shocking. As if a triple killing were not shocking enough for the public's voracious appetite. Already at the gate at the head of the pathway leading from the back garden was a second wheeled gurney and despite its cargo of two small children, the small group of story-hungry press men moved as one, silhouetted by the lights and appearing as a murmuration of starlings flowing this way and that as they thoughtlessly manoeuvred for a better angle. Then something strange happened, as the second trolley emerged from the garden the street became still, flashguns stopped, videographers turned off their bright lights as they saw the black outlines of two half size body bags. Even a ravenous press hoard was beyond recording the bodies of two small children as they joined their mother in the back of the inconspicuous van. The hustle and noise of the street stopped, neighbours stood still, and heads were bowed either out of respect or because they were too shocked to look. David also had seen enough, these were two young children who would not get to grow any older or bigger thanks to a psychopathic killer without an inch of human compassion, and he too lowered his head out of respect and closed his eyes in silent prayer. His tribute cut short when he heard the babble of a rabble rushing from front of house to rear. The news had reached them that the bodies were being transported from the cottage, and they had not stopped to think about the 'entertainment' that was being staged.

"Come on Gold..." He moved swiftly toward the mob. "We need to stop this!"

He had not needed to say a word, for Stella was hard on his hip and running straight for the tourists of gore. A few of the press-corps were aware of what was happening and even they had feelings, sometimes, and they formed a human barrier between those rushing forward and the van as it was being loaded. At the edge of the melee was a lone photographer who raised his camera to his eye, the lens pointing directly into the van. Stella Gold caught sight of him and acted swiftly as she snatched the camera away from the snapper with one hand while taking a fist to his nose with a forceful straight jab, Mohammed Ali would have been proud of the speed and accuracy.

"Ow!" Moaned the soft photographer. "That hurts, you can't do that." And then with great indignity he added. "I know who you are, you may be out of uniform, but I recognise you."

If that was supposed to impress or frighten Gold, it had no effect whatsoever. "I don't give a rat's arse. Have you no shame, this is the entire family of a lovely man who has done nothing but serve this community as a police officer and all you can think of doing is photograph his wife and children as they are bought out to the ambulance."

"We all have a job to do love, what's your name and number, I am not going to be manhandled by the likes of you." The glaring looks of disgust from his fellow journalists was enough to tell the thoughtless moron that he was treading on soft ground, on that realisation his voice dwindled until the last few words became just a whisper.

David stood, hands on hips, anger draining from his face, Gold appeared beside him again. It seemed these two were not to be separated for long on their private quest. No words were uttered between them, but David put a reassuring hand On Stella's shoulder. Together they watched as with tails between their legs the crowd slowly returned around to the front of the house. Finally, the ambulance doors were closed.

Nobody had their eyes on the black van as it pulled away, sorrowful looks were kept downcast.

From just behind them a soft voice spoke, so quietly and yet they both heard every word as if they were amplified. Standing in the same cone of light that beamed down from the one streetlamp was a slight man, short and slim with a kindly face which was half hidden by a pure white and bushy beard. His brown eyes burned brightly, showing patience, caring and, Stella thought, a huge amount of love and forgiveness. His skin was a shade darker than Kobe's but had that same olive hue, he also had a look of intellect and reserved temperament.

Those dark eyes looked up to David and Stella, quickly darting from one to the other with a vibrant liveliness and behind the sparkles in them he offered nothing other than charity and calm. Now he had their attention he introduced himself.

"I am sorry if I startled you both, I had not meant to sneak up behind you like that." Stella answered for them with a simple 'no problem, Sir.' He continued, "Let me introduce myself. I am the Imam from Officer Kaan's Mosque, and I am deeply sorry for his tragic losses. I assume you are friends and colleagues."

"Kobe will appreciate you being here to give solace." It was Gold that spoke, David did not know what to say to the holy man. "We will tell him as soon as we get to see him, which may not be for some time I am afraid." It was strange but as Stella spoke to the cleric, she felt the burning anger she had felt toward the mob, subsiding quite considerably. It was if the small man before her exuded kindness.

"I am the Imam at the Mosque, Ibrahim Omar." He gently shook their hands, taking each of theirs in both of his.

David introduced himself and Stella, explaining that they worked with Kobe. "Kobe is not here at the moment; he was taken to our Chichester station around half an hour ago." He continued, "I..." he corrected himself. "...we were about to follow him, but we thought he may like to know somebody was here to watch over his family."

"As it turns out it was good that you did, people can be like wolves on the hunt when they gather as a pack like that."

The Imam was a good few inches shorter than the lofty David and yet it was he who felt the lesser of the two men. Again, as he spoke David felt the urge to bend nearer, he spoke so softly but he realised that each word, even with the accent, was as clear as a bell being rung. The humble eyes carrying the pain for the absent Kobe Kaan.

"I didn't realise that Kobe had a local Mosque, I always thought he had lapsed with his religion, he doesn't talk about his beliefs often, but I do know that sometimes the job does conflict with his teachings, and it troubles him," David explained.

Stella looked on interested but felt as a woman she should hold her tongue. Even though she had spoken to him she was not sure how to behave at all in front of the Imam. She was however, intrigued by the Imam's wonderful beard, snowy white and bushy enough that it could have won prizes for size and condition. Trendy young men nowadays had the fashion for growing their beards longer and used all sorts of product on their carefully tended facial hair, and here was this Imam who had grown his natural, it was, she thought, an organic beard.

"Sadly, no. We did not see much of Mr Kaan, but he had visited us from time to time in the line of his work if he needed advice about investigations that may involve a fellow Muslim." David found himself liking the man. "I understand his wife Rae was a Catholic and the children were being left to make their own minds up later in life, but being a Muslim is not about coming to Mosque to pray, it is about what is carried in his heart.

"We are a family, and as such we must take care of each other," the Imam continued. "I was hoping to begin making arrangements for the swift burial of his family as dictated by Muslim teachings." David was about to interrupt, but the Imam raised a hand to stop him. "I realise that because of the nature of their passing this will not be possible as there are investigations to be conducted before we can regard how their next journey will be taken care of. All things needed, even for his wife." The Imam explained. "Even though not a Muslim, Rae Kaan will be treated with the respect and care due the wife of a follower, I understand she had no family of her own. In our eyes she was a sister in our family, the children our children also."

"Thank you, I will tell Kobe as soon as they let me in to see him and explain what you have said. One thing, you may like to know, is that the first officer on the scene heard Kobe outside the room where the bodies were discovered and he was repeating some sort of incantation, or prayer I suppose it was. The officer could not tell me anymore as Kobe was speaking Egyptian, something else I did not know about him."

"It was probably '*Inna lillahi wa inna ilayha raji'un*'." The Imam explained, "Verily we belong to Allah, and truly to him we shall return. It is the prayer for our dead, so he was not such a 'lapsed' Muslim as he assumed."

David went to say his goodbyes as he was keen to follow Kobe to the station. "Sir, Imam, sorry I have no idea as to the protocol and what I should call you." He blushed slightly.

"There is no need for discomfort my friend, just call me by my given name, Ibrahim." The cleric said calmly and without taking offence. "I understand the need for thorough investigation, but would you kindly tell Mr Kaan, that he can be assured that arrangements will still be made and that with the help of the community as soon as it can be allowed."

The kindly man with the white beard went on to explain that should Kaan not become available, they will make *'Dua'* and ask Allah to forgive the sins of the family of Kobe Kaan. Kobe may not have followed his faith closely, but he is still part of that family, as we are his family, and he will always be welcomed into the family."

David and Stella said their goodbyes and once again were offered the warm handshake, and the man never took his warm eyes off the two officers which they found strangely comforting.

They rushed back around the front of the house and followed the path back along the inlet of the huge harbour and conservation area. At one point as the path narrowed and the incoming tide was threatening to wash over the muddy trail, with no thought but instinct David reached behind to offer Stella a hand to keep them together and her safe and she took it easily. It was another moment amidst the tragedy and mayhem that calmed them both and they stayed hand in hand all the way back to the car.

CHAPTER 36

Tuesday morning, and the Councillor was reading the Chronicle on-line while sitting in his home office. Front page news was of a triple murder, in a village a short distance from the city centre, the number one suspect was a serving police officer, one DI Kobe Kaan. It was believed that he had slaughtered his entire family while in a rage, according to sources within the police, the paper said. Although the Detective Inspector had been released without charge, investigators were not looking for anyone else in relation to the ongoing case.

Sam, and his Centurion, were relegated to page five. Jackman was furious that his big story had been bumped from the front pages. He had worked hard to get the press interested. Even though angry he was happy with the photograph they had taken of him to accompany the story, it was always good press to get your mug in the media, even if it was only the local paper. He also pondered over the image of the statue that accompanied Nick Flax's words. Was it good enough to fool the casual glance, were the two statues identical twins? He touched the screen of his laptop and spread two fingers to zoom in on the statuette. It was near perfect, only an expert would tell and by then it would be too late. His plan was coming together nicely.

Yesterday he had inserted himself nicely into the story by turning up for Sam's press call. Now this morning on webpage five was the photo he had orchestrated, him with his arm around Sam's shoulder, like lifetime buddies with Sam smiling broadly for the camera, damn it felt good to be popular. Next year Mayor and then onto Parliament leaving this boring city and Barbara his tedious and nagging wife behind. There was no limit to what I can achieve with the kind of charisma I have, Jackman thought smugly.

Yesterday had been a good day, and his inclusion in the story was making today another good one. Monday morning and the photoshoot was well underway when he had arrived. As he breezed into the room, he was deftly brushing back a stray lock of hair that had dared to flop across his creosote tanned brow, he headed straight for Sam before the meddling reporter Nick Flax could get in the way. Fiona his driver had been told to distract the reporter and allow Jackman time enough to insinuate himself with the grubby little junk shop owner.

"Good morning, Samuel, glorious day isn't it." The ambush timing was perfect, his luck was changing.

Sam looked slightly bewildered, nobody had ever called him Samuel, not even on his birth certificate.

"Councillor Jackman, we met yesterday in the tea-room at the Antique fair..." Hand extended for a friendly shake, Sam thrust his out in thoughtless response. Jackman did not wait for an answer as he shook hands with Sam. "You, my friend, you can call me Kenneth."

Flashes went off as the local paper's one photographer got the first of his snaps, a Councillor, and the subject. Pulp journalism, but all part of his job.

Sam realised he was being addressed by somebody important and broke out his best smile, not a bright-bleached smile like the Councillor but a grin of off-white, tea-stained coloured teeth. Right hand, to right hand, a firm handshake, a brief pirouette, and a left arm across his shoulder from the Councillor and he had him in the perfect politician pose. The young news photographer continued snapping with renewed vigour when he realised this could make the Nationals and the strobe of his flashgun threw dancing shadows across the whole room. On the plinth alongside them, and well within shot was the Centurion, his six-pack stomach burnished to bright gold, his sword held high helping the menacing look of the artefact.

Sam relived and retold the whole conversation that he already had with Nick over the phone, but he was happy for his story to be heard again. Sam decided he would never tire of telling the story if there was someone to listen. Never out of earshot or camera shot, the politician's face remained excited and interested, but, if truth be known he wasn't listening to anything Sam had to say. His brain had been busy working out a way to get hold of the fake bronze and then to make a swap. How, where, and when? He had solved bigger conundrums, that is why he was the success he was, nothing left to chance. First, he and his driver, Fiona needed to take a short trip down the motorway.

His plans since then had unfolded perfectly.

Come Tuesday and Sam had decided not to open the shop. The previous day had been too exciting and exhausting, plus Nick had warned him that press from just about every publication, newspaper and TV show would be knocking down his door so it would be advisable to keep the shop closed for a few days. Sitting at his kitchen table with one of those sachet supermarket cappuccinos, he was listening to the heavy and comfortable purring of Wedgwood as he slept on by the Aga, his tummy full of the best cat food money could buy. He did not have a long memory but never recalled eating fresh fish before, and in tasty, meaty chunks. His bowl had been licked clean within seconds.

The peaceful, and happy morning was broken by a hard rapping on the shop door. Nick had been right, Sam thought. The impatient knock came again and not wanting the window in the shop door broken Sam peeped through the ragged velvet drape to see who it was, it would not be Nick, he had his own key. A face was peering through the dusty glass, and it took a moment for Sam to recognise the Councillor. Letting the curtain drop back into place Sam checked that his baggy pyjama trousers were not going to fall down his skinny torso and that his dressing gown was secured with a good double knot.

Jackman did not waste a moment and as soon as Sam had pulled back the bolt that he had to reach on tiptoe for and turned the lock the Councillor barrelled into the shop without waiting for an invite. The Councillor swept the room with greedy eyes and Sam felt sure that Jackman had a look of contempt that briefly flickered across his face, maybe Nick was right not to trust him.

"I hear you love a good cup of tea Sam, how about making us one then." He had seen Sam emerge from behind the curtain and without invite he headed that way, brushing the curtain aside as easily as he had brushed any courtesy that Sam was due.

On entering the kitchen Jackman sneezed, twice, loudly, and Sam was hoping that he was allergic to cats. Sadly, for Sam, it was just the dust from the curtain that had caused the sneezing. Jackman quickly found his seat, at the head of the table, and he plonked himself down into Sam's smoothly worn Windsor chair. Sam felt the hairs on the back of his neck rise with annoyance but said nothing as maybe this was the way all important people acted. He had not been around many VIPs and, despite not liking him, was impressed by the man's status, but also wary as Nick had warned him to be the previous day. Ignoring the rude behaviour Sam placed the kettle on the hotplate of the Aga.

Jackman did not want to stay in this mouldy kitchen for one

minute more than was necessary, and so began putting his plan into action.

"You say this bronze figurine is valuable then Sam." His eyes scanning the kitchen looking for the one thing that would get his fortunes back on track.

A whistling kettle stopped Sam's reply and it gave him a moment to try and figure out what the Councillor's game was. Two cups of Earl Grey were carried to the table in two simple china mugs, Sam was not getting any of his best china out for this surprise visit, mainly because most of his best crockery was chipped. Earl Grey was a black tea with an acquired taste, but the nose of its floral-like orange scent was enticing on any breakfast table.

Watching the impatience on Jackman's face was pleasing for Sam, but it was time to answer him. "Let us just say, it will be a life-changing amount, but nobody really knows its true worth until it goes to auction. Nothing like this has come up before." Again, Sam wondered what he was up to, he did not like the man one little bit, but it would be worth hearing what Jackman had to say, that which he felt was so urgent to get out.

"This may seem like a strange question Samuel," There he was with the Samuel again and he was wearing out Sam's name. "...where will you be keeping it until the Auction, you will need to be careful with something so valuable. There are unscrupulous people out there who would only be too pleased to relieve you of it."

"Well, the last two nights it has been tucked deep underneath my bed." Where was Jackman leading him. "And nobody would go near there, not with Wedgwood, my cat, on guard, he can be a vicious little bugger."

Both men looked around at a still purring and satisfied cat, curled up in his bed and unlikely to move until dinner time or an earthquake, whichever came first.

Sam had not really thought about where to keep it, it had been in his shop for close to 50 years now without problems. It was slightly different now though as half the world knew of its, and Sam's, existence, maybe Nick had been right about the publicity, and he should have kept quiet.

"Why don't we, the Council that is, look after it for you." One of Jackman's absolute best smiles. Sam sipped his scalding tea, just to give him a moment to think but Jackman remained ahead of him.

"This historic find is something that we, as a city, should take a pride in," the Councillor was in full speech mode now. "We should take pride in this find and we should show it off with all our other precious art and artefacts. We safely have on display at the Council building, as well as our art galleries, items that are valuable and all kept under the closest scrutiny. Even the Council's silverware, regalia and valuable gifts from visiting dignitaries are all kept on public display in armoured glass cabinets, all linked to a very sophisticated alarm system. Your Roman should be on display so the people of Chichester can view it, safely and securely of course, and join in the celebration of it being found after all these years." He was looking Sam right in the eyes, and Sam could not turn away from the gaze, Jackman had him right where he wanted him.

"I am not sure Mr Jackman,"

"Kenneth, please call me Kenneth." Sam misheard him.

"I don't really know you Benny..." For the first time he saw Jackman flinch and wondered what he had said that was so unsettling for him.

'Kenny, fucking Kenny' Jackman battled with the thought, as he hated what he felt was a pet name and very demeaning, he was a man of importance. He would not call the King, Charlie, for fuck's sake. But he had to let it slide, he was doing a sales job here and his plan would not work if he did not get Sam onside with some sort of exhibition.

"You loan it to the city, free of charge of course. As if they would charge somebody to exhibit something so valuable. I have checked with our people already and we do have a spare bullet-proof and lockable glass case." Now the part to seal the deal. "And we would be more than happy to host a press and patrons evening, with every big name, including the mayor, of course. That will allow people to see how we treat our most successful residents as well as getting you even more publicity in readiness for your auction. The more publicity you get the more people will want to own the Centurion, and the estimated price would continue to rise."

"I do like the sound of that, in fact a man from Bonhams, the big auction house is due here in about an hour's time to give me a pre-auction estimate."

"That is excellent news, then I can tell our Council bean-counters what to add to our insurance."

As Suddenly as he came, Jackman was now rising swiftly from his chair, he had no time to wait for a *'no'* from Sam, and as long as he did not hear a no then it would be all systems go. The sturdy Windsor chair scraped back on the flagstone flooring and Jackman was already flinging back the curtain into the shop. He had not drunk a drop of his Earl Grey, if the truth were known he was strictly a coffee man, as far as he was concerned only gays, actors and gay actors drank those speciality type of teas.

Sam bolted the door behind the fleeing Councillor and plonked himself down on a wooden piano stool and for once did not question the fact that he did not have a piano to go with it. He really did not like the man, but he made sense when it came to the security of the bronze. His shop was not the most secure on the street, the charity shops probably had better alarm systems, and who did anything these days if an alarm did go off, all people do is look around to see who, or what, was disturbing the peace and quiet and consider who to complain to about the noise. Only sophisticated alarms that went through to a security company were of any use, and Sam could not afford that.

His rightful place at the head of the table and back in his favourite chair Sam decided he would do it. The security would be good, the extra publicity would be more than welcome, especially when those who derided him in the industry would be even more envious now and so important as to have a second press conference. Sam had never felt so important in his entire life and as he thought of what the wonderful future would be holding for him, Wedgwood left his warm bed by the Aga and leapt onto Sam's lap, something he had not done since he was a kitten. Sam stroked him and he purred some more.

CHAPTER 37

Kobe Kaan's Tuesday morning was not so eventful in the physical sense, but in his head, it was a heavyweight scrum with both sides pushing against the other with no quarter given, it was full of drama, of harsh memories and above all, a blinding headache. He wanted to remember his family, of how beautiful they were, how loving and how sweet the hugs and kisses were mingled with the intoxicating sound of their laughter, but those thoughts were pushing shoulder to shoulder against the ugly sight of their damaged bodies, the yawning gap of their sliced throats and their blood-stained bodies. Although he did not want to, he imagined the sound of their screams cut short as the blade did its bloody work. It was heaven and hell in one complex drama of thought.

He did not think he would sleep but after being up all of Sunday night and suffering the indignities poured on him throughout that night and much of the next day by strangers in the job that he loved; he was exhausted. David and Stella took him back to her place, where they put food in front of him, but he did not eat, poured a wine but he was too scared to drink for fear of never stopping once the alcohol had numbed him, plus he could not help but think that he had angered Allah enough. He settled for a cocoa while Stella made up the bed in the spare room and she and David left him to disappear into his own painful world. Kobe lay there for a long time thinking back on his life with Rae and the children, thinking forward to the life he now must lead without them. There was no recognisable timeline, his brain skipped forward and backward, good memories, wonderful memories, and then the horror of recent memories and the massive weight of guilt he felt for not being there when they needed him the most.

Kobe felt for his wallet, there was a photograph of them in there, and he wanted to look at the undamaged version of them all night long. But his wallet was missing, taken by the investigators back at the station. Drifting through the thin walls of the neat apartment was the gentle sound of classical music, and the subdued chatter of David and Stella. David a good man, friend, and colleague, always strong and standing beside his Boss and friend and she, Stella had proven to be a great asset to the team, he hated to think of what might have happened if she had not become aware of the gun and dealt with it efficiently. She would make a good copper. He could hear them deep in muttered conversation in the room next door and it hurt him to know that whilst he was alone, others were beginning new relationships, or living comfortably in old relationships. He missed talking to Rae already.

It had taken only 24 hours to turn a world upside down and bring Kobe to a place where he was sleeping in a stranger's home and wearing strange clothes. Nothing would seem normal again. At moments he felt overwhelmed by the feelings that were flooding through his brain, his thoughts rushing in and out again, like the tidal waters that Canute had tried to stop, deluged with memories and awash with images. He wanted to see his family, touch them, and hug them goodnight. But he would never do that again. Eventually exhaustion and tiredness took over and he drifted into a fitful sleep filled with bad dreams, listening to the hushed conversation from the next room.

Eventually as a morning sun began to lighten his room he awoke. It surprised him that he had slept but he had woken feeling no less tired than he did the night before. It took a moment for him to recognise where he was and why he was there instead of in his own bed. And as surely as stormy waves crash upon a rocky shore, his memories would continually hit the immovable rocks of his reality. He cried no tears as the memories hit him hard, he had shed them all last night, Kobe's eyelids were still sticky in the corners from the tears shed yesterday.

He climbed from the strange bed, he was still in the gym gear which he had been given when his own clothes were taken for forensics, his trainers lay abandoned just inside the door. He bent to pick them up, almost losing his balance caused by the dizziness of standing up too quickly and put a hand against the wall to steady himself. His head was pounding from the effort of all the thoughts going through it, and he still could not control or anticipate which thoughts were coming and when.

Kobe opened the door and stepped out into a short hallway, plain carpets, and beige walls but with Art Deco images and frames hanging just inches apart. It felt to him, in his confused mind, as if he were misplaced. He was not who he thought he was, he certainly had no idea where he was, it was as if he was lost within a movie somewhere showing another time and another place. At the end of the hallway the bathroom, where first he relieved himself and then splashed cold water on his face waiting for someone to yell 'CUT', and the film would be over, and he could head home to his family. There was something wrong with that thought though, but his memory would not risk a playback. Back along the hall and past the room he had spent the night he passed another, bigger, bedroom with the door slightly ajar which meant that he could just see in, David and Stella, two of his team, were wrapped in each other's arms, faces close to each other as if in readiness for a morning kiss, he envied them, and that hurt.

There were hints of the taste for Art Deco throughout the small apartment, Stella had good taste and liked to live neatly. He looked in the fridge for some kind of juice to quench his thirst, but there was none, she was obviously not expecting guests, and then felt more guilt, this time for the intrusion into her private life.

Why was he here?

Kobe sat on a kitchen chair and slipped into his trainers, which seemed to suit the crumpled, slept-in jogging bottoms, and mismatched sweatshirt. The shoes fitted just right, and he wondered if they were his anyway, he could not recall seeing them before. He found the front door and pondered about what would be on the other side, if it were the real world, he wanted none of it. But he could not stay here, wherever here was.

He looked back down the hallway toward the bedrooms and heard another deep snore and that made him move with a little more decision, as he did not want to embarrass either of them by letting them know he had seen them sleeping, it felt weird. Twisting the catch he slipped through the door, closing it as gently as he could behind him.

A few stairs down and another door, which lead out to the street. He recognised where he was, a street or two to the canal and a few more to the station, he instinctively knew he should not be anywhere near his office now so turned his back on the familiar building and headed for the canal. There was a bench on the edge of the almost still water, so he sat on it with a view down to the first bend in the waters that were being rippled by a swift breeze, a brightly coloured barge sat tied to the quayside and it was lifting and sat solidly in the still water. He had no way of knowing but this is exactly where David had been when called about a problem at the Kaan house. It was at that moment he sensed something was wrong, he thought about getting home but had no idea where his car was. Then he remembered!

CHAPTER 38

The Councillor had arrived home with the slight but unmistakeable coconut smell of shower gel on his skin, the second night this week. Last time it was to remove the smell of his lover and her bed, tonight it was to remove the smell of tobacco smoke and that awful man he was forced to deal with. Probably did the man living in that squalor a favour by cutting his useless life short. He could not understand how any man could live like that.

Waiting for him with a mixture of sternness and hurt in her face, was Barbara, the long-suffering Councillor's wife. She would not believe he had showered at the council offices after a long day of debating, who did that. He felt that as usual lately she would be itching for a fight, but tonight he would not give her the excuse, he was far too stoked after the afternoon's events.

"Debates about street lighting and dog shit does not take a council a whole day to debate." She would tell him in that cold frosty tone, he knew his excuses were beginning to wear thin. Ultimately, he would have the last laugh, he will have made the big time without her money.

The sinning husband would be relegated to the spare room for the night, but after an energetic evening of delightful action with the surgically enhanced girl of the moment he would not be unduly concerned with his punishment, what with the sex and now a killing, the adrenaline was off the charts, and he needed a break. He would welcome the rest and space.

Jackman was expecting at least an hour or two of inquisition on arriving at their beautiful house on the outskirts of the city, he turned into the drive and the electronic gates opened automatically, then closed behind him, the prisoner back in his cage. It was her house really, and her car, in fact everything was Barbara's and each time he arrived home other than at the expected time he would expect an earful. There was no choice for him now, so he had to put up with the sniping and nagging, he would leave in an instant if he could, but his only money coming in apart from his council fees and massaged expenses was from her. In the beginning he had won Barbara over with smooth charm and an electric smile, but she was a means to an end, and for him the marriage had worn thin very quickly.

Barbara knew he did not love her, but she hoped he would learn how to, he was a rogue but that was what first attracted her. She only had herself to blame. She was not a stupid woman but in matters of love there are no rules or strict guidelines, so she preferred to bury her head in softness of her pillows and ignore his straying, and lying, the lying being the worst of his sins. She did not want to know what he did behind locked doors, but recently his latest bimbo had been bragging on social media about her dating a handsome councillor. Nowadays she realised she continued to put up with his behaviour because at her age she was frightened of being alone. Forty-five was no age at all, but she looked after herself, but if asked she would say she was not a handsome woman, she would call herself plain. On the plus side she was tall and elegant, long slim legs which suited the kitten-heels she loved to wear, and she always felt good when in public but when she arrived at home with nobody but her mirrors to notice she wore baggy sweatpants and a T-shirt, at least she was comfortable. The thing that made her stand out in a crowd though, was her lustrous red hair, copper waves that cascaded across her shoulders. Hair worn loose she looked fabulous, hair up and in a two-piece suit she took on a whole new business look and powerful persona. Growing up she thought she was pretty, but one abusive lover and one straying husband and she had lost all confidence in how she looked. Anybody could be affected badly if told often enough that they are unattractive and uninteresting.

Barbara had grown up in a wealthy family, her father Arthur Jackman, owning a building firm and heading up several charities as well as Chairing the local Round Table. Out of respect for him, when she married, she kept the surname as it was well respected and a good business tool. Arthur was well known in the community and well respected, he had tutored his children, Barbara, and her younger brother Anton, to respect their name and their upbringing. When they reached eighteen, he gave them both £5,000, cut them out of his will and stopped any allowance they had been getting and told them to make their own lives as he had done. That is just what they did, Anton apprenticed in one of his father's building firms and learned the trade from the bottom up, he worked any overtime that was going and lived frugally, by the time he had reached his 25th Birthday he bought his father out and allowed him to retire, although Arthur kept a seat on the board. The business had grown even stronger under Anton.

Barbara took a slightly different route, she went to college and lived for three years on a student grant which she secured with the security of the gift from her father. He did not agree with her choice, but it was her choice and he respected that. On leaving college she worked at several beauty and hair salons learning her craft, never staying in one job for long, but her father remained patient and trusted her judgment. Within five years of leaving college, she opened her first salon, which ran without any of the mistakes or bad business practices of her competitors. Every six months she either bought out one of the competition or opened another salon, she now owned salons across three counties and employed over two hundred well trained beauticians and therapists, both her father and her brother were proud that the family name had been cherished and built upon.

Barbara Jackman had worked hard for her lifestyle and her layabout husband who thought life was easy would one day take just one step too far. She had already bailed him out of two failed business ventures, he suffered a short attention span and knew nothing about the value of money, or how to work hard. As for a private life together, she may as well get rid of him, she was lonely already.

CHAPTER 39

One man was already counting the cost of loneliness. There would be no gentle nagging or ribbing for him that night, not even the playful sort that he had become used to living with Rae. That sweet gift of a happy family life had been brutally stolen away from Kobe Kaan in just one evening of violence.

To say he was lost would be a massive understatement, since moving in together they had only spent the odd night apart in almost nine years of happy times. Kobe had no idea how to manage the thought of being apart from her, or their beautiful children. Although he knew what his thoughts were telling him was unobtainable, he still tried to think of ways they could be together again. The Kaan family were his entire world, and they had been snatched away from him. His other love policing had been what had driven him to excel every day and now even that was gone.

Kobe had been released without charge after spending almost 24 hours in custody after being subjected to endless time-wasting interrogation by a senior officer who was just trying to get another feather in the cap of his inflated ego. Total exhaustion had run his body down to almost zero energy, his brain power was on low and fogged. He had tried to sleep, but each time he drifted off he was disturbed by vivid bloody dreams and terrifying memories.

In his dreams and memories there was always something wrong with the roses.

Given only a couple of hours of restless dozing, Kobe's body still did not feel refreshed, while his tired mind remained in turmoil. Stella Gold and his sergeant, David Martin had kept watch over him, risking their own careers in doing so, but even they had to give in to the tiredness that long hours of worry and caring bring. They too were exhausted and now slept heavily, and Kobe had glanced into their room seeing them tightly in each other's arms. Them being together pleased him, though he would not normally condone fellow officers sleeping together.

He did not want to intrude any longer, so he had decided he needed to walk and head for his own home.

Body and mind on automatic he walked the streets of Chichester, initially on empty pathways and with only the odd car passing him. Then when civilisation began to waken and begin their normal day, he chose to ignore other people who were about at that time of the morning. Those heading for work did so trudging with heads down, or the children heading out for school turned out in smart uniforms. He recalled he was supposed to take young Kobe and Molly to school today, or was that yesterday, he could not work it out. In a moment of weakness, he had volunteered for the school run, but that was Monday morning, and he had a strange feeling today was Tuesday, could it be Rae had taken them as she usually did. That thought pulled him up sharply in the middle of the shopping precinct, when the memory hit him that there was no Mum to do the school run, and no children to take. There was to be no school run!

The rattle of the shutters being opened on a Pret-a-Manger startled him. So quickly did he stop that an office worker in the universal uniform of dark blue suit and light blue shirt almost ran into the back of him. The person cursed his bad walking, but Kobe heard none of it as the disgruntled man rounded him and continued apace toward his work destination, already in a foul mood even before his arrival at his workplace.

With the opening of the fast-food outlet Kobe thought he could do with the taste of a decent cup of coffee, and a sandwich, his empty stomach growled in complaint. He would pause outside each of the coffee shops as they opened their doors, high streets these days were full of them. He would pat his empty pockets before walking on, it seemed that every three or four stores there was yet another chain coffee shop. None were the cafe that he called at every working day morning, and for the moment he could not recall where that one was, or what it was called, he did recall that on the walls they had photographs of the food, it was strange that the owner had felt that people needed to be reminded what ham, egg and chips looked like. In the mist of his mind Kobe did realise that it must have been near his office otherwise the coffees would get cold. Breaking away from his selfish random thoughts for a moment, he thought of Jemma waiting for her morning coffee as she started her shift on the front desk, he did not like to let her down. He had let her down enough already in her life, coffee was the least he could do for her.

Chimes rang out from the Cathedral belfry panicking the roosting pigeons who flapped away as a grey cloud and then dispersing in all directions away from the sudden noise, Kobe recognised the sound, and he meandered toward the famous building and its gardens. He had to change course around a crowd that had gathered outside the old town hall, a strobe of flashlights firing hurt his tired eyes and fear gripped him! How had the press found him so soon? The media vultures had discovered the body to feast on. He heard the fired questions of journalists all trying to be the voice heard, he saw more flashes as camera shutters were fired. He ducked his head, tried to cover his face, and then saw the target for the photographers and reporters, it was a strange little man holding a sort of bronze figurine. Life was continuing at its strange normal elsewhere, and it could have been the Centurion's blade that bit deeper into his aching heart.

At the centre of the North, South, East and West streets was an ornate market cross sitting at the intersection, the gothic structure had been given as a gift to the town back in 1502 by a Bishop and it was topped with an ornate gold weathervane that glinted in the sunshine. Locals almost ignored the building, it was as everyday as the bank they would go into or the Marks and Spencer store, Students and elderly sat inside on hard benches set underneath the ancient archways to watch the world walk by while outside street musicians busked for change.

Kobe could not decide on left or right, this was not a day for such decisions, so he rounded the old market building and kept straight on, more cafes reminded him he was thirsty, it also reminded him he had no wallet nor money. Eventually the street ran out of shops and crossing a road he recognised a cafe with photographs of food from the menu stuck to the window, and amidst the faded burgers and ham, and sticky toffee pudding was a garish poster for the circus, which was long out of date, the acrobats and clowns having long moved on to yet another field in another town. Kobe thought the children may like to go, even though Rae was not a fan. His heart felt like it would burst at the thought of his children with their excited laughter and their faces awash with joy.

Remembering he wanted a coffee, it was now a craving, the more you cannot have something, the more you want it. He slipped his hands into his empty jogging bottom's pockets; they were still empty. He spun around and continued to follow the road, left took him to, what used to be, his second home, where apart from sadness amongst its rank, business would continue as usual. Kobe could not even bear walking past the place, he did not want to risk being rearrested for even more questioning, and it was a dread fear that he may have to talk about events all over again. It felt to him as if he had been walking with aimless intent, but his walk was leading him to the canal.

"Mr Kaan, Mr Kaan." The mister part of his name holding a small lisp. He stopped and turned.

The girl who would make his bacon sandwiches and prepare his coffees was running after him with a cardboard coffee cup in her hand. On young legs, she quickly caught him up.

"Mr Kaan, we heard about what happened to your family, we are all very sorry." Should he thank her or be cross at the reminder of what happened. He managed a brief and quiet 'thank-you.'

"I saw you through the window and it is chilly morning out here, so I made you a coffee." She offered a small smile with the hot drink, the low sun glinting off her nose stud.

"I am sorry, but I have come out with no money..." He felt himself blush with embarrassment, something he never remembered doing before. He could smell the delicious aroma of the coffee.

"This one is on the house Mr Kaan, my boss said you are welcome to come and eat something, but we don't really open for another 20 minutes or so."

Kobe took the coffee and thanked her for both the drink and the offer of food, but he was not much in the mood for eating.

He soon reached a junction where he could see the canal down to the right, he thought it would be quieter along the scenic towpath, fewer faces to bump into, a conversation of any sort would devastate an already broken man. The canal was originally built to join Chichester with Portsmouth and then London, but some idiot had invented the railway and suddenly the ingenious network of waterways was no longer needed. What remained of that defunct industry and passion was a pleasant walk with wonderful wildlife, it would still bring back painful, but warm, memories as Kobe's family loved to walk the canal of a summer's evening. Kingfishers racing along just above the surface of the water in a flash of iridescent blues in search of a different feeding spot, on finding a suitable low branch he would sit and carefully watch for the silver flash of a fish swimming by its roost. The children loved it when the tiny bird darted into the water to catch fish, before bursting out again in a flash of summer colours and then stunning the fish by beating its head against the branch, it was brutal for the fish but fun for the casual observer. One Sunday last summer they had watched a much bigger bird, as a heron sat at the foot of the far bank of the canal which was only some twenty feet wide. Twig like legs partially in water, its long beak in a slow sway side to side as it scanned for prey. The four of them had sat on a nearby bench to watch, the lanky, grey, bird oblivious to the audience, and they did not have to wait long before in a flash of movement it folded its wings back, looking like a delta jet fighter and thrusting its head forward at lightning speed, barely making a splash as its beak pierced the water. When his head pulled back in his long-pointed beak, he held a wriggling silver perch which with one well-rehearsed flick he turned so that the head was in the position to swallow first, Rae had explained to the children that he did that so that when he swallowed it whole the fish scales were in the right direction to make swallowing easier. Young Kobe was quick to point out that Mummy had told them they had to chew their food and that it was greedy to swallow it in one go. Rae had feigned frustration while Molly had told Kobe, the brother one, that he was being silly. It was a marvel to all of them how these birds fished so well. They had spotted cormorants diving for fish and eels, moorhens and coots clicking with their beaks for the young to stay close to home. Molly thought the little rough feathered chicks beautiful while Kobe would laugh at the ugly little hatchlings, but all of them loved watching them dart around the water's surface like playful children. They would toss grapes or cornflakes for the many ducks to feast on, Rae informed the children that bread was unhealthy for them, Kobe junior pointed out that if that were the case why did she feed them toast in the mornings and sandwiches on family outings. It was always an adventure no matter the weather, on rainy days it would be waterproofs and wellingtons and there would be a lot of jumping in muddy puddles on the rough track of the canal path, and on sunny days it would be shorts and plimsolls, but they still managed to get soaking wet. Then it would be home with worn out children and smiling parents, collecting a pizza on the way from a local pub, for dinner, hot bath and a bedtime story before the youngsters were bedded down for the night. Kobe junior loved recalling the summer's day when a young fox with his ginger coat and fawn breast sat on the far side of the canal semi-hidden in the brown rushes, his colouring the perfect camouflage. The fox was waiting for ducks who strayed into range, but the ducks were far wilier than the fox and stayed a safe distance away. Young Kobe thought it a shame that the fox would go hungry so after that day he made his dad carry dog treats in his pocket, but they never saw the fox that close again.

Nor would they ever, now, the chances had all gone.

Pains of loss and anger coursed through Kobe's body as the thought of never walking the canal with Rae and their children ever again ripped him apart, as if an electric shock had passed through him each recalling of a happy moment. He would never again see them racing ahead to the next puddle, or feel Rae's nervous hand in his, always fearful of the children falling into the murky canal water. But they never did.

The memories hurt him, but they would not stop coming. He felt that it may have been too soon to walk the canal, but there was nowhere he could walk without firing up another memory, everywhere was familiar to him, the memories would have been as fresh as every other spot they had been. Back when they were still a family.

Kobe stopped on a bench which was by an old wharf wall, and as he stared across the canal and out into the evening sun, he could see the tall grey spire of the Cathedral across fields and in the distance. His eyes watered and began to fill, it was a tough time for a fox to appear on the other side of the wharf, a vixen with a young cub by her side. Mother and pup stopped and stared at Kobe before her cub began bouncing around like any playful child. Kobe reached in his pocket for dog biscuits to toss across the water, his young namesake would have loved to do the tossing, swearing blind that he had a strong enough throw to launch them over the canal. One day he would have that strength...

Kobe cried!

A woman walking her yapping Jack Russell neared the bench where she saw a man, a little too dark skinned and swarthy she thought fearfully. The man was crying, his head held in his dark-skinned hands. In a moment of bravery, she approached and asked if he were okay. Kobe acknowledged her, turned his head partially toward the old lady and muttered that he was all right, but thanked her for asking. With the dog hard on her heels she wandered off far quicker than she had approached, determined that she would notify the police about a man who looked very much like he could be a terrorist acting strangely on the canal.

Kobe was not a man to show his emotions in public, his upbringing had taught him that showing your feelings was not a public spectacle. It was four months of dating before Rae had got the new man in her life to kiss her and show her affection openly, that was something done in private and behind closed doors. His grief now though was in a deep and dark chasm that he could not climb from, every fleeting good memory was tinged with the fact that he and his family would never do these things again, no more mundanity of family life, no more bedtime stories and no more hugs, laughter, or affection, private or any other way.

The old lady with the yapping dog had stopped a little way past where she had spoken to Kobe and had bent to pick up the steaming mess from her dog in a plastic bag, she inverted the bag over her hand and peeled it back over the small stick of dog's business. Neatly she tied the bag off, before nonchalantly tossing bag and crap into the canal, at the same time managing to look pleased with herself for picking up the poo in the first place.

Kobe stood and began the walk back to the city centre and the canal basin where the barges that carried holidaymakers on a there-and-back tour of the canal were moored. As he made distance between himself and the woman, he felt he had been rude to her when she offered her sympathy after seeing him in distress, but she had spoilt her copybook by throwing the freshly packaged turd into the canal, so *'fuck her'* he thought. The moment of anger was a relief from the pain of grief, but it was only a split second of respite.

Tears that ran freely down his face dried on the stiff breeze that he now walked into, making his cheeks sticky and cold, new tears over old. When he needed numbness, he only got sensation from his body, hunched shoulders ached, legs were shaky and sore, hands tingled and his heart dried to a small tight prune, laying wrinkled and hurting in his chest, where a great hole now resided where his soul used to be. He turned the corner in the canal where it widened out into the basin and saw the pub from two nights ago that held such hope and celebration.

If only he had not stopped for that drink, alcohol kills, and that one pint killed his family.

Kobe had no idea how long he had been wandering but the sun looked lower in the sky and an evening chill was settling in. Clothes that he was wearing were inadequate for the conditions, he was still wearing the sweatshirt and sweatpants from his locker at the station and on his feet his comfortable and scruffy Converse High Tops. He needed to go home and change, but he no longer had a home and even if he were allowed back in the house most of his things would have been bagged up and taken away for forensics. Caspar Jones would have made sure of it, in the search for evidence that did not exist, Kobe hated lazy police officers like Jones, not because he was being accused by him, but because coppers like him always took the line of least resistance no matter where it led, and that laziness usually took investigators in the wrong direction.

Nowhere to go, Kobe had never been in a situation like this before. Aimless, homeless and, for all he knew at that precise moment, jobless. He had no money to go anywhere, no bank cards or ID, not even his warrant card or a phone. The only thing to do when you had nowhere to go, was quite simply to go nowhere, so he just sat on a bench that had a viewpoint sweeping across the canal basin. He did not know it of course but it was the same bench that two nights before had seen the beginnings of some kind of relationship between two of his team and where they heard of his troubles, before rushing off together to go to his aid. Although he did not want company, he could do with them right now.

Kobe was a mess, with a brain full of mental rocks weighing him down.

CHAPTER 40

Sam thought it a grand affair, one of the grandest that Sam had ever been to, and he was the centre of attention.

Uncomfortable in a suit and tie, white button-down collar shirt that pinched his neck, and a pair of shoes so shiny Sam could almost see his face in them. The jacket was tight on the shoulders, as fashion dictated apparently; trousers too tight around the arse and crotch, again a fashion essential which he also disapproved off. He felt claustrophobic and strangled in his new clothes. 'How am I supposed to sit down in these clothes' he had asked Nick, the answer had been simple, he was not going to be sitting down.

Sam longed for his corduroy trousers and baggy jumper, his new and trendy jumper, which was smart, but Nick had told him no, and it was a firm '*NO!*' He had tried to fight the inevitable when Nick brought a tie into the big store's dressing room and his friend had won that battle too. Sam felt guilty about the complaining as Nick had used his own credit card to dress him for his big moment in front of the press, but he would get paid back in full, as soon as the bronze was sold. Sam had promised his friend.

The press was out in force, thanks to Nick who had called in favours with old colleagues, he had even got a few National boys down. Sam was astonished, he was going national, everyone would see his good fortune, and his detractors would now choke on their own words. Sam did have what it took to succeed, and at that time he actually believed in himself. The nerves and self-confidence flew out the window as soon as he had to stare out at those firing cameras and the pushy journalists who were shouting questions at him. To make it a decent light for the images Nick had taken Sam and the Centurion out in front of the old town hall where anyone with a minute to spare had to go and see what all the fuss was about, people loved an impromptu pantomime, and the bigger the crowd the bigger Sam's smile grew. Although the question-and-answer session was being held inside the building, where the bronze would be on display, there were still straight-out-of-college youngsters, with mobile phones recording, firing questions at Sam. Nick had explained that some were videoing the event and producing Blogs that would be viewed around the world. Sam for his part, spent the rest of the morning wondering what a 'blog' was.

Despite being strangled by the collar and tie, Sam felt good in his new suit, and he held the Centurion up with pride, sunlight throwing off a golden glint to the toned torso of the Roman. Photographers clamoured for the best shot, each shouting to Sam to lift the statue higher, lower and could he kiss it like a player with the FA cup. Sometimes Nick felt embarrassed by the antics of his own profession, pushing and shouting, trying to get that one comment they could and would blow out of proportion, always looking for the dirt. It seemed as if the British media had forgotten how to celebrate peoples' successes.

It was mixture of feelings that Nick had while watching his friend beaming from ear to ear at the attention, Sam had never excelled at anything and now he was getting his moment in the limelight. But there was always a price to pay for success and Nick hoped his friend would cope with that cost when it came. There was nothing he could do for now except stand off to one side and be there for Sam.

For his part, Sam was now feeling like a rock star or a movie idol, especially when the TV presenter from the BBC, a well-known face in the region, pulled Sam away from the throng to do his piece to camera. A tiny, furry, microphone was clipped to the lapel of Sam's new jacket, then the camera operator focussed on Sam's sweating face, the antique dealer had never known such nervousness and he could feel the beads of perspiration popping from his forehead. Euphoria was a quickly spent commodity and Sam was well out of stock after 20 minutes of a life spent in the spotlight. It is said that everyone has their five minutes of fame, Sam had overspent by fifteen minutes. He searched through the crowd for Nick, fearing he had left, leaving Sam on his own to fight off the gaggle of reporters. He was thinking he should have listened to his friend and just enjoyed the moment of quiet victory, but he had to tell the world, brag about his success, he wanted to both feel good deep inside and make his detractors and piss-takers feel the pain for a while. In the back of his mind, he had a sudden and random thought, what if it came to a point where he wished he had never found that bloody Centurion with his sword held high.

Everyone moved back inside to where it became a little more civilised, there was even tea and biscuits as well as very thin looking sandwiches, and the City's Mayor was in attendance. She was standing almost isolated at the end of the long hall, where only the day before yesterday Sam had been haggling unsuccessfully for some porcelain figurines. The mayor looked resplendent, but swamped, in her bright red coat with an itchy black fur collar. Around her neck and dangling down across her chest was the gold chain of office which was the only thing shining brighter than Sam's Roman. The local dignitary was looking as awkward as Sam felt, mainly because she was mostly being ignored, while sipping on a cup of tea from the council's best cups and saucers. All the while Councillor Jackman, the man who had somehow started all this fuss, was holding centre court telling those who would listen how he was the one responsible for bringing Sam Cobby to the fore on what had been a quiet news weekend, hence the press fever for a feel-good story.

Although crowded on three sides by the press, he remained busily watching everything from the centre of the room and looking as slick as ever as he stood just to the side of the press mob and answering their probing questions. A huge and well-practiced smile on his face, every now and again his hair was carefully brushed back into its waves of black and grey, by running his hand through the thick mane. He wore a loud pin-striped, blue suit, which on his slim frame looked elegant. Every now and again he would casually slide a hand into his trouser pocket causing his jacket to pull back and show off his red braces. Unlike Sam, the Councillor flourished in front of the camera, every move was a careful pose, his hair was both casually swept back and yet given freedom, it was as if he was born to be in front of the cameras. Sam was envious of the easy confidence. Handsome and full of charisma and charm, every arrow that Sam was missing from his quiver. He could see the local Councillor on the national stage in the future, as an MP or something in the Government.

Nick, for his part, was keeping to the edges of the event, but always keeping the line-of-sight clear so that Sam could see him. He was wary for his friend and ready to move in and rescue Sam if he got in too deep. Nick did not want to jump too soon and spoil his friend's moment in the sun, but he did want to protect him. He was also keeping a close eye on the slimy character from the council, the main difference in Nick's thinking, as opposed to Sam's, was that the bad apple in the council chamber would one day end up in the dock, and he hoped it would be one of his stories which brought him down. Nick had seen characters like Jackman come and go but this snake appeared to be protected somehow, no matter the work he put in he could not find the chink in Jackman's persona or history, well at least nothing provable.

So absorbed had Nick been in watching the throng around the Councillor, he had failed to notice that Sam had been stranded to the side-lines. He now looked limp and bedraggled in his new suit, such was the pressure of the morning's press call.

"Nick..." startled he turned round.

"Sorry, Sam, didn't see you creeping up on me."

"Bloody good journalist you are, losing sight of the main character in the real-life drama." Sometimes Sam liked to wax lyrical.

"I was keeping an eye on you, but I got distracted by the smooth politician over there."

"You two as redundant as I feel?" This time they both were startled as the mayor surprised them.

The diminutive woman swamped by her black and red robes of office and the chain seemed to be dragging her down, like a lead weight on a drowning man.

"My office for something a little stronger?" They did not need asking twice and they followed her out of the main hall.

"I know its a bit early, but..." She poured three whiskies into cut glass tumblers and without a word she quaffed hers in one gulp. Sam and Nick decided to sip, and even then, Sam choked a little on the burning brew.

"Thirsty, Madam Mayor?" Nick said in a friendly tone.

"I hate these fucking events..." she said, removing the heavy chain from around her neck and dropped it on the velvet covered couch in her office, she replied. "It's Sheila in here Nick, cut the pompous shit."

Sam did not expect such a common response from someone in public office, always thinking they should always be on best behaviour. Sam felt down in the dumps and Nick could not help but notice.

"What's up Sam, why so glum on your big day?" Nick placed a hand on Sam's shoulder.

"I didn't expect it to be such a big deal, I thought a couple of reporters and maybe a photographer." He looked toward the mayor to see if he should shut up and be more appreciative. But Sheila was just pouring herself another drink. "I am a bit overwhelmed is all, did you invite all of these people Nick."

"No, I didn't Sam..."

"I think our rising star did that all on his own Sam." said Sheila joining in. "Every time our Councillor Jackman sees a chance for lifting his profile in the press, he goes full bore. There are a number of us on the council who would like to see him gone, but he has been voted in and there is not much we can do about it. Do you not have something on him Nick?" She asked with a hopeful expression.

"Nothing we can use sadly, but one day, I am a patient man." Nick's determined look said the opposite.

Sam's look was a little less confident. "If I am honest, I am glad he has hogged the press, I about had enough of them today. Present company excepted Nick."

"I was asked to turn out with all the regalia and pomp I could manage because the National press was coming, and they don't usually come down here except to write theatre reviews, but it seems I am surplus to requirements anyway."

"Where is the statue, Sam?" Nick asked.

Sam simply nodded toward the main hall, where Jackman stood in front of the bronze Roman. "Look at that cocky shit, making out this is all down to him..."

Back out in the hall the slick Councillor was busy stealing as much thunder as he could get away with. As soon as Sam had run out of steam with the press, Jackman had stepped right in. Believing himself to be the consummate politician he shook hands and laughed all just the right times, that loud, fake, laughter echoing around the building. Mr charisma was playing to the crowds, and he loved it, strong in the belief that they loved him in return.

He lifted the Centurion from its pedestal as if it were a new-born from the crib, cradling it in his arms as he led the media pack and invited onlookers toward a glass display case sitting emptily alongside those holding the Council's treasures and silverware. They followed on as if they were the children following the Pied Piper, Jackman loved it when everyone played to his tune.

"Ladies and gentlemen of the press I am proud to put this wonderful find on display here in the council offices until it goes to auction, we would love to keep this treasure here but it does have an owner, as you have heard this morning," he stopped long enough to point at Sam, and it made the shy man feel guilty as if he had stolen the statuette and kept it away from the display. Embarrassed, Sam turned away and took a large sip of his warming scotch.

Jackman continued, "Hopefully the public enjoy it for the time that it is here, as it is a truly beautiful thing."

One journalist had the temerity to ask the question that they all had been ignoring.

"Mr Jackman, how can we be sure that this is not another fake, or even the same one that was on Antiques Roadshow." He held up his phone which was on record for video and sound, to later be transmitted as a Blog.

"I too was worried about that; it is easy to be concerned when there has already been one fraudulent piece." he was loving the game of tag between himself and the media. "So late yesterday I had both our museum curator and an independent assessor from our local and highly respected auction house and they both assure me that this is the real deal."

There was a small ripple of applause and once again photographers' flashguns lit up the room.

From his inside jacket pocket, with a magician's flourish, he pulled a soft velvet duster and used it to wipe any fingerprints off the Roman's body. All clean he opened the display case and placed it inside, twisting it this way and that until he was satisfied with its position. Sam, Nick, and the mayor watched from the door to the Mayoral Chamber. Jackman locked the case and easily slipped the key into his own pocket. Nobody noticed the sleight of hand.

"Can we go now?" Sam pleaded with Nick. "Not that I haven't appreciated what the council have done for me Madam Mayor, sorry, Sheila, but I would kill for a cold Guinness right now."

"Give me chance to hang up my superhero cape and put the chain away and I will join you." The Mayoral robe was already slipping from her shoulders.

"Not enjoying the event, Sheila?" Nick asked with a hint of sarcasm.

"Off the record Nick?" Even friendly council members needed assurance when opening their mouths in front of reporters.

"It usually is when we speak, but yes, off the record."

"I do not trust that slimy little man as far as I could throw him. And I am sorry for you Sam that he hijacked your big day."

"I was getting a little tired of it myself, I did not realise that it would be such a big affair. But I always do like a good buffet." Sam replied as he lifted a quarter sandwich from his suit jacket pocket and popped it into his mouth. It lightened the mood in the room.

Leaving the building they took a swift turning to the left and the trio entered the Tudor fronted Old Cross Inn and Nick ordered three pints of Guinness while Sheila and Sam settled themselves into a pair of matching green leather wingchairs, in the corner of the bar where they could watch all the comings and goings. It was late morning by now, but the lunchtime rush had still not descended on the popular watering hole. Nick being the last to the table was relegated to a green leather topped stool. Sam loosened his tie, but then decided to take it off, feeling relieved as he did so.

"Cheers everybody and thanks for today, it was nice to feel like a winner for once.!" Sam raised his glass, Nick just saying *'cheers.'* and Sheila offered Sam sincere congratulations, before adding "...old Mayor Cobby would have been proud of you Sam."

That comment had Sam bristling with pride, it was not a feeling that he had experienced very often.

They chatted about nothing for the duration of the first pint, which is when Madam Mayor made her polite exit but not before opening her purse and buying two more pints for a thirsty journalist and a knackered antique dealer.

Following her departure, Nick was the first to break the silence and leaned into Sam to speak, the bar was getting livelier now with lunchtime drinkers, and sandwich eaters. "Sam, I have a favour to ask." It seemed earnest so Sam took it seriously.

"Do you have a problem Nick, anything you know that my friend, if I can help I will..." Sam began to prattle.

"It's nothing to worry about Sam, well not for you." Sam looked intrigued rather than worried now. "The thing is I am going to ask Suzi to marry me..."

"Shouldn't you have asked her that before you got her pregnant, it might have been a good idea to do it that way around."

"It's before she drops the little one, I thought better now because if I wait until after the birth it may look like I am just trying to do the right thing."

"Hope he gets his looks from his mum, cos he'll be an ugly

bugger if he looks like you." Sam laughed; it was the first time today that he had felt at ease.

"What's wrong with you people, Suzi thinks it's a boy as well, it's going to be a beautiful girl that looks just like her Mum."

"Be a bugger if she comes out with long sideburns like her dad, won't it."

"Will you let me get to my point Sam, rather than taking the piss at a delicate moment."

Sam made the twisting movement of turning a key in front of his lips and then throwing the imaginary key away.

"I want you to be my Best Man, Sam, please."

Sam's glass was halfway to his lips, and it stalled there, he had a look of shock. "Have you checked this is okay with Suzi, Nick. Congratulations and all that, but bugger me, don't you know anyone better."

"Not really, and at least you have a new suit to wear."

"I was going to return that and get your money back." he said sheepishly.

"Seriously Sam." Nick did not often look nervous, he was a man that was usually full of confidence, but not today.

"I suppose you will want me to wear the tie again as well." Sam realised he had ribbed his friend enough. "Well, I suppose if nobody else has volunteered, it may as well be me."

"Thank you, Sam, I can think of nobody better."

"Try telling Suzi that, but It would be an honour my friend."

CHAPTER 41

Kobe had never felt more like a drink than he did at that moment, and it didn't help that he kept passing Off-Licences and supermarkets with brightly coloured posters in their windows offering cheap lagers and even cheaper ciders. Still, when you had no money in your pockets, cheap was still too expensive.

Kobe had never drunk heavily, partly because he was a Muslim but mostly because he never liked the taste that much, even at university when for his fellow students it was a cultural thing to get pissed every weekend he mostly abstained. His father was an Egyptian Diplomat of some sort in the UK, which is how Kaan had come to be born in England and never followed the rules of Islam very closely, if he was born only half Muslim then he should only need to follow half the rules, was his argument. Kobe's English mother was a non-practicing Catholic, so if he fell on one side or the other with religion he would follow his father, but not too closely. Kobe became non-committed to religion in general and neither parent felt it right to force him, just let him find his own feet. As he grew older, he grew closer to being a Muslim like his father, but never really took that seriously either. Now he was feeling that he must have pissed some one's God off because the retribution for his sins was way over the top. Kobe Kaan was angry at all gods, no one god was to blame, but if a god by whatever name existed, they were truly out of order. So right now, he fancied a drink, what else could they do to punish him.

They had taken everything away from him. He worked hard, both as a family man and in his chosen career. Now it seemed both were gone. He no longer had his family and how could he return to work for an organisation that felt he was the guilty party even before looking for anyone else. In the words of Kobe Junior whenever he ever got grounded as punishment, 'It sucked, big time'.

Many people in times of drama and trauma call out to the nearest god for help, even if they are non-believers, but Kobe felt he was way beyond help or redemption. His teachings told him that suicide was sinful and detrimental to one's spiritual journey, well circumstances had knocked anything spiritual right out of him. So, he left the colourful advertising posters behind him and just walked. He felt hunger and that brought on a further bout of guilt.

Guilt because his family had suffered because of something he did, guilt because he still had feelings such as hunger and thirst, while his family would never feel anything ever again. Thoughts would leap around in his head arbitrarily, one moment a beautiful memory from the past, the next the sight of his family on their bed and dead beneath bleeding roses. Images were strolling through his memory bank like a quickly scrolling computer screen. Would there ever be a time where he wouldn't see their deaths, every thought seemed to be cutting deep wounds into his heart and soul.

An experienced police officer is never far away from the questions that ruled their every working day, who and why? And what was to be gained from any crime, especially a cold bloodied murder such as this. Punishment or warning, or simply over the top revenge? None made sense, and for a detective something had to make sense. Even career criminals had a code, and except in extreme cases the code was never to involve families, family was off the table for most criminals whom even amongst the worst there was still some honour. Kobe was a copper in a small city in a beautifully landscaped and genteel county, of southern England. Major crime was not a problem they never had to deal with big crime in this attractive part of the world, apart from the odd drug raid or, an even rarer, crime of passion.

The sun began to fall lower in the sky and Kobe followed it, he had nothing else to aim for. He felt grubby and a little cold from being out in the same sweat clothes all day. There was no home to head for, and for the life of him and try as he might he could not recall where Officer Gold lived, not that he wanted to bother her and David for another night of lodgings anyway.

Once more, as if being attracted by a magnet he found himself on the canal path again, not remembering how he had got there or how he had crossed the busy by-pass. The footpath was narrow and uneven, every now and again he would step into a large dip along the dirt path and recall seeing Kobe and Molly on wet winter days jumping into them when they were full of rainwater, the lower half of their bodies would be caked in mud and soaked, which was also the fate that befell their parents who were always close to the jumping action. It made them all laugh, and suddenly Kobe felt half a smile on his lips but dismissed it immediately, he had no right to smile, ever again.

Kobe crossed a country lane to continue along the path. On the far side of the canal moorhens moved in and out of tall rushes, robins in the bushes sang loudly at him but he did not notice, and small flitting birds chased from the trees on one side the waterway to the rushes and willow trees on the other. Normally Kobe would see all this wildlife and point it out to the children, who would ignore him, or feign interest, before running off and finding another puddle ripe for jumping in. He could hear Rae beside him gently yelling *'Don't get too close to the water's edge!'* but they would run on regardless with Kobe junior always keeping a wary eye on his younger sister.

As he walked, he did have some lucid moments but even they were all about the burning question of WHO, or indeed WHY? Kobe Kaan had a strong analytical mind, which is just one of the reasons he was good at his job, and when he was able to force cogent thought to the fore he would try and calculate those two questions.

Throughout his career he had been the cause of many villains being put behind bars, their criminal trades out of business, but none had ever threatened his family. There were no big hoodlums or gangsters from organised crime, and anyway retribution meted out on police families was mostly the work of fiction and the movies, not for a copper from a small city on the south coast. His thoughts kept flipping in and out of detective mode. If nobody else was looking for the killer, then he would.

And without a thought for the non-violence belief of the Muslim faith he decided they would not reach the stage of being charged and tried, that would be too good for the likes of them, him, or her!

But why, it won't bring them back? He asked himself as his mood dropped again.

Who? Who would do such a foolish thing as attack a serving police officer's family? The last time he had dealt with anyone who was off the planet when it came to morals, was with two brothers who both turned out to be psychopaths, back when Kobe was still a Detective Sergeant, a case which saw him promoted and given his own small team of officers. One brother had taken the easy way out and dealt with the problem in his own way and taken the *easy* route out of trouble. Lucas and Jacob Tubb had given the police a right run-around, and it transpired that they both had the tendency to beat anyone to death if they were crossed, and yet on the surface were two very normal, and well educated, young men. Jacob, the younger and half-brother of Lucas was found bloated and floating in the harbour a few days after his disappearance by the two-man crew of a small sailing boat, the gruesome discovery ruining their day of sailing. The coroner had concluded that Jacob had decided that enough was enough and drowned himself. Previously Lucas had been sent to Broadmoor, a hospital for the criminally insane, from where he managed to escape and give Kobe a chase across the South of England.

It was eventually believed that Lucas was innocent with all suspicion then falling squarely on the brother's shoulders. Lucas was accused of killing a girl in a public garden alongside the cathedral, and then kicking her body under a bench in a poor effort to hide her. The sad, young and pretty victim had remained unnamed and unclaimed despite Lucas writing a book on the whole story, and even pleading on the flyleaf for someone to come forward and claim the girl. It was a best seller and the book brought him, along with his co-writer and journalist girlfriend, a certain amount of celebrity status. Kobe felt that the investigation had never reached a satisfactory conclusion, but sometimes one just had to go with the flow.

Kobe had stayed in touch with Gill Harmon, the girlfriend, but she always denied knowing about his violent tendencies and had heard nothing from him since they parted ways. Kobe, who had a gut feeling for such things believed her. His gut feeling about Lucas was that something was not quite right about the lad all along and eventually he knew his gut would be proved right. Had he come back for revenge? Could it be that Lucas Tubb had returned, Kobe didn't think so, but there was no way of knowing with a psychopath.

CHAPTER 42

The reception had long been over, and the journalists gone back to their respective offices to submit the story of a humble junk shop owner who found the greatest artefact in a very long time, and the photographers had downloaded their digital images and sent the high-res results to a myriad of agencies and newspapers. Everyone's work for the day was done including the remnants of the buffet being thrown away and all the crockery having been cleaned and stowed back in cupboards. Sam was back above the shop, with his cat who now seemed far more affectionate as he was being fed well, with his owner sleeping off the effects of an exciting day and three pints of Guinness. Nick was back at his home sitting and chilling with Suzi, massaging her feet, with music from the smooth old soul singer Isaac Hayes playing in the background.

Barbara Jackman was also sat at home, wondering as usual where her husband was for yet another evening. The last time she had seen him was on that evening's local news channel where he laid the charm out thick and plentiful in a story about a rediscovered bronze masterpiece. She hated to admit it, but the wayward man did look his usual ruggedly handsome self on screen, maybe he would make it to the House of Commons after all. She felt that he had conned her enough with his lies, wrecked their marriage with his affairs, and ruined her feelings of self-worth by having an open affair with a surgically enhanced bimbo 15 years his junior. Maybe it was with his charming ways that he managed to pull the wool over the electorates eyes as well.

The old town hall had long closed its shutters and the caretaker had locked up for the night. The caretaker was £150 better off when he left work that day, and all he had to do was forget to set the alarms, the Councillor had promised to do that when he left later that evening, he apparently had work to catch up on. In the Mayor's Parlour Kenneth Jackman sat in the Mayoral swivel office chair with his feet up on her highly polished antique desk. He sipped the last remnants of the sparkling white that had been put out for the press junket, he was not about to waste good Cava on the plebs from the press, even if it was the cheap stuff. Across the room on a little two-seater couch was his driver and minder Fiona Webb, she sipped on sparkling water, alcohol would poison the temple that was her body. Although all was quiet out in the corridors Jackman decided to leave it for a half hour after the caretaker had left with his beer money and a distinct lack of knowledge about what was going on back at the old town hall.

Kenneth broke the silence when he felt it was totally safe to do so. "Have you got it with you?"

Webb dragged a holdall around from the side of the couch. "All safe and secure." She thought for a moment before adding. "I presume you have worked out how we get away with this, Mr Jackman." The name was said with a sarcastic tone.

Webb led the way back into the outer office where the Centurion was on display. The main lights, as they would expect to be, were out but a blueish glow came from the lights that twinkled off the glass of the surrounding display case, shining like stars in a night sky. The real Centurion, with his sword held high, glowed with the cold of the display lights, it all looked a little spooky but that just made what Jackman was up to even more of an adventure as far as he was concerned. The glass walls and shelf of the display case had all been cleaned and wiped once the bronze was locked in there, in readiness for public viewing the following day, so both Jackman and Webb wore soft white gloves, dressed in black and wearing the gloves made them look like a pair of snooker referees.

Jackman drew the copy of the key from his pocket, the original was locked in a secure key case in the building manager's office. There was a moment's hesitation, not for second thoughts, more to enjoy the experience of a well worked plan, then he slipped the key into the chrome locking device and it turned easily with a satisfying click. With the tip of one finger on the top lip of the door he opened it wide, he may have gloves on, but he did not want to leave tell-tell smudges on the glass. The longer his exchange of the statues went unnoticed, the more chance of getting away with it, Jackman smiled at the simplicity of what he was carrying out. He would not get full market value, but it would still be enough to live the high life with his surgically enhanced lover as soon as he could clear off to Spain and leave this rain sodden country behind. Neither would he miss his harpy wife who controlled the purse strings, that was just embarrassing. It was demoralising, a grown man having to ask his wife for spending money.

As he lifted his gold looking treasure, Jackman felt like Indiana Jones in the movies, for a moment looking around to see if a huge boulder was being sent his way by some ingenious booby-trap. Fiona Webb rolled her almond eyes at his antics, knowing exactly what her boss was thinking. For a fleeting moment she thought of taking the Centurion for herself except, even given her wickedness, despite her infamy she did not have the contacts that Jackman had for selling something like this. Jackman handed her the real Roman, his short sword glinted menacingly as it passed the cabinet lights. It may have only been a 100 or so years old but it was the uniqueness that captured Webb's imagination, the fact that this piece of work came from Herbert Bayer who was better known for his geometric sculptures from the Bauhaus Movement in 1920's Germany. For Jackman it was all about the money, for Fiona Webb it was about the history and the sheer beauty of the artwork.

"Wake up, Fi, give me the fake." Jackman said impatiently in a heavy whisper, although nobody was near to hear any voices.

He was the only person to ever get away with calling her Fi, to her ears it made her sound common, and she was anything but. In her right hand she held the real Centurion, with her left hand she reached into a holdall where, still wrapped in a protective towel, lay the fake that had been discovered on television. For a moment she thought of doing a double switch and fooling Jackman while he was busy looking around the room as if searching for police to emerge from the shadows.

Webb hefted the fake and then the real deal, she took a moment to hold them balanced in her arms, they looked the same, weighed the same and carried an equal amount of gravitas, and they were both things of beauty. Webb could not fathom how even the experts could tell the difference. Then without another thought she handed the fake bronze to Jackman who quickly placed it into the cabinet moving it slightly to the left, twisted it counterclockwise and back again, once he had it positioned perfectly, he closed and locked the cabinet door.

Nearly there, a few more seconds and they were away free and clear.

Despite his rush to get out of the building he caught a glimpse of the valuable original just as Webb wrapped it in its protective cloth, he gently gripped her wrist before she had chance to finish so as to take a closer look. She wanted to slap him and looked at him angrily, Webb hated being touched or manhandled, but she let it go. One day he would pay for all these indiscretions, but now was not the time. Even she looked down at the statuette and marvelled in its golden sheen and for almost a minute they were both mesmerised by the artistry and beauty of the ancient soldier. They shook themselves from the artwork's grip on them and Webb finished the wrapping before placing the swaddled item into the holdall.

Jackman took another look at the fake now standing bravely with his sword held high and walked around the cabinet to check it from all sides. He needed to assure himself that he had repositioned the fake perfectly, photographers and cameramen had snapped and filmed it from all angles and Jackman was not about to fall short on his mission by leaving something disturbed that would alert people to the theft. People were strange, they could not recall their passwords but put an anomaly in front of them and it would stand out like a cow in a cornfield.

"Time to go, Jackson." Webb urged and tried to make it sound as if said with respect. "It would be a shame to get caught now."

Although he did not like the fact that she had just told him to do something, a pet hate of his as nobody told Kenneth Jackman what to do, or when, he moved immediately. Only Barbara had carte-blanche on ordering him around, but that would not go on for much longer. Once he had moved the statue to the Dutch buyer who was waiting to pay his asking price, he would have money of his own and be able to just leave her nagging self behind in this shitty place while he lived the high life on the Costa del something-or-other. The buyer did not care where the rare bronze had come from, he just wanted to own it and place it in his private collection.

They strolled out of the building with no sense of urgency, Jackman because it felt like he owned the council and its chambers, and Fiona because there was nothing she feared. In fact, they walked the corridors with a jaunty step. Jackman's Oxford brogues squeaked with each step and Webb's stilettos clicked on the bare floors, as burglars they were inept, but as international art thieves they excelled, or thought they did.

It was a little after midnight when they got back to the Jaguar and the streets were quiet, even so they had walked in the shadows to avoid showing up on the city-centre CCTV system. On reaching the car Jackman stowed the Roman in the boot and covered him with a blanket and Webb said he could take the car as she felt like an early morning stroll back to her flat across the road from the city's world-famous Festival Theatre.

"Good work tonight, Fi." And he was in the car and gone.

Webb was glad to see the back of her boss tonight, she knew how inept he was and wondered how his wife had put up with him for so long, some women were just so weak, but she didn't pity them, weak women maddened her. This little adventure would be so worthwhile, just as soon as she received her cut for her evening's work she would move to Paris and set herself up as a professional assassin, for that covert work she did have the contacts and she had discovered a real liking for the job. Webb liked the sound of that title and she pondered on her new life as she walked past the theatres where, outside the studio theatre, the Minerva stood. A proud statue of the Roman goddess of war. An important goddess for both Romans and Greeks she carried a shield and sword, it seemed apt that they had just stolen a Roman warrior and here stood his goddess looking even more powerful. Webb liked that, being a strong female warrior herself.

CHAPTER 43

The sun began to rise, as did the chill temperature of early morning, both telling Kobe he had been walking and thinking for the entire night, yet he didn't feel tired. Truth be known, Kobe felt nothing physically. All he could feel was an overwhelming sense of loss that bore a hole right through the core of his very being. He was still wearing the same sweatshirt and bottoms, they carried the damp of the night that should have chilled him to the bone, but there was nothing, no physical feeling. Only the sun rising made him realise his physical being was under attack as well as his mental well-being.

Walking streets that he recognised only vaguely, had been a lonely vigil, but he was going to have to learn to live with that. The fact he was now being surrounded by the busy rush of workers heading for their office shifts and shops did nothing to alleviate his loneliness. Is this how it would be for the rest of his days, he thought, no matter the company he kept there would still be loneliness. The suffering was immeasurable. As the streets filled, he was jostled as people with a tight timeline to their day ploughed a furrow through the crowds, even in the broad precinct they still bumped into each other. Their collective day had only just begun and yet they were stressed and angry already.

Total strangers, shoppers, and shop staff heading for their 9am opening and even the women pushing expensive, designer-built buggies, heading for morning coffee, all looked Kobe up and down while making up their own minds about the down-and-out beggar, penniless and looking for a begging spot so he could afford the next drink. Beggars were a blight on the streets of their beautiful and historic city. Faces showed their displeasure before the owners detoured around him with loathing in their eyes. Nobody cared for the homeless alcoholics, they only had themselves to blame, nobody gave Kobe a caring look or thought as he trudged his way through the day. He caught a glimpse of himself in a dark shop window, the glass acting as a perfect mirror, Kobe did not recognise the broken man standing there in the reflection. His head and chin showed thick black stubble, the sweats he was wearing were limp with damp and blackened with the debris picked up from benches and walls he had brushed with throughout the previous night and most of the day. His once white trainers were now dark with puddle water and scuffed, his posture was hunched. How he, and life in general had changed in the few days since that drug raid. To Kobe that felt a lifetime ago, hours dragged into days and days would eventually drag into weeks. When there was nowhere to go and no specific time to be there, the hours on the clock were totally meaningless, sunsets meant colder stretches of time, sunrises meant maybe a little warmth.

Another day had passed, and another night, Kobe looked drawn, and pale skinned, despite his usual olive complexion. Hunger forced rumbling sounds in his gut, yet he did not feel like eating. He had slept for a few hours propped in the corner and shadows of an abandoned shop doorway, in the current financial climate the homeless were spoilt for choice and could go downbeat, or upmarket with their choice of abandoned shop doorways. As the first glow of daylight crept across the ground before gently flooding into his doorway, where reluctantly it woke him. The fitful sleep had left his thoughts in a murky morass, even more so than on previous morning since his gruesome discovery. He had to think for a moment to discover where he was, and why he was there. Aches and knots in his muscles made moving awkward, but as he moved, he noted a cardboard coffee cup by his side and a triangular sandwich packet, it must have been left by some charitable unknown. Coffee aroma filled the doorway as an expensive perfume could entice, and Kobe could not resist picking the cup up and sipping, hot and fresh, white coffee which tasted good that morning and he sipped it carefully. A kindly, elderly lady, with purple rinse and thick woollen tights, dropped two, single one-pound coins into the doorway and begged the homeless and scruffy man not to spend it on demon drink. Advising him at the same time of where to go and get help finding a bed for future nights, apparently there was a storm coming. Kobe thanked her although he wanted to throw her charity back in her face, but then thought that would be rude. Her phrase had him thinking and indeed there was a storm brewing, when he found out who had killed his family, the storm he had planned would possibly wipe them out, after making whoever did this to suffer as Rae and the children had suffered at the hands of their murderous torturer. It wasn't revenge for himself, he did not place himself in a high enough status for that, it was for those three lives cut so cruelly short.

He also knew he could never return to his beloved police force once he had handed out his style of justice.

Shame was now added to his other alien feelings, he did not want others to see him this way, especially any of his colleagues from the force, so, it was time to move on. Apart from anything else he did not want to talk about recent events, talking about it made it seem even more real and now his lucid thoughts were shutting down. He dropped the empty coffee cup in a bin, and ripped open the sandwich packet, but after two bites he felt nauseous, so the remnants were dropped in the next bin along.

Shops were opening, with alarms being turned off, several with electronic screams before the correct digits were punched into a keypad. An ancient grocer, blue apron, and grey hair began displaying his wares in the old ways when shopkeepers all displayed their produce with pride, an art, apples being polished and displayed in neat rows, carrots and oranges bright on sloping display racks and a box of exotic pineapples propped up on one end, all their leaves curving upwards like green crowns. A security shutter, thrown open rattled in its runners and made Kobe jump, he looked around startled, before looking down at the ground once again and walking onwards, the last thing he wanted was to catch somebody's gaze.

Light spilled from one of those chain pubs that served an inexpensive breakfast as well as long cool pints of beer that were being supped before most people had chance to get to work. Kobe had never understood the need to drink that early in the day, well maybe he understood a little now. Outside the pub sipping on a half pint of what looked like lager was a blonde woman, with hair like straw that was piled up in a ramshackle bun, her face hardened and lined by life was coated in thick make-up in an attempt to hide a variety of sins. One hand, decorated with iridescent orange varnish on bitten nails, lifted a skinny rolled-up cigarette to her lips, she drew hard on it to extract the most smoke from the least amount of tobacco and blew the smoke into the air. Her other hand was resting on her bare thigh, white, skinny, long and mapped with blue veins beneath a mini skirt that barely covered the lady's arse. She sat one leg crossed over the other and was looking with a venomous stare at her partner across the table, who had similar mapping of blue veins but across his bulbous nose. He took large swallows from a pint tankard, more manly than a straight glass, on just one visit to his mouth the glass was half emptied of the bitter local ale.

His arms and face were covered with various tattoos. Under one eye he had just three dots, showing that he had been in prison, it's meaning unsure, but most prisoners believe it to mean death to the police. Kobe noticed things by instinct and as the man took a second large gulp of ale, the letters ACAB were written in upper-case across his four fingers, a well know acronym standing for All Coppers Are Bastards.

Kobe felt both sympathy and anger at the couple, the chances were that they had children at home, and what sort of life would they give their offspring... But at least their youngsters were still alive. As tears filled his eyes and he walked on, even if he had the £4.99 for one of the pub's popular breakfasts, he felt sure he would only vomit it back up.

He kept walking out of the town and toward the harbour via the canal path again, this time he would walk all the way, it seemed that each time he walked beyond the shopping precinct he headed toward the marina following the pathways he had walked with his family. He tried to let his mind wander and follow its own route, but he had an idea of how to stop the suffering. He recalled how Jacob Tubb had taken his own life when the going got too tough for him. The man was a psychopath who had beaten to death the family Nanny, by all accounts a loving old lady who had virtually raised the boys and then stayed on as the family housekeeper, remaining loyal to Jacob and his brother Luke. As the investigation continued and DNA was checked it was discovered that after a secret affair with the boy's father, it was the nanny that had given birth to Jacob. Unknown to him he had murdered his own mother. Totally unhinged he viciously beat and raped the police Family Liaison Officer, PC Jemma Costello, who had been assigned to him. The assault had left her close to death, leaving her scarred and frightened by life itself. Kobe had blamed himself for the assault as with his enquiry team thin on the ground when it came protection, he had left her alone with a violent killer. Then still a DS, Kaan swore to catch the man and as he and the team closed in on him, Jacob Tubb saw no way out and chose the easy option. Instead of the shame of arrest and imprisonment for life, he went for swim in Chichester Harbour with no intention of ever reaching the shore again.

Kobe now headed for the same beauty spot. He too had begun to see it as the only option.

CHAPTER 44

"Ladies and Gentlemen," The auctioneer had reached the finale of the sale. "...now for our final lot of the day, of which there has been much interest, both here and on the internet. We will also have several telephone lines open and will be taking bids from the floor." he announced.

A white-gloved porter carried the Roman Centurion, with his sword still held triumphantly above his head, with great care to a podium to the right of the Auctioneer's rostrum, and just in case anyone had missed what the man with the gavel was alluding to, the porter with an elaborate flourish of one hand pointed to the Roman that gleamed powerfully under the room's lights. The gladiator looked powerful under the lights.

"We have potential buyers, online, on the phone and of course here in the saleroom." he repeated. his voice was pompously that of a private school well-educated Englishman and he exhibited a smarmy smile that he mistakenly misjudged as charm. "We have many offers on the book already, you have all seen the news and heard the provenance of the bronze, that had been missing, believed lost forever in fact, and rediscovered by one of Chichester's finest antique dealers, a man with a solid reputation and a keen eye."

Sam, in the same suit and white shirt Nick had bought him minus the hated tie, was stood at the back of the room with his friend alongside him as he always was totally rapt in the proceedings and almost missed the actual words that were being said on the podium. Nick jabbed him in the ribs with his elbow, and Sam realised what had been said about him.

"Did he just say what I thought he said?" asked Sam.

Nick with his finger over his lips, told Sam to shush.

"Put your hand down Nick, he will think you're bidding." he said with humour and a little too loud, bidders in the back rows turned to see who was interrupting proceedings. Sam blushed.

"I can begin the bidding..." A dramatic pause so the auctioneer could milk every second of his appearance on stage. "...two million, one hundred thousand pounds." The last two words he pronounced as 'thowsand' and 'pownds'.

Sam giggled but he wasn't sure if it was the staggering amount that the sale had begun at, or the awful voice of the auctioneer. But the giggle died in his throat as the bidding climbed quickly. The last auction Sam had been at climbed in ten-pound increments, this sale was leaping at one hundred thousand a bid, it flew toward three million, slowed slightly as it passed that mark and sped up again as it approached three and a half. These were figures Sam had only ever dreamed of, beside him Nick supported his friend at the elbow as he saw his knees begin to buckle under him.

The excitement and tension in the ornate London auction room held a thickness to it. Nick in journalist mode realised his pen hand was shaking but hoped his shorthand would be legible. Although surrounded by fine artworks Sam could not take his eyes off the gavel, held in the finely manicured hand of the auctioneer, as it hovered above the rostrum top. One part of him wanted it to drop so it would bring an end to the almost painful euphoria he was feeling, but he also wanted it to stay aloft because if it was not being brought into use, he was getting richer. Sam was hypnotised as he followed the gavel with his eyes as it pointed to bidders in the large audience and then to the bank of phones, before travelling onto the computer folk, it was a busy gavel pointing this way and that as the bids continued to flow.

Sam felt out of his depth, he was in awe of the proceedings, the feeling like that of a drowning man struggling for breath. On beyond four million, Sam thought he would faint, he was hyperventilating and feeling light-headed.

The gavel was used to point out a bidder at the back of the room. "Four million, two hundred thousand, to the gentleman at the rear of the room." a slight pause by the smart auctioneer to look at the half dozen phone lines being occupied, another glance at his computer screen. "Four million three on the telephones." With hardly a moment to breathe in for the auctioneer. "Four, four, thank you Sir..." he nodded toward the rear of the packed room.

Sam could not take anymore, and he turned and fled from the hall, Nick saw him go and almost followed, but he had a job to do and, he would have to tell Sam at what figure the sale finally reached.

Thankfully there was a bench just outside the auction rooms and Sam sat there, elbows on knees and watched the traffic rush by, taking deep breaths and inhaling the exhaust fumes. He longed for the clean air of his hometown, where he realised life would never be the same again. No more counting pennies, no more wondering if he could feed Wedgwood, or himself, again. There would be no more living above the shop, no more cracking his shin on coffee tables that would not get out of his way. It brought on a mini panic attack and once again he battled for breath. He had lived above the shop all his life; he knew nothing else. Sam had watched the city grow and change, around him, from childhood he had watched as the fortunes of the area grew and then falter again before, becoming the wonderful place he knew and loved. His life was as permanent in the city as the Cathedral's, where sadly, sometimes, he felt as old and grey as its walls.

If he had been listening, Sam would have heard the round of polite applause, celebrating the price his statuette had achieved, the clapping filtered out into the street signalling the end of the sale. Sam never heard the clack of the auctioneer's gavel as he concluded the bids. It was a huge day for Sam, but back in the imposing building it was just another day in the life of a London auction house.

That beautiful Roman was no longer his, and he felt sadness at the thought of it moving on, while hoping it had gone to someone who would care about the soldier with his sword held high. One thought lifted his wilting heart, he would buy his friend Nick and his partner Suzi a nice house where they could bring up their baby, one with a nice garden. That was unless what he had witnessed inside the auction house was just a dream made up by a head that had always been full of dreams.

Now that his dream of success had happened, what would his future dreams be about?

His reverie about dreams and the style and position of Nick's house were stopped short as his friend flopped down on the bench alongside him and let out a long breath.

"Well!" said Nick, with what sounded like the last piece of air in his lungs.

"Well, what? Nick. Well, what?" Sam was not known for patience.

"Five and a quarter!" Nick swivelled to look his friend in the eye.

"Thousand?" Sam was in denial.

"No Sam," he shook his head and offered a smile for Sam to

share. "Five and a quarter million. Five million, two hundred, and fifty thousand pounds, Sam."

"But they take fifteen percent of that? Don't they?"

"Plus, VAT Sam, don't forget the tax. Plus, when your yearly accounts are totted up you will owe the taxman some of your income." Nick was enjoying this.

"He can join the queue, Nick." Sam leapt up from the bench as did Nick and they hugged on the sidewalk, cheered loudly, and laughed with abandon. Passers-by continued walking without reaction, London was a place where men hugging and cheering on the footpath was an everyday scene.

Just over thirty minutes, the auction of his statue had lasted no time at all. Even after all the taxes, fees and paying Nick back for the travel costs and hotel, he would be left with somewhere around £3,000,000. That thought, for Sam, was an unimaginable figure and he felt another panic attack coming on. He found it tough to breath.

He staggered back onto the bench, his breathing rapid, his head swimming and his heart pounding. Nick sat back down with him and told him to breathe gently, "In and out like you do every other day." Finally, Sam began to get it back together.

"When do I get the money Nick? I owe you for the suit and the hotel and stuff." This was how Lotto winners must react with the jackpot, a mixture of euphoria and fear. Every day from now on his life would never be the same. "Fuck! Nick, fuck! What am I going to do with all that money? Fuck, Nick?"

"Anything you want Sam, anything you want." and the two men burst into laughter once more, and Sam still had no idea when he would get his money.

Nick wondered how his friend would cope, money can bring disaster and sadness as well as joy and it was how you handled it that would determine which way round it would go.

The nearest bar to the auction house was a trendy wine bar, even though Sam was now wealthy he still preferred a good old-fashioned pub, he was determined that money would not change him. Nick bought the drinks while Sam found a table in the corner, and they drank a cold European lager straight from the neck of the bottle, Sam would have preferred a pint of West Country cider. It felt effeminate to be drinking posh Belgian beer out of a bottle, but then he recalled that he was rich and posh now. All around them London office workers sipped cocktails and wine spritzers, young men with bushy beards and small buns of hair atop their heads drank out of bottles. Every time someone new entered or left the bar there were hugs and cheek kissing, associates one kiss on each cheek, best friends went for three. Sam wondered what ever happened to the good old handshake and proper hairstyles.

"Could we have not found a decent pub and a good pint Nick? I may be a millionaire, but I still like the simple things in life" Millionaire, it sounded good hearing the word.

"That's the trouble with you rich people, never bloody satisfied." both men laughed, clinked their bottles together in a toast and sipped on the cold watery beer.

Two young woman, attractive and with good figures entered the bar. They may have been pretty, but they still felt the need to enhance their modern look with tight miniscule dresses and a mass of make-up. The pair were on show, and they sauntered past and looked down their noses at the two out of place, out of town strangers. Nick thought nothing of it but it made Sam feel even more uncomfortable. He shrunk into the jacket of his suit and felt his cheeks burn red.

"If either of those girls knew what you were worth now Sam, they would be sitting on your lap and nibbling on your ear." for a moment Nick thought of inviting the girls over to help Sam celebrate, but just as quickly thought better of it. "No matter how much money these city traders and arseholes have made today, not one of them have made the profit you have Sam. It will take them a lifetime to come up with that sort of money, and then they will have to live with the stress that they suffered making it. You are a winner now Sam, and you have earned it."

As bars full of trendy youngsters is apt to do this wine bar was beginning to get a little loud, raised voices, fake laughter and indecipherable music that charged over their heads was becoming a hubbub of colourful noise. It was so loud that Nick and Sam could not hear each other and so stopped talking and swallowed the last of their factory-tasting beers, it was time to head home, which both were pleased about. Sam had never wanted to get back to his shabby shop quite so much before, and for his part, Nick was desperate to get home to the pregnant Suzi. He missed being away from her, and their unborn.

As they emerged into the street from the darkened wine bar it was almost a shock to discover it was still daylight and one with bright sunshine beaming down through the gaps between the tall buildings. Over the sounds of traffic and the wailing of a passing ambulance Nick faintly heard his phone ringing and felt the vibrations in his pocket, looking at the face of the phone he did not recognise the number that was ringing, but for a journalist this was not unusual, so he answered its electronic jingle.

"Say that again." Sam picked out the, more than a, hint of concern in Nick's voice and his friend looked at him with a face that had aged in moments. "It's the auction house, they have asked us to pop back in." He said with puzzlement in his tone.

CHAPTER 45

Having lived on the edge of Chichester Harbour for several years Kobe knew all the beauty spots, by feel rather than a tide table knew how the tides moved in and out at those spots. He also knew the tide movements and the speed with which they travelled, but the water was too far out when he arrived at the muddy bank. He was unable to walk out into deep water from where he intended to reach for his family one last time. The Quran states that God will judge everyone by his or her deeds and heaven awaits those that have lived righteously, hell awaits those who have not. With all his sins and misdemeanours Kobe could only hope for the former.

As he waited there for the tide to come in and swallow him up, he also remembered that it is Allah who determines when an individual dies, and as the hours passed, he began losing his resolve, Kobe decided with reluctance that he could not risk another sin so quickly. Plus, he had things to do here on earth, especially doing right by his family, they still needed him – alive and caring.

After changing his mind standing by the mud waiting for the tide to return, some of Kobe's old grit and determination returned, if he had gone through with the plan that a few minutes ago seemed the best way to go, Rae would have thrown him out of paradise herself.

The change of plan meant that he would have to face people again, hardest of which would be at the station. He began the lonely walk back into the city centre, retracing his steps along the canal where sunshine glinted like diamonds on the surface of the water and swans glided majestically leaving barely a ripple behind them. Across the road and up the gentle hill until the station came into view. They had his warrant card and keycard, so it had to be through the front door, and as she usually was, it was Jemma behind the counter. Kobe thought he saw tears in her eyes as she looked up and saw him. He felt embarrassed when he realised how down and dishevelled, he appeared.

"Mr Kaan, I am so sorry to hear about your family." Kobe fought back the desire to cry as well. "I was here on the night they brought you in. I brought you a coffee, but I think you were too distracted, obviously, to remember." She took in the sorry sight that used to be her Boss and mentor. "Should I buzz you through, or if you're suspended, I don't suppose I can?" The girl was flummoxed and showing the nervousness she felt at uncomfortable moments.

Despite his troubles Kobe offered a calming voice.

"You had better not Jemma, and thank you for your kindness, I do remember the coffee it was very a sweet gesture." Kobe could not go into detail, it would be too much for him, so he just settled for saying. "I think this is the last place the people upstairs want me to be, so would you be kind enough to call David Martin and have him bring my belongings down please, I currently don't have a phone, my wallet or any money."

Without hesitation Jemma turned and picked up the desk phone, through the Perspex window that separated the entrance from the front desk, Kobe watched as the light caught her face. He could clearly see the physical scars left behind to remind her every day of her attack. Around her mouth and one eye the skin was puckered and white, her nose now slightly bent at the tip and on the cheek nearest to him, the distinctive mark made by Jacob Tubb's signet ring, that was as red and angry as if it had only happened yesterday. Kobe Kaan would be hounded by the guilt of not getting to her in time and for not figuring out that Jacob was the killer he had been after. Sometimes being a copper was hard, and maybe, just maybe, it was time he retired anyway. He had no heart to return to a job that had led his life down its current route.

"He is on his way down Mr Kaan."

"Jemma, when will you start to call me Kobe? I am not your boss anymore."

"Will do, Kobe." It felt strange coming out of her damaged mouth, she had always known him as Mister. "Mr Martin said he has been worried since you left this morning, he had no idea where you had gone."

"I wasn't sure where I went either." He then added. "I am sorry, I was not able to bring you your coffee this morning. I had no money." He felt ashamed, to add to all the other shit feelings he was having, by pleading temporary poverty.

"That's okay, Mr Martin brought one in for me, and he said he will keep doing it until you come back."

"If they ever let me back." Then it dawned on him. "Or if I want to come back."

David Martin burst through the door as if on a raid and pulled Kobe into a huge hug. It was the first time he had ever hugged a senior officer and he imagined the street artist Banksy would do a wall mural of two police officers hugging just like one of his early pieces that is still on a Brighton wall.

He had a plastic bag holding Kobe's belongings but explained because of his suspension he was still not welcome in the station. On 'Ghost's orders' apparently.

"The miserable bastard still doesn't want you around," he explained. "He still thinks you are good for it, so we're to have no contact with you."

"I guessed as much. When you have no idea what you are doing you latch onto the nearest branch then just hang on for dear life." Kobe responded.

"Who's Ghost?" Jemma asked.

"Casper Jones," David explained. "He becomes invisible when the hard work comes around. He is one of those on the job who never makes a mistake, or so he thinks."

Jemma looked appalled with the fact that someone could think it was Kobe. "Does that mean you could lose your job Mr Kaan." she couldn't help herself when it came to the respect she held for her bosses.

"Might as well, I've lost everything else."

Neither David, nor Jemma, knew what to say to that, what could anyone say. With a brief thank you Kobe turned and left Chichester nick, he knew in his heart and his mind that he would never be back. He truly had lost everything he cared about. David Martin disappeared back through the security door before he was spotted, it made him feel as if he was betraying his friend and boss.

By the end of that harrowing day, with his wallet back, he had bought himself some clothes, just the essentials, found a quiet B&B that he knew of from his days as a uniform. and where he knew he would be left in peace and it was there that he finally showered, his first in three days, it felt good having the steaming hot water run over his body. Looking in the mirror he thought of shaving his head and chin again but decided there was no vanity left in him to care about how he looked. It was still daylight outside, but Kobe was exhausted, his body was giving in to the fact that he had not slept for nearly three days, so he pulled the curtains and lay on the bed.

He was woken by the sound of a vacuum cleaner out in the hallway, it was an audible reminder of his home and family life. After splashing his face with cold water, he remembered to take his watch from the plastic bag of belongings. After clamping the bracelet to his wrists, he checked his mobile phone and slipped the keys to his Alpha Romeo into the pocket of his new chinos. How to retrieve the car though, he did not want to go anywhere near the house to pick it up, but the car would become useful as well as carrying memories of when he and Rae first began dating. He had allowed her to drive it back to Chichester from the country pub where he had taken her for a meal. Not being used to its power she nearly wrecked it on the first bend, and all she could do was giggle. Kobe had frozen in fear, that his potential new girlfriend and his car could be gone in one wild moment, he wasn't sure which he cared about the most back then and when he realised it was the girl with the almond eyes, he knew she was a keeper. But he never let her drive it again.

Aware he was asking his friend for yet another favour he texted David and asked about his car, the reply was swift, almost before he laced his new Timberland boots. 'Car in compound, will call and tell them to release it to you. Take care Kobe, here if you need us.' Kobe assumed he meant Officer Gold, and he was happy David had found someone. His DS had stopped trusting woman after one suspect had poisoned him, that kind of thing would put most men off.

Kobe left his room and the kindly landlady, who like a landlady of old wore a wrap-around apron all day, greeted him as she brushed down the stairs.

"Would you like some breakfast Mr Kaan? Cook has gone for the day, but I can knock you up a quick bacon sandwich if you like." She was always grateful to Kaan, who was then a young PC, had thrown her violent husband out of, what was, her house and warned him never to come back, and he hadn't. "I heard what happened to you and your family, you are welcome here for as long as you need the room."

"Thank you, Molly, that is kind, but I am laying off the bacon sandwiches for a while." He smiled at the kindly woman and gently touched her arm, the human contact felt good. "And, if its okay I would like to stay for a few days at least, I know I cannot go back to my house."

Kobe suddenly felt strange, as if walking into a cold room, something had sent the shivers through him. Then he realised it was the name, Molly, he had said the name out loud, and it shocked him to feel the name cross his lips. His darling Molly, gone, as with everything else. And now there was another Molly, his God played strange tricks.

Molly was a no fuss kind of woman. "The couple in the front room will be gone later today, it's a bigger and much more comfortable room. It won't feel so claustrophobic in there. I will move your things across when I have had a chance to clean it and change the bedding" Kobe was about to tell her not to bother but he knew arguing would be pointless.

"Thank you..." He tried to say her name again, but it just would not come to him, so he repeated himself instead. "Thank you." And he walked down the hallway and out into the depressing world again.

To any onlooker he appeared to be a man on a mission, walking with purpose and striding toward town, head down and face hidden beneath the peak of a baseball cap. Kobe had woken with a purpose, he was a copper, born and bred, and you could not just switch that off. If Casper bloody Jones wasn't looking in the right direction than he would.

CHAPTER 46

"Mr Cobby, this is a fake, a very good one but a fake none-the-less." The Eton and Cambridge educated voice belonging to someone born with the proverbial silver spoon in their mouth. Sam never took a liking to him from the start, and he thought the man must be stupid as well as unlikeable. "You should really have checked its provenance before bringing it to us." Now it really did sound as if the Chairman of the auction house was talking down to him and it was pissing Sam off, good, and proper.

"I did have it checked by the local, and well-respected, auctioneer. Indeed, a very well-respected man in the trade and it was he who suggested I bring it here as it was a little too big for a regional house." Sam had his arguing head on now. "Then you stand there like a pompous twat and tell me he, and my father, had got it wrong."

Nick butted in, trying to calm a volatile situation. "Excuse me but how can it be a fake? It was authenticated by an expert, your own expert came down and checked it, it came with printed provenance and history Surely, your in-house expert checked it properly, before the sale." Nick made a salient point. "We went on your judgement." Nick's normal smooth manner peeled away like poorly fitted veneer; he prodded a finger toward the head of the auction house.

"Well, we did value the item as genuine when we came down to Sussex to do our first valuation but his is not the statuette that we valued and with all the publicity and the paperwork we trusted you a bit too soon to bring up the object we valued."

"You mean you couldn't wait for a fat sales commission and get some publicity for your gallery, but Sam came here in good faith, you had plenty of time to ensure all was right." Nick was bristling while Sam stood there stunned by events.

"It was the buyer's expert, which he brought for authentication that spotted it, apparently the signature on the base was not correct and when we double checked he was quite right."

Sam was once again being belittled, and he hated it, and he was not going to take that sort of treatment anymore, not from anyone, no matter who they were. The man in the blue pin-striped double-breasted suit stood a full foot taller than Sam, but he was not going to be intimidated, well, not until Nick pointed out that a pair of burly security men were stood behind them. The Chairman stood, pushing back his leather padded swivel chair as he did, bent at the waist and looking down on Sam, in every way possible. With his hooked nose and thinning hair which was brushed back from his forehead it made him appear like a vulture over a dead carcass. Only this time Sam was the carcass!

Even though the sword was still held high over the centurion's head he looked a little less triumphant than usual and Sam wrapped his small fist around the bronze's waist and hoisted him up, almost as a weapon. The two security guards fearful of what the little man was going to do moved in quickly and nervously. Nick stepped between them and Sam, but the downcast dealer lowered his army of one, spun on his heels and left the building, two burly security men scurrying behind him and behind them a red-faced Chairman who had just lost out on 15% of five and a quarter million.

Seeing Sam was shocked and crestfallen, as they reached the door out to the street, the Chairman eased down the temper a little.

"I don't know what has happened from the time we examined it to now, but that is not the bronze we valued, since it was the buyer's expert who noted the flaw, we have checked the photographs our expert took down in Chichester, and the signature is definitely different." Then the accusation. "I have no idea how or why you would think you could get away with it, but it is obvious that you have swapped the statuettes!"

As they left the impressive white-fronted building the security guard began closing the heavy door right behind them, and the pompous arse was just a foot or two behind them and he seemed to be braver now he was protected by bulky security. "That is not the Statuette that we had valued!" Standing upright to his full six foot six with dark eyebrows moving independently of each other the Chairman pierced Sam with his own short sword. "And please be aware we will be sending you an invoice to cover our lost commission and *will* expect it to be paid."

The door crashed shut before any response could be given. To Sam it sounded as if it were a prison cell door that was slamming closed behind him. Sam and Nick were left standing on a dusty pavement looking at ornate oak doors that were locked to a world that Sam had only dreamed about. His dream had not lasted long and had quickly become a new nightmare.

The weather was as sombre as their mood and drizzle began to fall, making the dust at their feet turn a darker grey. It was as if life was adding insult to injury, and they stood there puzzled and silent. Sam was holding the centurion by his raised arm, and it dangled by his leg, in the same way as a child holds his teddy bear, it felt twice the weight as the last time Sam had held it.

"I don't understand what just happened Nick." Sam said as they began looking around while trying to recall where they had parked Nick's car. "They said it was real, they all did. I just sold it for more than five million quid." It sounded even more ludicrous an amount when said out loud. "I must be the shortest millionaire on record. Fifteen minutes of fame and money and suddenly it's all gone again."

Nick walked on but Sam had stopped and dropped to the kerb too stunned to cry, argue, or walk on. With both feet in the gutter, he sat on the cold and damp kerbstone and placed the soldier in between his freshly shone but battered shoes, raindrops begun to spot on the comfortable Oxford brogues. With his head down he watched the dribbles of rain splash and run down the polish.

Nick joined him at the pavement's edge, and they watched unseeing as the London traffic raced on by, both lost in their own world of thought and fully aware that Sam's world had just collapsed. With feet resting in the cycle lane, it was not too long before a Lycra clad irate cyclist swerved around two pairs of legs and verbally abused them. Sam muttered a heartfelt '*Fuck off!*' but the cyclist was gone just as quickly as his millions.

Drivers were used to seeing strange sights in their city so no one else paid any attention to the two grown men and a Roman centurion sitting on the roadside in the rain.

"I am as baffled as you Sam," Nick was now driving them home, the grimy London streets left behind, the guilty faced Centurion hidden from sight in the boot. "...but at least I am starting to have an inkling of what has gone on here." Nick took a brief look at the disconsolate Sam sitting beside him as the car cruised down the motorway. Nick was glad to keep his eyes on the road, looking at his friend was too painful.

"What Nick?" Sam had never known such anger or disappointment and wished he was once again the no-hoper that everyone took the piss out of, then he realised that was exactly who he was again. "What the fuck has gone wrong here because I am struggling to understand. Three experts tell me it's the real McCoy, I know my father was sure of what it was, and then soon as we sell it, it's another dud in my life of dud deals. The money was almost in the bank and now I am back to being the joke in the trade."

Sam never felt older or of less value in his life, and Nick had no words of comfort for somebody he cared deeply about.

"Sam..."

"...It's not even the money, you understand that right!" Nick didn't have the chance to finish. "Don't get me wrong five million quid would have come in handy, less what the sharks all took from it as commission, but it's still a good payday, right."

"To say the least Sam." Nick tried to lighten the mood. "I am out a new suit, a tank of petrol and one night in the Holiday Inn, and you are worried about your bank account." Sam knew what he was doing and at least tried to smile.

"I cannot miss what I never really had Nick." Sam was quieter now and Nick could just about hear him over the sound of tyres droning on the motorway tarmac. "It was the respect, after all these years of being the butt of everybody's jokes, being the sad little man in the junk shop, finally, just finally I was getting some respect. Something I have never had, even at school I was the kid with the dad who had a junk shop.

"I know it would have been a begrudging respect they offered, but at least there was some and in time hopefully I would be treated as one of the gang. I only ever wanted to fit in, it was not the money that would change my life, it was the way people saw me." Sam was feeling sorry for himself, and Nick could not blame him for that, this time.

Sam turned his head away and looked at the Armco barrier rushing by as the last few words had caught in his throat and Nick guessed there were tears. He didn't blame him for crying and thought nothing less of the man for letting his frustration and sadness out. He turned the radio up slightly, tuned to a jazz channel that was playing laid back tunes with Miles Davis on trumpet and John Coltrane on sax, it was a beautiful sound.

With the anger abated for a while Nick wanted to share his thoughts with Sam but he gave him a few minutes to recover, the Trane had just completed a solo and Nick turned Miles down a tad so he could talk. His journalist hackles were up and his news gathering brain was in full cry. The hounds were on the scent. Sam sniffed some of the snot back and wiped his nose in the back of his hand, he never claimed to be stylish.

"Councillor Kenneth Jackman, Sam, the only fucking explanation." Sam's head snapped around to pay Nick attention, he never swore, Suzi didn't like it and Nick only used the 'f' word in extreme frustration or anger, and right now he was fuming. "It could only have been him. He is a slimy bugger at the best of times. An auction house the size of the one that took it on, do not make mistakes this bad, when their expert checked the bronze in the cabinet it had to be the real deal. I also believe your dad would not have got it that wrong. The house's reputation is on the line with everything they sell and if it had not been the fact that the buyer bought his own expert a switch would never have been discovered. Who was the only one who had access to the cabinet and who had the idea to display it in the first place. He was right it was a secure place, up until he grabbed the key."

Sam was trying to work out what his friend was saying, thinking too hard was not a favoured hobby of his, but that afternoon he was giving it a good go.

"One flaw in your plan Nick, how did Jackman get a copy made so quickly to make a switch, it's not possible. Especially a statuette of that quality." Sam was thinking straight now, the foil to Nick's thoughtful thrusts. "He may well have had access to the statue, and he may well be a slimy bastard, but it would take weeks to copy something that intricate and beautiful. There is a reason it was so sought after; it was bloody good and made by genius artist."

Then, as if dark clouds had parted and crepuscular rays of sunshine had beamed down, Nick's thinking cleared. Outside the car it started to rain again, and Nick switched on the wipers and waited for the windscreen to clear, as well as his mind.

"A fake was already available, not only that we have seen it!" Nick's voice was ecstatic, up at least an octave or two.

"What, where do you mean?" Sam's voice had also risen almost to the point of being tainted by helium.

"On the Roadshow Sam, the bloke on Antiques Roadshow." Nick was talking fast now, with the same speed as he could type words, and he usually typed a story quickly. "How hard would it have been for somebody to find out where the guy lived, and I would not mind betting he was local. In our newsroom we had his name and details sent through on our daily newsfeed, if we had wanted to run the story, we could have gotten to him easily. The Councillor used his influence and position to find out where the guy lived and then went round and paid him a visit, offered him a decent amount to hand the statue over. The bloke was so disappointed with the valuation he would have wanted rid of the thing. Kenneth bloody Jackman had a ready-made copy."

"But how do we prove it Nick, saying it is one thing but getting proof is a whole different ballgame as you know only too well." Sam was excited by the revelation, but everything else had gone wrong, why should it go right now. "Jackman will just laugh in our faces if we confront him."

"We need to go and see the bloke Sam, find out from him if Jackman, or anybody else had been around to buy his fake."

Sam felt a little sorry for the fake Centurion dumped in the dark of the boot. "Let's find him Nick, let's go and ask him." Then Sam had a charitable thought, another reason Nick liked the older man. "If we can get this sorted it might be nice to give him a cut of the money, I will hopefully get one day, if I can get the real one back. Let's face it I would never have even looked for mine if I had never seen his. Maybe he will let me buy the fake so that I will always at least have a Centurion with me, fake or not."

"Sam you are a good man."

They both fell into silence, not bothered by the rainy trip home. Nick turned the stereo up again just as Miles Davis began a wailing trumpet solo.

CHAPTER 47

Kobe felt better after turning back at the water's edge, Rae would have been disappointed in him if he had taken such a cowardly way out. His mind was still in the depths of despair, but he was fighting it and as he did whenever disappointment hit, work was the answer. He armed himself with pens and a notebook, normally it would be a whiteboard at work where he would do his calculations. Kaan had an analytical mind, but his memory was not as strong as he would have liked, although that said he wished he could forget some of the things he had seen.

He flipped over the cover of the A4 pad and took one of the pens, red to begin with, and he wrote a column title...

Possible Candidates...

A line straight down the page...

Motives and opportunities...

Another line, another column...

Helpful Contacts...

That would be in and out of the force, he guessed despite the rumours and his questioning he would still have friends serving who would help where they could.

He had set up office in one of those chain pubs that served a cheap breakfast along with pints of beer, a strange habit to be out drinking when most people are arriving at work, all the down at heel men sitting around the bar and at outside tables with cold beers could not all be night workers having a pint after a hard shift. The breakfast did look good though, just in case of anymore retribution he pushed the bacon to the side of the plate, but without thinking and warding off hunger he ate the pork sausage. It was fuel for the body more than anything else, plus he would think clearer if his stomach wasn't growling at him all the time.

He flipped over to the next page, three columns again...

Revenge...

Diversion...

Personal...

As he wrote the heading to the third column, he swapped red

for a blue pen and wrote...

Of course, it was personal, you attack someone's family, that is as personal as it gets...

Going back to the first page, he wrote down in the contacts column...

David Martin

Stella Gold

That big bugger with the door enforcer, *Murphy*

And one that surprised him, not even sure why his name came out so early in the list, but he had written the name down in heavy blue capitals...

NICK FLAX...

Press and police always had a very tenuous link, it was a balancing act. The local paper was a fine source of information and a useful way of getting messages out to the public whether that be something as simple as 'lock your bike, cars, and doors, or as tricky as have you seen this man who is wanted for serious assaults. The dark side of the union between the two organisations was when the press overstepped the boundaries and printed stuff the police wanted to keep silent for operation reasons, and sometimes they would be like sharks on a feeding frenzy. Throw them a fish of a story and they would attack trying to swallow the whole shoal. But one journalist always stood out as being sensible and fair and he had been with the paper for as long as Kobe could remember.

Nick Flax was a rare breed in the reporting industry, he would fight for his stories and for the facts as much as any journalist but did so with polite firmness rather than aggression or by breaking trusts. Kobe had always liked the way the man worked and his attitude toward the truth, he was not a bottom feeder like many of his kind. It was a two-way street with him as well, if he thought some information, he had unearthed would help the police, he would hand over his notes and quite rightly he would be there with phone recorder in hand when it was time for the debt to be paid by giving out the odd scoop. Outside of work Kobe had bumped into him at several functions but chats had been brief, he liked to keep journalists, even the decent ones, at arm's length. Although he did not know him well personally, he somehow knew that Flax was a contact he needed.

As the day wore on and he drank more cheap coffees to keep

his mind buzzing and alert, it was a bit late now, but he did think he should have drunk decaf. Time after time, he mentally walked himself through the crime scene as he had seen it back on that, so recent, Sunday evening. First time around his thoughts were foggy, part of his brain trying to bury the horror, but he needed to see it as it was, and see it clearly. As he mentally walked through the house, all he could hear was the silence, when there should have been the noise of children playing and music coming from Rae's studio room. And instead of a pretty little waterside cottage all Kobe could see was the blood-spattered walls and his family lying dead in each other's arms. Rae, beautiful with pale porcelain skin and slender hands and each time he thought of her his thoughts would always go to the vicious slash in her throat and the way her life's blood had leaked down and into the white duvet. Molly and little Kobe, both young and innocent, their life too allowed to leak out, what sort of animal would take a knife to an innocent's throat?

Molly, small and inquisitive, a proper daddy's girl and yet could usually be found next to Rae and holding on to her skirt hem or onto little Kobe's hand, the two of them inseparable and although his son was the older of the two it was Molly who would always stand up and protect her brother. But it was Kobe Senior's job to protect his family and he had failed in this single most important function.

Father, husband, and policeman... he had failed. Three out of three.

The bereft father closed his eyes tightly, trying to get the final images out of his head so he could walk the crime scene properly, it felt easier thinking of it in those terms rather than as their home. He clenched his fist and forced himself back to the moment when he climbed from his Alpha, the back gate he could see in his mind's eye was open, the secure catch undone, Rae would never leave it like that. Mentally he swivelled his head to take in the surroundings that he knew so well. Three hundred and sixty degrees, did something catch the corner of his peripheral vision? It was your job to notice the unusual, the suspicious...

THINK MAN!

Was anything out of place, was anybody out of place, did some anomaly go unnoticed in his eagerness to get into the house? But instead of evidence such as fingerprints on the gate-catch it would be a mess of prints as he was certain he had touched it that evening, for God's sake even the first officer on the scene probably touched it and then he recalled seeing Martin and Gold across the street. They would have tried to get in to see Kobe, so they probably touched it. First on the scene, the officers name avoided Kobe's thoughts, David Martin would find out his name and maybe even make contact for him.

Concentrating this hard had given him a headache and his eyes watered, he tried to stem the flow but with no control he was suddenly crying, almost sobbing aloud. Fury as he had never known before burned deep into his heart. He grabbed up the debris that was his impromptu office and staggered from the bar almost unnoticed, other customers had been there all morning and had seen it all before, nothing much stirred them into action, except for maybe a late Manchester United goal. Stumbling out of the door and into the street he bumped into a table with an almost matching pair of old ladies, both nursing half pints of lager, they had been checking out the tight arses of young men on the street full of shops but stopped just long enough to curse the drunken bastard who had almost spilt their beers. It always surprised Kobe that old ladies like that with their big handbags and perms knew such language, he recalled once seeing a legend on a T-shirt 'Looks of a mermaid – mouth of a sailor' ... It seemed apt with those two ladies.

Along the street a little way there was an arch of grey stone that led along the back of the Cathedral, and he hurried down it and rushed to get away from the throng of the city centre. Another arch, this time of red brick, and he realised that he was in the Bishop's Garden, a popular beauty spot with manicured lawns and flower beds which were always alive with bees and butterflies, a robin, feathers ruffled, strutted along the lawn edging pecking at the grass for grit and insects. There was an empty bench, unusual at lunchtimes as on days like today workers from around the town centre sat in the gardens for their lunches, so he sat down and watched. Re-honing his skills of people watching.

Looking around he saw an air liner with twin vapour trails fly way over the top of the cathedral tower and he could hear a choir rehearsing from inside, he found it reassuring until he recalled an interview from when he was a DS, where the man they had thought responsible for a murder had described that very scene. This was the spot where Lucas Tubb was accused of murdering a girl that had remained unnamed, despite in-depth enquiries to discover who she was. It was a complex case, one of the toughest of Kobe's career.

Kobe quickly opened his note pad, and under suspects wrote...

Lucas Tubb, right at the top of the column. Under that he wrote...

Drug mastermind?? (doubtful)

He had raided two drug houses in a little over two weeks, it was suspected both were operated and run by a mystery man who was remaining anonymous, and he must be royally pissed off with the break in his income chain.

The park where he was trying to think clearly was beautiful, birdsong in the air and a choir singing in the distance, the sun was warm and an exhausted Kobe nodded off, it was an easy sleep, no harsh dreams. So tired his brain just shut down and he slept, he didn't fight it when his head started drooping, he just allowed the tiredness to take him.

CHAPTER 48

Sam, puzzled and as unhappy as he was by the events of the day, found himself relaxing on the journey now they had left the motorway. All around him was the scenic splendour of Sussex, it had stopped raining, and the lush greenness of the South Downs was a fine antidote to the grime and noise of London. For once he was pleased that Nick never drove quickly, in fact he never did anything quickly, it is part of what made him such a good friend and a calming influence. Sam hadn't noticed Nick continually glancing across at him.

"You look pretty relaxed for a man who has just lost a bloody fortune." Nick said with his eyes flicking between Sam and the road.

"Can't lose what you never had Nick." Said Sam philosophically. "I am not sure of what to feel to be honest. It's all a bit surreal but I know one thing for certain, my Centurion was the real thing. They confirmed it was real," Sam said in anger as his thumb pointed back the way they had just travelled from. "…my own dad said it was real. But then something happened between the valuation, and it being released from that glass cabinet and us taking it to the auction. Never having had much money, it feels very strange to be almost given a few million quid and then have it taken away again before it even reached my overdraft!" he paused… "Like winning the lottery and losing the ticket."

Eventually, Sam took his eyes away from the scenery and gazed at his friend's profile as he drove. "There is one thing that baffles me, Nick." He never gave his friend time to ask what. "Why does Suzi allow you to keep those bloody bushy sideburns, I was born 20 years before you and they were out of fashion then, Christ, they were out of fashion when Charles Dickens was a boy."

The tension that had been in the car since leaving London, was lifted, and both men managed a smile.

"I would like to say that Suzi has no say in the matter, but we both know that would not be true." Nick took on a look of resignation. "In fact, I have promised to shave them off before the wedding."

"You will be telling me next that she has also bought you a jacket without patches on the elbows." Sam added, as his friend turned his head to show that it had already happened, and the smiles turned to quiet laughter. But the respite from the disaster of the day would not leave their minds or their lips.

"I know what happened Sam." Nick broke the mood again. "That slimy bugger Kenneth Jackman happened, that's what. I thought at the time that he was a bit too keen to put the statue on display and now I know why." He could not keep the anger from his voice, Nick had become a journalist to right wrongs, and his friend had been mightily wronged. "I reckon we go and see Jason... whatever his name is." Nick never usually forgot a name, but his anger was getting the better if him.

"Benny, Nick, Jason Benny." You said back when I first found mine that the guy was called Jason Benny." Sam helped.

Nick slowed the car for a road junction, "Here we go Petworth, five miles." The car bumped across the shallow rise of a mini roundabout and the lady on the Satnav in a matronly and slightly patronising voice ordered them to... *'leave the roundabout at the second exit...'*

"Stupid woman, full of attitude and then tells me which road to take after I have taken it." Nick berated the dashboard. "Bit bloody late now, dozy mare!"

"Back to the wonderful Mr Benny, Nick."

"Yes, of course Sam, sorry." Nick was back on track road wise and conversation wise. "If we pay him a visit, I bet he has either sold his Centurion, which we now have in the boot behind us, or has had it stolen. Meanwhile I would bet my journalistic life on the fact that it was Jackman who obtained it by fair means or foul and that he now has your Centurion stashed away somewhere while he quickly looks for a buyer."

The soulless voice in the dashboard told anyone who cared to listen that they should drive straight on at the next junction.

"You sound almost resigned to the fact that it has all gone wrong for you Sam, you should be as livid as hell." Nick flicked a look sideways.

"I have been disappointed so often in my life Nick, you know anger is not something I do often. It seems to take too much energy." Sam thought for a moment, and Nick did not interrupt so as to not break his thoughts. "I suppose it is good to point the finger though, and neither of us is going to point in any other direction. But it's partly my own fault because I didn't do as you warned, I insisted you tell the story. If I had just done what you said and kept it all quiet, I would be a multimillionaire right now and you would still be an impoverished journalist." Sam picked at a piece of stray thread on the cuff of his new jumper, it began to unravel a longer strand, so he bit it off at the cuff.

"I understand why you did it, Sam, you wanted to tell all those that doubted you and bullied you that you were a somebody after all." His left hand left the steering wheel and nudged his friend in the thigh with a very light and supportive punch.

"I was simply showing off Nick, so I am partly to blame in my own spectacular downfall." The smiles and laughter of a few moments earlier had been forgotten, even the magical scenery was ignored. "Can we take a drive to Portsmouth tomorrow, Nick, or do you have to get back to the office."

"The office can wait, I will just tell them I am on a story, which is partly true." Said Nick, expecting the last half hour of the drive to be taken in silence, then a thought hit him. "Mind you, it's only a short diversion from here to Portsmouth and Suzi is not expecting me back until tomorrow, she thinks we are still in London celebrating at some swanky restaurant."

"You know where he lives?" Sam sat up straight in the passenger seat, all attentive now. "I just remembered I had to get his address and phone number when I wrote the story, with everything else going on I had forgotten, you recalling his name jogged my memory. Shouldn't take too long to get there and find out if we are right and then we can go and confront the thieving Councillor."

At the first opportunity Nick turned off for Portsmouth and thirty minutes later he pulled into the rundown estate where Benny lived, he slowed even more than usual to look for the road. But he needn't have searched quite so hard for in front of them the road was closed off by police cars and personnel. Blue and white police tape was stretched taught across the road but was twisting and flapping in a stiff breeze and that with the blue flashing lights at the end of the road of poor semi-detached was creating a psychedelic strobe effect, it was almost hypnotic. Behind the tape Nick suddenly noticed a uniformed officer frantically waving him past the end of the road, checking his mirror he could see why as he had a tailback of cars behind him, the area had gone into full spectator mode. Just beyond the roadblock Nick saw just one parking space outside the cordon and immediately pulled into it, even though it was half blocking another house's driveway.

Locking the car behind them he and Sam walked smartly to the cordon tape, Nick knew the officer who had been waving them forward.

On reaching the tape they could see beyond and smell the charred remains of a serious fire, ringlets of smoke still floating up from number 13.

"That must be Benny's house Sam." Nick informed him.

"Maybe he was so disappointed about his valuation that he set fire to himself." Sam guessed.

"If that was the case, he would have done it months ago when his episode of the Roadshow was filmed, not nearly three weeks after it was aired."

"Good point."

"Stay there a minute will you, please Sam."

Sam wasn't really listening as he watched a collection of worker bees swarming around the outside of the house. Some in protective firefighter clothing, some in police uniform while others strode in and out of the remains of the house in blue paper forensic onesies, their faces covered with surgical style masks, it was like the pandemic all over again. Nick approached the officer standing sentry at the gate.

"Hey Pete, how are you doing?" Nick enquired.

"Bit off your beat down here aren't you, Nick."

"I was just on my way to do an interview for a story I have been working on." Nick tried to keep his voice calm and professional. "I know you can't comment officially Pete, but off the record, what has happened here?"

Pete looked all around to make sure that no brass was watching or within earshot, too many plods had been censured and sacked for talking out of turn to the wrong people. "Just a house fire, Nick, nothing too odd or newsworthy about it. Although there is a crispy bloke in there, first on the scene threw up his lunch when he saw it, forensics are not best pleased having their crime scene spewed on. You can still smell burnt flash down here, so I would probably have done the same if I had found him." Pete tucked his hands into the armpit holes of his stab jacket, a regular stance of today's beat officer, it was relaxed without putting hands into pockets and looking slovenly, feet apart and with a straight back, he looked like a man you would not pick a fight with, but Nick knew him as a gentle soul who bred canaries in his off-duty time.

"Is it number 13?" Nick had to ask.

"Yeh, why?" Pete had an enquiring look. "Did you know the bloke that was in there, then?"

"If you want to earn some Brownie points with your bosses, tell them to look at the fact he was on television, say you just recalled seeing him with some fake bronze statue being valued on Antiques Roadshow."

"For real?"

"For real, Pete. His name is Jason Benny." It was Nick's way of paying the officer back for his little bit of help.

Nick rushed back to his car, almost dragging Sam behind him. He didn't speak until they arrived back in the car where an angry householder, already pissed off with the disruption in his street, was complaining he could not get his own car out of the drive. Nick waved him off with a brief apology, got behind the wheel and drove off throwing dust from the road up behind him.

"You going to tell me what is going on or not Nick?" Sam asked impatiently.

"Sorry Sam, just pulling it all together." He said still breathless from both shock and energy expelled.

Nick gazed across at Sam and as they passed under a streetlamp, he could see the worry lines on the old man's face. In fact, in that split second of light he had never seen Sam look quite so old or stressed.

Sam kept his eyes on Nick, expectant and fearful, this day continued to spiral out of control, and it scared him about what could, or would, happen next.

"Well!" Sam sounded like a whiny child.

The next junction was a roundabout that would take them up onto the motorway out of the city and Nick would not be able to drive and explain to Sam what he had seen, heard, and smelled. The aroma of burned flesh imprinted itself on Nick's mind, there was nothing else quite like it. He circled past the motorway slip road and parked outside an old pub, now converted to flats but still with the shining green tiles which was part of the signature of the now extinct brewery company 'Brickwood's'.

Sam looked grey as Nick turned to face his friend.

"It's a fire as bad as it can get and our man with the statue is still in there."

"Dead?" As soon as Sam opened his mouth, he knew it was a stupid question and just flapped a hand at Nick for him to continue.

"An old contact of mine, Pete Collins, was on the tape boundary and he told me what he could, which wasn't much, but with what he said, and I heard between the lines are two different things." Away from the fire now he sniffed hard to try and shift the smell of burnt flesh, the in-car air freshener hanging from the mirror had no effect whatsoever. "Forensics are on site, it is a crime scene, and they have found a body. The house was the one we were looking for and it had one single occupant. Pete, said a traffic copper was first on the scene and the smell from the body caused him to lose his lunch."

"Was it the fire that killed him?"

"I pushed my contact as far as I could, but experience tells me we will not know actual cause of death until the release the autopsy results. But I do get a very strong feeling that it will not have been the fire that got the poor sod."

"You do realise that your chum is PCPC, don't you?"

"What?"

"Your copper chum you just spoke to, PCPC, PC Pete Collins."

"I have just told you all the gruesome details and that's what you took from it. PCPC!"

Sam was not smiling. "Different people have different ways of dealing with shock, Nick. I have just chosen a diversion to get past the bits that I didn't like..."

"And what bits in particular didn't you like Sam?"

"All of it Nick. Every fucking bit of it." Sam's voice was trembling. "I don't like one little bit of it. This bloody Roman is just causing too many problems. It's one thing to embarrass me, but to set fire to some poor bastard in his home because of it, that's going too far."

"Whenever money is involved, there will be someone not entitled to it trying to get their grubby hands on it, and people have been murdered for far less than five million."

"And I don't suppose they found a figurine have they, not in a blaze like that appeared to be?" Sam was not a big man to begin with, but he seemed to be shrinking in his seat.

"Pete did not say, and I doubt if he was getting that sort of information even though he is on duty there, forensics don't give lowly

Plods details." Nick explained. "But I did give him the heads-up on the Roadshow angle and the fake statue, because I don't think they will find one."

"Simply because we have it in the boot of this car." Interrupted Sam.

"Which means I am driving around with vital evidence in my car." Nick realised. "It will earn Pete some good behaviour points when he tells his Skipper."

"Did you mention the wonderful Councillor Jackman?"

"No point," responded Nick. "...we have no proof he was involved. Just as we cannot prove he switched the real Centurion for the fake which he has stolen from that poor bugger back there." Up until now Nick had shown fear and anger, but now he sounded resigned to the events that had unfolded, he had never been so close to a story. "I have been doing my job for close to half my life now Sam, but I have never come across such a twisted, sick story in all my assignments, and there have been some nasty ones. But nothing even comes close to this, and I am sorry you seem to be in the middle of it, Sam."

"I put myself there, Nick, you told me to be careful in what I was doing but my damaged ego wouldn't let go."

"And it's not over yet, not by a long way. We must find something against our bent man-of-the-people Councillor, but before then we have something even worse to worry about."

"What on earth could be worse? Nick, it's about as bad as it gets so far."

If it was possible the journalist in Nick took on an even more serious look. "Jason Benny was no doubt murdered." Sam didn't take his eyes off Nick. "They will eventually realise that a fake statue has gone missing from the burnt-out house."

"Surely, we will want them to do that won't we? Otherwise, the Councillor will get away with it." Sam said.

"A fake Bronze has gone missing Sam, and somebody has just tried to sell a fake bronze of the same description at a London Auction House for something over five million pounds. And none of this links or leads, to a nobody, and supposedly wealthy, City Councillor from Chichester." Nick had summed it up perfectly.

"FUCK!" said Sam as he too summed his feelings up perfectly. "Take me home please Nick, I need to feed Wedgwood."

CHAPTER 49

Kenneth Jackman's ears should have been burning 30 odd miles away as he sat in his, very macho, study come man-cave at the remote country house he shared with his wife, Barbara. A pair of lazy, chocolate brown Labradors lay like bookends at either side of his large leather topped desk. The room should have smelt of expensive cologne and cigar smoke, but Jackman never cared for either.

The Councillor sat smiling a self-satisfied smile, he had pulled off a masterstroke. He swung to-and-fro in the swivel chair while holding and stroking the bronze flanks of a very expensive Roman Centurion who continued to hold his short-sword high in possible anticipation of a battle that was to come. It was feeling like a sexual thing, as if he were stroking the flanks of a beautiful lover with smooth cold skin. He revelled in the weight of the bronze idol, felt the thrill of its cold metal, sliding his fingers down the entire length of its rippled torso. He couldn't help himself; he used the tip of his index finger to test the sharpness of the sword and flinched as it broke the surface of his skin, a bubble of blood appeared on the soldier's blade, probably the first time it had tasted blood. At that moment the Statuette seemed alive to Jackman, his Roman Warrior was the sexiest thing he had touched, even more than his surgery enhanced lover. Even though behind closed doors, he felt himself redden with a little embarrassed guilt.

Annoyed at himself he banged it down on his mahogany and leather topped desk, then regretted it as he realised, he could not damage the statue, this was his future. Despite his erotic urges toward the inanimate object his main thought was not for the beauty, or craftsmanship that he held in his hands, it was all about the money and the freedom that money would offer him. He estimated that he could get maybe two, hopefully, three million on the black market, and there was something very sexy about that. It would mean that he would no longer have to rely on his fucking wife's money. The smirk that had been on his face disappeared as he thought of his wife, who he had come to loathe. It was her money that kept him tied to her, maybe when this was over, he should let Fi loose on the miserable, overbearing, sexless bitch. At Least if she were dead, he could keep the house and still walk Malteser and Twix the two Labradors, but on second thoughts he had no idea what he would do with two poorly behaved dogs when he got to Parliament. On the plus side being recently widowed would certainly get some voters onside.

CHAPTER 50

Another strange bedroom, another bed, how he longed for the old bed of recent memories. Waking to the sound of gulls screeching, of the warmth of Rae next to him, snuggled into the back of him with flesh warm and smelling of sweetness. Always the delicious fear of two very lively children running into the bedroom with sunshine pouring through the cottage windows and leaping on him and waking him from a drowsy peaceful dream.

They were all gone now, never again would life feel that good.

Even before being fully awake in the alien environment, he tried to work out where he was, the smells were different, the sounds, instead of waves crashing against a shore he was hearing branches rubbing together in high winds, of crows calling and robins whistling a repetitive song. Opening his eyes, he looked around the bedroom and noted rustic French style furnishings and walls of sepia-tone photographic images from a long-ago era of jazz musicians, all smoky bars and Zoot-suits, saxophones, and pianos. Then he recalled the previous evening and why and where he was.

Strong sunlight poured into the room and dust motes danced in and out of rays, from somewhere else in the house he could hear the muted sound of a blues guitar wailing out its twelve-bar refrain and a strong smell of coffee. Checking his watch, which was on the bedside table, he noted it was a quarter after ten as he slipped the metal strap over his wrist and clamped it closed. He could not recall sleeping that late for a long time, his body obviously needing to refresh itself. His new clothes, which he had purchased a few days before were over the back of a chair and he slipped out of bed and slipped on just jeans and a denim shirt. Shaking and straightening the duvet would do for bed making, opening the bedroom door he was pleased to see a bathroom in front of him, eagerly he stepped inside and peed, and like any man in a strange house he was worried that the fart he released could be heard throughout the house. Washing his hands and throwing cold water over his face he checked in the mirror as he used his wet hands to push back his hair that had grown over the past couple of weeks, it was strange feeling as he had been shaving his head for many years. He noted at the sides his jet-black hair of old was showing signs of grey streaks.

He followed the sound of the music, and it led him down a corridor, off which there was another bathroom and two more bedrooms, the door at the end opened into a vast kitchen where Rob Berry, the barrister and bluesman, and his wife Anne were spending their morning. Rob stopped picking at his favourite Les Paul Gibson guitar and placed it in a stand beside his chair and greeted Kobe warmly and without ceremony. The detective stood awkwardly in the doorway expecting to be fussed over as he had been lately by the kindly landlady of the B&B where he had been staying. Robert had not moved from the chair.

"Good morning, Kobe, I trust you slept well." The smile was one of pure bonhomie. "Coffee in the pot dear boy, help yourself, cereals and bread in the pantry." Apparently, mornings in the Berry household were a relaxed affair and it made Kobe feel more at ease.

"Just coffee please Robert." And he poured it black from the filter machine into a mug that was just sitting there waiting for him. First sip it was bitter and hot on his tongue.

"Sorry but we like strong coffee in the mornings."

"Just how I like it, thank you." And Kobe pulled out a chair from beside the refectory table and sat with elbows on the battered and stained-by-life surface, his coffee mug balanced in both hands.

Rob remained in his chair and picked up the guitar again, resting it in his lap, and with the volume low he played a gentle jazz riff, that Kobe found soothing. The lack of conversation suited Kobe, so that it gave him time to recall how he came to be there in the barrister's kitchen, fur on the tongue and fuzz in the brain told him alcohol had a big part in the story. It seemed that the part-time Muslim had failed again in cleaning up his religious faults.

After a meeting the previous afternoon, the kindly lawyer, on hearing that Kobe was currently in a guest house, took him home for dinner. It was a generous act, that was further enhanced by Anne Berry, Rob's wife who was a locally known author still awaiting a best-seller. She had welcomed the impromptu visitor into their home and had prepared and served a delicious dinner without complaint even though Robert had sprung the last-minute guest on her. Kobe had not eaten a home cooked meal since the last Saturday he had dined with his family. Last night he had been ravenous and recalled he had eaten the meal in silence as across the table the warming and homely sound of a husband and wife as they chatted about their respective days. It was one of the things that Kobe had wrestled with while on the job, he always tried to get home to meals with the family, it was something he missed growing up as his parents were too busy with their political social circle to eat with him. Kobe ate with the servants. When he married and despite the heavy commitment of being a serious crimes detective, Sunday dinner was sacrosanct with him, and he always tried to get home to eat with Rae and the children with roast dinner served at six...

With blame in his heart, he thought back, the one day he was an hour late was the one day he should have been an hour early.

Previous thoughts of their dinners together were always gentle and beautiful, that was until that last Sunday, and now those memories tore a bigger hole in his chest. Loss is a physical thing, not just a mental one and the pain for Kobe was intense. In the days that followed the discovery of his family the pain and vision of what he had seen had not lessened, it had only increased and hardened like a growth deep inside his very core, a growing cancerous tumour of hate and loss.

Last night had been an all too brief date with normality and feeling the warmth between the couple, who if truth be known he hardly knew, was comforting and cheering but it also scared him. How could life carry on without Rae and the children, he had thought better of taking the easy way out because he knew his wife would have been disappointed in him and he never liked to see that on her face. How does one carry on knowing you will never again see the children's cheeky grins and hear their infectious laughter. He had even started to take an interest in football which his son was mad about, Kobe was a rugby lover, and now he had learned all about who Messi and Ronaldo were.

Sipping his hot coffee, he tried to think of happier times, but it seemed that even his memories had been murdered along with his family. Each time he thought of precious moments they were invaded with the images of bloodstains among the roses and across the snowy duvet. He felt as if he were about to cry again, it seemed to be his latest hobby, but the sound of warm conversation over the soft sound of a guitar gently strummed held him in its enticing grasp. The Berry household was, he tried to describe it in his mind, normal was the best compliment he could come up with and strangely it cheered him slightly.

Kobe hadn't noticed her light up, but Anne blew out a puff of smoke which was blown inward from the open window rather than out of the opening before rising to join a cloud hanging just below the nicotine-stained ceiling.

"Apologies for the smoking, Kobe." The voice was husky from years of the demon weed. "It is one of my few real and illicit pleasures in life..."

"Along with drinking and swearing." Robert interrupted without any reproach in his tone.

"...I have tried to give it up but that only got as far as just cutting it down to just five a day, dammit." She resisted using a stronger expletive. "Rob has his music, I have my ciggies as my sin, but apparently the devil likes hard guitar sounds and not the demon weed.

The cigarettes carried a strong aroma and Kobe noticed a packet of Disque Bleu on a Welsh dresser, they were a French brand with a rich aroma all of its own and it reminded him of his childhood as he father smoked the same brand. Kobe found the pungent smell quite attractive, add to that the smell of his coffee and the sound of the guitar his senses were enjoying the hits this morning whereas they had been dulled over recent days.

Anne rose from her chair, an old and battered armchair with odd dots of scorch marks on the arm, and grabbing the ashtray headed out of the backdoor.

"I will take this out into the garden, it's a pleasant morning, it will give you two chance to talk as I am sure you have things that need to be sorted." Before she disappeared out onto the patio, she added with a tone that was not to be argued with. "Kobe, you are welcome to stay here as long as is needed whether that be until you have found somewhere proper to live or you have healed enough to move on. We will enjoy the company and it will be no imposition on us as this house has been bereft of visitors and good companionship for too long." She paused long enough to indicate Robert with a nod of her head. "Since John Lee-Hooker there retired we don't get many visitors."

Kobe liked the idea of being around people but there was no chance to thank Anne before she vanished in a cloud of smoke out into the garden. His coffee cup was empty, and he felt comfortable enough to just head for the filter machine and refill.

As he sat again at the table the guitar stopped playing and was placed back in its rack, the amp switched off, the sudden silence added gravitas to the morning and Robert took a worn wooden chair across the table from Kobe and dropped a large folder and yellow A4 legal notepad on its surface.

Robert began without preamble... "I think we should hold a press conference, Kobe."

It was not the opening gambit that Kobe expected but he responded by going straight into business mode. "I have some savings Robert, but I don't think I will be able to afford your fees and thank you for the offer of accommodation, until I get the house sorted it would be much better than the B&B, if you and Anne are certain."

"It was Anne's idea, but I think it a perfect solution and as she said, the company will be nice." He went on to add, "There are no fees, I retired some years ago, and I do this for fun now, plus it keeps me from getting under Anne's feet. It was either that or join the tennis club with her and that's not going to happen. Be assured I will give you my best attention as I hopefully did with all my clients, so if you are happy to retain me." Robert had a smile above his grey, goatee beard that must have won over many a juror in his trial days. "As for living here, if you don't like strong coffee, blues music or cigarette smoke, then to be honest, you are buggered."

"You mean like everyday life?" Kobe said softly, humbled by what this man and his wife had offered him. "A slice of everyday would be wonderful after the recent days I have had. So, thank you."

"No thanks needed my friend." His smile really was great tool for liking the man.

Polite business out of the way, Kobe knew it was time to get down to the tough stuff. "You say, hold a press conference, what good will that do? Do I really need to tell the world about my loss and the gruesome details?" Kobe asked, a little nervous of what the answer would be. Even as a DI he hated the obligatory press conferences.

"It is fairly obvious that someone out there means you harm." He explained. "Another good reason for you being here." Then he took that statement one step further and it truly frightened the normally stoic policeman. "And, I have the feeling that they, whomever 'they' might be, may not have finished with you just yet. Your family was not just a message sent. It was way too extreme for that."

"Let them come I say, I have nothing left to lose." Kobe's logical mind went back to business. "What about me, have I been cleared so I can go back to work yet?"

Across the kitchen table Robert shook his head. "Even if cleared, you would not be going back to work without some sort of therapist to say you are good to go. You have suffered too much trauma."

"Even *if* cleared..." Kobe was astonished that he was still a suspect.

"Despite your airtight alibi, backed by everyone in your squad as well as the pub landlord and his staff, Ghost Jones still has you in mind for it." Robert looked as if he had just bitten on something sour. "That man has no finesse whatsoever or any skill in policing, he is still laying the blame firmly at your door. He is like a dog with a fucking bone!"

The expletive sounded strange coming from a barrister's plummy accent, but it contained Kobe's attention totally on the now, and not on the past days.

"I even got hold of the Assistant Chief Constable, apparently the Chief himself does not speak to retired lawyers, and he confirmed he was happy with Casper Jones and the way the investigation was being handled, which makes me think someone either knows something we don't, or someone high on the food chain is bringing pressure to bear.

"Is it likely that they know something we don't?" He had to ask the question.

Years of interviewing suspects and witnesses had taught Kobe when to shut up and listen. This was one of those times, so he just answered with a very firm but succinct '*No*'.

"Good, my thinking is that we hold a press conference, we will do that in one of the hotels close to the station so that the public know you are not in hiding out of guilt, plus there is no need to advertise where you are staying, although I have had to alert Jones' of your whereabouts." Robert was making sense so far to Kobe. "A friendly press will take the pressure off you and put it back on those trying to discredit you. By taking the bull by the horns, so to speak, and giving up your unshakable alibi to the press, sympathy will be on your side and not on the side of whoever is playing the tail wagging Jones' dog."

Kobe, for a moment, thought of something he always knew from experience, lawyers and barristers in particular loved hearing the sound of their own voices. The thought brought a little smile to his lips, and the movement felt strange.

"I know what you are thinking, we solicitors do love the sound of our own voices." Then he let out the loudest guffaw of a laugh that Kobe had ever heard, it reverberated around the kitchen. A voice from out in the garden shouted with warmth but serious intent.

"Calm down Robert, remember your heart and what the doctor said about you getting over excited." Anne rapped on the window to ensure she was being heard.

"You didn't complain the other night, dear."

"That was different, I was the beneficiary of the excitement." Anne chuckled and then coughed, hacking slightly like a true smoker.

Kobe had been out of touch with everyone over the last few days. "So can I assume I am still suspended?"

"Yes, you are my dear boy, but I have got them to reinstate your pay. I pointed out it would not look good on them if they suspended you without pay, so they capitulated."

Kobe was getting angry by now, the force he had worked hard for, sacrificed for, and put his life on the line for, were now treating him like a remorseless killer, acting as judge, jury and executioner.

"I am getting the distinct feeling, that even when this is over, I am still not going to be welcome back on the job." Kobe felt hurt and even more broken than he did a few minutes ago, when would life stop stealing from him?

"Actually, to be correct, they have not suspended you now, they have put you on sick-leave, or compassionate leave, if you prefer."

Kobe reacted to his anger but kept his voice low, he never liked to scream and shout, it wasn't his style. "Suspension by the back door, to keep me well out of the loop without garnering bad publicity." Kobe then referred to the lists he had been making.

"When talking to the press I know of someone who has always been fair with the police and still did his job of bringing us to account for our actions. Nick Flax, strange reporter born way out of his time but a good journalist none the less."

"I know Nick from the old days, and I agree with you, I will make sure he gets an invite and a front row seat."

Robert then got out the question that he had been dreading to ask, but it was a vital question. "Any ideas as to who would want to do this to you, a case from the past maybe, or even a current case where you have gotten too close to someone powerful?"

"I have thought of little else these past few days..."

"I can only imagine, dear boy."

"...and while we are always open to threats against ourselves in this job, it is very rare that they are ever carried out, for obvious reasons." Kobe spoke with well-considered confidence and intelligence. "And, unlike in the American cop shows where they go after the family, this is not the Mafia and families are usually not the part of any revenge pattern, our little island is too small and the criminal fraternity, despite the fact they are criminals, will not normally countenance a copper's family being hit. It's just not good for business."

"The biggest cases in the past few months have been on two, very busy but still low key, drug house raids." Kobe continued. "In fact, that's what we were celebrating, when I should have been home protecting my family. I should have been home, I could have stopped whoever it was, but, no, I had to be in the pub celebrating just doing my job!"

Noticing the tears forming in the corners of Kobe's eyes, Robert stopped the questioning and walked across the kitchen to the coffee pot, but then changed his mind. He opened the cupboard door above the coffee pot at eye level in front of him, its door was a distressed mixture of blue-green and the wood was visible where the peeled paint looked as if it had a touch of designer chic, but all the doors in the kitchen had been sourced from a French street market, they were the real deal in a room that appeared to be purchased from an old château. From the shelf in the cupboard, he pulled a bottle of 25-year-old Macallan Single Malt, liking the flavours of chocolate, spice and cherry syrup that accompanied the warmth and depth of Scottish malt whisky. Two heavy crystal glasses clunked together as he pinched them between closed fingers and he then casually tucked the expensive whiskey under his arm and he walked back to the table, making sure to just lay a comforting hand on Kobe's shoulder as he passed him. Kobe sniffed back the tears and wiped his eyes with the back of his hand.

Kobe carried on from where the conversation tailed off. "The drug raids, even if it were to do with them, were too recent. One was around a month ago and the second the morning of..." His voice tailed off; it was too painful to say the details of that day out loud. Robert got it, immediately.

"I understand, Kobe, and tend to agree with you although we cannot just dismiss it out of hand." Robert said, trying to keep things moving along. "If I recall the news of the day following the first raid, your team had confiscated close to one million in street drugs. That must have hurt somebody, hard, and that somebody must have a supplier who would still want paying. It's probably a long way to the top of that career ladder."

Heeding the words, and mentally labelling them to be dealt with later, Kobe continued thinking out loud.

"Then of course, when we first met, we had that high-profile murder case of what the press dubbed 'The case of the Unnamed Girl'. First chasing one brother only to get that wrong, then losing the younger brother to suicide, before discovering it was Lucas who had carried out the murder in the park, and then it transpired that both were deranged killers."

"Lucas and Jacob Tubb." Robert interjected, stroking his goatee carefully in thought. "I recall it only too clearly."

"Of course, sorry I forgot for a moment that you represented Lucas." It was Kobe's turn to take on a thoughtful gaze. "Were they not the sons of a family friend?"

"Lucas was my Godson; his father and I went to college together." Robert explained. "I was just glad at the time that he was not around to see what his two boys had become. Tragic for everyone concerned."

"Then as you know we never found Lucas again, he was into the wind after his chat-show confession."

Kobe looked Robert in the face, catching his eyes with his own. He had a good poker face and did not show the emotion that he knew he must always feel about the brothers.

"Young Jacob was always the troublesome one in the family, he was a half-brother to Lucas, following an affair his father had been having with, as we found out later, the Nanny to Lucas." Robert was finding the discussion hard, but he had done nothing wrong, merely defended the boy that had grown up knowing him as a family friend. "It was tragic when Jacob took his own life, and I think his father would have found that more disappointing than the violence that emanated from him. He raised his boys to be strong and independent."

"I have to admit, even though I was involved in all aspects of the case, that the book Lucas wrote about his experiences, before finally remembering he was the killer all along, was a damn good read." Kobe recalled. "He actually painted me as a very good copper, which I appreciated, even after I got him locked up in Broadmoor..."

"We both thought that was the right way to go after reviewing the evidence. You and I both share the blame on that one I think," Robert confessed. "...it seemed at the time that it was the best place for him."

"I presume like me; you have no idea where he actually ran off to." Kobe continued. "Never heard of or seen since, seemed to vanish in thin air from the TV studio. I did wonder when making my notes over the last day or two if he was mad enough to come back and get himself a taste of revenge."

"The boy was certainly deluded enough." Robert took over the train of thought. "I wonder if he still has that level of violence within him? He would have to stay well below the radar to avoid recognition, the world is not that big a place."

"I have no doubt he is still capable of killing, even though we got him sectioned to Broadmoor, wrongly as we first thought. We thought it strange at first that the doctors there thought him capable of such violence and more."

"I do have one lead for you Kobe, which I think we can follow up on without hindering, or particularly helping Casper Jones." Revealed Robert.

"Which is?" Interest sparked within Kobe's dark eyes.

"I am still in contact with Gill Harmon..."

"The journalist girlfriend!"

"Yes, we befriended her and helped her avoid the press after Lucas went missing. The book was a runaway best-seller even after the TV show, in fact even more so. People are so morbid for chasing the gruesome details of events like that."

"You said you were still in contact." There was excitement in Kobe's voice as well as impatience. "Where is she, will she talk to us?"

CHAPTER 51

"How do we get to him Nick." Sam asked. "People like Jackman always seem so untouchable. They just rise above trouble and seem to gain a momentum on success because of it. While us poor buggers at the bottom of the heap must keep eating the shit that is served us. Well, I want to pick something new on the menu." Sam's voice was low, firm and filled with ambition, but although talking a big game his voice was tinged with defeat.

Depression was weighing heavily on both sides of Sam's elegant refectory table in his dimly lit kitchen. With his thoughts ranging between depression and revenge, Sam had little time to think of how the money he never had would have changed his life.

"As always with my job Sam it's the difference between knowing and proving, same as with the police." Said Nick explaining the obvious. "And, even without asking we know he will have an airtight alibi, for both the theft and the killing of poor Mr Benny, who just had the bad luck to get caught in the middle of all this."

"I never thought this would turn to murder Nick, I feel a little responsible." Sam said sincerely.

"It's nobody's fault but that conniving Councillor's." Nick almost spat the words out. "We have to get him by coming at him from another direction."

"Surely with all the sources you have at the paper, there must be something we can use to get him." Sam was plucking at straws, but he saw Nick's expression had changed. "What? What is it, Nick?"

"I, and by I, I mean me and the paper, do have something..."

"Is it something we can use Nick, maybe even as leverage if you can't publish a story about it? Something we can use without putting your career in the toilet, you have Suzi and your little one to think of now."

"It's something solid, so no flushing careers away, but I will admit, I am not going to enjoy using it." Nick's expressions were changing every few seconds as each thought caught his mood, now it was solemn. "It is photographic proof of his lack of morals after shouting about family values to get elected. Even my editor is loathed to use it as we are first and foremost a local family newspaper. It's one of the reasons I like working for him, traditional values. Which there is a shortage of in the media these days."

"If he has been caught playing away, then maybe we should use it." Sam quickly caught himself. "Sorry, that was very selfish."

"About time you got a little selfish Sam, but the trouble is that this time it will cause a lot of hurt to a lovely person who does not deserve it."

"Surely, if you have something on him, he bloody well deserves it to get out." Sam did not mean to sound angry, but it was how he was feeling. The tone was involuntary.

"With every story Sam, there are innocent bystanders, look at poor Jason Benny. That man was just an unlucky spectator to something he didn't even know existed and now he has been killed. Most of us are unaware of the consequences each time we do something, most times all is okay, but then other times we topple the first domino, and the stack just falls way and topples even faster the further it runs. Like you, he had no idea that lives were about to change while others ended."

Sam chose not to interrupt, as he knew his friend would eventually get to the point.

"...Barbara Jackman, the Councillor's wife, what we have will devastate her. I have known her a long time and she is a lovely lady, loyal, strong, and not without influence but she would become another of the innocent victims knocked down in the rush."

"If she is that smart, Nick, surely she should know about him and his antics!" Sam argued.

"Like I said, she is loyal and always looks for the best in people. She has always had an inkling but stays blind to the truth because she wants to believe in her husband. She even has no awareness of the fact that the money she put into her husband's business was used to set his girlfriend up in her waterside apartment."

"If you have proof Nick, then put it in front of him." Sam suggested. "Scare him, into doing something rash."

Sam moved forward to the edge of his seat as if he were watching a late-night horror movie and the background music had begun to build to a mysterious crescendo. Elbows on the scuffed surface of the table, his hands supporting his head on a tired neck, Sam looked a mixture of determined and beaten.

After a 'long' minute of silence, Nick finally explained. "For a few months now, we have been holding some very clear photos of Jackman and his 24-year-old, pumped up, blonde girlfriend in some very naked and compromising positions. They were sent to the paper anonymously and the paper has been loathed to use them for both bad-taste and legal reasons. We are not one of the National tabloids, just a local newspaper that is reliant on local advertising for its survival, and many of those advertisers would not want to be linked to such a sleazy and graphic story. They were obviously gained by the photographer going onto private property, and we have rules we have to adhere to these days, The Chronicle probably would not survive the scandal."

"Could you get hold of them, the pictures?" Asked Sam as if it needed quantifying.

Nick, then shocked Sam, "I have them." And he patted the brown, canvas shoulder bag that hung over the back of the chair and went everywhere with him. It contained reporter's note pads, pencils, and an old-fashioned Dictaphone that Nick still liked to use, and on that evening, it also contained a plain A4 manila envelope holding the images that had been gained illegally, probably.

"Then let's go," He was already out of his chair and aiming for his coat. "...let's go threaten him with exposure unless he comes clean."

"We have to be smarter than that Sam, a few risqué images are hardly likely to scare him into admitting murder and theft." Nick took a deep breath, he never did enjoy the shock/horror/probe style of modern journalism, one of the reasons for staying on a local rag. That and the fact he never wanted to move away from Chichester, even less so now seeing as how Suzi was pregnant. "He will know that The Chronical would never publish them."

"Then what do we do? We can't do nothing."

"Sadly, I know what we must do, it's his wife, Barbara, that has to see them. Another innocent bystander caught in the crush." Nick was genuinely concerned about hurting Barbara Jackman, one of the reasons Sam admired Nick so much was his gentle heart.

"Will that do any good?" Sam asked.

"The money is all hers, she basically controls all the Councillor's finances, and she holds the purse strings tight. Which is why I think he is taking the risks he has taken, apart from the fact I think he enjoys seeing himself as a villain, I am sure he has RHS!"

Sam asked quizzically, "RHS?"

"Robin Hood Syndrome, except he conveniently forgets to pass on the loot to the poor."

Sam merely tutted.

"Once the purse strings are finally cut, he will have to come out of hiding and take some risks, especially getting rid of the Centurion. He won't easily find someone to buy it, not without advertising the fact he has it."

The following morning, before the dew had been warmed off the daisies in the back yard, Nick and Sam set out to shake the Councillor's world. Nick knew that Jackman would be following his normal daily routine and would make an appearance in the council chambers, he liked to be seen to be doing his job. Not that there was any council business to be done, as most councillors had day jobs and businesses to run, he just liked to hang around council chambers and feel important. Practice for when he got to the Commons as an MP, he would tell anyone who bothered to ask. Sam put down a fresh tin of food for Wedgwood, compliments of Nick as Sam had not opened the shop for over a week now and money was in short supply. Now he waited at the end of the precinct ready to be picked up by Nick, when he saw somebody look closely through the dusty window of his shop, and then rattle the door to see if it would open, the man peered through again, hands cupped over eyes so they could see through the dusty glass. The potential customer was eager. Sam was torn between opening the shop or continuing to wait for Nick, but at that moment his car appeared at the end of the precinct. And so, the adventure to get Sam's rightful property back, and some justice for Mr Benny was about to begin and Sam was looking forward to getting some payback.

Apart from brief hellos as Sam climbed into Nick's car, the drive out of the city was done in silence and Sam watched out of the window as the size of the houses grew larger, and the gap between them grew longer the further they travelled into the Sussex countryside. At the end of a pretty, little village Nick turned left into a country lane, three or four houses and a trendy barn conversion later it was just farmland for as far as the eye could see. Nick cruised to a stop and Sam saw the house through a gap in the hedgerow, a curving gravel drive led to a brick and flint farmhouse and Sam was in awe of the stylish 180-year-old property, alongside the drive Sam could see a tennis court and he imagined summer parties with guests in tennis whites sipping Pimm's on the lawn. It was a different world to the one Sam was used to living.

"Any second thoughts Sam?" Nick stirred Sam from his imaginings and looking at his friend with a stony face he continued to give Sam an option to quit. "Every action has an opposite and equal reaction, or something like that. What I am saying is that what we are about to do may well come back and bite us in the arse, Sam."

"Maybe I will settle for a nice cup of tea at the local farm shop, then." Sam showed his nervousness, normally in life he was not a man to pick a fight.

The two close friends looked at each other and had a moment...

"Fuck it!" Nick blurted out and shoved the car back into gear and turned into the driveway.

"Don't let Suzi hear you talk like that." Sam teased.

"I think she will understand for this one."

The curved drive was long enough that Nick changed into second gear before reaching the front of the imposing house. They both took a large breath to steel themselves for what lay ahead and without another word they alighted from the car and stood on the flagstone doorstep. Nick gripped the metal ring that connected by levers to a doorbell, and it gave an antique clang that echoed from inside the house.

"Will a butler answer the door, do you think Nick?" Sam was joking but still half expected it to happen.

The door opened and Sam's jaw slackened, and he felt his mouth dry. He knew he was gawping, staring open-mouthed, but he could do nothing to hide his stunned expression. Barbara Jackman was the opposite of Sam in almost every way, tall, elegant and with glossy jet-black hair that cascaded down to rest on her shoulders like the hood of a shimmering cape which framed her stunning facial features perfectly. Almond shaped and deep blue, her eyes beamed with light and emotion. Her make-up was sparse and perfectly applied, it flattered her features rather than hide any flaws, sharp cheek bones and a pretty nose above a perfect mouth, that Sam was currently imagining kissing. This all took a split second for Sam to notice, and he felt himself blush.

"What do you want Nick Flax?" It was a well-educated voice but with a slight Sussex burr. "Looking for more dirt to try and spread about my husband." Sam liked how she was loyal, even if it was misguided. "I don't know how you dare bring whatever accusations you have today to my home, especially as we both know that he is in Council Chambers today. I would rather be surprised at seeing what your paper will concoct in print than have you standing at my door."

Sam was stood slightly behind Nick and as Barbara Jackman was standing on her doorstep she appeared to be looking down from a great height, he felt like a schoolboy sent to the Head's office. She eyed the little man, and her gaze was intimidating, Sam really had wished they had gone to the farm shop for a cup of tea now.

"And who is this nasty little weasel, your photographer." Sam felt the insult hit him like a well thrown spear, and to hear it come from such a goddess almost made his heart bleed.

"Barbara..." Nick was stopped from saying any more.

"It's Mrs Jackman to you, you lost the right to call me by my first name a long time ago. Especially here on my own doorstep." Nick didn't shrink at the barbs, and he realised he had something going for him, and Sam... she had not slammed the door in their faces quite yet.

Nick did not change tack or shirk from his mission. "Barbara, this is my friend Sam, I am not here as a reporter and whatever you say to me, should you choose to say anything at all, is off the record and will never appear in any story, you have my word."

So far, so good, as she remained on the doorstep, the door half open. "I do need to talk with you though and have something to show you. It is something you do not deserve to see but I promise that the time is right for you to see it and I hope you listen to me." he added, "I wish there were another way, but there isn't."

He stopped talking and waited, Sam remained standing slightly behind him, his mouth still open as if ready to catch flies. Nick felt as if Sam were about to speak, but a sharp look toward him from Barbara stopped any words before they even formed in his mouth.

With a poker face, Barbara Jackman stood quite still, arms folded defensively across her chest, she was wearing a classic twinset adorned with pearls and matched with stylish linen trousers. A slight breeze found its way up the driveway and flicked hair across her face, Sam saw it in slow-motion, as she brushed it back behind her ear with an elegant hand. He was smitten with this strong and impressive woman.

Finally, on realising that neither man was going to be put off, she stepped back and ushered the two men into her house.

"This better be good Nick Flax." It was a threat, but a gentle one.

Head down to avoid eye contact Nick brushed past her, followed by a cowed Sam who felt some sort of electricity flow between them as their arms touched in the close confines of the doorway. Even now that he was up on the doorstep beside her, she was still a full six inches taller than the small antique dealer. Sam felt diminutive beside the formidable woman, but strangely for him not intimidated.

Barbara led them through to a smart kitchen, almost garish with red cabinet doors and chrome appliances, in this room it was a different century to the rest of the house. Sam imagined it was a house that saw a lot of entertaining. In the centre of the kitchen was a massive oak refectory table that he admired professionally. Long and heavy legged, its polished top was made of just one piece of rich wood, and at one time it must have been hewn from a mighty tree for a monastery or castle, Sam valued it at around two grand. Its shiny surface further polished by the arms and hands that had rested on it for over two centuries.

With a nod from the lady of the house they both pulled out oaken chairs, with seats worn smooth, and sat on one corner expecting Barbara to sit at the far end just to intimidate but she chose to sit alongside Sam. He had already felt small sitting up to such a magnificent table, now with this imposing woman beside him, he mentally shrank. The whole experience so far Sam found to be intoxicating and he felt out of his depth from the moment that they had driven onto the gravel drive.

He was way out of his social depth as well and just sat quietly waiting for Nick to do the talking.

"Now that you have my attention, what is it you want to tell me? And be warned this better be both off the record and off the charts as far as any accusations you make." The look from her was adversarial and Nick agreed again it was.

Sam sat silently, allowing his friend to tell the story in the way that only a trained journalist could do. Barbara sat with her elbows on the table, her fingertips together to form a steeple. She occasionally sipped at a cup of coffee as Nick spoke, she had not offered one to her guests. Sam would have loved a tea right now even though he could clearly smell the intoxicating aroma of her filtered coffee. Sitting next to her Sam also got a distinct whiff of a sweet and flowery perfume, it was pleasant and smelled expensive, for her part it was as if Sam didn't even exist even though he was sitting alongside her, Barbara appeared as if she was listening intently to Nick.

Nick began at the very beginning and told her everything, to her credit she did not interrupt. When Nick reached the part about Jason Benny and his untimely death, he heard her take a sharp intake of breath, and as much as she wanted to defend her husband, she waited for Nick to reach his conclusion.

Even Sam could see her impatience and had the strong feeling that the reporter would soon be on the end of a tongue lashing while he was being put in his place. The lady had yet to be convinced. Being married to a man in the public eye, even if it was on a local level, she was used to seeing journalists as piranhas feeding on the flesh of the well-known. Sam noted the glowering looks she aimed toward Nick. Sam didn't even consider that he was talking out loud and would be heard by Barbara, but as he was alongside her that was doubtful. He had not thought his action through and was glad he was not in her eye line.

"Are you sure you two used to be friends?" he said without thinking it through. Now he received a contemptuous glare, as she turned her head to look down at Sam. There was no immediate answer from either of the adversaries, but he had to give her credit where it was due, she was giving Nick the chance to tell the whole sorry story. Barbara briefly interrupted Nick for the first time.

"Our friendship was a very long time ago, Mr Cobby." Now he was certain she had heard his whispered comment.

Finally, the tale was told, and Nick leant back in his chair, the old oak spokes on the Windsor chair creaking in complaint. Nick had finished up the story with the auction and how they were embarrassed at being told they were trying to sell a fake as original. Nick left it unsaid about who he believed had switched the figurines. Barbara read the silence perfectly. Sam just sat there nodding, as if it were needed to confirm Nick's telling of the story so far. So quiet was the room that he thought he heard church bells from the far side of the village ringing in muffled tones.

Although his friend had done all the talking it was Sam's mouth that was dry, he was frightened of saying the wrong thing in front of this woman. He was intimidated by both her attractiveness and by her composure.

Sam watched her elegant fingers un-steeple themselves and she placed them palm down on the table, looking as if she were about to use them to lever herself up and into standing position. Barbara was pushing down hard, and the knuckles of both hands turned white with the effort as she used the pressure to control the tension she felt. With an unblinking gaze she switched first to Sam then back at Nick, she might not have had the chair at the head of the table, but she was definitely in charge.

"Total bollocks, Nick Flax!" She blurted out. "Almost believable, but absolute bollocks!"

Sam was shocked that such a beautiful and delicate mouth could come out with such profanities. It was spoken with such venom that Sam was also surprised by the fact that her next words were tinged with disappointment.

"Where is your proof, and why would he steal this statuette thing, we have plenty of money as you well know, my business is good, and my father left me well cared for thank you very much." Her voice was now faltering as if her support for her husband was floundering. "Maybe some of what you say is true, but *murder,* are you insane? That poor man's death was tragic, but you surely cannot believe that Kenneth had anything to do with that. Proof Nick, where is your bloody truth?"

Reaching into his constant companion, the brown canvas satchel, Nick pulled out the buff-coloured envelope. "It gets worse, Barbara. I know you are trusting and loyal, you always have been, and I have kept these away from being published for some time now as it is not why I became a journalist."

He opened the neck of the envelope and drew out a half-dozen 10x8 photographs, all in glorious colour. Sam tried to get a peek at the salacious content, but Barbara was too quick in picking them up. She looked at each image, placing them one by one face down on the table, keen not to have to share her shame. She gazed at the naked flesh, the entwined bodies, the passionate expressions of the surgically enhanced girl and her cheating husband. Barbara remembered the girl from one of the garden parties the previous summer, she was introduced as a secretary from the council. The bastard had brought his bit on the side to her own home, to meet and mingle with her friends, then she recalled that Kenneth had disappeared for a half hour, or so, and his excuse was that he had been talking shop with the then mayor.

Both men could see the pain behind her eyes, but she remained strong and showed no outward emotion. Sam was getting more impressed by the minute, how he had always longed to meet a woman like her, but she would eat him alive. Her cheeks flushed pink, she could not control anger and disappointment that well. Barbara Jackman was a loyal and trusting woman and she expected the same from the people in her life, she knew her husband was a bit of a rogue, it was one of the things that attracted her too him, he was not a wimp like most of the men that chased her.

Eventually, the hurt painted itself on her features and her eyes took on a watery brightness as tears began to build. She had no idea of her husband's infidelity, he had always been a flirt, but she had, foolishly it now seemed, trusted him. She had an upbringing that taught her that if you dealt with people fairly, that would come back to you as a reward.

"I know you won't believe me Barbara..." Nick reached across and put a hand on hers, which was now balled up as a fist, expecting her to pull her hand away but she left it there. Sam wished he had done that first. "...but I am sorry I had to show you those images, I took no pleasure in it. The last thing I want to do is hurt you and I also know how much you value your marriage." To console her Nick gently squeezed her hand, only this time she pulled her hand away. Barbara Jackman hated being pitied.

"If that was the case, why did you show me those disgusting pictures." She had to let her anger out somewhere, and Nick was the closest.

Tears began to form in her eyes, but by sheer willpower and pride she held her emotions in check, saving it up until the company at her table were gone. Only then would she let them fall. Sam saw the hardening of her jawline and was even more impressed with this woman.

"I showed them because your husband needs money." Nick added. "And he is desperate enough to do anything."

"He does not need money; we are very well off as you well

know." She reacted quickly and barked the words out at Nick. All the while Sam remained quiet and watched the verbal match going on beside him.

"Yes, but it is your money, and I know how careful you are not to flaunt the fact." Nick continued. "He paid for his girlfriend's breast enlargement, and the flat these photos were taken in, it's not hers. His name is on the lease and it's not cheap renting on the waterfront. She is the proverbial 'kept woman'." Thankfully Nick did not create the speech marks with his fingers in mid-air. Sam loved it when his out-of-date friend used old-fashioned phrases.

Barbara said nothing, she was waiting for the information to sink in before she reacted, but she was in for an even deeper betrayal.

"She is not the most tight-lipped girl in the world, and she told me that Kenneth is waiting on one big score and then he is going to move in." Her jaw was now firmly clenched, and both men noticed the facial muscles harden. "He is making all sorts of promises to her, promises his wallet cannot keep. Which is one reason why he needed the money from the stolen bronze. Apparently, keeping the attention of his teenage lover and a payday worth more than three million pounds are well worth killing for." Nick paused for the last sentence to hit home, which it did with devastating force.

"Killing for?" Anger was now her overriding feeling, her emotions really were on an emotional rollercoaster. "I know what you said earlier about the fire, but how did this go from a sordid affair and embezzlement of my money to killing a man and setting fire to his house for Christ's sake." Again, Sam forgave her for cursing. "You don't just mean killing, you are talking murder!"

Again, Nick explained the story of the Antiques Roadshow and the fake, and how Sam discovered that he owned the real thing. He told Barbara his thoughts on how Kenneth had obtained the fake bronze and probably carried out the switch, explaining that it was only guess work at that point but there was no other explanation for all that had happened.

"If that was the case, why didn't Kenneth just buy the bronze? He didn't have to go and kill the man, for God's sake." Her stoic defence of her husband was becoming harder.

"Even though the version that he stole first time round was a fake, the Roadshow experts had still valued it at a few thousand pounds, and he just didn't have the money, and he couldn't get that amount from you without raising your suspicions." Nick was speaking softly now, fully aware that each of his voiced thoughts were hurting somebody he used to consider a friend. "Kenneth, in personal terms is broke. So, he needed to get the fake without paying for it and I doubt if he had the courage to do it himself, so he must have had the poor bloke killed."

"See, this is where your story falls down." Barbara cut in. "He has invested in several successful companies and has his own substantial income. I don't see how he could be broke."

"I have been pondering that over the last few days." Nick had not even told Sam what he was about to say. "I know for a fact that in the last month I have overheard Kenneth talking of a slight cash flow problem and that has triggered a memory of something that was brought up in recent editorial meetings. The timing of his shortfall links with another story we have covered, police have carried out two raids on Chichester drug houses and seized a massive amount of narcotics. Whoever, was the power behind those enterprises must owe the importers a fair old amount of back pay and you don't mess with those sorts of people."

"Now you are saying he is a drug dealer!" The shocks just kept coming, she felt like a boxer being held against the ropes and pummelled.

"This is stuff we have known for an age at the paper, but we have never found the proof. Even the police have been unable to find any..."

"Maybe that's because there is none to find." Barbara was still fighting for a little sanity. "Did you never think of that?"

"I am on good terms with DI Kobe Kaan, senior officer of the County's Serious Crime Unit, and he has been working on bringing Kenneth in for some time." Nick explained. "The cash flow prior to the drug raids is interrupted, just as your husband suffers a cash-flow problem."

"Go back a step Nick," Barbara was still angry, except now it was under control and not aimed at Nick or Sam. "You keep talking about this valuable bronze, what does it look like?"

Her expression had changed instantly, as if she had reached that eureka moment.

Nick looked at Sam, and finally he had a dog in the show that he could parade around the room. At last, he was able to speak. "It is a magnificent Roman Centurion, bronze, about this high..." he indicated with a handheld above the table's surface. "He has his short sword..." he never got to finish.

"Held up high as if he has just won a battle." Now both men sat with mouths wide open as they knew what was coming next. "I have seen it! Right here in Kenneth's home office. I don't usually go in there, that's his territory, but I needed some paper for my printer. And it was there shiny and as clear as day on top of his filing cabinet. I just thought it was something he had bought to brighten his office. I was quite pleased, thinking that finally he was getting a taste for artistic things." She shook her head. "What a fool I have been."

Sam was about to say something else, but he never had chance to get the words out.

"Would you two mind leaving me alone now, I need time to take this all in." She pushed back her chair and stood, Sam was again impressed with the way this woman looked and carried herself.

With the storytelling concluded for the moment, it was a different Barbara Jackman that showed them to the door and bid them goodbye. Her manner toward them was now as friends, she shook hands with Sam, he liked the softness and warmth of her grip, but she hugged Nick and kissed him on both cheeks. Sam was a little jealous, and it bothered him because women such as Barbara Jackman were way out of his league, even if she hadn't been married. She watched from the doorway as Nick climbed into his old car and turned the key to start the engine, much to his embarrassment it belched, pushing out a blue-grey cloud of exhaust fumes. The rear wheels struggled for grip on the gravel drive, and they spun throwing out handfuls of gravel. Even before they had reached the gate, Barbara had closed the door, double locked it, and slipped the security chain into its slot.

Barbara Jackman had closed the door and locked herself in to think over what was left of her damaged life. Her soon to be ex-husband would never be allowed back into, what was after all, her house.

With the world and its witnesses now securely outside, the tears began to flow. Barbara, thought about her life to date with Kenneth and despite his flaws, she had genuinely loved her husband, and had done so since the first day she met him. One huge regret was that they had no children, Kenneth had never seen himself as father material, why would he, he was still a boy himself, Barbara thought. She had given up her chance of motherhood for him, and now it seemed she had also given up her bed. So much for loyalty. Now she wondered if there was any love left, at all. There was certainly no trust left, that was for certain. She walked back into the kitchen, expecting to see the photographs still on the table, but thankfully Nick Flax had taken them with him. Discarded and cheated on, she had never felt so unwanted or ugly. Despite her successes in life, all her achievements, she now thought of herself as a useless failure. Her self-worth was at zero level.

In the car driving away from the desolation they had caused as messengers, Sam sat quietly, he was thinking exactly the opposite about the woman he had just met, he could not remember meeting a woman so beautiful, so elegant and so strong.

Sam Cobby was besotted!

CHAPTER 52

Kobe needed to feel pain, the physical kind.

The mental anguish, and that harmful emotional pain that resides deep in the chest had to be replaced as he could not function properly with that overwhelming ache. It was making it difficult to see his family as they once were, he was tired of every sleeping and waking moment seeing them as the killer had left them for him to find. Curled together arms over lifeless bodies, spooned into each other's backs like lovers frozen in time, their skin as white as the duvet, the duvet now as red as the reddest roses on the wall. Huddled together in a macabre tableau, it had to be left as an image meant to cause maximum suffering for the man who discovered them. The husband, the father and friend, now with that image imprinted indelibly for ever on his mind, at the start of every thought and every moment in sleep, all were filled with nightmares.

Their bedroom had once been such a place of joy. On Christmas mornings all the presents would be around the foot of the king size bed, and not downstairs around the tree. The children would rush in, far too early but that was okay, as the children began ripping apart some of the smaller gifts Kobe would head downstairs. Tasks would go in order, quickly eat the mince pie, being careful to leave a few crumbs on the mantle shelf and drink the glass of milk put out for Santa, the carrot would go back into the veg rack, make coffee for Rae and himself and make chocolate milkshakes for the two Christmas monsters. A selection of mini pastries picked up late on Christmas eve put on a plate with a few paper napkins. Crumbs on the bed were not only to be expected, but a part of the ritual.

With the tray laden with coffees, soft drinks, and chocolate nibbles, he would thump upstairs to warn them he was coming, there would be an overdose of laughter and giggles, happiness and if the presents were what was wanted or even unexpected there may even be a few tears. Next Christmas there would be nobody in the bedroom, no toys around the bedpost, that family home within the home, a place of love, hugs and sheer unrestrained joy. None of them really liked the turkey and trimmings tradition, it was more a day of snacks with Rae's speciality Bacon and Egg Muffins for lunch. A perfect day spent in Christmas pyjamas, enjoying the unique relationship that is family.

Now it was as if reality had thrown a dark cloak over everything except the bedroom scene that burned Kobe's every thought. He thought of revenge, of showing as much violence toward the killer as had been shown his family, police training and Muslim teachings were off the table now. Kobe Kaan needed to find those responsible and make them pay. He was filled with a rage like he had never known before.

He had begun to drink, to excess, every day. His favoured scotch now tasteless and without the burn in the throat, pointless. No matter how much he drank he felt neither the buzz of alcohol nor the numbness of mind he sought.

Another brightly lit shop front offered discounts on the cheap beer of the day, or money off today's featured wine. None were of the strength needed to calm Kobe's moods so he walked in and purchased the first bottle of whisky he found on a shelf, he didn't care about the age, the barrel it had matured in, or if it was a fine single malt, it was whisky, that will do. No sooner was he out of the shop before he unscrewed the metal cap and swigged from the bottle neck, he never even registered the burn it left in his throat anymore or the flavour.

He wanted, no, needed, to feel something other than this unending mental anguish that had been forced upon him. If the killer's objective was to break Kobe Kaan, then he would have been pleased with his work.

Kobe wanted to stay away from the centre of the city, the little bit of pride he had left meant he did not want people he knew to see him like this. He wanted neither their pity nor their help. In the end he just picked a street and walked down it.

At the end of the road there was a rowdy crowd of feral youths blocking the way. As idle youth are want to do, they jostled and passed obscene comments to young women who had no choice but to walk near them, or cross the busy road, the girls kept their eyes on the ground and just hoped to get through the group of half a dozen or so street idiots. As he walked by, they shoved at an old man and laughed raucously as he staggered on his walking cane and tried to keep his balance. For a moment Kobe noticed something other than his own situation and moved toward the teenagers, taking a another shot from the bottle neck before screwing the top back on. He was about to get the physical pain he longed for. His normal thought would be to flash his warrant card or just walk away and let uniforms know about the disturbance.

Approaching the six teenagers, all but one with their grey hoodies up and hiding their faces, the odd one who seemed to be the gang leader wore a baseball cap back to front as was the trend. Kobe looked him in the face and noted that the kid's nostrils and mouth were surrounded with open sores, in the gutter beside him was an aerosol of spray adhesive.

"Why don't you fuckers leave people alone?" Kobe spat out as a challenge, before barging into baseball cap, knocking him out of the way. "It's bad enough being a young woman or elderly lady in this society and not being able to walk safely along our streets, without you dickheads making life worse." Kobe was now face to face with the biggest boy in the group, that would be the one to put down first.

"Fuckin' 'av 'im Kev…" The runt of the litter called out from the shadow of a hoodie. The face turned and became lit by the overhead streetlamp, Kobe noticed the runt was a girl, the face with dull eyes had been attacked by acne.

No further prompt was needed, a shove in the chest came from the tall boy, followed by an ineffective blow from the girl, her bony fist merely bouncing off Kobe's head. It was a signal for them all to join in. Wildly, they were throwing punches at his upper body and kicking his legs. Kobe's every instinct was to fight back but he swiftly buried that thought and kept his arms by his side. Years of being a streetwise copper had taught him to never begin a fight he couldn't win, well this fight he was not even going to try. He was an open target for their casual violence.

A punch to the face and he felt his nose give a little and he tasted blood on his lips. As suddenly as the onslaught had begun it stopped as Baseball Cap yelled over their fighting screams, he was calling his minions to heel.

"STOP, STOP…" He yelled at his tiny crew of miscreants, stepping between Tall Boy and Acne Girl. "He's a fuckin' copper, he is setting us up for something."

"You sure?" An insubordinate gang-member yelled back, though why he was shouting Kobe was unsure, you could have thrown a sack over the entire mob.

"Course I'm fuckin' sure, he done my old man for robbin' the post office a few years back." he pointed an accusing finger at Kaan.

Both Tall Boy and Baseball Cap stopped throwing blows and looked up and down the poorly lit street for police back-up and saw none but it did not ease the fears of being set up. Despite not seeing any uniforms bearing down on them, discretion was the better part of valour. They were already dispersing and, on the run, when Tall Boy called out the order to disperse.

"Move it, the bastard is trying to set us up."

His five followers split in all different directions, pulling their heads further back into their hoods to avoid identification. Baseball Cap was the stockiest and carried some strength and he hung around just long enough to land one more, this time powerful, punch into Kobe's face. Kobe felt the top lip split as it caught on his teeth, and the strength of the blow caused him to drop to one knee.

"Come back, please, there is no back up." Kobe pleaded with them to stay. "It's just me." He was now sobbing with frustration.

Acne Girl had turned around to come back and have one more dig at The Man. Kobe was on his knees, she aimed a kick into his ribs, she was feeling braver now he was down, the leg did not carry any strength but the hefty Doc Martins she was wearing did the damage. Kobe felt a rib go, and he gasped in pain as the wind was kicked from his body.

Then they were gone.

Kobe was distraught, he could not even get a crowd of young apprentice gangsters to hurt him. What was wrong with this fucking city? He thought, as he remained kneeling on the pavement trying to catch his breath. But the pain was nowhere close to what he wanted to feel, sore lips, an ache where his nose was flattened and a heavy throb from what was probably just a cracked rib. He was turning out to be useless at most things these days, could not protect his family, could not get street idiots to beat him up, and then the real pain hit him, and hit him hard. The whisky bottle that he had only just started was broken on the pavement its contents dribbling down into the gutter.

Using a low garden wall to help him up, he stretched the rib and wiped the blood away from his nose and mouth with the sleeve of the charity shop jacket he had bought earlier. Body checks over he staggered off in search of another off-licence or supermarket.

It began to rain, and something did feel strange to Kobe, it was a chill drizzle and it slicked down his short growth of hair. Something he had not felt for several years, it dripped from his hair and down the neck of his light jacket. He stood at the kerbside wiping raindrops from his face with the palm of his hand, but at least his tears were hidden now. The reactionary wipe took his hand down across his nose and it increased the throbbing from that part of his face. He welcomed its dull ache.

Shop lights further along the road gave him a target to aim for and he began walking, feeling the rainwater seep into the thin trainers he was wearing. He wondered how homeless people managed in this lifestyle of the streets; it was bloody uncomfortable. The thought of comfort took him back home and winter fires in the hearth, curtains pulled closed against inclement weather. Strong winds blowing up the harbour and the relaxing sound of the sea working its way to land.

The lights from across the road shone like a beacon leading him onward to his own holy grail. He noticed a couple in a doorway, arms around each other, she was reaching up for a kiss. It was Baseball Cap and Acne Girl, and he was jealous of them and their teenage groping. Neither of them noticed the freshly beaten man as he walked by their doorway. Arriving at the shop he was disappointed to discover there would be no drink on sale. Displayed on the window were silvery words linked with gothic knots and symbols, swirling Celtic designs mingled with mythical dragons. Once upon a time tattoo parlours surrounded naval depots and dockyards but nowadays, they could be found on every high street, no longer offering 'Love You Mum' but now exhibiting fine artwork and the same elaborate designs that sports stars and movie idols boasted on their inked skin. In modern times the ink artists were creating walking galleries of art.

He gazed through the window, pondering, being voyeuristic toward the young woman having a dagger drawn the length of her upper arm. A bright red heart, pierced by a dagger with blood dripping from the stiletto point before fading out, just before her elbow, on the third or fourth scarlet droplet. An artistic dagger through a bleeding heart... Life had a strange way of emphasising things.

Kobe knew that if Rae were here with him, she would have flipped if he even mentioned a tattoo. Despite her artistic leanings, she hated the sight of body ink. For her art belonged on paper, canvas, even cardboard and hardboard, plinth, and pedestal, in galleries and not strolling around the city centres on bare-chested show-offs. Watching the tattoo artist work though was giving him thought, the pain from the fight had diminished, even the rib had stopped aching, and any further discomfort would be gone by morning. What he needed was a short, sharp pain, that left a constant reminder He hated how he felt now but another fear that consumed him was that one day he may begin to forget, and he must never forget. He needed something he could tug at, or fiddle with when the mental pain became too much to bear, he needed something physical.

He pushed the door open, expecting a bell to tinkle overhead, but instead all he could hear was some loud music that he recognised as the Foo Fighters, blaring out from two massive speakers at the far end of the shop. A pretty, young Goth sat behind a counter, lips black, eyelids black, hair black, clothes black and dark ink tattoos covering both arms and her neck. A black crucifix was tattooed at her temple and Kobe wondered what was so wrong with just looking pretty. As he moved closer, he noted a huge black ring that she sported in the extended and stretched lobe of one ear, fitting into a hole a bus could drive through. He pondered as to whether Rae would have room for complaint if he had that fitted, it would surely hurt.

The girl lifted a small remote control over her shoulder and the Foo Fighters lowered their volume to a less painful level.

"Evening Sir, can I help you." Well-spoken and polite, obviously well educated, the lifestyle choice puzzled him even more, but what did he know he was over forty now, 'old' as his children always reminded him.

"I take it you do piercings?" He could not believe he had just asked that as he nodded toward her various pieces of inserted silver.

"We do, what were you thinking of, nose, ears, something more exotic like a Prince Albert?" Kobe knew what that was and was not about to have his cock manhandled and pierced, she noted the panic in the customer's eyes.

"What is the most painful?" It was a strange question to ask, he felt, but she did not miss a beat.

"I would go with nipple." She answered quickly. "Mine hurt like hell, even more than the one in my clit, that one was quite exhilarating."

She added with a cheeky smile, a small diamond reflected light on the face of one of her top teeth.

"Well, I haven't got one of those so I will go for a nipple please." He thought a moment about which side of his chest the seatbelt crossed. "The left one please."

"Just the one..."

"For now."

The Goth girl looked over her shoulder, and over a low wooden barrier where another client was laid having a massive landscape produced on her back. Kobe could only see the sweating bald head of the man working on her.

"Dad, can you do a quick nipple piercing?"

Kobe, worried on those words for a moment, *'Quick nipple piercing...'* This was his body they were talking about so flippantly, a very delicate part as well. Were piercings, the fast-food of the body art industry? He wondered.

The bald man stood up and arched his back straight. "Marnie and I could both do with a break; give me five minutes and I will fit him in. Just the one, is it?" He added looking at Kobe, he could just nod his conformation.

Five minutes later, medical forms filled out and signed he was ushered through a pair of swinging doors, cowboy saloon style, and into the piercing chair. It sounded like an archaic punishment for witchcraft without a licence.

Kobe removed his jacket and T-shirt, both damp with the rain and the bald man sat and wriggled to comfort on a stool that looked small against his massive arse. Kobe was amazed it survived the assault, if he wanted to feel pain maybe he could just get the man to sit on him. Kobe could not avert his gaze from the gap between bald guy's wife-beater shirt and his trouser belt which disappeared under his overhanging belly. The daughter looked across from her stool behind the counter and smiled appreciatively at Kobe, with his rain-damp body which was well toned and an olive brown hue. He failed to notice the teenager's leering gaze.

Bald man collected his tools from the steriliser and pointed to both Kobe's nipples asking the silent question.

"Left one please, the seat belt would rub the right." It was getting surreal now, the statement although factual felt strange and incongruous seeing as how he wanted to feel pain. And, yet there was hope for some relief later.

Bald Guy seemed almost disinterested as he grabbed a clamp, with two metal loops at the business end, and squeezed it onto his nipple, the discomfort deep, but warm. Kobe felt the clamp being held steady to keep the redundant man-organ still. A sharp pressure on one side, and then a second or two of searing pain that strangely came with both pleasure and pricking discomfort. The flesh went unyielding for a moment and Kobe foolishly looked down; he saw what appeared to be a size 12 knitting needle pushing hard to break through the brown flesh. His nipple bulged on one side as it tried to defend its well-being and Kobe felt a trickle of sweat run down from his armpit.

"Don't worry mate," Bald Guy said. "...been doing this for 15 years now, ten of those in this very shop." The boasting gave cause for concern as nobody confident of themselves never needed to brag about their skillset mid-job.

Suddenly the skin broke, Kobe took a large intake of breath, as the needle completed its journey through the dark skin of his delicate and now wounded, nipple. No sooner had the brief agony arrived than it disappeared just as swiftly. The skin had been invaded by a huge sweating man with a sharp implement and Kobe chose not to utter a sound, but his brain had other ideas.

"Fuck me, that stings!"

"Wuss." Came a not-so-subtle cry from the Goth on the counter, Kobe couldn't argue with that.

For a mere millisecond he felt what he had yearned for, but it also taught him the humility of wanting to feel such pain. It was nothing compared to what his family had suffered, even the earlier fight felt juvenile and petty when reflected on. It belittled his family, not help him to assuage his suffering at being left behind. In that split second of pain his thoughts ejected the image of their dying and was replaced with the sunlight of their living. He saw Rae and his children on the village green that sat alongside the sailing club and the waterfront, flying beautiful kites on the breezes that flowed in unhindered across the water's surface and up onto shore. He felt Rae sitting alongside him, the diaphanous material of her dress gently brushing his skin as its folds caught the breeze, making the hairs on his arms stand on end. There were roses on the summer frock, and suddenly he saw blood running from the petals.

As quickly as the memory arrived in his minds-eye, it had disappeared again. But at least it gave a drowning man a raft to cling to.

Another spike of localised pain brought him back into the Bald Guy's world as the chrome pin was pushed through the hole that had just been driven into him. Bald Guy screwed a small silver ball onto the screw thread end that was poking out of his nipple.

"All done, here is a leaflet on how to keep it clean and how often to clean it." Bald Guy was all business and then gone, back to Marnie and the Constable style landscape being inked into her skin. He felt like saying, 'don't worry love, he's been doing this for 15 years now', he thought it, but stopped himself from saying.

He paid £25 for the privilege of being stabbed in the tit, and another £25 for the thin stick of silver that now filled the hole. He touched it to ensure his money's worth, and sure enough he had got what he paid for.

In that moment of pain, and the seconds that followed, he had a brief vision of sunshine and family summers. For a brief second or two the winter of his life had moved away as if clouds had parted to order. He left the shop and before he could close the door behind him the Foo Fighters with a thrashing rhythm once again raised the volume, probably to hide the screams of the clientele.

Kobe had done with physical pain, it changed nothing, he just had to learn to live with the painful images that filled his thoughts and his heart. Now his only thought was the creator of all this mayhem. Who, and why had they done this to his family. It was unwritten law that families were to be left alone, it was a coward's way of dealing with things. Come tomorrow Kobe would start asking questions among the local criminal fraternity. It was only a small city with only very few serious criminals working within its ancient walls. Somebody would know something, and they would talk, murder was the sort of behaviour that was bad for everyone's business.

CHAPTER 53

Somewhere between ten and eleven o'clock on a fresh Friday evening Kenneth Jackman headed toward home, Fiona having collected him from his girlfriend's paid-for apartment. Each time Fiona saw the girl he was playing and paying with, she thought that if he ever dumped her, she would move in on the girl as she had the serious hots for the surgically enhanced bimbo. Jackman was unsure of the exact time as he had left his Rolex Oyster Perpetual watch on his girlfriend's dressing table, at six grand a throw he hoped she did not see it as her fee for the evening's entertainment, that would have been a tad expensive even with her sexual gymnastic display.

Ensconced in the comfort of the rear seats of the Jaguar he hoped that Barbara would not be in a frisky mood, his friskiness was all used up. The luxury car purred out of the city and into the countryside, Jackman almost falling asleep cocooned in its warm and cosy cockpit. Arriving at his front door he almost stumbled from the car, before leaning in and telling Fiona,

"Not too early in the morning Fi, may need a little recovery time." Jackman smiled; it was a not very subtle boast.

Fiona did not answer, just drove away as soon as Jackman had closed the rear door. She hated so much about working for the Councillor, she didn't like him much for a start with his grabby hands and innuendos, he was a wanker and she wondered what women saw in him. He was everything she hated in men, arrogant, pushy, selfish, and worst of all, he was weak and sloppy. She had sorted out too many messes and loose ends for him since going on his payroll two years previously. Back then he was having trouble from an irate drug dealer, lately it seemed the man was always having trouble of one sort or another for her to sort out. She had enjoyed that first job, even keeping one of the dealer's broken teeth for a 'memory drawer', with his fingers broken he would not have been able to pick it up for himself anyway. When her boss had mentioned a bonus for her efficient work, she decided on beginning her shoe collection. The upside of working for the weasel Jackman, was that she did love hurting people, scaring them, and best of all, killing them. It was the ultimate high and left her with adrenaline coursing through her veins. One day though, she knew that Jackman would become his very own loose end, and she would really enjoy tying that one off. Worst of all, out of all his annoying habits, and there were a lot, was that she hated being called Fi! She would happily reverse the Jaguar over him for just that transgression alone.

As the car disappeared down the driveway, brake lights blinking on, then off again as it was manoeuvred through the gates, Jackman was momentarily distracted by thoughts of his driver and what she would look like naked. She would have smallish boobs, but that was okay, he liked all boobs, big, small, and in-between, slim waist and hips and he took a bet with himself that she was probably totally shaven down there, but as she was a confirmed lesbian, he would probably never have a chance to find out. She would not be totally naked of course, she would keep on the five-inch stilettos, the ones with the red soles and those killer heels that he had bought for her.

He would never do anything about his lustful thoughts, he had thought on several occasions of asking if she would like to join him and his girlfriend in a fun-filled threesome, but he knew only too well that, as she always put it, batted for the other team only.

"One night with me, and I would change your mind about that, lovely Fi." It was the drink talking. Shocked that the words had come from his mouth, rather than just in his head, he turned toward the front door to ensure it wasn't open and Barbara, his wife, was not standing there listening. With his index finger over his lips, he shushed himself.

He fumbled in his pocket for his house key, while with his free hand he hefted and scratched his balls through the thin material of his chinos. There was a tender spot where his enhanced lover had played a little rough, he had liked that, it was a new diversion, but now away from the bedroom it made him wince and he dropped the keys onto the gravel drive. Bending to pick them up he almost toppled forward onto his face, but with a wobbling step he regained his balance and retrieved them. Now held firmly between thumb and index finger he took a deep breath and readied himself for the arduous task of getting the keyhole on the first thrust of key-tip. A step forward, good start, the second step a little trickier as he had to mount the low tile-covered step to reach the front door. He missed it, the toe part of his shiny loafers getting scuffed as it connected with the front of the step which was only three inches high. He was still laughing when his face collided with the door, his only thought, 'ooh, there's the door'. He stood up straight, aimed, prodded, a miss, a second aim, another miss, third attempt and the tip of the key met its target and slid in easily. 'Just as I did earlier...' he chuckled, he was not sure if the comedic line had been thought or spoken. The key was being twisted but there was no movement, no turning motion and no key ridges engaging with lock mechanisms, he slid it almost all the way out, before thrusting it back in again, and sexual thoughts drifted haphazardly through his mind making him giggle like a schoolboy seeing pictures of naked boobs for the first time. In and turn, simple enough, but nothing happened, and he slid the key out to check it was the right one. It seemed to be and this time it took him four attempts before the key sank to its hilt in the mechanism, but still, it would not turn. Fearing the lock may have been tampered with he rang the bell, and for good measure thumped on the door and called his wife.

"Barbara, some bugger has busted the lock, can you let me in please." The deep breath he took just before shouting in the letter box seemed to have allowed him to avoid the bad taste of being discovered as drunk.

Jackman, worse-the-wear for drink was getting cross, things always worked for him, its just the way he was made. Years ago, he made his first play for the boss's daughter and a year later they were married, she was boring and controlling but he made it work. With his past business ventures, he had been doing well, until outside influences made mistakes, losing most of the money he had made from supplying building equipment, that was how he had met the pretty Barbara, who was working in her father's construction company. Marrying her had stopped him from going broke, but now he had his own strong enterprise going and apart from a couple of recent setbacks, he was making his own money. Get those setbacks sorted, and the drop in cash flow reversed and soon he would not need Barbara, and her interfering ways, or her money anymore. Okay, things may have been a little slow financially recently, but now with that bloody bronze soldier in his grasp, everything would not only be back on track, but he would be ahead of the game. Things were looking up, apart from this fucking front door and the key. He thrust it in again, turned it hard and it snapped, right where the circular head met the ridged shaft.

Only one option left, he got down on one knee, just like he did when he proposed to Barbara. It wasn't a proposal as he knew he already had her captivated and in love with him, he was ruggedly handsome, and because of his expensive tastes in clothes, watches, and cars he looked a good financial catch as well. Oh, and of course he was an excellent lover, with a magical touch. The thought of proposing again while down on one knee was funny, and he laughed as he pushed the sprung flap in the waist high letterbox open, shouting louder than necessary through the oblong opening.

"Barbara, BARBARA..." His voice echoing down the vast hallway that led to all the downstairs rooms and the broad staircase at the end that led to the bedrooms. "My key wouldn't open the door, now its broken, have you left the latch down?"

The flap in the letterbox sprung back and closed hard, nearly taking one fingertip off. "That fucking thing is dangerous, nearly took my feckin' finger off." He said at the front door and with a leering laugh, he added. "And I need all my fingers for pleasuring you women." He thought that as a comedian he was hysterical.

He waited, looking up at the stained-glass portal at the top of the door to see if any shadows crossed it. None did. So, he opened the flap again, waiting a moment before shouting and listening for any sound within. Barbara could not be out, she never went anywhere, boring bitch. All he could hear was the sound of some TV drama or other, the music was building to a crescendo, there would be a fucking crescendo here as well if she didn't get her finger out and open this fucking door. With drunken slurring that was exactly what he should shout through the letterbox, she would know now that he was well pissed, and she had better get her fat arse down the hallway and let him in. But what he yelled was...

"Darling, there seems to be a problem with the door lock." He whined, get in the house first and then give her a piece of his mind, that's the plan to go with.

Finally, he heard the TV stop, and the echoes of the low heels on Barbara's 'comfortable' court shoes clacking on the hallway's highly polished, parquet flooring as she neared the door. Keep your temper Kenneth, you need to get in the house first, then the bollocking for making him stand out in the porch as if he was being punished for something.

"Who is it?" The question was intended to needle and wound her cheating husband.

She was taking the piss, surely. "It's me. Who the fuck do you think it is?" Oops, that was a bad move, he was supposed to keep his temper.

"Who did you say again, I didn't catch that?" To his drunken voice she sounded way too calm.

"Don't fuck around love, you know who it is." He tried to keep his voice level and calm. "It's been a long day at the council, and the lock seems to be broken."

"It seems that the one who has been fucking around is you. I have seen the photos." She sounded almost cheerful, knowing that it would wind him up even more. So, you no longer live here." Her tone was as cold as her heart felt that night and although she wanted to sound composed, the words did catch in her throat. Barbara would never let her husband know, but a tear slipped from the corner of her eye and touched her cheek.

"You cannot lock me out of my own home, its not right." It was the first thing he could think of to say, he needed a moment to recompose himself. Then quickly in defence. "...and I don't know what you are talking about." That sounded believable, his drunken mind thought.

Kenneth Jackman was known for his swaggering confidence, bordering on arrogance, but a hint of fear gently clutched at his heart as he saw his comfortable lifestyle being locked away behind that formidable front door that kept his wife from getting the beating of her life. Nobody treated him this way. This was not just sentimentality on his part, truth be known he couldn't give a flying-fart about his marriage, not now he had a way to his own fortune which was near and within his greedy grasp. He just needed a little more time to manoeuvre his way out of the current financial pickle he had found himself in. Unconcerned about his wife's feelings he had been given another problem tonight, tucked at the back of the bottom drawer of the filing cabinet in his home office, which was behind this locked door, was a foot-high bronze statuette of a Roman Centurion with a short sword held aloft, and worth around £3million to him.

On the other side of the door tears were now falling one after the other down her face as she tried to control her breathing well enough to speak without the bastard out on the porch knowing how hurt she was.

"This is not your home, or your house, never has been." Barbara stated. "It is my house, my home, I own it, lock stock and barrel!" Anger was all that was stopping her from breaking down or, even worse, giving in and opening the door. "I was born here, grew up here and it was left to me, in my name. You have given up the right to live here, or even be here in fact. So, get off my front porch and off my property before I get my friend the Chief Constable to have you removed." She wouldn't use her friendships like that, but it sounded convincing.

Now Jackman's wife had become as immovable and unfeeling as the door he needed to get through. And neither were going to give.

"For fuck's sake Babs, stop pissing around and open the door so at least we can talk about this, what is obviously a mistake." He was wincing for using the shortened name for his wife; she hated it. It had been a bad move on his part, but pride would not allow him to apologise for it.

Despite his verbal mistake he heard the door latch click open and Jackman let out a sigh of relief, she had come round. It would take some working out to get her back on side and he may have to sleep in the guest bedroom for a night or two, but by then the bronze would be on its way to its new owner in Holland and the money would be on its way to his bank.

Ready to step though when the door fully opened, he clenched his left fist, punch her in the arm he thought, not in the face where people would assume as to what he had done, bruises must not show, that would give any battered wife ammunition. Thoughts of entering the house disappeared as soon as he had them, he heard the security chain rattle in its chrome holder and the door stopped with just a two-to-three-inch gap between jamb and door. Something was being slipped through the gap, it was his passport.

"That is all you own in this house, so take it and fuck off!" Barbara never swore, despite spending her life around the men of the building trade, this must be serious. Jackman began to feel panic rising.

For her part Barbara continued to bait him. "You own nothing in this house, not your clothes not your office toys, nothing. Everything has always been in my name for business purposes. I will have all the relevant receipts and paperwork ready for when I divorce you and leave you without any more of my money or any rights with regards to this house or anything in it, Kenneth, and I mean anything..."

What did she mean by 'anything', that sounded like she knew, but how could she know. The Centurion was tucked away, hidden in his office, and she never went in there. Until now! Panicked thoughts were racing through his head, suddenly he was sober.

As quickly as it had been partly opened, the front door on his old life was firmly slammed in his face, Kenneth was now left without money, without a home, or a wife but that part was okay, he always had his girlfriend. But how long would she stay around if she knew he was broke, although he had paid for her double-D breasts he could hardly demand those back! Even the tenancy of the flat was in her name, he had merely paid the rent. She rented the apartment, and he rented her. She would be nothing without him and have nowhere to go, without him. Kenneth imagined the spare clothes that he had in the wardrobe and drawers being scattered on the wharf side, thrown from the first-floor apartment in the marina, and being blown down along the pontoons and into the filthy water. His wife, that bitch Barbara had really left him with nowhere to go.

Thankfully for Barbara, and with what little pride and feeling of self-worth she had left because of her straying husband, he could not see what was happening on the other side of the door in a house now empty of joy and love. She had slid down the wall next to the chained and locked door and was sitting on the highly polished floor and hugging her knees up to her chest. Her heart had broken for the second time that day and she was now sobbing for the loss of her dream marriage, which had been fractured bit by bit over recent years. She always knew her husband was not perfect, her father had even warned her to protect her but had always given her room to make her own decisions, good or bad. It was the roguish charm of the heavy equipment supplier that had first attracted her, but she always believed that he would remain honest and loyal to her.

She had been such a bloody fool!

The homeless lothario, in his expensive designer suit and his hand-crafted Italian leather shoes, stood just off the porch swaying slightly on the gravel drive, when the nausea took over and he hurled his stomach contents onto the drive mixing his earlier dinner with the gravel. He felt giddy with the remaining effects from the earlier alcohol intake as it now mingled with the stones on the drive. It had been a fine red wine, a St Emillion Premiere Cru with its warm, earthy tones, that he and his lover had shared while naked on the soft rug of her lounge, under the huge picture window that gave a view of the lights and boats in the marina. It wasn't just his wife that had caused the upset.

As his predicament sobered him further, he thought of the people he owed money too. His suppliers were not as nice as he was in business, and they would want paying, sooner than later being their motto. It had only been minutes, but he had already forgotten all about Barbara and was only concerned about himself and what he could do next. There was no point going back to the waterside love nest because if she found out about him being kicked out, she would expect him to move in with her, and Kenneth was not going to share his £3m with a bimbo like that, she would spend it way too quickly.

First thing to do was get away from the glaring security lights of the house so he crunched his way down the drive, the security sensor picking up his movement and opening the gate. As he walked past the sensor and out into the tree-lined street, the gates closed behind him, and he knew without checking that the entry-code would already have been changed and the only auto-sensor he had was in the Jaguar, so he had no way of getting back in. Fi was not supposed to collect him until morning, so he took out his mobile and called her to turn around and come back and collect him, there was no answer. He had no way of knowing of course, but Fiona was already busy with her latest conquest. She was busy making love to her surgically enhanced lover behind the picture window that looked out over the marina.

With no other option he decided to call an Uber, he needed to get to a cashpoint swiftly. There was only a £20 note in his wallet, and he never carried change, it spoiled the cut of his expensive trousers. There was a need to be hasty in getting what cash he could out of an ATM, because he had no doubt that his canny bitch of a wife had already closed that avenue off to him. If she had locked him out of his home so easily, she would have no qualms about locking him out of their joint-account and his money. Now he was off the property the security lights went out, and he looked back at his house and home where windows were lighting up as Barbara moved through the house, he half expected to see her on their bedroom balcony and throwing his clothes and possessions over the railings, but that would litter the drive and lawn and that would not look good come daylight when the neighbours could see.

Kenneth had not been thinking straight and he watched patiently until eventually the house, room by room, returned to darkness. Barbara despite her perceived lousy mood looked to be heading for bed. Finally, the lights in their bedroom flicked into darkness. Give her a few minutes to fall asleep then if he was quick, he might just get away with it. He took his jacket off and threw it over the gates, then climbed the ornately designed metalwork before dropping down back on the driveway again. Grabbing up the jacket he sprinted across the expanse of front lawn. He never ran anywhere but was now thankful that his girlfriend had kept him fit and active along with visits to the gym twice a week, the security lights suddenly burned bright again, lighting every blade of grass and white-shirted man within range. There was no time to worry about being seen he just had to run and hope.

He reached the timber framed car porch within seconds of landing back on the property and fumbled with the key safe hidden on the back of one of the mighty oak uprights. They were hanging in there, maybe he had saved at least part of his awful night. Grabbing the spare keys to the Range Rover Evoque, he headed for the bulky but smooth looking car, which was Barbara's, well up until that moment anyway. The doors unlocked with a click of the remote and Kenneth was in, engine started and reversing out of the space when he saw the first fresh light from inside the house.

He pulled the lever back to 'D' for drive and sped toward the gates, gravel crunched under the tyres as he raced to get through the gate sensor before Barbara deactivated it. The luxury car curved its way down the drive, Kenneth did not lift his foot from the throttle, just hoping the automatic gates would be swift enough. He took a moment to check the rear view and was surprised to see that the front door had not opened, and that Barbara had not chased him. Shame, as that would have been a lot more satisfying.

Eyes back in front and he saw the gates begin to part and swing inwards, he was still determined not to hit the brakes, to be honest he didn't give a shit, it wasn't his Range Rover. The nose of the car made it through, and Kenneth kept going, almost through, then he felt the car kick sideways a little and that jerking movement was matched by the grinding of metal on metal, as he threw the car to the left in order to head up the lane and not into the ditch opposite, the rear end had caught the gate. Scraping down the side the car which almost came to a halt as the rear bumper caught the metal upright of the gate frame, from the steering position Kenneth felt the lower rear panel begin to give. Metal tore and fittings snapped but the powerful engine did its job and pulled the vehicle away from too much damage, Kenneth was home free and away from his snarling wife.

Jackman was struggling to focus properly, so he opened his window and allowed the night air that rushed in to clear his head. He had thought he was sober, but now with hedgerows and the odd house rushing by in a blur of colours the nausea was returning, and a headache was beginning, but he dare not stop, if he was to save what funds he could from their bank accounts and credit cards before his cards were cancelled. He fought the car as it tried to head straight on as he approached a sharpish bend, he took his foot off the throttle, but it was not enough to slow the car sufficiently to make it around the dogleg. He hit the brakes and tyre smoke rose from all four wheels, in what racing commentators would refer to as a lock-up, it seemed his fast actions had overruled the ABS. Still at a little under 30, the large Range Rover slewed around the sharp bend. Realising he was still drunk he took better care in watching the speedo and the roads ahead, now he pootled along at a steady 40 miles per hour. He had made a clean getaway, all he had to do now was figure how to get the Centurion out of the house. It would be a lot harder than stealing the car.

His only other way to some cash, and it was a huge amount, was at a terraced house in the heart of the city, and the fucking police had stolen all that, and labelled it evidence.

Some of Kenneth Jackman's biggest mistakes in life was to underestimate people, or more to the point, overestimate his own shrewdness and intellect, tonight he had underestimated his wife, the formidable Barbara Jackman.

The trickiest part of his inebriated drive would be going through, or even around, the city centre. He chose the shortest route, to go through, going around would be longer and therefore bring about more chances of being stopped by police. Even his pull as a councillor would not help him get off a drink driving charge. He liked his thinking, short route it was then. Once beyond the centre it would be plain driving to the marina. He would have preferred to stay at one of the lovely boutique hotels that Chichester was well known for, but if his credit cards had been cancelled, and he was certain Barbara would have thought of that, then it would be embarrassing for him as a councillor standing at a hotel reception being refused admission. Why pay for a hotel when your girlfriend had a lovely waterside apartment, plus all the comforts of home with her luscious body on hand. On reflection he decided to head there, at least he would be welcome there.

As he drove into the centre he passed the old Army MP barracks, now converted into luxury apartments, and he thought one of those would be rather smart when he got hold of his millions. Not a bad place to commute from to get into London when he was elected to parliament. A couple more roundabouts to clear and then he would be safe, he hoped that he had not damaged the rear of the Range Rover too much, he liked his cars to look good, and he liked to look good in his cars. It briefly crossed his mind that he may have to let Fiona go, until he sold the bronze anyway. He knew she loved working for him so maybe she would be happy to wait for her money, and more of those bloody shoes she loved so much. One more roundabout navigated, he drove toward the next with the grey stone, high wall of the Bishop's Garden to his left and in that moment, he smiled broadly, where else would she get work like she performed for him, she was hooked to him if she wanted to keep being who she was.

Then he saw them...

CHAPTER 54

Jackman saw the blue lights the moment they were switched on.

So intent was he on keeping the powerful Range Rover below the speed limit and in a straight line, he hadn't even noticed headlights behind him. It seemed as if the whole interior of the Range Rover was having its cream upholstery washed in a swirling blue light. Hope was still working for him, and he expected the police car to swing around him and fly off into the distance, the *whoop-whoop* of the two tones killed any hope. An older, rusty car drifted around the scene of a posh car stopped by police, for the man in his old Ford Mondeo it was manna from heaven, and he laughed as he lowered his mobile phone from his ear to below the steering wheel until he had passed by.

No parked kerbside, Jackman wound down the electric window and waited for the instruction to step from the car and blow into the bag. He cursed himself for underestimating his wife, the bitch, who sat on several charity committees along with the likes of the current Mayor and, more importantly, the county's Chief Constable. Then he realised that the drink driving was the least of his worries, she had left the keys in the hidden key safe on purpose, that was why she didn't come out of the front door as he drove away, she was too busy reporting the theft of her car. As soon as he had fallen for her little plan, she would have been on the phone.

Looking on the bright side, he would at least have somewhere warm and dry to spend the night, even if it was to be a hard narrow bed with no young warm body next to him. A good night's sleep, released in the morning and time to think about taking his revenge out on all those who had brought about this hiccup in his plans.

Someone would pay dearly for this night.

A night sobering up in the cells, the shame of having to be seen by a duty solicitor. It seemed that Barbara had thought of everything even the family friend and old retainer of a solicitor obviously warned off from being called out. The Councillor's patience was wearing thin in equal amounts to his rising anger and hatred. Theft of a car? The police settled for a verbal warning, it was classed as a domestic dispute, and they didn't really want to know anything about it. A charge of driving while under the influence and at almost double the legal limit, there was no way of getting beyond that one but luckily, he had a chauffeur driven car waiting for him once released.

Having spent the night in the cells, and they didn't have cashpoints in there, so he presumed that all avenues to any money had been well and truly closed. First thing he did was to check on his phone with the mobile banking app. He should have checked last night and moved money from the joint account but was too drunk to think about that. He did have a stash of cash at the marina apartment which would cover him for a few weeks, but he had to pay up almost all the £20 note in his wallet for a taxi out to the marina. Maybe things were not as bad as he thought while incarcerated, he had more than a few quid tucked away, he had a warm, enhanced, and appreciative girlfriend with a flat that even Barbara could not take away from him.

He would get through this.

Looking across the crowded marina he took a deep breath and enjoyed the sea air as it drifted onto his senses. The aroma of the sea was one of those smells that you could taste. Things were not that bad, he was going to leave his wife anyway to start a new life elsewhere, he still had the bronze hidden and ready for sale, and he still had a loyal assistant in Fiona as well as a very lively, if not very intelligent, girlfriend.

The thoughts had cheered him a little, and just as he began to feel that things could always be worse crossed his mind, they suddenly were. Through the glass side wall of the apartment building, he could see tall and slender legs, followed by a slim waist, enhanced breasts and flowing bleached blonde hair sweeping across a pretty face, struggling down the one flight of stairs. Tottering on impossible heels, that he had purchased just as 'bedroom shoes', she struggled from step to step and behind her, bouncing down each riser, was a wheelie suitcase, overladen if he judged weight by the way she was struggling with it.

She shoved the door open with her delicious, apple shaped arse, then turned toward a waiting taxi without even seeing him. Stunned by what he was seeing, he did not think of calling out. The taxi driver, smitten with his attractive new fare, leapt out and swept her suitcase up into the boot of his car. He had tried to look cool and macho, but the weight of the case almost caused his hernia to play up and he struggled to get it over the lip and in. He hoped she had not seen his weakness. Men do seem to lose all reasoning when confronted by a pretty face, especially when a globular bust such as hers was on show in a tight white T-Shirt, nipples bursting to poke through in chill morning air. Her thought had always been why go through the pain of the boob-job and not show them off. It was that same cool breeze that a moment before Jackman was breathing in and appreciating, that now made her nipples stand erect, he already missed them. The cabbie was even more impressed, and Jackman was jealous of the way the scruffy driver coveted, what was essentially, his property.

The pang of jealousy startled him into action, and he rushed over before she could close the door of the taxi. Before swinging the door closed, she swept a stray length of hair and tucked it behind her ear, she did have a beautiful profile Jackman thought, and then he noticed her tears and bloodshot eyes. She looked both lost and angry, but it did not match his anger as he had all night to nourish it.

"Where the fuck are you going." His voice carrying real venom, the like of which she had never heard from him before.

The taxi driver thought of intervening before then thinking better of getting involved.

She gave him a thunderous look. "Home to my Mum, where else do you think I can go you shit!" The hair fell across her face again but this time she left it there.

Yachtsmen preparing their boats in readiness for a day's sailing stopped unfurling sails and coiling ropes to see what all the fuss was on the marina wall. Locals heading for the waterfront cafe for breakfast stopped and gawped.

"And where is your car, why are you getting a taxi?" He had bought her the second-hand cream mini a few months ago but was still paying the hire-purchase.

"Repossessed earlier this morning, some bloke came and took the keys off me before lifting it on the back of his truck and fucking off with it." Jackman had always liked her soft spoken and gentle accent before, now it was a raging, hard-edged Northeast intonation, as the curtain came down on her cosy life with the Councillor as a lover.

"But why leave the flat, I have nowhere to stay, I was going to move in with you." His voice was pleading, but she didn't hear it. "That was what you said you always wanted."

His eyes had dropped, and he no longer looked at her tear-streaked face, but at the pair of breasts, that he had also paid for, that were trying to poke their way through the thin material of her top. She noticed, she always had.

"That's all I am to you, isn't it. Just a pair of tits, just because you paid for them it doesn't mean you get to keep them." In the front of the cab the cabbie almost chuckled aloud but held himself in check. He had not had this much fun in years and thought he should write a sitcom about it. "I aint got a flat no more, another geezer came round earlier and said your wife was my landlady, apparently, she owns the whole building and he had a court order saying that the funds to rent this place came from your criminal sources and so he gave me notice to quit, and a couple of grand for my trouble if I left this morning instead of staying here to see out my two-month notice. The bloke gave me two thousand in cash to move out right away, and what with me having to start again, I wasn't gonna refuse that. He told me just to pop the keys through the letter box which is what I done."

With that she pulled the door shut and told the cabbie to head for the station, she had a train to catch. Jackman wondered how he would get into the flat to get his nest egg, then he realised why she had wanted to leave so quickly rather than punish him further. She must have found huis stash of money and taken that as well.

It was just a few days ago that he walked through the columns of the old town hall and climbed into his chauffeur driven Jaguar and felt like the king of all that surrounded him. an attractive and wealthy wife, a great lifestyle, dreams of making it to Westminster via a year as Mayor of Chichester, a lover tucked away, and power, and he loved the power part. He had no idea which he would miss the most, but then decided he would miss that power the most, as well as the expensive tits.

From an extensive and very costly wardrobe, he was left with the clothes he stood in. No doubt he would either be suspended or deselected as a councillor, so there went any power, and influence he had. All that was left was a pending prosecution for drink driving, and the press coverage announcing his downfall to anyone who cared to read about it. Apart from the local rag's Chief Reporter, he always prided himself in the fact that he had a good working relationship with the press, they seemed to like his handsome face on the front page.

He was not sure he would get so much good publicity anymore, ambitions of becoming Mayor and then an MP were placed on the backburner; for now.

There was only one thing left in his favour, and as soon as he could get the Centurion out of the house he would be back on the rise, making sure he left all his detractors far behind him. He always fancied living in a hot climate and with somewhere around the three million mark to live on, it would be a good lifestyle far away from drizzly Chichester. All he needed was to find a new owner who was not too bothered about provenance, and his Dutch contact was just that type of person.

His days of decline were beginning to take over and he still needed somewhere to stay, there was only one option. He thought of phoning first, but that may put her on the back foot and give her a chance to say no to him staying overnight.

For the past couple of years, he had been a good employer, almost friendly some would say. How could Fi deny him shelter when they had been through so much together.

CHAPTER 55

Fiona lived an hour away by foot and by the time he reached there his feet were killing him, he could not recall the last time he had walked so far. The doorbell was harsh, like nails on a blackboard, but it seemed the norm for apartment blocks to have such ear-grating announcements. Fiona's voice sounded tinny as she asked who was there, which Jackman thought was better than the long moment of silence that followed, he said he needed to see her. At least the Jaguar was parked outside, it was leased in his name, and he doubted Barbara could do anything about that. At least if Fiona decided enough was enough, he would have the car to sleep in. It was a comfortable ride, maybe it would make a comfortable bed; the thought did not shake him from his thunderous mood. She buzzed him up and as the door swung open Jackman breathed a sigh of relief. At least one thing that day was heading in the right direction.

Outside her second-floor apartment he rapped on the door with his knuckles and a shadow crossed the spyhole as the person on the other side checked the caller was who they were expecting. Jackman was surprised she took that care, she was the scariest person he knew, who the hell would call on her to do evil. The door opened just a crack and Jackman heard the security chain rattle in its slot, it was the second time in 24 hours that had happened, and it was starting to piss him off, but he knew better than to show annoyance as he needed her help.

"What is it boss?" Fiona looked over her shoulder and back into the apartment. "I am a little busy."

"She has kicked me out Fi, I have had a hell of a day." This was not the time to beat around the bush. "No clothes, bank cards cancelled, just out on the street."

His driver/assassin was not someone who knew much about sympathy, he offered one of his charming smiles, but it came across as sleazy and creepy. Fiona remembered that even sharks smile sometimes!

"That smile may work on some women but not me, Kenny." She emphasised the shortened version of his name knowing how much he hated it, as she did with her own name.

Fiona had strong feelings that her career in this town was ending, especially with this employer, so there would be no more Mr Jackman to order her around or leer at her in that disgusting way. She prided herself in knowing when to move on and Jackman was not a risk, she was willing to take much longer.

She was being discourteous, and Jackman hated that, but there was little he could do about it so he tried a different tack.

"Things are a bit tight at the moment, for obvious reasons." Jackman tried to sound calm. "But I can get some money from the bank in the morning, I have a private fund that Barbara has no idea about." He lied, masterfully he thought. "I need to take the Jaguar tonight if that's okay, unless you can offer me a couch for the night." He didn't bother with the smile this time.

"As I said I am busy right now, so no can do on the putting you up for the night. Hang on a second." She closed the door, leaving an uncomfortable Jackman standing in the hallway. Fiona reopened the door and handed the car keys over; she also gave him two £20 notes. "You can pay me back when you have been to the bank."

"Before you go, I have one last job for you, if you feel its something you can do." He knew he was pushing his luck. "I still have the bronze statue and even if I must sell quickly, it will still fetch £3m, or more. If you do this one last task, I will give you £500,000 for an hour's work."

"I will say yes when you pay me back my forty quid."

As she was about to close the door on him, he glanced over her shoulder and through the narrow gap, he watched dumfounded as a girl with long and slender legs walked past the narrow slit in the doorway. She was wrapped in a white towel with her blonde wet hair cascading over her shoulders, the towel did nothing to hide her enhanced breasts. Would this day never end Jackman thought, the way it was going so far it was more likely to get worse, but he had no idea how.

CHAPTER 56

For the non-partisan it had been a good match, a hard-fought draw with just two goals apiece. That left both sets of fans disappointed at the score but happy with their team's performances. So, it was a happy band of football fans leaving Portsmouth's ground at Fratton Park that Saturday afternoon. Nick Flax had much to write about, disallowed penalty claims, dubious offside calls by both referee's assistants and a red card for a particularly nasty high tackle that saw the Plymouth Argyle central defender sent off and his damaged opponent carried off on a stretcher with just a half hour left in the game. As far as Nick was concerned, and he had never followed any particular team, it was a fair result, and he would say so in his report in readiness for Monday afternoon's Chichester Chronicle.

Nick ambled toward the train station lost in the middle of the home crowd all sporting blue and white scarves, hats, and football shirts. Police patrolled on the outskirts of the group that Nick was with, and they were a happy bunch chanting and clapping as they headed away from the ground. The police were ever vigilant, it would only take one small spark to ignite bloody warfare and hand-to-hand street fighting between the two sets of fans. With all their eyes on the ground and the electronic surveillance from the closed-circuit television the police failed to notice one person in a blue hoodie moving against the tidal flow of fans.

Nick loved his football, not any team in particular, but just the game for the footballing skills and the atmosphere, to him it was truly the Beautiful Game. With the match report pretty much finished in his head, he was looking forward to getting home to Suzi, her wonderful bump growing daily. He had mentioned to Sam that she was getting as big as a house, but he would have never dared say it within earshot of his pregnant partner, he was not that brave. For Nick his day now consisted of the train home and whizzing past its two stations, kiss and hug Suzi and then quickly write the story and send it over via E-Mail. Change into sweatshirt and jogging bottoms before getting the Saturday night pizza delivered, now including anchovies which was demanded by Suzi and her pregnant desires. Feet up and all in time for Strictly Come

Dancing on the television.

Hands deep in his jacket pockets, laptop held in its brown, canvas, man-bag and hanging from his shoulder, Nick shrunk his neck down into his collar to keep his face warm, it was a chilly afternoon. He was smiling at the thought of getting home to Suzi, how he loved her, the baby was a bit of a shock to begin with, but he loved the idea now. Soon to be married, soon to be a father, what a wonderful time of life it was.

Amidst all the blue clad supporters Nick was an easy target to spot in his battered wax jacket with its leather elbow patches, and the person in the blue hoody swimming upstream against the tide kept her aim dead straight toward him. Her face was set with determination, she had spotted her target and now it was time to act. It may have been the last job she did for Jackman, and she had thought twice about it, but half a million in her bank, and the job was an enjoyable one. The crowd that carried him along was thinning out as supporters reached their cars, caught their busses, and generally dispersed in all directions. Nick looked up and saw a face he thought he recognised heading toward him, for a moment he thought it might be a friend of Suzi's homing in on him to reveal bad news, but he could not recall seeing her face at the baby-shower or any of their house parties.

Suddenly, the face was in front of him, bodies centimetres apart, and Nick felt himself instantly worry for Suzi. Would she cope without him? Would he now get to see his child grow? He had no idea why these thoughts had entered his head, like the face directly in front of him, they had just appeared. With her stilettos on Fiona was eye to eye with her target, and Nick could see a calmness deep within her soul and yet there was vile venom with her intent.

Unblinking she told the fearful reporter why she was there, and although her voice was as soft as a feather falling on snow he could hear her, understand her, feel the menace in her voice.

"You have upset my employer with your callous and thoughtless actions Mr Flax." Her stare and her tone both froze him to the spot.

The crowd that surrounded them had disappeared as far as the two of them were concerned they were standing alone in the middle of the road with their confrontation. The forgotten crowd as waves drifting around shoreside rocks. Although a hardened journalist with decades of experience Nick still hated confrontation, of any sort, and yet here was

Councillor Jackman's driver and right hand, who he suddenly recognised, getting into his face, and looking for a reaction.

"Well, if your employer will play away in full view of everyone while spouting moral rhetoric." He responded boldly and with more bravado than he felt. "He leaves himself open to fair comment by the press." Unlike Fiona's whispered threat, Nick's voice was loud, loud enough to be heard over what was left of the chanting crowd and he wondered how he had heard anything the messenger had said.

Fiona standing in front of the reporter had brought Nick to a halt at the head of an almost unstoppable flood of people. Firstly, it moulded itself around the two stationary objects, and then the force of the flow began pushing forward again, like the onrushing tide, relentless, now crashing over immovable rocks, one unstoppable the other immovable. The flow of football fans was unceasing, and Nick struggled to hold the wave of people back and himself steady, Fiona was protected by his body.

As he had halted so the crowd behind pushed forward in a concertina effect, nobody had told the mob at the back that the front had come to a halt. They surged forward.

Pushed forward, Nick first felt himself lifted by the mob behind him, he rose to tiptoes. Then there was a click, somewhere around his belt area. A soft click like the latch on a well-oiled door or gate. He saw Fiona's eyes open wide in excitement, the iris as black as the blackest night and fully dilated. Then he felt the sharpness. The blade entered between his ribs, expertly positioned.

His killer had felt the blade slide in and up to the hilt, it went deep and passionate. It was as if a part of her had entered her secret lover. For her it was a sexual climax!

Nick's final feeling was of a warmth flooding across his chest as if a cup of coffee had been spilt on his shirt. His final thought was of Suzi's beautiful face, and a baby whose face he would never see.

CHAPTER 57

Fiona felt an onrush of adrenaline, like nothing she had felt before, as if a lover had found a new erogenous zone on her body that would help her achieve orgasm, something that as of yet none of her lovers had managed to do, and she longed for that release.

Even though this final act had not been planned, Fiona had adored the moment, she was only supposed to scare the reporter. Maybe the fact that it was spontaneous was what had made it so special, she was certain she felt a wetness between her thighs, she was certainly tingling there. Despite the many lovers she had tried over the years, both male and female, the latter being her preference, none had ever pleased her this way before. Fiona was wrapping herself in the warmth of her actions with the sensual act, the blade a stiff appendage penetrating her victim, her lover.

She had watched the light go out in Nick Flax's eyes, felt his body crumple downward, the knife exited his ribs in a smooth withdrawal as she moved away. As his body sprawled on the floor the crowds continued to push, they stepped over his body, on his body, they trampled on him.

Until a girl screamed.

Fiona had simply turned around, allowed the crowd to take her away from the body. She kept the hoodie up over her hair and shading her face, eyes down toward the ground, no CCTV camera would see her face, and the bloodstained clothes would soon be gone. She wanted to turn around and revel in the skill of her workmanship, wanted to feel that near orgasm again. The knife, which she would have loved as a memento, she let slip from her fingers to the ground, she wished she had licked the blade to taste her victim, it was free from prints and stolen so there was no way to trace it back to her. A job well done; she took great pride in her work.

Fiona, through the sexual haze she had created, finally realised that murder, instead of just threat, was by far the more satisfying to her, both sexually and mentally.

Thoughts travelling quicker than the speed of light had her

wondering if it really was safe to leave the knife with the body, no harm could come of it, and it was far better to be found there and not in her pocket. It would just be put down by police as an assault following a football match, sadly in these times a stabbing at a match had almost become the normal.

The scream from the young girl who had stumbled over Nick's body in the crush to get 15,000 people all home safely was heard by officers on both flanks of the supporters, which were thinning out at this point.

When the throng had gone and the road leading to the football stadium had been closed off, much to the annoyance of many people trying to get home after work or shopping, a little more about events quickly became apparent. Nick was found lying around ten to twelve feet beyond where the biggest blood patch was situated. Common sense thinking said the Nick had been stabbed and then carried along by the biggest part of the crowd before being deposited where the teenage girl had fallen over him.

Nick had died without really knowing why, nobody kills because they showed a wife some saucy images of her husband taken after too much wine and not enough sex. He died where he fell and it had been his last match, and it had been a disappointing 2-2 draw.

Suzi had lost a future husband, their unborn baby a father, and Sam had lost his only friend, and all because a Roman Centurion now had blood on the short sword that he held aloft in victory.

The story in Monday's Chronicle would not be about a football match played in the next city along the coast, but of their chief reporter who had been fatally stabbed and fallen to football hooliganism, the scourge of the English game had reared its ugly head once again. As well as being the cover story, the inside front page would be taken over for the Editor's Opinion, which was usually just half a dozen column inches on page three. He would begin his week with a page long tirade about the state of this most English of games. In his harsh words he would call for there to be better security checks and stronger crowd control on match day. People had cowered in their homes for far too long on Saturday afternoons, and things needed to change.

In his comfortable office at the Town Hall, Fiona was telling Jackman that it was an unfortunate accident, that could not be foreseen. She had failed to realise that all accidents are unforeseen, by their very nature.

"If you will excuse the pun..." Jackman liked his humour dark. "...it is one less thorn in my side. "And Fiona my deadly girl, don't worry about money, as promised, and so well negotiated by yourself, a big lump of the value of the Centurion will be coming to you, as soon as it's sold. To be honest I will be glad to get shot of it, and you should see about a million coming your way. Just call it a thank you for all the fun we have had."

Fiona imagined herself and her long-legged, big-breasted friend on some Caribbean sandy beach drinking ice cold Pina Coladas. Murder was such bliss!

Across town in the kitchen behind his shop, sat Sam and Suzi. Although she had never seen why he and Nick had the friendship they did, she was now comfortable with the old man and being thankful for his company. They talked about nothing except their shared passion for Nick, a kind and generous man who they both loved.

A week later and Portsmouth were playing at home again, but this time there was no Nick in the Press Box, only a spotty young reporter fresh from Journalism School. At the same time the fans were flooding into the ground and walking over a dark stain in the road that nobody paid attention to. It was more than coincidence that at that same time a hearse bearing Nick's body, was drawing up at the Chichester Crematorium. Several cars followed the hearse to the front door, the solemn building was very church like in design and set amidst attractive lawns and gardens, the perfect spot to end up after a life lived, be it lived well or badly. Immediately behind Nick's coffin was a very pregnant Suzi and alongside her an attentive Sam. She did not want to get out of the funeral car, it would make saying goodbye to her partner all too final. Sam was wearing the same suit that Nick had bought him a month before so he could be smart when his statuette went on show at the council offices and again when he wore it to the auction. It still felt uncomfortable to wear, and Sam still went tie-less.

The service was brief, the crowd large, many of the seats taken by colleagues from the Paper. Nick was popular and would be missed by many. For the second week running a huge portion of the paper would be given over to its Chief Reporter. This week he could command the centre page spread in Monday's Chronical, his story and his funeral. His editor, a portly, slightly scruffy man, gave the eulogy, mentioning many a memory of Nick the man and Nick the reporter, even the leather patches on his tweed jacket came in with a mention, they raised a small smile from both Sam and Suzi, she grabbing, and gripping the old man's hand numbing his fingers. It was also mentioned that Nick was wearing his favourite jacket that day as well, and that snippet had the room in tears. The paper had also provided a grand spread, a buffet served at the old council offices where this whole story had begun. Sam and Suzi stayed for just a few minutes and then snuck away. Sam grabbed a pair of scotch eggs on the way past the buffet table in case he felt hunger later.

Outside Sam stopped to check that Suzi was okay, and whether she was up to going home on her own. Nick's editor had followed them out and said he would take her home. They left Sam in the precinct as they headed for the Editor's car, Sam heard him as he made a promise to Suzi.

"Anything you need, anything and at any time, call me at the paper." He told her earnestly. "Nick was not just a reporter; he was my friend as well." He wanted to say more but he thought it not to be the appropriate time.

Sam felt like walking and not heading to his depressing home, the sun had broken through, and it was a nice afternoon for a funeral. As he headed down the pathway toward the Bishop's Garden, Sam noted a black Range Rover with a single passenger inside, parked near to his shop. The door opened and elegance stepped from the vehicle, dressed head to toe in black apart from a golden scarf with images by the artist Klimt on it. Barbara Jackman stood staring at Sam and nervously he walked over to her. He thought he had never seen anyone so beautiful before.

"Why didn't you come into the service, I know you liked Nick?" Sam asked her.

"Hello Sam, it didn't seem right."

He was about to ask why she felt awkward about seeing Nick off, when she cut him short.

"Could we talk Sam?" She asked, he nodded, and they continued walking toward the Bishops Garden and a bench in the autumnal sunshine.

She was so much taller than Sam, but it did not bother him, he felt comfortable in her company.

"What can I do for you Mrs Jackman?" He asked as soon as they had found a bench under a pergola that in the summer had been covered in red blooms.

"Barbara please, Sam." Her elegant hands were on her lap, the nails perfectly manicured and with pale blue varnish that stood out against the black. "There was good reason for me not coming in…" she paused, just slightly, "I think it was Kenneth that had Nick killed."

She blurted it out, there was no way to say it politely or slowly.

"Your husband?" Sam blustered for a moment he was rendered speechless.

Finally, he began firing questions at Barbara, none of which she seemed able to answer. In the end, because it was just a feeling she was harbouring, rather than proof or reason, they ended up just talking about Nick. It was wonderful conversation. She told how she had met Nick many years before not long after he had joined the paper and back then his main assignments were what he called 'fluff' pieces. Many assignments were about the charities she was linked to and involved with. Eventually, she told Sam, Nick had written a moving and glowing piece about her father after his death, they had been friends ever since. Sam told her of his unhappy life as a junk shop owner, and of his friendship with Nick. He told her the story of the Roman Centurion, leaving out the bit about his certainty that it was her husband behind a switch of the bronzes. He was enjoying her company and did not want her to leave if he accused the Councillor of more wrongdoing.

After that the two of them had then sat in silence for over an hour, before Barbara had to leave. She bent slightly to give Sam a peck on both cheeks as a goodbye. As she walked away, Sam sat down again and watched her leave, strutting like a catwalk model down between the garden's bud laden, rose bushes. He wished the farewell kiss had been on the mouth. When her lips had brushed his cheeks, they had felt plump and warm, they seemed to indicate more affection than he expected.

As the path went under an arch of red bricks she stopped and looked back toward Sam, and he waved an awkward wave. She turned and was gone, maybe the affection he felt from the kisses was just in his mind.

CHAPTER 58

Sam sat in his kitchen and the light was fast disappearing at day's end, filling in darkening shadows in every corner of the room. It was a growing, moving thing, that crept nearer to him and with each passing minute was painting his mood in perfect dull shades of blacks and greys. Sam could not see a future life in any other colours. There would be no more rainbows, a life bereft of bright spectrums. Sam thought the greatest pain he would feel was when he lost the fortune that was never his, but to then lose his only friend and the world a good man, that was almost too much to bear. Selfish feelings racked him with guilt as Suzi and their unborn child had lost so much more and Sam could not help but think it was all his fault. He wished he had never found that bloody Centurion, it was a jinx.

It was now Sunday evening, the time when Sam felt his loneliness the most. On the table in front of him sat two teas, as it always was on a Sunday evening. A simple English Breakfast tea, with lemon – not milk, for Sam and an Earl Grey for his friend. Nick's cup was placed on the other side of the table where he would sit and discuss the price of antiques, he would tell of Suzi's growing bump and the latest ideas for names, she was still firmly against naming him, or her, Samuel, or Samantha. Both drinks had long turned cold, and the screen on the television remained black and blind. The season's last episode of the Antiques Roadshow had been aired the previous weekend, even if that had not been the case Sam doubted, he would have watched it tonight. It was too hard, his feelings still too raw.

Sam smiled inside when he recalled Nick always telling him that old age was a state of mind, but tonight Sam felt truly old. Old, alone, and friendless. He was sitting in a gloom that had now descended fully, remembering his friend and their many conversations, he missed the intelligent voice of companionship. Life with just Wedgwood for company had always been satisfactory, Sam didn't have much and never wanted for much, the thing he wanted most in life had been to be left alone. And in that regard his wish had come true. That was until Nick came along and as their friendship grew so did the feeling of warmth in his home, something not felt since his father had died. For a few years now, no matter how quiet his week had been there was always a chance that the back door would open and in would stride Nick, complete with patched elbows, and he would head for the kettle. It was only the previous Christmas that Nick had bought Sam a new kettle, one that plugged in and ran on electricity, it even lit-up a see-through tube in blue and showed off the water level, science gone mad, and not only that but it was cordless as well. Sam had joked that he had never seen such a magic thing in all his life, meanwhile Nick threw the battered old kettle that sat dented and blackened on the gas hob in the trash. Sam still preferred to us a non-electric kettle on the Aga's hob but in deference to Nick he plugged in his modern kettle.

Sam loved his flavoured teas but had to admit that it took him some time until he had become used to the awful smell of Nick's Earl Grey, and now he missed it. His home and shop felt empty again, when Nick had lost his life... NO, he had not lost it, it had been snatched from him, denying him that chance to see his new child, to marry his sweetheart. It was all too cruel, and Sam missed him, Nick had become a huge part of Sam's life. The rooms, especially the kitchen, seemed empty cold and sparse, even Wedgwood was more miserable than before, which was saying something. Nick was a young man with an old mind, and Sam ancient in all regards, but they were a perfect foil for each other. Wedgwood almost as if on cue rattled in through the cat flap, totally ignored his owner and went straight to his bed alongside the Aga.

It was turning out to be a busy evening as a tentative rap on the frosted windowpane in the back door shook Sam from his recollections, he saw the shadow of an average sized person, it could have been anybody, and the door slowly opened. Sam for just a second or two hoped it would be Nick, but a soft voice eased the shock that Sam had felt, but it would be a while before his heart rate slowed down to its usual crawl.

"Sam, Sam, are you in there?" It was a woman's voice and for a moment Sam did not recognise it.

He did not move a muscle, "Go away!" he was close to tears having thought it may be Nick. The voice was not Suzi's, so Sam was not interested.

In response to the broken-hearted command the door was pushed open further, not closing as Sam had hoped and there was no sound of retreating footsteps disappearing along the path. As the door was pushed fully open, it squeaked, a sharp noise that did not help Sam's mood. Finally, a head appeared around the door edge, and in the dark Sam recognised a face he had been thinking about a great deal. Sam found it hard not to smile as he recognised Barbara Jackman, her long slender neck wrapped in a black silk scarf, her hair tied back.

"Did you not hear me?" Sam was still being curt, even though he found the face beautiful.

"I did Sam, but I need to talk with someone." She sounded desperate. "It seems that now I have kicked that cheating bastard Kenneth out of my house and life, I have nobody to talk to. It seems I have scared away the few fair-weather friends that I had and thought of as true friends."

"Well, they may come round when the dust settles, but I have lost the only person I got to call friend." Sam's voice seemed to be weakening in its resolve. "And he will not be coming back any time soon."

Not sure if she was welcome or not, Barbara remained in the doorway half in light and half in silhouette, holding it open as if still deciding whether to walk in or run away. Scared to stay, scared to leave.

Sam relented. "Shut the door then if you are coming in." Sam still did not feel hospitable. "Kettle is on the side there, tea and cups in the cupboard above it."

Barbara had other ideas. "Have you got wine glasses, or tumblers? I brought a nice, earthy, red wine and thought we could maybe drink a toast to Nicolas." She held the bottle up by the neck, showing it off as if Sam needed reminding what a bottle of wine looked like.

Sam had never heard his friend referred to by his full first name, it sounded alien and yet it suited the man more than just Nick.

"We can drink to something, I suppose, but Nick is out of bounds to you until I am more certain of who you are and what you want with me." Remaining sharp in tone he realised that secretly he was glad of the company, and she was company that was pleasant to look at, better than just a miserable cat. His eyes could not stay on the wine, he was drawn to her eyes, which were jet black in the dim light of his kitchen. The fact her features were slightly lost in the dimness of the room made her seem even more intoxicating and desirable, like Salome in her seven veils.

Sam was about to say something, unsure if it would emerge as friendly or sharp, he would just have to wait and see how the words jumped from his mouth, but his house guest beat him to the punch.

"He was my friend too, damn it! Sam!" said with a sharpness that also carried hurt with it. "And, Jackman was my mistake, I always thought him a decent man, even if a little reckless sometimes. My only fault was that I closed my eyes to his failings."

Needing a diversion to give him chance to form the correct words and put them in an order that made sense, he spoke to the only other thing in the room that would listen.

"Alexa, turn the lamp on." He ordered.

Somewhat seductively, and robotic, she replied... *'Turning lamp on.'*

"Condescending piece of work isn't she." Barbara said sounding jealous.

It eased the tension between them.

The energy saving bulb took a while to warm and lighten the room, and Sam watched as Barbara's skin began to glow with her complexion of a golden hue. He was besotted and promised himself not to talk to her so sharply again, the events as they had unfolded were not of her doing. The dim lamp was one of those modern energy saving jobs, it was taking an age to light the room and was battling with the growing darkness in search of dusk, it was a fight it could not win. Enough finally slipped through the tasselled lampshade to brighten Barbara's face and light the wine bottle. Sam pushed his chair back, reached over, and pulled two twisted stem wine glasses from the dresser, each a collector's item, and worth about £400. From a drawer in the table end, he drew a corkscrew and handed it to Barbara, he didn't want to dent his manhood by struggling with a recalcitrant cork.

He continued from what she had said about turning a blind eye. "If by 'failings' you mean his thieving and murdering, then that was a very blind eye. Nelson with his one good eye would have been proud of you."

She had no reply and no defence.

Pulling out a chair, trying to keep the table between her and Sam, she elicited another sharp response.

"Not that chair! It's Nicks." Even saying his name caused his throat to close and his tear ducts to open.

Gently she pushed the chair back under the table and moved to the next one around. Once seated she opened the waiter's friend and with the deftness of a skilled sommelier, expertly screwed it into the cork, using the lever attachment on the bottle rim, the cork slipped out with a pleasing 'POP'. "Beautiful glasses…" she said as she poured the rich and fruity red.

"They are Georgian, date from around 1760," Sam informed her, his tone now back to its normal softness. "…the stem has a pair of opaque spiral bands encircled by a 16ply spiral band. The bowl is only small, but the wine should taste good out of them." He looked lovingly at the beauty of the stems, hardly noticing the rich ruby filling.

"Nicholas always said you were good with your knowledge of old things Samuel." She replied before taking her first sip and savouring the grape nectar.

He liked hearing his full name, his father had always called him by it, saying it was lazy to shorten such a strong name. Coming from her glossy painted lips, she made it sound almost poetic. Suddenly and without warning Sam realised he was comfortable in her company, and for the first time in weeks he felt himself relax.

So comfortable was he, in fact, the warm feeling of friendship he was feeling lasted until the next morning.

CHAPTER 58

"Who would want to harm your family, and in such a brutal way, and thereby injure your whole life." Robert Berry was used to saying things as they were, it was a solid courtroom tactic he used, designed not to confuse a jury. "Any one of your past successes with villains and miscreants, I presume."

Robert and Kobe had strolled out into the garden and away from Anne and her cigarette fumes. Over the weeks since they took him into their home, the two men had become easy in each other's company, Kobe loved the frankness of the barrister's words, while he enjoyed Kobe's inquiring mind.

"I keep asking myself the same question." His head was down, and his forehead furrowed with deep lines. "In all my years, I have never been concerned that anyone would go for my family and punish them for my sins, or any of my team's families come to that. It's not like we are dealing with the mafia here, this is Chichester for Christ's sake, not New York." In frustration Kobe kicked at a molehill that was on the edge of the lawn and broke its uniform mound amid the mower lines. "Basically, we put away the idiots, the unlucky and the bad men; if we can catch them." Kobe looked at the mess he had made with the freshly dug soil of the molehill.

"Little buggers, no matter how we put them down, they still come back." Robert said.

Kobe stopped his pacing and just looked at Robert, the barrister understood the quizzical look. "Oh, not the criminal buggers, I was talking about the bloody moles. Mole traps are too messy, breaks the poor sods' backs. Anne thinks the traps are nasty, so she has banned me from using them. I suppose she is right though; traps do seem cruel."

Kobe joined in easily with the sudden change of subject matter, it seemed less harrowing than talking of his family all day, people would soon stop listening to anything he had to say if it was about his woes and losses all the time. But Robert was easy to talk to.

"When I was at university I used to help with a landscaper at weekends, it was a welcome break from using the brains all week, nice to add some brawn as well." Kobe knew he was waffling, it was like learning to talk again, and he enjoyed the memory. "He would pour petrol down their tunnel runs after covering as many ends as he could find, and then ignite the fuel. The explosion and the flames would kill them."

"Makes my mole traps seem almost humane." Berry interrupted.

"Thing is, I don't think he ever got any." Kobe continued, "All it would do was to scare the moles into next door's gardens. Next door wasn't his problem, he had been paid to rid them from his clients' lawns and he succeeded in doing just that. He stopped doing it though, after a nasty accident..."

"Don't tell me he blew himself up, that would be too funny, and good karma."

"Worse. He would drop a match down the hole in which he had just poured the fuel down, then block that hole by putting a disused paint tin over it and hold it in place by resting a foot on it. One time he was a bit slow in putting his foot down and the petrol ignited and the only thing that stopped the can from going into orbit was the gardeners face. The can broke his nose, and the following flame took out his eyebrows and fringe. I was sacked for laughing too loudly and for too long."

"That must have been some sight, and yes, it was good karma." Robert said with gentle chuckle.

Kobe chuckled himself at the memory, but that split second of thoughtless mirth hit him with a ton of guilt and his face immediately returned to its sad demeanour. What right did he have to show happiness, even if it was only a second of forgetfulness with amusing memories.

"Maybe that's it?" Robert explained as if in a eureka moment.

"What?"

Robert stopped navigating his huge garden, and sat himself down on a wrought iron bench, ornate with curlicues of metal on the back and legs. "Maybe you had just sent the moles off next door." Kobe seemed to catch the drift, but let his barrister, who had fast become a friend, continue. "You have just had two very successful drug raids in the past few weeks, haven't you?" Robert didn't wait for an answer but continued to think out loud. "Have you completed your enquiries or is there someone further up the food chain that you wanted to discover?"

After a moment or two of fidgeting with his feet Kobe sat on the bench alongside the friendly barrister. The view from there was toward the house and back down the lawn with its converging lines of mower-tracks, which was pleasingly geometric.

"Intel was telling us that the drug-dealing family we took out on the last raid were the top dogs. I don't believe that now and did not believe that back when we were planning the raids. The old lady and her dippy son never seemed smart enough to me, not with the amount of product we found on the premises. Nor did they have the wherewithal to raise the kind of capital needed to fund such an operation. Plus, this was no regional haul of product, it was at least ten times, and more, for the needs of Chichester."

"Copper's intuition, or smart thinking, either way it's a constructive thought." Robert cut in. "Don't forget that your intel failed to discover that someone had a gun, a big miss in my book."

"It would be feasible I suppose, for there to be a, so called, mastermind behind the drug houses, and the amount of cocaine, and other drugs, we discovered was way too large for a little old lady and her son, no matter how smart or stupid. It was something I was going to bring up on Monday morning when I debriefed my bosses. But of course, that didn't happen."

It was always the same, his mind would lead him off on other travels before making a sharp U-turn and return to the image of their bloody faces and the bloody roses. As he felt his eyes begin to tear up, a friendly but firm grip on his shoulder brought him back into Robert Berry's Garden.

"From what you tell me, and from stuff that finds itself being talked about around the courtrooms, the raid that Sunday was far too big for local dealers, and that they must be just middlemen. Surely the sheer weight of contraband you found was far too big for an area such as Chichester. Somewhere such as Brighton I could understand, but our sleepy little city. Unlikely..."

"Those were my thoughts at the time." Kobe responded. "And we did have a third raid in the pipeline."

"What if your first raid was an annoyance. The second a sizable loss for your middleman." Robert said thoughtfully and Kobe could see where he was going with that statement.

"And, if that second raid had left the local top man with no income to pay off his suppliers for such a large haul, then he would be in serious trouble..."

Robert picked up where Kobe had left off. "If he, or she, did not have the money to pay for that shipment, then there would be serious repercussions."

"Serious would be an understatement my friend." It was like a tennis match as the two men lobbed ideas over the net and back again. "There must be an importer somewhere in the background, or at least a money man who would want his pound of flesh, there is no way he could let a loss like that go unpunished." Enjoyment is probably the wrong word, but Kobe was feeling better now his brain was working again, doing something positive and not just drinking to salve his sorrows.

"I know you trust your team, Kobe, but it is no big stretch of the imagination that there was always the possibility of an intel leak about raid number three, and that would have any organisation panicking about the huge losses, of both revenue and stock."

"With the kind of money in the drug industry it is always an assumption that somebody can be bought." Kobe, replied. "And, you are right, I do trust my team. But I would be a liar if I said the thought of a bent copper in the midst had never crossed my mind."

"And by getting rid of the police officer in command of the raids, they would put a stop to their drug losses." Robert pondered.

Kobe went quiet for a moment. Even with his enquiring mind working hard, he had still managed to hold back thoughts of his important work being the reason for their deaths, even though it was the most obvious reason. He felt his brain would simply explode if it had been his fault. Now, with Robert Berry, it had been said out loud, and it could not be un-said.

Kobe leaned forward, elbows on knees, as a drunk would when planning on expelling the evenings alcoholic intake. His shoulders shaking as he became trapped in a fit of sobs. Robert stayed where he was, one leg crossed over the other, left hand in his lap. With his right he put a caring hand onto the rising and falling back of Kaan, A gentle reminder that he was not alone. No words were spoken, Robert knowing that when he was ready Kobe would pull it together and begin thinking of the 'why and who' again. It took a few minutes, but Kobe returned to the brainstorming.

"We thought we had broken the back of the drug ring." Kobe began again as if there had never been a break in the conversation. "As well as knowing there were three shops dealing like a legitimate business, the thinking was that the third raid would be the nail in the coffin for at least a few years. If nothing else, it would curtail the money flow which was a not a healthy prospect for any dealer." Kobe strengthened his mental resolve with a large breath, then continued. "For a low level, street corner dealer, a loss of product or money would probably mean a bit of a beating from his supplier and then back on the streets selling again. But we are talking serious money here, and some serious players. That said, it would still be bad business to hit a police family, it would bring hell down around their ears. That's why we thought we had rid Chichester of them, and why the get together for drinks, because we had something to celebrate."

That thought took Kobe back to that night. "If I had not stayed on for that drink with the squad that night, if I had gone straight home, instead of feeling obliged to stay and buy the whole squad drinks. My obligation should have been to my family, if it had been they would still be alive." His voice cracking with remorse and emotion.

"I know it is tough, but you cannot think like that my boy, that way madness surely lies." There were no words of truer comfort he could offer.

Robert quickly moved the subject on, not wanted Kobe to ponder on things he could not change. "Apart from the third raid, did your squad have anything on-going, where somebody would like you distracted?"

"There are two cases that come to mind where somebody may not like me very much."

"Only two?" Sarcastically asked Robert. "You can't have been a very good policeman."

Kobe almost got away with ignoring the comment, but he couldn't stop the smirk that grew on his face. "One is the drugs, and the other you know only too well, a case I think that will never be closed."

"My darling Godson you mean."

Kobe just nodded.

"That one got right away from me." Kobe shook his head, still in disbelief. "I knew Jacob was bad, but Luke had me fooled..."

"Luke had us all fooled." Robert shook his head. "I still feel shame that my own godson could carry out murder and then walk away. Not even have the courage to own up and pay for what he did."

"It has always worried me that one day he may just come back to haunt me." Kobe admitted. "I put him in Broadmoor, that must make anybody mad. Plus, because I was caught up in chasing one brother, I let the other loose on one of my officers. I put her in harms way and never got back in time to save her from a very nasty assault, which she is still paying for, some two years on. Like most investigations we were stretched thin with manpower."

"He basically has fallen off the face of the earth, I can't see him coming back." Robert hoped what he said was true, with all the bad things Lucas had done, Robert still loved him, but would never forgive him. "I still meet up with Gill, his girlfriend..."

Kobe said he remembered her and that she also became one of his victims.

Robert continued, "... we meet for coffee and lunch occasionally, she is busy writing a novel now and is pleased at how it's going. I would have thought if Lucas was anywhere near, he would at least try and contact her. I reckon his love for her was real enough."

"There is one other candidate, but it's only guesswork on my part." Kobe was grasping at straws.

"Well, talk it out, it may spring something into a clearer view. If I recall you always talked things through with David Martin, your DS." Robert was intrigued, as a solicitor and barrister he always had an enquiring mind, and he was enjoying working things out with such a well-respected detective.

"A little while ago, the Leader of the City Council reported that there were discrepancies on the expense accounts, and not small ones either. In fact, he said some were very high."

"Surely that would be easy to check, with an individual who put the expenses in being the culprit." Robert said playing devil's advocate.

"You would have thought so, but when we looked closer it wasn't just one councillor. There were four, and all-over different periods."

Robert pondered this for a moment, and as he always did as habit when deep in thought he stroked his goatee beard. "Now that is curious. One I can believe, a couple of councillors, at a stretch. But four bent councillors on a planned assault of the county's expenses bank.

No, I am not seeing that."

"Exactly, my first thought when I was told, was that it would be one councillor in particular..." Kobe continued.

"You suspected one in particular?" Asked Robert in his best court voice, it had a serious resonance and confidence to it.

"Not really, no..." Kobe thought carefully, he was not used to sharing with those outside the job. "Well, maybe one!"

"Would it be inappropriate to ask who?"

Kobe looked Robert straight in the eye, the man had a perfect poker face. "Yes, it would." Kobe held back for a second or two, Robert knew when to keep quiet. "Councillor Kenneth Jackman! No evidence yet, just my gut instinct. And he is a man living well beyond his means."

"His wife, Barbara I think, isn't she the money in that household." He went on to tell Kobe that he had met both at different times and at various functions. "Always liked her, never took to him."

"Not many do apparently." Kobe looking as if he had a nasty taste in his mouth. "When we checked the expense sheets of all the councillors, there was a little fiddle here, and little trying it on there, as would be expected. Then there were the four suspect councillors, and they were tearing the arse out of it."

"But Jackman's expenses claims were clean and perfect." Robert guessed.

"You catch on quick Mr Berry." Kobe noted. "He was the only one struggling to make ends meet and yet he was just about the only one that came out clean, that does not make sense to my copper's instincts..." Kobe was about to add more but Anne Berry called from the house.

"You two, I have knocked up some food for you so come and get it while its hot." Then added for her husband's ears. "I am off to my yoga class Robert, be home around nine-ish. Now you boys play nice while I am out. Kobe, I trust I will see you again in the morning."

They both called out their thanks and began to walk back up the manicured lawn, Kobe suddenly realising that the sun had now dipped behind the trees at the bottom of the garden and that there was a cooling chill to the evening air. He also realised that he had not been feeling the pain quite as much for the last couple of hours, it was a welcome release that he knew would not last.

Entering the house through the patio doors, they discovered

Anne had left them a lasagne, with the mozzarella still bubbling on top and a delicious looking side-salad.

"I only married her for the cooking." Robert winked, but Kobe could see what they both meant to each other. Whenever he saw 'Rob' Berry playing his blues guitar on Chichester's precinct, Anne was always there with him, reading a book or taking money for his home-studio recorded CDs that were for sale.

"Could he, Jackman I mean, be the one responsible for your tragedy?" After a few mouthfuls of the meal, washed down with an inexpensive but crisp white wine, Robert started the brainstorm up again. "It seems a bit excessive for a few quid on expenses."

"I asked myself the same question, I know there are more questions to ask so that I can link everything together." Kobe put down his fork, "I guess I won't be doing that anytime soon either." He took a deep breath and piled back in with the tell-all question. "But why would somebody slaughter my family, for making a few quid on the side, it's disproportionate and doesn't make sense."

"Maybe, there is more to it than a little fiddling." Robert had retired from his work as a barrister a little over three years ago and he was enjoying the mental athletics he was sharing with Kobe. "You said four others were at it, so what if Jackman had something on them and was forcing them to hand over what they fiddled, allowing him to put in clean expense sheets and make some money without being implicated."

"Good point but what sort of hold could he have to make them do that?" Kobe asked, his mind was usually sharper than this, but it was if his thoughts and reasoning were lost in fog.

"When I was a practising barrister the Jackmans, and I moved in similar social circles. The wife Barbara was on several charity committees, as is Anne, and we occasionally chatted. I always found her to be a real lady, both elegant and clever. But he was a different kettle of fish. An obnoxious and slimy character, the sort of bloke that when he shook your hand you checked to make sure your watch was still on your wrist. The purse strings are definitely hers."

"Which a man like Jackman, he would not like that at all." Kobe interjected.

"No, he wouldn't. I was always impressed with how she carried herself. I met her father a little before he died, and he was a real no nonsense kind of man, and it must have rubbed off on her. It made her comfortable with her wealth and it surprised me when she started dating the councillor. He wasn't anything back then, just a struggling estate agent with delusions of grandeur. They met, she fell in love with him, and he fell in love with her money, and the rest, as they say, is history."

"He is too smooth for my liking as well and I would have no trouble in believing he was on the fiddle, but a triple murder. That's a stretch!" The words caught in his throat, but he kept it together. It was early days, but he was finding the conversation therapeutic. Or so he thought!

Just the mention of the killings, brought the pain crashing back through his body and it made him physically shake as nausea coursed through him. He leapt from the dining table, knocking the chair over in his haste, before only just making it to the downstairs toilet before he vomited most of the meal he had just eaten. The retching racked his body long after his stomach was empty, leaving his throat sore and his ribs and abdomen aching badly. When it stopped, he slid down the wall and sat on the bathroom floor, allowing the nausea to ease, and then he cried, large sobbing spasms bending his body. He was tired and did not know how much more of this he could take. He missed his family but the only mental image he could drag up, with them in the picture, was the death scene he found in their bedroom.

Robert could hear all this and wanted to go to him and comfort him, but he knew this was something that Kobe had to work out himself. So, he made do with clearing the table, putting the leftovers in the fridge for another day. He boiled the kettle and made two cups of peppermint tea, hoping that if Kobe could stomach a hot drink the peppermint would calm his nausea. A few minutes later Kobe reappeared, face red and eyes bloodshot, and apologised for what had happened. Robert said nothing, except to point out the peppermint tea and the two men sat quietly back at the dining table and delved into their own thoughts. It wasn't that Robert was cold to human emotion, just a lifetime in courtrooms had left him with a poker face when it came to strong feelings, he was used to hiding any personal feelings in the courtroom.

At nine on the dot Anne came home and found the men in the lounge, she thought Kobe looked exhausted. She walked toward Robert and kissed her husband on the top of his grey head before sitting next to the grieving Kobe and hugging him. She sat with her arm around his shoulders, and he lay into her, he had no tears left but Anne held him tight until finally Kobe fell asleep, like a trouble child. Only then did Anne let him go, he stayed asleep so Robert just covered him with a blanket and the couple left him there, hoping that a little of the real Kobe would return by morning.

Sometime during the night Kobe had woken up and taken himself up to the spare room, the next thing he knew was that sunlight was pouring through the window and Anne was knocking at the bedroom door so she could deliver a cup of coffee to their guest.

He sat up in bed, sipping the gloriously rich coffee blend, he felt the fug lifting from his brains. He had dreamt during the night, but it felt real. As if his brain was calculating things that had been said and thought through the previous evening. Kobe thought through them again as he sipped his coffee.

Four councillors, previously of good character according to reports, all caught over-egging their expense accounts. Jackman, well known for having a bad character, offers spotless expense papers, for the first time ever. Conclusion, but not proof, is that somehow Jackman has his fellow councillors on a string, and they are paying him from their increased expenses, in the hope nobody would check. Three of the four councillors were married with children and no rumours as to any playing away for any of them, the fourth was openly gay and devoted to his toy dogs. Lifestyle blackmail was not the answer, not for four such different men, so what connected them to Jackman?

"Drugs!" Kobe's sudden thought made him say it out loud, and he so surprised himself he spilt coffee on his bare chest. If he wasn't awake before, he was now.

Kobe quickly put on his jeans and a T-shirt and still barefoot raced downstairs where he found Anne and Robert in the conservatory sipping their own coffees and chatting while watching the sun rise over the gardens of their neighbours'.

Robert looked up at the excited Kobe and said, "It's the drugs!" He smiled knowing that was the same word on Kobe's lips, he had enjoyed stealing the policeman's thunder.

"My thought exactly." Said Kobe, Robert told him to carry on and expand his thought. "Jackman is married to money, but that hurts his ego too much, so he has to make his own..."

"Keep going," encouraged Robert.

"Suddenly he is short of funds, he cannot go to his wife because she will ask questions." Kobe was in full flight now, like a bird released. He had missed being a police officer. "We discover, during raid one, that there is a big haul somewhere else in the city, weeks later a second raid we discover the large stash in a hidden room of an indistinct terraced house. Following raid one, seemed to be the time that Jackman began bleeding money, it just so happens that our four councillors may well have a drug problem, which Jackman knows about, so he blackmails them into making imaginative expenses claims."

"How does that affect your family, by anyone's standards that was a bold and stupid move." Anne interrupted, but then regretted it.

"Getting there," with his mind now on the target he was able to separate thought from grieving. "Jackman is the drug master we have been searching for, and because he supplies the drugs, he knows who the end users are and hence who to blackmail. Following raid number two when he discovers that a third raid could well be happening, so he sets in motion the murder of my family to throw any enquiry into disarray."

Anne again, "That is rather drastic action for a local drug dealer to take, isn't it?"

"That's what was bothering me." Kobe responded. "If it were just that, a local dealer, no matter how busy, it would have not been a big enough deal. You would just ignore the inconvenience and open shop elsewhere and keep on trading. But what if, and stick with me here, Jackman wanted to move up to a bigger league. It was no secret his ambition was to become an MP and head for the House of Commons, but that would cost big money and his income was already dented from the original raid."

Robert was too fired up to sit back. "So, the big boys allow their local dealer to play middleman." Kobe was nodding furiously. "Chichester Harbour would be a good place to run a smuggling enterprise, Jackman would take his motor yacht out on a sea jaunt, pick up the dope from either another boat or from a designated drop off point out in the English Channel..." Robert hesitated with the last part of his train of thought, now he looked for help.

"I think a drop off point," Kobe continued. "a fishing boat over from the continent, drops off a row of creel shaped lobster pots, all containing waterproof packages. Jackman comes by and picks them up, empties the contents, because it would not look good for a pleasure craft to carry the pots on deck."

"So, he leaves out them for the next run." Anne joined in.

"Exactly!" Kobe agreed. "Only now, instead of just enough dope to feed West Sussex, he now has enough stock to feed the addicts of most of the south of England. It just so happened that we were earlier with the raid than he expected, and it crossed over with what happened to my family." He put a hand up to stop his hosts from interrupting him. "Jackman was desperate, the first raid hit his pocket hard, a second raid would destroy him financially and put him in hock with some British, or even, European drug cartel and they don't play for fun. He had to stop any follow-up raids somehow."

"Surely, especially if he is scared of his wife, he would not have the guts to do that himself, far too dirty a job for his smooth hands." Robert added, excitement was high in the room, and he was loving every minute of it, all they had to do now was impress a jury.

"I firmly believe the attack on my family, and the raid happening on the same day, was pure coincidence. And, as for his bravery when it came to the dirty work, did you know his driver..."

"That's a young woman, isn't it?" Anne asked wanting to stay within the conversation.

"Yes, Fiona Webb and she already has a record for violence and quite a few more close run-ins with various police forces that haven't been taken to court because the witnesses where too scared to talk." Kobe shook his head at the thought of the woman, any woman, being that violent and that cold-hearted. "She is a nasty piece of work and more than able, and willing, to carry out attacks like that."

"So, we now have two suspects in the pot for the murders, how do we take this a step forward." Robert concluded.

"Who are they both, then?" Anne asked, feeling a little stupid. "I understand about Councillor Jackman, but who else?" Both men could see in Anne's face that she had yet to figure out who the other suspect was.

Both men realised that when they were discussing the alternative, they had been in the garden, and she had been at her yoga class.

Kobe left it to Robert to break the news. "Lucas, my love. My

Godson Lucas, not the beautiful boy we thought he was, and he is more than capable of murdering that beautiful family. Anne's chin dropped and she was made speechless by the accusation.

"Lucas and Jackman, then. So, what do we do next?" Robert asked, but Kobe never had an answer.

CHAPTER 59

Sam was first to wake, which he did with a strange mix of feelings, his emotions were running riot, his ego – well he wasn't sure what his ego was doing, one part of it was going 'well done Sam', while the other was telling him to apologise for not lasting very long. His big moment, and it was over in seconds rather than minutes. Sam thought to himself that they never showed that awkward part of lovemaking in the movies, the hero with supreme stamina would last for an age, his love interest after several orgasms would be both satisfied and exhausted. Sam felt he had lasted all of thirty seconds and then fallen asleep.

His bed was normally a cold and lonely place but now it was full, shared, and warm. He thanked the good-housekeeping gods, it was only a couple of days ago he had changed the bedding, he could not recall the time before that. In fact, leading up to Nick's funeral he had blitzed the place, a year or more of dust was moved around and vacuumed up. Nick had often said he would be much happier if he kept his home neater, and it turns out his friend was right about that as well. Sam had not had a woman in his bed for many years and had given up the hope of finding anyone that would be willing to take on this lost cause.

Sam rolled onto his right side and took a long look at the face that was on the next pillow. A gentle face, strands of black hair whispered over a delicate nose and chin, her lips were just open, the mouth soft and sweet. Sam wanted to kiss her but did not want the spell to be broken. He was with a beautiful woman and the bedroom smelled of sex, his bed was warm, and he had that nice empty feeling in his testicles. If she woke the dream would disappear in a flash, she would regret her actions, take one look at Sam, and run off with pure shock. He was so worried about what would happen next, he failed to notice her eyes had opened.

"Don't worry Sam, I am not going anywhere." She had read his face perfectly.

He investigated a pair of deep blue, sparkling eyes, the only time he had seen that colour before was deep in the clean waters of a Cornish harbour with a name he could not pronounce, with sunlight and blue skies giving the water that oceanic, azure, blue and then painting it with a liberal splash of sparkles.

"You saw me worrying, did you?"

"You were frowning, Sam." She smiled and his heart leapt. "Not a good look for a girl to wake up to."

Her head remained on the pillow; her hair fanned out like a black halo. Hygiene crossed Sam's mind, had he cleaned the toilet bowl during his spring clean, he prayed it was clean and sweet smelling. What a thought to have when you have one of the world's most stunning creatures lying next to you.

He stuttered a little, the last time he was this nervous was at that disastrous auction and look how that turned out!

"I-I w-was wondering whether to a-a-apologise to you or not."

"Why would you apologise Sam, I am a grown girl and I know what I am doing." Barbara propped herself up on one elbow, her hair flowed down over her shoulder, and the quilt slipped revealing a pert breast with a dark nipple, Sam took a sharp intake of breath, and hoped she didn't notice.

"I didn't last very long last night, and I know I was clumsy." Sam hung his head; shame made his face colour up. "It has been a very, very long time, and even then, I was not that experienced."

"Me neither Samuel Cobby, I am not a good time girl you know."

Sam panicked, thinking he had insulted her, but she cut him off before he could say anything and dig a large hole for himself.

"Stop fretting, I am just teasing you Sam," She liked saying his name, it was easier and softer than saying Kenneth, there was no worse name to utter when lost in the throes of passion, and her soon to be ex-husband would never let anyone call him Kenny. She thought of him as a pompous prick, but then felt badly about herself for thinking about him at a time like this.

"Shall we start again?" She could see and feel his mixed emotions. "Good morning, Sam."

"Yes please. Good morning, Barbara." There was obviously no embarrassment or regrets from that side of the bed and Sam thought, one out of two is not bad as he felt both.

His regret was that he had not lasted longer, not because his ego was dented, but because it was such an amazing feeling being inside of her.

Wide awake now she wriggled closer to him, one hand snaking up behind his neck, it felt soft and warm to the touch, her body felt damp and sticky, the after-effects of their earlier love making. She seemed to engulf every part of him, and the hand pulled his head down toward her mouth and she kissed him deeply and he was conscious of his bony body against the softness of her skin. She allowed her tongue to slide into his mouth, an invitation for him to respond in kind, and it felt good, for both of them. Sam had never been with such an intense lover.

"Better?" She asked when their lips parted.

"I may have to keep coming back, I need the practice." Sam said, Barbara shook her head and her hair once again tumbled over her face, he wanted to experience that look every morning from now on. "I am sorry though, I am not used to waking up next to someone, and never someone as beautiful as you."

"You don't have to pay me compliments Sam, just be yourself, I was attracted to you as well don't forget." She let out a small giggle. "In case you hadn't noticed, you have pulled, as I think they say nowadays." She leant back a little so he could see the earnest look on her face. "And it was not the wine that got me here, Sam, I wanted to be here."

"I was wondering." Sam admitted.

"It has been a while for me too, with all his philandering and so-called business trips I have spent many a night alone. Sometimes the nights he lay in bed next to me where some of the loneliest. I just needed the impetus to throw his sorry arse out of the house." Sam liked the way she said arse, it was as if the 'a' and 'e' were not needed. It had a charm about it rather than ass, as in the one you rode.

Sam felt like saying something glib to ease his embarrassment, but instead he held her close and kissed the top of her head, from her response of squeezing in even closer to him he knew immediately he had chosen the right option. With the pair of them wriggling in such close proximity Sam felt himself responding again. They kissed, hard and with tongues, and Sam was stiff. He felt her hand slide down over his stomach and encircle him, the grip firm and confident. Affectionately and slowly, she began to move her hand up and down, the grip of a woman feeling good in its rarity. It being an age since anyone had touched him there. He let himself go, and relaxed into the warm sexual feeling, suddenly it mattered not who had been the last woman or when his penis had last been gripped.

"I better be gentle with him..." She said with a wicked look in her deep blue eyes. "Wouldn't want to break him after all those years out of action, especially after we just got him working again."

"You seem to be in charge, so I am just going with the flow if that is okay." Sam said but found it difficult to form words because of what she was doing below the blanket, he had never felt anything so blissful, she tugged on him again, a little tighter this time, and it elicited another sharp intake of breath. "You seem to be ready!" She said, her voice husky with her own passion rising.

She rolled Sam onto his back, then she straddled him, with her hand between her thighs she guided him into her. They both gasped at the sensation and while their bodies engaged so did their eyes, and they remained like that for some time.

Sam would not have to apologise this time for not lasting very long. He had never known such blissful satisfaction.

CHAPTER 60

Kobe did not want to move on, he had no idea where there was to move-on to, one senior officer told him to take whatever time he needed, the job will be there when you get back. Another told him to see the events of the past few weeks in a positive way, then he would soon be able to *'kickstart'* his new life, his one-word reply summed up his feelings,

"Bollocks!" He thought about adding a *'Sir'* but decided that the moron did not deserve the title, or the respect.

Casper Jones and his spotty acolyte had been ordered back to where they came from as finally, Kobe was cleared of any blame, though he would never absolve himself. The final act, the bodies of his family were released so he could prepare them for their next life.

He had always had some sort of belief in the afterlife, but right now he could not figure out how all that worked. Three beautiful, and blameless, lives had been snuffed out, bright lights to burn no more, and somewhere deep within his soul he knew that his life as a police officer had caused those lights to be extinguished. Whatever scenarios he and Robert Berry had painted after a whole day of talking, exploring, digging into the facts, as well as the gut-feelings, none of them were provable. Even with all his experience as an investigator, he had no idea where to start a profitable investigation.

With nowhere else to go he slouched into the town centre, every coffee house, cake store and restaurant reminding him of times he and Rae had been to them, every toyshop and sweet store brought back the images of excited children, every street and every store held some sort of memory, and he recalled laughter, joy and even some soppy romantic moments. His heart would break all over again with every new memory. The pain was still intense and all consuming. He walked with head down and eyes cast on the paving slabs beneath his feet, for fear of seeing someone he knew and having the same conversations over and over.

Continuing to wander in such an aimless way seemed pointless. Kobe forced himself to stop and watch the world around him, just to feel normal for a few seconds. So it was that outside of an artist supply shop, he sat on one end of a bench with the enticing views of an old-fashioned cafe that seemed to have had a rebirth of popularity with all things retro being the latest rage, he and Rae had gone in there just the once and discovered it was not their cup of tea. Next door, the art shop window full of everything budding or professional artists would need, easels, pencils, brushes and of course works of art by local artisans who had purchased the very things on display. He recalled the joy on Rae's face when walking past one day they had spotted that one of her works, a landscape of East Head, a nature reserve of sand dunes, course sea grasses and rough wooden poles roped together to form a barrier between walkers and nesting birds. One summer's evening they had made love somewhere in those dunes, the fear of getting caught adding to their excitement, it was a painting of those exact dunes that spent two weeks in the shop window and now hung in their harbour side cottage. He could not stand the thought of someone else owning it and so purchased it himself, Rae was astounded to arrive home from the school run one afternoon to discover Kobe hanging it over their fireplace. Kobe doubted he would ever go back in there to retrieve it, or anything else they had shared as a family, in that place which was now a broken home.

Watching busy people rush by in the precinct and the memories he had conjured had given Kobe a headache, his temples throbbing. But each time he closed his eyes he could see Rae as he wrapped her in five pristine white sheets, it would be three for each of his children, he placed her left hand over her chest, the right laid over left and her blonde hair in three neat braids. The linen cocoon pure, clean, and as bright as a new laid snowdrift. She had looked so pale and beautiful as he wrapped her in the inexpensive shrouds, the wide mouth across her delicate throat where the killer had sliced her life away, still angry, and raw looking, in one vicious sweep of his blade. The mortician's Y-shaped incision stitched roughly as if by an amateur seamstress, that made a cruel mark down her porcelain torso. He cried at the vandalism to something so delicate and beautiful as he secured the funeral ropes around her breathless body. He wanted to run away but had to stay strong as he still had his children to prepare for Salat al-Janazah, the funeral prayers.

At the time of carrying out these last rites for his beloved family in preparation for their next, and last journey, it did not seem as a chore, even when he gently washed their bodies clean as tradition and teachings required, each one washed three times before he added non-alcohol perfumes to their greying skin.

He was certain that some sort of Paradise awaited them, they had led faultless, blameless lives. Kobe doubted he would be allowed in, but hoped a benevolent God would overlook his transgressions in payment for his suffering here on earth and his work as a police officer. He still felt he was a little further ahead in the plus column, plus, he was supposed to be a forgiving God. Being used to having control of most things in his life, it was a struggle having no control whatsoever with how his life would end. Would he meet with his family again in Paradise or would it be an eternity alone in Hell, it was aptly named. Would there be anyone left to pray to Allah for mercy for him?

With his eyes closed he could see them as clearly as he did when he had finished readying them for their onward journey. A mother and her children, the two bundles side by side looked so small, so insignificant and yet they had brought so much love and joy into the lives of those around them.

Eventually the fear of being spotted by work colleagues or friends grew too deep and it was time to leave the town centre. That's when the thoughts hit him that maybe it was time to head onto somewhere new.

There was nothing to keep him here...

People, friends or otherwise, was the last thing he wanted to mingle with, he could not stomach any more pitying remarks, or even another of the dozens of invites or so for him to join friends at their homes instead of moping all alone. Even the Chief Constable invited him to some large dinner party his wife was organising. One particularly thoughtless sergeant had even offered up that his attractive sister was single and looking for someone to date, it was 'never too early to get back on the horse, Kobe'. He had no idea how he resisted the urge to just thump him, maybe it was because he wanted to remain in the plus column when he came to be ready to move on.

As usual Kobe ended up back at the canal basin, outside of the pub where his troubles all began when he stayed late with his team to have a drink, they say pride before a fall, and whoever *they* were, they were right. He followed the towpath as it curved at right angles and took him away from town and into the countryside where nothing except ducks, swans, moorhens, and coots went about their own business, ignoring the humans that walked past.

The path went into shadow as it travelled under the main by-pass, but within a few paces it was back out into autumnal sunshine. He still had memories of walking here with the family, but they were all memories of fun and joyous laughter, much less painful than the city centre. With no concern for time Kobe walked on until he reached the marina, stopping briefly at the Boathouse Cafe and Bar to rummage in his pockets and find enough change to buy a cappuccino to go. The server recognised him, but not wanting to intrude she made do with a brief nod and a sympathetic smile. Kobe appreciated her reserve. As he left the bar to continue his walk a voice from behind, called out for him.

"KOBE, Kobe, over here!" But Kobe ignored it, he did not even want to turn to see who owned the voice. He was not in the least worried if it caused offense or not. Just before getting out of hearing range, he heard the grumpy complaint. "He must have heard me, the ignorant bugger..." Kobe, usually polite, just did not care anymore.

Just before reaching the lock gate, he saw the mooring where Lucas Tubb had kept his father's motor yacht, which he used to escape in. Despite there being a clamour for mooring spots, 40-feet of pontoon remained empty, maybe yachting types were superstitious about where they moored, or it may have been than the yachtsperson was out sailing that day, not that Kobe gave a toss either way. He had not been to this part of the canal infrastructure since the case with the two brothers, both violent psychopaths, and both avoided capture, one by taking the easy way out and committing suicide by drowning in the harbour, the other by just disappearing. If Kobe still had his authority maybe he could discover if the young man had returned to wreak havoc and prove to be the one who had killed his family.

Kobe knew at that moment there would be no closure until he had proven either Lucas Tubb, or Kenneth Jackman were the guilty party. If he could find proof, it may even be that neither of them would ever see the interior of a police station, or court.

Over the busy lock gates, where people stood transfixed by the wonder of a lock gate opening and closing, small things to excite small minds. Beneath him and circling outside the gates, looking like they wanted to get in, were a pair of swans and swimming in a line behind the cob and the pen were three cygnets, their plumage still a dull grey/brown colour. It would not be until next year that they started to show the snowy white plumage that made them such beautiful birds.

He found a quiet spot on the calm shore of the broad waterway, he stood alone, well away from the main tourist and hiker track. Surrounded by the picturesque scenery that has given the harbour its fame, he recalled every heart-wrenching step of the farewell to his family. Looking out toward the mouth of the harbour and the endless sea beyond his eyes were unfocused as yachts skipped back and forth across the impotent waves of the conservation area as they headed out into the English Channel and his mind so troubled with hard and hurtful thoughts, he did not register anything he saw. A two-man dingy swung around close to shore and as it did, they raised a spinnaker of deep blue, it's strong image on the water twice as its reflection sailed alongside, Rae had once painted such a scene and the picture had sold quickly during the local art club's annual exhibition. This day, Kobe failed to register any of it. Unfettered tears ran down his unshaven face as he felt his wife and two children drift skyward, their memories lost on the wind for all eternity. It is forbidden for Muslims to be cremated but Rae, was Catholic, and the children were being raised knowing both faiths so that when they were old enough, they could make their own decisions. Rae was specific, she did not want to rot in a hole in the ground and Kobe knew she felt the same for the children. There would be no box or urn on the sideboard for them either, Rae was a free bird and she deserved to fly free over an area she loved to paint and walk. Kobe knew this was one more transgression for him when it came to the reckoning of his plus and minus columns, but his wife's wishes came first. Up to this point he had followed his own teachings; the rest were Rae's wishes.

Kobe opened the simple cardboard container and held it up to the gods.

Their ashes were quickly taken on the brisk breeze and Kobe was pleased to see their remains twist and mix together, they would be together for eternity, but his jaded beliefs found it hard to feel that they were bound for a heaven or some afterlife paradise as he had once believed.

Cliché would say that life was a cruel mistress, and there was good reason for such dogmas, she in her cruellest of moods had a way of leaving life-partners and parents behind to mourn for the loss of loved ones who should never have been taken first. What sort of God would take three such beautiful and innocent beings so cruelly and painfully. Kobe could not understand God's plan. Especially such a cruel plan, as sitting by the water's edge trying to understand it all he had one last, heart-breaking, realisation. As they were being murdered, either his children had to watch their mother being slaughtered, or poor Rae had to watch as her children were sliced open. Kobe knew now where his destination was, it was an eternity in the Hell that he was feeling now.

As with many small families, it seems that there is only one person left to make arrangements and settle their life's affairs, even with little ones there was things that needed to be done. Kobe was the one left behind, and for a man whose career life was one of working out complex logistics, he was finding it hard just making sure everything was done right, he knew Rae should have been the one left behind, she was always superb when a family crisis occurred. So it was that Kobe was the one left behind to deal with their funerals. To settle affairs, tell the respective schools his children would not be back for next term, or any other term. Rather than be cruel and do it by telephone Kobe had visited the schools, then the charity shop where Rae volunteered for two days a week. It was hard but had to be done, the hardest part, taking all the sympathy with each contact. He had to wait while they said what great little students they were, how loved and with so many friends in class, playground, and shop. They were loved so much, and they would be missed. Although tough, in a way it was also comforting as it kept his mind busy, and he did enjoy hearing the love that his family received every day from fellow pupils and staff. Rae was better at this sort of stuff, Kobe could organise a group of rag-tag, tough old coppers with ease, but organise the children and everyday stuff, that was Rae's expertise. There was no Rae now to smile, kindly, and tell him he was doing okay. As well as the good will the odd person staggered him, and with his job people no longer surprised him, but one beggared belief. As he was leaving the school yard, he passed the mothers outside the school gates and as he closed the gates behind him one of them sidled through the crowd, heavy make-up, with bleached-blonde hair, tight top and skirt way to young for both her skinny legs and her age, approached him at speed. With eyes shining out from within heavily mascaraed lids, she looked up at him, a sickly smile on her mouth.

"You know that there is no need to be alone at a time like this."

She placed a hand on his arm, there was no mistaking the intention. She was hitting on him.

Kobe wanted to swear and curse her, he could not believe how some people behaved. For a second or two, he thought to tell Rae when he got home, but then he remembered, there was no Rae, nor going home. He chose to say nothing, just ripped his arm from her grasp and noted that one fake nail tore away and fell to the ground. She was left standing outside the school gate with other mothers watching and judging.

God and all he stood for had abandoned him, he had taken the people he hated saying goodbye to in the mornings and loved going home to at the end of the day. He was the police, the father, the husband and his number one job in the whole world was to protect them, to ensure the safety of those he loved, to keep them from harm. Both his names translated to 'King', none of his family were supposed to go so early. The king could not protect his people!

With one last task to perform, and his was the toughest by far, Kobe's only duty now was to discover who and why. It was one of the many reasons he had for leaving the Job why he left the building where he had served as a PC and then a DC and DS, before rising to the rank of Detective Inspector. It was where he excelled, been applauded and where he did a job that he cared for and had been good at. He truly hoped he had made a difference to the city he called home, but none of that mattered anymore.

Despite the teachings of non-violence that had been hammered into him since birth and as he grew into adulthood, he could now see himself crossing the invisible line in the search for those who had delivered such despair to his door. There was a certainty in his mind that blood would yet be drawn in his search for who had both done this and who had ordered it. Nobody would blame him, but there were rules that could not be broken, and knowing he was likely to not just break, but shatter those rules he could no longer continue to serve as a police officer, not with such hate and desire for retribution in his thoughts and heart.

There also no forgiveness in his heart for the officers he had served under, instead of understanding, they had arrested him and suspended him from duty, calling it compassionate leave. It was the Deputy Chief Constable who had delivered the news, and as he did so he kept a fake look of concern for a fellow officer on his face, but Kobe could see in his lying eyes that the 'leave' card was just a cop-out. The DCC was just covering his arse when he told Kobe of the decision to offer 'compassionate leave' while the investigation was underway. Kobe had sat in on many interviews, and nine times out of ten, he knew when there was a liar across the table. Kobe saw a lying face that day. So, he was on compassionate leave, Kobe told the Assistant Chief Constable that he no longer had any compassion. None!

Kobe was on his own, in every sense, and it was something he was not used to. He had always had his parents, fellow officers and then Rae and the children, he had never known what loneliness was. But he knew now.

As to the future, he knew without doubt that lines would be crossed. Previously he always had a keen idea of where to draw a line in the sand, it was what made him such a good investigator, now he was not so certain. Worst of all, for a man with a clear idea of right and wrong, Kobe feared what his final actions may be. The bacon sandwiches, the odd pint of Guinness could be forgiven by his God, they were just weaknesses of a frail human nature. Now Kobe knew that if he found those responsible then he was about to create the gravest of sins within his religion.

Motionless on the edge of the water, sitting on the grass with his knees tucked up to his chest, Kobe recalled the teachings from the Quran, teachings that had been driven into him with the repeated rattle of drumsticks beating out the rhythm of rat-a-tat-tat on a snare drum. Teachings he learned everyday as a boy; *'And whoever kills a believer intentionally, his recompense is Hell to abide therein; and the wrath and the Curse of God are upon him, and a great punishment is prepared for him...'*

Well, he was prepared to suffer God's wrath, it could be no worse than what he was suffering now. Mentally he was now prepared for whatever fate had in store for him and was fully prepared for an eternity in Hell, for it could not come close to the hell he was suffering here on earth. Kobe was already serving his punishment.

"Bring it on, you bastard!" Kobe hollered at the clouds.

CHAPTER 61

Barbara had been gone most of the day, she had told Sam she had things to do, including a meeting with her solicitor which would take time as there was a great deal to discuss and sort out, there was also the bank to sort out and the locks to get changed on the house. He hated saying goodbye to her, fearful that she would not return, and that the last 12 hours had been a dream.

Sam missed her and had done so from the moment she left his home above the shop.

Christ, I am a soppy bugger, he thought. It felt like the statue debacle all over again, first the elation and then the devastation of losing, and he had lost enough already in recent weeks. A statue found and lost and now his long-term friend lost in a pointless killing. The previous days had been tough to endure and yet last night was glorious, enlightening and an event he would treasure for life, and he wanted it again. He wanted to feel that sense of being worthwhile again and again.

While sitting at his kitchen table awaiting the return of the delicious Barbara, he had to wonder if he had been a pity shag, or a revenge fuck. Then recalling her beautiful eyes and the way they looked at him, he knew this woman was not even close to being shallow. He saw on kindness and caring in those deep blue eyes, glinting like an azure sea.

Sam fed Wedgwood and no longer had she cleared her bowl than she was out through the rattling cat flap again. There was gratitude for you, two girls pleased in the space of a few hours, and both had disappeared through the door. As Sam was at the sink, clearing up breakfast things and washing up the cat dish, he heard the shop door rattle as somebody energetically tried to get in, he shouted that he was closed for the day. What he didn't say was that he was too knackered to open the shop after last night's horizontal gymnastics. He wanted to tell Nick about what had happened with Barbara, Sam felt sure he would have approved. As he was finishing up the back door opened and Sam thought, cheerily, that is must have been Barbara returning. His expectant smile soon disappeared; it was the wrong Jackman.

Without preamble Kenneth went straight into attack mode.

"Where the fuck is my statue..." before adding, "...and my wife."

Sam, not normally a brave man, went on the offensive. "I notice you put your wife second on that short list, she deserves better than that and should be your number one priority. Which is probably why she kicked you out." He said surprising himself with that splash of bravado.

Jackman was across the kitchen quicker than a skater on ice and Sam felt himself pushed back against the stacked Welsh dresser, plates fell and crashed onto the flagstone floor shattering around Sam's feet. He felt his body yield to the bruising assault, the base of the unit hit him in his lower back while for his mid-back and neck, the shelves caused the damage. Sam was not a fighter and pushing back got him nowhere, two inches away from the dresser and he was rammed back into it again.

Jackman was taking no prisoners he was desperate.

"I will ask you one last time, where is my fucking statue?"

"It's not your statue, it's mine, left me by my father." Sam responded. "Even if it was here, I wouldn't tell you, same for your wife, but as it happens neither are here. Maybe if you find one, you will find the other." Sam was angry. "Now get out of my fucking kitchen before I do something I may regret."

Although Jackman had the element of surprise, he was not used to people fighting back with him, especially as he normally had his minder, who also seemed to be missing this morning. Sam's new-found confidence seemed to take the wind out of Jackman's sails, and he backed off a little. Sam thought, and hoped, he was leaving but Jackman had just made room to enable him to throw a punch. His clenched fist flew up from waist level and caught Sam in the solar plexus and pushed its way beyond his ribs and into the spongy gut, the blow forcing the wind from his lungs. Sam double over, retching as if he were about to throw up. He waited for a follow up blow, but it didn't arrive. He slid down the cupboard section of the dresser and ended up sitting on the cold flagstones.

"Stay away from my bronze statue, and my wife. If you make me come back here it will get nasty for you." It was a line from some movie or other that Jackman had heard but it seemed to fit the situation.

The back door rattled as Jackman slammed it behind him, so

hard that Sam was surprised that the window remained in its rotting frame. However, he was relieved to know that Jackman had gone, Sam was not built for fighting and after just one punch he was breathless and nauseous. He heard the broad tyres on Jackman's Jaguar screech on the road at the end of the precinct, the wheels spinning angrily, fought for grip. Sam was puzzled about the statuette though, if Jackman didn't have it, who did? And, if it was Barbara, had she slept with him to just make sure she kept hold of it, even if she knew where it was.

Sam began to haul himself up from the cold floor and was struggling to stand, his right leg weak as usual making simple manoeuvres a trial when he heard the door open again. He thought it was Jackman returning to dish out more violence, but Barbara's soft tones cheered him, despite the ache in his gut.

"Sam, what happened?" Barbara dashed to his aid and helped him stand, and once again he was embarrassed in front of this perfect woman.

"Your husband happened, that's all." Sam responded as he regained some of his cheeriness. "He came here demanding his statue back. Oh, and he also asked after you, as an afterthought. Apparently, I have both and he wants them back. Had no idea about the statue but I told him he wasn't getting you back. Then he hit me and hightailed it out of the door."

"Poor Sam," she patted his cheek mockingly, "...let me make you a tea." She fussed around him. "Would it be Roobush or a nice peppermint for physical assault."

"Roobush please." Sam's back and gut hurt, but with Barbara back in his kitchen, it seemed to make aches and pains disappear."

"Well, you were right about one thing, you have me, and I am not going anywhere." She turned and hugged him around his neck which caught the growing bruise from the collision with the high shelf on the dresser, but he wasn't going to complain. "As for the statue, well he is on the end of the table, Sam."

She released the headlock of a hug and moved to one side and there was the Roman Centurion with his sword held high in victory sitting on the far end of the refectory table. Sam was certain he saw a brass smile on his rigid face.

"I have no idea if it is the real one or the fake one Sam." She spoke. "But I found him in a carrier bag hidden behind files in his office cabinet at home."

"He is not very good at hiding stuff then is he."

"He knows that I never go into his office, just as he never goes in mine. Mind you that's because I lock the door to mine and have the only key." Everything she says or does made Sam feel warm inside, her voice as sultry as her looks.

"Yes, that would be the real one, I still have the fake here, in fact it's in the shop window with a £2000 price tag on it." Sam shrugged. "Thought I may as well make some money out of this fiasco." He walked to the end of the table and hefted the statue to feel the weight of the bronze in his hand once again. "I wonder if the auction house would like another go, or if the high bidder from the auction will still want it."

They both looked at the resplendent Roman once more.

"Personally, I think he is an ugly bugger, and can't wait to sell him. Have you seen the size of the Roman nose on him." Sam said jokingly but meaning it.

"Never fancied him myself either, I prefer my men to have softer features and slim bodies. I don't go in for all this six-pack lark..."

If she was going to say anything else about what sort of men she liked, she was cut short as the back door swung open again, Sam's doors had never been to busy. It was the young girl from the charity shop who had so kindly patched his damaged head a few weeks ago.

"Mr Sam, you need to come straight away." She looked panicked and upset, tears filled the corners of her pretty eyes, the black Egyptian style make up sweeping up from the side of her eyes was in danger of running. "It's your cat..."

Sam forgot about his aches and bruises and ran after the young girl; Barbara was right on Sam's heels. The girl stopped at the kerbside and looked down, Sam was soon on her shoulder, and he stared down at Wedgwood, his back at a strange angle, head twisted around, tongue out and eyes glazed and sightless. Barbara put a steadying hand on Sam's shoulder, there were no words. Sam bent and picked up his long-time companion, and as superior as Wedgwood acted, Sam loved her. She had kept him sane all these lonely years.

"I am sorry Mr Sam, I was just going to work and saw her there, I knew she was yours, we loved her too, we used to feed her occasionally in the shop, it's probably a cat thing but they are always hungry." She was babbling, uncertain of what to do next. Sam could not speak so Barbara thanked the girl for her kindness, which gave the young girl an excuse to make her exit.

Barbara looked down at the piece of road where Sam had picked Wedgwood up from, there were broad, black, and broken tyre tracks where the car tyre had gone over the cat. They were broad tracks like those left by a badly driven Jaguar. She knew without too much thinking that this was another thing that her husband had to answer for.

Barbara spent the rest of the day with Sam, watched as he lovingly found an ornate cigar box for Wedgwood and buried her in the small rear garden behind the shop. There were no words of farewell, Sam had not spoken at all since the discovery. At teatime the kind girl from the charity shop popped round to check on Sam and seemed happy that someone was with him.

As Barbara opened the door for the youngster to leave, she turned and looked at the crestfallen Sam and told Barbara. "He is a lovely old man..." Barbara wasn't sure he would like to be called 'old man', "...but he always seemed lonely. He occasionally called into the shop to see if we had been donated anything of value, and always paid a fair price, not what we put on the ticket. Are you, his girlfriend?"

The question that had raised from nowhere surprised Barbara. "Yes, yes I suppose I am now, but it's not been very long."

The girl nodded sagely. "Well look after him, nobody should be alone especially now he doesn't have his cat."

She meant well, and as Barbara ushered her back out of the door, she told her. "I intend to look after him. I hadn't realised it until the last day or two, but I have been lonely as well. I think we are going to be okay together." Barbara had no idea why she had confided in the teenager, but it felt good to realise that she too was no longer lonely.

She made Sam another Roobush tea, and herself a proper cup of good old English breakfast tea, she would have to experiment with all these different tea flavours. Teas brewed, she sat alongside Sam, and they stayed like that for some time, sipping tea in silence. Barbara had never had a relationship where the silences were comfortable, she always felt as if conversation was served in a never-ending supply, silence meant discomfort. After a while she looked along the table and there was the Centurion staring back at her, his sword held high in that arrogant warrior stance. She broke the silence.

"I still think he's an ugly sod, nose is far too big."

It took only those few words to knock Sam out of his stupor and bring him back to the real world. There was still no smile on his lips, but a sparkle appeared in his eyes and Barbara noticed. Sam appreciated that Barbara had stayed with him.

"Thank you for staying here, I appreciate the company." He placed his hand on hers, he half expected her to pull away, even though they had spent the night together, but she not only left it there, but also put her own hand over his as well.

"If you will have me, Sam? I will stay a lot longer, don't ask me how come I feel this way and don't try to overthink it. I just have a feeling we are just what the other needs."

Sam was stunned, but it was a nice shock. "No argument from me. I would like that a lot, and not like that pig of a husband of yours, it's not because you have money, I find myself genuinely caring for you."

"Well, the money part is no problem." She nodded toward the Roman. "Once he has sold, we will both have money of our own, not that it would be an issue to me if you decided to keep him and still ran this charming shop."

Nobody had ever called the shop charming before now, and it was just another thing that he liked about this beautiful woman, she did not judge but accepted things the way they were. And they remained sat there, at the table, long after the sun had set.

CHAPTER 62

Kobe was back inside his favourite greasy spoon cafe. At the counter Stella Gold was ordering three coffees and three rounds of bacon sandwiches, while sitting at a Formica topped table in the corner David Martin was bringing his old boss up to speed as far as the investigation was going into his family's murders.

Gold was soon back and placed a tray with three hot drinks on the old-fashioned tabletop, one cappuccino, one latte, and a simple black Americano for boring David. As she went behind him to take her seat she ran her hand with affection across his shoulders, Kobe was pleased for them.

"Do you need sugar, Boss?" Stella asked.

"I am no longer your boss Stella; it is just Kobe now."

"Old habits and all that, but I will try and remember." She was pleased that Kobe had the strength now to offer a small smile.

"I really am taking medical retirement. After the cock-up over my arrest in front of the press and the fallout of that, the brass at the top were worried I would sue them." Kobe explained. "So, they are putting it down as Aggressive PTSD, which according to the force doctor, I actually am likely to be suffering after everything that has happened."

"Will you not miss the job; it is pretty addictive you know?" Gold enquired.

"After what the job has cost me." There was no anger in the tone, just disappointment, although he tried to keep his voice level. "Why would I stay in a job that has cost me so much, my family deserved better, and I let them down."

"Full pension I hope Kobe." David queried, trying to divert the conversation away from Kobe's family.

"Full pension and medical pension benefits as well." He looked a little shy about telling them the next piece of his news. "I have put the cottage on the market, and I am going to move away as soon as it is sold. I would never have been able to stay there again anyway. I will use the money from that to buy a small place wherever it is that I end up."

"Any idea where?" David asked.

"Just going to drive, and keep on driving, until I find somewhere that feels like I belong."

"Well let us know when you get there." Gold was all smiles; she was in a happy place. "We will need to know so we can come visit."

She looked toward David as if posing a question, he just smiled back and shrugged.

"Plus, your Godson will need to know where you live." Stella added, softly.

It took Kobe a moment or two to fully realise what she had said, and when it sunk in, he could not help but smile, it seemed as if weeks of bad memories and thoughts had been washed away. It may have only cleansed his mind for that moment in time, but it was a welcome relief. He spent the next ten minutes asking them about their future, was marriage on the table, what would he, or she, be called and he begged them not to burden the child with the name of Kobe. He also told them he would be happy to be the Godfather, it felt to Kobe as if a little bit of life had returned. The balance that is the universe had got a little of its equilibrium back.

The bacon sandwiches, an inch thick and oozing grease, arrived and Kobe realised it was the tastiest thing he had eaten in weeks. Up until that point food was just a method of refuelling his body. They ate in silence but all three were smiling.

Plates had been removed and second coffees served when they got down to talking shop. It was not good news for Kobe, but it was movement in the investigation. As David explained, Stella stayed out of the conversation unless new partner needed reminding of some salient point or other. She sat alongside him with one hand on his thigh and the other holding her coffee mug. They made a good team.

"It has been more complex than we first thought." David began, not wanting to falsely build up hopes of an imminent arrest. "In a roundabout way it is linked to the theft of some valuable bronze statue, and the murder of the Chronicle reporter Nick Flax..."

"I read about both of those stories," Kobe interrupted. "I liked Nick, he was a good reporter, one of the decent ones who got the stories right. His partner was pregnant as well, wasn't she?"

"Yes, Suzi, and she is close to giving birth. Really sad, after the news of his death she nearly lost the baby through shock." Said Gold.

"Wasn't he just unlucky to be stabbed during a football incident?" Kobe asked.

"That's what everyone assumed," said Gold. "The plods on duty at the game thought that and had dismissed it as such, until video surveillance saw the killer arrive against the flow of the crowd and leave the scene keeping the face hidden by a hoodie. With the supporters dressed either in bright blue or bright green one person in a dark blue hoodie was hard to miss. But we will get back to that when everything will knit together."

David continued telling Kobe about the Roman Centurion, explaining how it is believed that Jackman was responsible for switching the real bronze with a fake. The fake that he had obtained after murdering a Portsmouth man who had appeared on the Antiques Roadshow.

"Wasn't there something strange about the murder weapon?" Kobe asked, his mind as inquisitive as it had always been, after years in CID it was part of his DNA.

"Yes, he was stabbed, and even though crispy by the time they got the fire out, it was clear from the autopsy that it was the cause of death. At first, they could not figure out what had pierced his heart. Then the coroner remembered a case in Europe where a victim had ripped off his drug lords and died in the same way, right down to the fire to tamper with cause-of-death."

"Don't keep him in the dark David, it's not a thriller plot, tell the man." It was clear to Kobe who was the boss in their relationship, just as Rae was in charge in their house. Kobe felt guilty for enjoying the afternoon a little too much. It was a guilt that would always raise its ugly head, he would never get used to it. He looked on enthralled with the conversation.

"It was a stiletto." David explained finally.

"What, as in a dagger?"

"No, as in a stiletto shoe." David paused a moment to let that sink in. "The medical examiner believes that the blow turned a very expensive shoe into a murder weapon, it had been thrust into the chest by some sort of karate kick. Apparently, it took a good aim and a massive force to drive it through the ribcage and into the heart."

"Fuck me!" Kobe swore, something that was rarely heard from his mouth.

"That's what everyone else has said as well." David continued. "So not only have we a strange murder weapon, narrowing the killer down to a woman, but also, it has now been discovered, there are several more killings with the same M.O. across Europe."

"Interesting but what has this to do with my family." Kobe was growing impatient.

"I will get to that I promise, but bear with me a little longer."

Kobe nodded, not wanting to waste any more time asking questions.

"The murder in Portsmouth was not drug related, which was unusual for this type of killing." David got back on track. "It was to do with this bloody bronze statue of a Roman that keeps cropping up. The Portsmouth man/victim, as you know, was on the Roadshow, where they proclaimed his bronze to be a fake. Then a Chichester man, who runs a bric-a-brac come antique store in the precinct discovers he has the real one. That goes on show in the old Town Hall, organised by everybody's friendly Councillor Kenneth Jackman..."

"Always knew that snake was up to no good, just couldn't prove anything." Kobe said, adding his own thoughts.

"...by the time the dealer, Sam Cobby's bronze gets to the London auction house that too has become a fake, making poor old Mr Cobby a laughingstock. And the only person who has access to the statue while on display..."

"Kenneth bloody Jackman!" Kobe said showing he was following the story so far.

David took a sip of his Americano before it turned cold, so Stella asked a question of Kobe.

"Do you remember that Jackman loved swanning around in his shiny new Jaguar, and who his driver was?"

"Always annoyed me that, the flash bugger had a better car than the mayor."

"Also had a more attractive driver as well." Stella fed the bait and she waited for Kobe to bite. He had lost none of his intuitive skills.

"A slender, dark haired young woman..." A slight pause as he pictured her. "And she always had a penchant for wearing black stilettos, those expensive designer ones with the red sole if I remember. I recall Rae saying that if a chauffeur could afford to buy them why couldn't she have a pair? Not bloody likely on my DI salary!"

"Well, it seems that in the last few days the Jaguar has been reclaimed by the leasing company for non-payments of fees going back six months." David continued.

"What's he reduced to now? Driving his wife's Range Rover?" Kobe asked.

"Well, here he is the funny thing." David was torn between just stating the facts as they were, as he would if he were reporting to Kobe back in the days when he was boss or tease him a little with snippets so he could work out the story himself.

"Don't tell me he has gone missing now." Both Stella and David nodded together in affirmation.

"We were looking at him for the theft of the Bronze, valued at around five million for some unfathomable reason, ugly bloody thing if you ask me, made by some famous long-ago-dead sculptor. Then there is the death of the Portsmouth man, we were having to work with the Hampshire lot on that link, but they were not being very helpful, apparently having their own thoughts on the death and who caused it. It then seems that our friendly journalist, Nick Flax, in trying to get a story on Jackman that will stick without getting the paper sued, may have gone a little far. It transpires that every Sunday night, Flax, and Sam Cobby meet out the back of the shop to drink fancy teas and enjoy the Roadshow, they have been friends for several years.

Kobe could not stay out of the conversation; it was ingrained in him to make conclusions based on the facts. "If I am hearing you correctly, Cobby gets the bronze stolen and Nick does his best to help his friend, probably with facts held on file by the paper."

"Right so far..." said Stella between sips of her latte.

"They both know that Jackman is to blame but the only thing the Chronicle has on the Councillor is the fact that he has been having a secret affair, that everyone but his wife knew about. Barbara Jackman and Nick Flax are friends of old as the reporter has covered a few of Mrs Jackman's charities. The paper never used some photos that had come to them from a source unknown as it was dubious at best using them legally and the editor thought it would lower the family style of the newspaper. Flax grabs the photos from the archive and goes and visits his old friend Mrs Jackman and shows her the photos of her husband doing bedroom gymnastics with a surgically enhanced blonde..."

"You know the sort..." interjected Stella, "...all tits and lips!"

"Nick Flax rubs salt in the wound inflicted on Barbara Jackman by informing her that Kenneth paid for the bouncy tits and sticky lips."

David continued. "Adding insult to injury he was also paying the rent on their waterside love-nest with money from his wife."

"The man is a legend and a gent." Kobe said with his words coated in sarcasm. "Please tell me you have something on him!"

"Getting to it, but cutting a long story short, Barbara Jackman changes the locks and kicks him out with just the clothes he was stood up in. Good news is we are now also looking at him for blackmailing other Councillors and forcing them to hand over their fiddled expenses claims from the council. In fact, these councillors are of previously good character and good expense claims. Which again baffled us."

"For him to be so panicked that he commits murder and steal a valuable antique, he must have some serious cash flow problems." Kobe was firing on all cylinders now. "Plus, you say he was blackmailing his fellow councillors and fiddling expenses."

"Actually, he was the only one *not* putting in bogus expense claims, which is why it stood out." David explained.

"And what would cause a well-to-do, high-living, local businessman and Councillor to suddenly have cash flow problems, so bad that he has to resort to theft, blackmail and murder." Stella posed the tantalising question as she could see from Kobe's expression that he was putting the seemingly unrelated facts together.

"Putting two and two together, I would say a couple of drug raids, could cause a major cash shortage for the main dealer. Especially with the amount of dope we secured during the raids, it was far too big a haul for our little city." Kobe was feeling mentally stronger than at any time since he found his family, and he tried mentally to keep their death's out of the mix for the time being. He could see where this story was heading and was enjoying the brain-storming chase. "Plus, Jackman had to have something on those bent councillors, and drugs would be the obvious blackmail subject if he was their drug source."

"Spot on, Kobe. Not only has he now gone missing but also his deadly driver with the stilettos."

A sad look crossed Kobe's face. "Is she also responsible for the stabbing of Nick Flax."

"We think so." David concurred. "It wasn't a shoe this time but looks like the blade was a dagger type flick knife, one was found at the scene but obviously no prints. CCTV did catch someone close to the driver's description walking toward the stadium a few minutes after full time, and again walking away some ten minutes later. We are certain it was her from her stature and walk."

"Do you think we will find Jackman alive." Stella asked, changing tack for a moment, her eyes darting between both men.

"I doubt that very much." Kobe answered, it was hard to get away from the fact that he was no longer in charge. "Sorry David, Carry on." David understood.

"Not much more to tell, really." David concluded, but he knew his ex-Boss wanted more.

"You can't stop now, what about my family." Panic made his voice quiver. "Did Jackman order my family killed, did that skinny bitch in high heels kill them?"

Kobe brought his fist down hard on the table, it shook the mugs and teaspoons, everyone in the cafe looked around. The owner began to make his way over from the griddle where he was tossing burgers, but David held his hand up to indicate all was okay. The owner, come cook, decided that he was better off with the spitting griddle. Stella reached across the table and put a relaxing hand on Kobe's forearm.

"We don't think so." David said sternly in the hope his words were getting through. "Her method with knives, and heels, has always been stabbing. It seems to be her signature, the drug gang's way of sending a message to those that cross or cheat them. Hence why we have seen her work turn up several times across Europe, she has been a busy girl.

"So, if it is Jackman, he had to do it himself." Kobe was struggling with the news that they were still not sure who had slaughtered his family. He thought on a little further, "Although I want somebody nasty to blame, if it were me, I would say that he does not have the balls to do the dirty work himself."

"That's our opinion as well." David wanted to keep Kobe away from the investigation, so he moved the subject carefully away again. "Sam Cobby now has his bronze statue back, and its off again to be auctioned, this time protected by the Auction House themselves. He has also had the very recently available and attractive Barbara Jackman in tow. It seems that amid the disaster they have found love..."

Kobe opened his mouth, about to interrupt. David stopped him by answering the question that crossed his mind.

"We have checked and there is no impropriety on their part.

Apparently, the Jackman marriage has been rocky for some time, he did not have the stamina for two women. Barbara was trying hard to save their marriage, but Jackman was enjoying the highlife far too much. Trouble was when she cut him off from the family fortune, he could not stop the wild spending and was getting further in debt with the drug gangs. They used that to force him to take bigger and bigger shipments which would then be moved on to destinations across the country. Jackman was using genuine council business trips to move the product in the boot of his Jag."

"Clever and virtually impossible to track, we were just lucky to get the intel from a street dealer who would rather risk being discovered for grassing on his dealers, than spend time banged up."

"When I joined the force, I never realised this world was so fucked up." Stella's brain was getting ready to explode with the things she was learning in that cafe close to the railway station.

"Let me see if I have this right!" Kobe wanted to sum things up, trying to see where his family came into the overall picture.

Over the past few weeks Kobe's mind had gone from a dense field of fog, with little clarity apart from the horrific tableaux of his family's death scene, but now he was slowly getting back to the way his mind worked when he needed it on the job. He needed to find that clarity, now more than ever. David and Stella remained quiet apart from the odd nod of the head or a quietly spoken confirmation.

"Jackman has been the brains behind the drug trade in this city for some time and done bloody well to keep it from our radar. I can only assume because of the European contacts who kept him on a tight leash by having his driver keep him in line." David nodded. "By sheer chance or fluke, we raid two drug dens in the middle of town, which it turns out are both run by Jackman. This leaves him short of cash to pay his puppet masters in mainland Europe, so they tighten the screws on him, forcing him to become the distribution agent for the whole of the UK."

"Right so far." David confirmed.

"Already deep in the shit, he gets lucky when he hears of this bronze statue thing and so he comes up with a plan to get it for himself and make close to £3 million on the black market. That's a lot of money for a lump of metal, even if it is an old lump." Kobe took a breath. "If he can get his hands on that sort of money he can leave his wife for the busty girl on the waterfront and pay off his debts while still leaving some for him to keep on doing what he was doing or set himself up somewhere else.

"That poor bugger, Nick Flax, tries to do right by his friend, Cobby was it?" Stella and David nodded in unison. "And he gets killed for his troubles. Sometimes these lives that we live just do not play out they way they should. And we are supposed to believe in benevolent gods, its not right. The girl in the high heels has gone missing, Jackman has gone missing, nobody is being made to answer for my family, nobody is going to answer for Nick Flax's murder, and the poor sods like us are left behind to just wonder and hope before moving on to the next case."

"That's about the size of it, Kobe, I know it sucks, but you know I will not stop. Don't you?"

"I know David, but you two need to think about your careers, so don't do anything stupid on my account. Nothing is going to bring them back, so all I can hope is that some day one, or all, of them will be found. What goes around comes around, right." Kobe was fighting hard not to scream and lash out, but he no longer felt he had the strength.

"You taught me well Boss, and you always instilled in me not to give up. I will keep shaking trees until some rotten fruit will fall." David saw that statement as a vow to Kobe, never to give up on him or his family.

"I know he was always a longshot, and was never really in the frame, but, what about Lucas Tubb?" It was a last gasp attempt, the hail-Mary from the quarterback.

"Nothing Kobe, I don't think he will ever come back here, for any reason. He got away free and clear, why would he risk it?" David shrugged.

"Thank you, both of you." Kobe gave the biggest smile he could manage; he had a lot of love for the couple in front of him who had stood by him through all the bad hours. "I am going to my car now and begin driving, I will let you know where I end up."

Apart from one bite, Kobe's bacon sandwich remained untouched on the table.

The three of them stood, David went to pay the bill while Kobe hugged and spoke to Stella. "You two make a fabulous couple, take care of him please." He nodded toward David. "And take care of my Godson, or daughter, she or he will be my new family, so updates please. I may not know where I am going, but for you two I will always be contactable."

David returned. "What are you two talking about?"

Stella answered. "He told me to leave you as soon as possible and raise my child on my own."

David and Kobe hugged, it was strong and meaningful. Kobe kissed David on the cheek, and it felt natural to both men. Stella, he kissed on both cheeks, and he felt a teardrop slide down his cheek, it took a second to realise that the tear had fallen from his own eye and not Stella's.

"Speak soon." David said.

Kobe turned and walked out of the cafe and away from the city he had tried to protect, he felt like he had let the city and his family down. Too many people had died while he was on duty, he had failed them all.

CHAPTER 63

He thought it would be harder but as he drove away, he did not even as much as glance in the rear-view mirror. David had kindly gone to the cottage and retrieved a few cherished items for Kobe. What David did not tell Kobe was that the very walls of the once pretty cottage still reeked of death, professionals had gone in and cleaned the place from top to bottom, but David could still detect that metallic odour of dried blood. It would never be a sedate home again, not after the events there.

The farewell hug with Kobe had been brief, the only words spoken apart from the obvious goodbyes was when Stella held her ex-boss, she whispered in his ear,

"Don't ever forget we are here; your Godson will need you."

Kobe leaned back and looked her in the eye, it took just a nod to know that it was going to be a boy. He would have to admit to a little jealousy, one family just beginning, and his complete and perfect family gone.

He climbed into his Alpha Spider, its red body gleaming in spring sunshine, the engine burst into life, burbled slightly and then smoothed out. It had been six long and hard months since his family had been taken from him, the time was right to move on. Next to him on the passenger seat was an ornate wooden box from the cottage and that he had found washed up on the harbour shore shortly after moving to the village. The box contained a few photos and keepsakes. In the foot well a holdall with a few clothes and toiletries. Kobe Kaan no longer needed or wanted for much; it was time to restart his own personal engine. A brief wave and his two friends watched as he sped away to wherever he was going, all they knew, and all that Kobe knew was that on the outskirts of Chichester he took the third exit on the roundabout and onto the busy A27, the dual carriageway would carry him West.

He stopped some two and half hours later outside the town of Honiton, he knew it as a pretty, town that for many holiday makers was just a spot on the way to somewhere or on the way back. This was not where he would stay. The Grazing Cow was a pleasant roadside cafe that served wonderful cakes and good breakfasts, but hunger had not hit him yet even though he had not eaten since getting up, he was too eager to leave the old life. Maybe he should have got the bacon sandwich to go! He settled for coffee and a shortbread biscuit, but on seeing the inside of the cafe was bustling with holiday bound families, he asked for his coffee to go. Needing a rest from driving he leant on the wing of the car.

Two girls left the cafe, faces thick with make-up, eyebrows as black as night even though both had dyed blonde hair, lips were pumped up and painted with purple gloss. Kobe knew he was getting old, but he noted that the skirts were too short, and the tops cut too low. Rae had always told him, legs or tits, a girl doesn't have both showing at the same time. They glanced across at Kobe and burst into girlie giggles, he now knew how woman felt when men leered at them. He didn't realise it of course but he was looking good himself, his hair had grown, black and glossy, with two grey streaks at either temple, his face sported the beginnings of a salt-and-pepper beard. He was lean, not eating properly for a few months would do that and his clothes consisted of a pair of green cargo trousers and a black sweatshirt with no logos, his favoured Timberland Nu-Buck boots were on his feet.

He deposited the drained cup and the biscuit in a nearby bin, he did not fancy the shortbread after all. He climbed in over the door and slid down into the bucket seat and continued west. After a short trip along the M5, which he hated even though he could blow any remaining cobwebs out of the engine, and he was back on the winding road toward North Cornwall. Either side of the road the scenery changed from green farmland and wooded areas to the vastness of Dartmoor with its dark hills and almost barren heathland, it held a tough exterior that still held a hint of romance thanks to stories such as Jamaica Inn.

Finally, he was on single lane roads, winding between farmland and rundown villages, there seemed to be more cattle than people. As he drove from Devon and into Cornwall, he felt the pressure that had been upon him for all these months slide away. It was as if the border left the old world behind him. Kobe let out a long sigh, steam released from the pressure cooker of his life. He recalled a family holiday when he was a child, normally they would fly to Egypt so that his father could visit family and friends of old, he would also renew his important contacts within the Egyptian Government, as far as his father was concerned it was they who decided on his future. His father well suited as a diplomat. Both parents wanted to remain in England, his father liked the freedom, and for his son he wanted an Oxford or Cambridge education. Kobe's father wanted him to live in a free society, not the closed life that was Egypt at the time, Kobe had always thanked his father for that bequeathed gift.

A signpost to Bude, brought back memories of the single seaside holiday he had as a child, swimming and body surfing in scary waves, ice creams and fish and chips on the waterfront. The fish and chips were like some exotic foreign food to the child Kobe. It sounded idyllic now and so he followed the signs. At last, the road ended, all that would have been left would be to follow the coast road to somewhere else with sea, ice cream shops and bakeries with Cornish Pasties. It had been another two and half hours of driving since coffee and as well as some food he needed somewhere to stay the night, although it was not yet the busy holiday season, he might find it tricky to get a B&B or a holiday let cottage for the short term.

He put the top up on the car and locked his few belongings inside. The car park was alongside a canal that led to the sea and a curving sandy beach backed up by steep dunes. He did not recall the canal from his childhood holiday, but it was a perfect setting. The thin crowds seemed to be heading toward the beach, pulling behind them small trailers filled with all sorts of ephemera, umbrellas for keeping the sun at bay, or the rain away, brightly coloured windbreaks, for privacy and shelter from onshore breezes, ball games from cricket to football and badminton all catered for and enough food to feed a dozen beach trips. Not knowing where else to go he followed them, seeing the hampers that were obviously filled with food, he began to feel hungry.

Up ahead was a floating restaurant in a converted barge, easily named The Barge, clever he thought. They advertised fish and chips, with the fish line-caught out in the bay by local fisherman, it was a natural assumption to believe that the chips would be carved from Cornish potatoes cultivated by local farmers. It only seemed fair. There was a picnic bench out front with nobody claiming it, so he took a seat, ordered his food and a black coffee from the hatchway and while he sat there, he watched a family with cream teas. A gentle argument was being held about the delicate matter of cream first or jam first on the scone. A local walked past them, her chocolate Labrador pulling at the leash eager to get to the beach, she knew the correct way, it was a religion in these parts.

"Rolo, sit and wait boy." The dog obeyed, but still showed signs of impatience. "You are in Cornwall, it is jam first and then the cream, they do it a funny way round in England. But you will get deported if you get it wrong here." Then with a command Rolo was released again to pull his informative owner toward the beach.

Half the table with voices raised boasted that their knowledge of the 'Cream Tea Debate' was the right one, the others begrudgingly admitting defeat.

Kobe's food was delivered, and he tucked in, as advertised the fish was fresh, it was, he had to admit the finest fish and chips he had tasted. He ate his meal and watched the families on the beach running around with ball games, rushing into the sea and out again as they narrowly avoided surfers on their long boards. Adults dipped a toe before retreating to the beach towel, the water was still quite chilly for the pampered city folk. On the far side of the beach, he could see the busy sea pool, a natural rock-pool filled to overflowing by the incoming tide and enjoyed all year round by locals.

He was envious of the family groups and their happiness; it brought back memories of the good times as well as the images of the bad times that would stay with him until his dying day.

CHAPTER 64

It had been a little over two years, well two years, four months and two days to be precise, but it was only Kobe Kaan that was counting and even he could not recall the times of day, from kissing his family goodbye to saying prayers for them, it was a blur. In all that time he had still failed to find a kind of peace and he knew that pleasant feeling would allude him for many years to come,

Every morning, rain or shine Kobe would walk the canal. When he first arrived in Bude, a great place to land as the road sort of stopped there with only the Atlantic Ocean beyond, he spent the first few nights in a comfortable bed and breakfast establishment, before finding a small one-bedroom flat, the size suiting him perfectly, and which overlooked the very canal he walked every day. He had discovered very quickly that Bude was a place where everyone said good morning, and he smiled every time he said it or it was said to him, the friendly locals quickly became what he referred to as his 'canal-pals'. Learning their dogs' names long before he remembered the owner's names.

He still took coffee, and sometimes breakfast, at The Barge on the canal. In winter the inside was warmed with a charming log burner in the corner, and in the summer, it was cooled by the sea breezes that blew along the canal from the surf topped water. Kobe had quickly become part of the regular customer base, all friendly and all chatty. Conversations held at the Barge and along the canal carried him through the day and he never felt lonely. He still missed his family of course; every minute of every day and the pain of their loss had never eased.

A couple of times a month he called Stella and David, his godson, named Toby after nobody, was not yet speaking but he recognized Kobe each time the three adults spoke on Zoom and giggled all through his parent's conversations, Kobe thought they made a beautiful family. David was now a Detective Inspector and, apparently heading for great things. Stella was a stay-at-home mum but studying with Open University for a degree in Psychology, with an eye to becoming a mental health counselor. Kobe thought she would be good at it. Toby's favourite playmate was Suzi's son, who she had named

Nick. David and Stella had kind of taken them under their wings.

Every time he called; he asked the question. 'Had they any leads on who had killed his family?" He never expected any answers in the positive, not after all this time. But one evening in the middle of April, when he called Stella and Toby were nowhere to be seen. David stared at the screen; his face painted with a serious demeanor.

Suddenly his screen flickered and at the other end sat David.

"I have news Kobe." The look and tone of his voice was not good news, Kobe didn't answer, just waited. "A body has been found, in the woods on the Goodwood Estate."

Goodwood was known for its horse racing, golf course, car racing and vintage aircraft, including two Spitfires. But it was also a place with great views from its hills and great walks in its woodland.

"Go on." Spoken so softly that David hardly heard the words. Kobe's heart was in his mouth.

"We are 100% certain that the body is Kenneth Jackman. DNA gave us the definitive ID but Barbara his ex-wife has identified some of his jewelry."

"Cause of death?"

"Only a rough cause, after so long, but it looks as if he was beaten to death by something wooden and heavy, probably a pick-axe handle."

"Just desserts I would say." Kobe felt no guilt for thinking that way, even if he was not responsible for the deaths of his family, Jackman's greed for money and thirst for power saw others killed, and that does not consider those who died and had lives ruined by his drug dealing.

"And still no evidence to point us toward him being the one responsible for Rae and the children. Sorry its not better news, Kobe."

"And, no sign of that psychopathic bitch who did his killing for him, I suppose."

"None that we can confirm." Replied David. "But there have been reports from European mainland of similar gang-related murders. That has become the problem of the French and German police now."

"She does like to get around, doesn't she?"

After a few pleasantries, Kobe offered his thanks and hung up on the call, he would spend the rest of his evening dredging up the past, partly as a husband and father missing his family, but also as a copper, mentally going over the case, time and time again. But still he never reached a new conclusion. Although he regularly checked with David and searched the internet, he discovered that Lucas Tubb remained a ghost, no sign of him or anyone matching his description. One of them was responsible and it broke his heart that he would never know.

It was now mid-June, a hot and busy summer, the heatwave had lasted almost a month already and Bude was swamped with the tourist traffic, or Emmits as they were known to locals. The Barge kindly saved his two-seater table in the corner so that every morning he could have his coffee and read his newspaper, which he bought from the old-fashioned Crescent Stores at the head of the canal, with its old, curved frontage which was decorated every morning with things needed for the beach, balls, blow up dinghies, buckets, and spades. It was Post Office, grocers, paper shop and gossip central.

Kobe strode down the gangplank of the barge, almost feeling like an Admiral waiting to be whistled aboard. There was something strange this morning as he wandered past the service counter, he noticed somebody at his table. He knew that if they were very busy, he had no right to the table, but the dining area was half empty, which was usual a few minutes after their opening time. Kate was the owner, her blonde hair flowing down over her shoulders and with her usual bright and wide smile, she would cheer up anyone's day, and as Kobe walked between tables and counter, she poked her always smiling face around the side of the chrome coffee contraption.

"Sorry Kobe," she began in hushed tones. "But she says she is an old friend, and she knew you came in here every morning."

He told Kate, no problem and was intrigued to discover who it was claiming to know him. If truth be told he was fearful of it being someone from his old life. Kobe had made a clean break on purpose.

As he approached the table, he could see the back of his unexpected guest's head. Black hair, cropped slightly to accommodate the hot weather of summer, Kobe half recognised her, or thought he did, but doubt halted him for a moment. It could have been the stiletto killer they had been searching for, he tried to see under the table for her footwear, but her feet were tucked too far under. He took a deep breath and moved in. Body tense, expecting the worst, he placed a hand on her shoulder, it was partly a gesture of friendship and partly a way of holding her down if it turned out he was about to be attacked.

The touch startled the woman, and she turned her head sharply to see whose hand it was. Kobe knew at that instant who it was. The woman had an overriding fear of being attacked again and found it hard to keep her nerves on a tight thread, and when she lifted her face toward him, he could see the scars around her lips and her eye. It was Jemma Costello, the last person he expected to see. She offered a broad smile, which stretched the scars around her mouth.

Kobe took his seat, always one facing into a building, he never sat with his back to people, sudden noises behind him brought on panic attacks, since he first began suffering from PTSD. What a nervous pair they made, but he was genuinely pleased to see her.

"Jemma, what brings you to Cornwall." He tried to make it sound as a greeting and not as an imposition. "You are looking well."

"I am feeling well," she said, "better than I have in a long time. Never thought I would travel this far from home again." She let out a large breath in the hope it would relax her further.

Both were nervous of the meeting, neither comfortable around strangers. Kobe had realised some time ago that why he enjoyed Bude so much was because bumping into people was a fleeting thing, he was never expected to stand and chat idly for too long. It appeared that Jemma was just the same.

Kate bought Kobe his usual decaff cappuccino, foam almost overflowing and sprinkled with chocolate dust, just how he liked it. Jemma said no thank you to an offered second cup of her favoured latte.

"I felt strong enough to travel so I wanted to come and see how you were getting on. David Martin, he's a DI now you know, well, he tells me about your Zoom chats, and he let slip you were in Bude." She knew Kobe didn't want anyone from his old life knowing his whereabouts.

"That's okay, I always ask him how you are doing as well. He told me he still must bring your coffee in every morning no matter what shifts he has been on."

"David, just like you, feels obligated. Even though I have told him not to bother."

And so, their idle chatter about everyday life carried on through two more coffees each, there was a lot of catching up to do. They stayed until a noisy family took over the V shaped bow area just behind them, their children using the walkway along the centre of the barge as a racetrack and parents just shouting at each other rather than have a conversation, the noise did neither Kobe nor Jemma any good in their mental state. People were so thoughtless toward others.

Without words they left the barge and walked to the end of the canal, over the lock gate and began climbing the hill to 'Compass-Point' where a red brick folly with slit windows built in to allow coast guards of yesteryear clear views in both directions along the cliffs and coastal path. Its carved points of the compass around the top were slightly off by a few degrees from a time when crumbling cliffs meant they had to demolish, rebuild, and reposition the small building, it was rebuilt with the windows dictating its position and not the compass points. It was a popular and well protected part of the coast path that the locals loved. There was a bench looking out to sea alongside it. On the horizon a white ship, Toyota, written large along its flank, carrying cars to a destination somewhere near to Bristol. All that sea and only rarely would anyone see a ship on the distant horizon, there were usually small fishing vessels in the broad bay, but rarely anything the size of the car carriers.

Sitting in that beautiful spot and looking out to sea, their silence was comfortable, Cornwall was one of those places where just-to-be, was enough. The only sounds they could hear were the distant hum of the 'Emmits' on the beach far below. It was the Cornish name for tourists, or ants as they resembled that social insect in the way they swarmed over land. None of that mattered as the main sound was the continual crash and wash of the waves as they crashed into the Cornish coastline after travelling across the Atlantic. At night Kobe slept with the windows open just so the sound of the surf would act as a lullaby and help him sleep.

"I have missed you Kobe," Jemma broke the silence. "I always looked forward to you coming by the front desk every morning with my coffee and a smile. You always looked me in the eye, most people find it hard to take their gaze away from my scars."

Kobe thought she was going to finally blame him for what had happened to her, which he was okay with. In trying to be in two places at once, he left her alone with Jacob Tubb, who turned out to be a vicious killer and rapist. Kobe had missed that side of the man and he had always blamed himself for what had happened to Jemma.

He began to apologise to her, yet again, something he had tried to do and repeated often when he was back in Chichester.

"I missed you too, even now I buy a coffee and think of buying two." He confessed to her.

"Ever since David accidentally told me where you were, I have wanted to come and visit." Her voice had a tenderness to it, which Kobe had not picked up on before. "But I knew you needed time to mourn your beautiful family."

Kobe, said nothing, what could he say. He was leaning back on the bench, his eyes gazing out to sea and thinking of Rae and how she would have loved this place. Unexpectedly, Jemma reached across and placed her hand on his thigh.

"I think you know I have always loved you, Kobe," The words shocked him so much he was frozen for a moment, he could not even move her hand from his leg. "And you cared so much for me when I was hurt, I knew we were destined to be together. I just had to remove the obstacles that kept us apart and then wait for you to heal. So, I am here for you now, and we can be together forever."

THE END

ABOUT THE AUTHOR

David spent 20 years as a freelance feature writer and photographer working in the lifestyle magazine sector. Now retired he spends his time figuring out new ways to kill his victims and put his heroes in perilous situations. Born and raised in Hampshire, England, he now lives on the North coast of Cornwall where he plots and writes his thrillers while drinking coffee in the waterfront cafes. Blood Among the Roses is his third novel with the hero Kobe Kaan.

David came to novel writing late in life and loves the daily effort of putting words to paper, not to mention thinking of new ways to murder perfectly nice people.

Printed in Great Britain
by Amazon